Arthur Schnitzler

Bachelors

STORIES AND NOVELLAS

Selected and Translated from the German by
Margret Schaefer

IVAN R. DEE

Chicago 2006

www.ivanrdee.com

Library of Congress Cataloging-in-Publication Data:
Schnitzler, Arthur, 1862–1931.
   [Short stories. English. Selections]
   Bachelors / Arthur Schnitzler ; selected and translated from the German by Margret Schaefer.
      p. cm.
   Includes bibliographical references and index.
   ISBN-13: 978-1-56663-611-7 (cloth : alk. paper)
   ISBN-10: 1-56663-611-6 (cloth : alk. paper)
   1. Schnitzler, Arthur, 1862–1931—Translations into English. I. Schaefer, Margret. II. Title.
PT2638.N5A2 2006b
833'.8—dc22
                                                            2006012726

Contents

Foreword

FREUD CONFESSED he felt baffled by the question, "What does a woman want?" calling female psychology the "dark continent" of psychoanalysis. He found male psychology more readily transparent and more readable. Yet Arthur Schnitzler's narratives, whose penetrating acuity Freud himself acknowledged, make it apparent that the Oedipus complex by no means tells the entire story of male psychology, and that the psychology of men, too, is a dark continent.

In the narratives collected here, the Viennese dramatist and writer Arthur Schnitzler illuminates that hidden world. He grasps more clearly the subtle connections between love and anxiety, sexual passion and fear of death that Freud, his contemporary, only hinted at. And he is more aware than Freud of how much social forces impinge upon individual psychology. Yet, though he reveals a depth of understanding and empathy for his male protagonists, he does so with an unsparing eye that will please many a contemporary feminist. And one of these stories, "Casanova's Homecoming," contains perhaps Schnitzler's strongest positive portrait of an emancipated woman.

The four narratives in this volume convey to us the inner life of bachelors from diverse ranks of society: Lieutenant Gustl is a young lieutenant who has risen to the rank of officer in the Austrian army from a penurious lower-middle-class background; Alfred in "The

Murderer" is a young lawyer with an independent income, a member of the city's upper middle class, the very prototype of the socially desirable mate; Emil of "Doctor Graesler" is a middle-aged doctor looking for a wife; and Casanova is—well, Casanova is Casanova, *the* historical Casanova, in fact—not exactly an aristocrat, though he has given himself a title, but certainly a member of what one critic has called "the erotic elite," who hobnobs as easily with the aristocracy as with street prostitutes.

Although these men inhabit quite different social worlds, they are brothers under the skin. Despite their status or success, they are inordinately subject to feelings of humiliation and shame and exquisitely sensitive to what they consider slights to their honor and self-esteem. Lieutenant Gustl ("little Gus") takes umbrage at the slightest stray remark or inadvertent gesture and is ready to duel anyone he believes has insulted him. Alfred has such a need to regard himself as loving, kind—and irreplaceable—that he can't bring himself to terminate a relationship with one woman to marry another, and resorts to ever more desperate stratagems to find the "kindest" way to solve his problem. Fearing self-exposure and humiliation, Emil Graesler flees from a potential marriage to an independent and attractive woman he loves into the arms of a much younger and undemanding "shopgirl." And Schnitzler's Casanova is an aging roué who sees himself in his moments of self-recognition as an old, shriveled-up man who can no longer attract the women he desperately needs to confirm his erotic and worldly power.

It was "Lieutenant Gustl" that secured Schnitzler's position as a major fiction writer as well as a dramatist. Published in 1900, the same year as Freud's *Interpretation of Dreams* and Thomas Mann's *Buddenbrooks*, it was no less groundbreaking in both content and style. It became Schnitzler's most famous novella as well as the occasion of a major literary scandal. It was the first major piece of European literature to use the literary technique of "stream of consciousness," a form of interior monologue which captures the fragments of fleeting thoughts and feelings, perceptions, memories, and dreams that flicker unceasingly through a character's mind. Although inspired by the French writer Eduoard Dujardin's experiment with the technique in a novel of 1888, Schnitzler's more sophisticated use of the method anticipates that of Joyce and Virginia Woolf and Faulkner by more than twenty years.

In "Lieutenant Gustl" the portrait of a young, arrogant, bigoted, and anti-Semitic Austrian officer was so compelling and convincing that it offended the Austrian military, which saw it as an indictment of the Austrian military officer class and of the practice of dueling. A military court convened to sit in judgment of Schnitzler's novella discharged him dishonorably from his reserve army officer status, a position he had held for twenty years. He was also widely attacked in the press. In an ironic twist of the sort that makes life seem an imitation of art, one of the reasons the military court discharged him from his commission was that he did not answer one of his critics by challenging him to, yes—a duel!

The judges' sentiments were not unfounded. The novella does show the absurdity of the practice of dueling, which at the time was still tenaciously defended by the Austrian officer class as a mark of status. Only about 5 percent of the Austrian population (primarily military officers, aristocrats, and upper-middle-class professional men) were of a high enough social status to be "*satisfaktionsfaehig*," that is, "qualified" to duel. Gustl's dilemma is that he cannot avenge his honor by dueling with a baker who he feels has insulted him, as the baker is not of a sufficiently elevated social class to duel. And the story is also an indictment of a large segment (80 percent) of Austrian military officers, all those from a lower-middle-class background whose rank was achieved through attendance at one of the cadet schools that enabled youth of that class to rise to officer status.

But at the same time the work is more than an indictment. Schnitzler understands the social and familial conditions that produced the kind of socially insecure, bigoted, and belligerent man who embraces anti-Semitism and other prejudices—against socialists, for example—to defend against an uneasy fear of social failure and humiliation. Gustl cannot see beyond the ideology, the chauvinism, and the absurd code of honor that have been drummed into him. That these principles all require him to commit suicide in order to save his honor is of course the irony of the story. But though Schnitzler paints Gustl as an obtuse and deluded bully, he understands how he is also human and pitiable.

The other novellas and stories in this collection were written and published ten years later, between 1910 and 1918. In "The Murderer," published in 1911, Schnitzler again takes up the theme of an upper-middle-class man's relationship with a woman of a lower social class that he had treated earlier in many of his plays and narratives. But this revealing narrative is a darker, more extreme version of the theme. It is a chilling account of ever more desperate deceptions and betrayals. With a keen and unsparing eye, Schnitzler shows how kindness and self-interest, extreme vanity and self-loathing, love and rationalized cruelty, can be two sides of the same coin.

"Casanova's Homecoming" and "Doctor Graesler" were written just before and during World War I. Although Schnitzler was one of the very few Austrian writers who courageously opposed the war from the beginning, he does not deal directly with it in his works. Life for Viennese men of Schnitzler's class not directly involved in the war continued much as it had before the conflict began. This war was still fought at the front, in the trenches, between soldiers, not with the indiscriminate bombings of civilians. (That "civilized" practice was first used by the British against Iraq in 1928.) But as if aware of a world at war and the passing of an era, there is a sense of impending decline and loss, and a nostalgia for a greater and more glorious past in both these novellas. Both deal directly with the theme of aging and its attendant losses—worries that increasingly preoccupied Schnitzler personally as he himself aged in a world about to disappear.

"Casanova's Homecoming," written during the war, is set in eighteenth-century Italy and is loosely—very loosely—based on the memoirs of the historical figure of Casanova, the famous eighteenth-century Venetian lover. But its atmosphere of melancholy, nostalgia, and at times desperate and overwhelming sense of decline reflects not only Schnizler's preoccupation with his own fears of aging but the years in which it was written. Schnitzler's Casanova is not that fabled dashing and handsome figure that the very name evokes. This Casanova is fifty-three—Schnitzler's age at the time of its writing, an age already "old" in Schnitzler's time—and down on his luck, reduced to writing hypocritical scurrilous tracts against Voltaire and his own convictions in order to curry favor with the Venetian authorities. Only through his reminiscences and "creatively invented" stories about his own glorious past do we see that Casanova was once a man of great intellectual power and sexual magnetism, famous as a lover of many women and friend of the highly placed in every large city of eighteenth-century Europe. At the time of the story's action he is a man who must resort to chicanery and trickery to get what he wants, a mere shadow of his former self. How much like the Austrian empire itself, which after the war changed from a huge multinational empire to a smallish "head without a body"!

Like "Lieutenant Gustl," "Casanova's Homecoming" provoked a literary scandal. This time the charge was obscenity—a charge that Schnitzler had faced before with his 1900 play *Reigen (La Ronde)*. "Casanova's Homecoming" was one of three works seized by police from the offices of an American publisher in New York in 1922, along with D. H. Lawrence's *Sons and Lovers* and *A Young Girl's*

Diary, a memoir of the sexual experiences of a Viennese teenage girl with a foreword by Sigmund Freud. Schnitzler's work does of course deal directly with sexual and erotic material, true, but it can hardly be considered a paean to the notorious lover. The novella's first sentence sets the mood and announces the theme as it describes Casanova drawing "nearer and nearer to [his native city of Venice] in ever tightening circles, like a bird gradually descending from its airy heights in order to die." The mood is one of nostalgia, melancholy, and the inevitable coming of death.

In "Doctor Graesler," published in 1917, Schnitzler portrays a rather conventional middle-aged bachelor, a doctor who performs his duties perfunctorily and prefers to travel from health resort to health resort to practice medicine rather than settle down to a more serious permanent position. Still a bachelor at forty-eight, he finally begins to search for a wife and a more rewarding kind of medicine when his sister, who had kept house for him, dies suddenly. Schnitzler, himself a doctor and the son of a doctor, often made a doctor either the main protagonist in his works or the wise and rational onlooker who comments on the action. For example, Fridolin of "Dream Story," Otto of "Flight into Darkness" (translated by me in two earlier volumes of stories, *Night Games* and *Desire and Delusion*), and the protagonist of his eponymous "Professor Bernhardi" are all doctors. Like them, Dr. Graesler thinks of himself as a rational, responsible, and compassionate man. But Schnitzler subtly undercuts Graesler's belief that his cautious reserve and his careful weighing of choices are signs of his autonomy and his power of reason rather than rationalizations of his fear and indecision. The ending of the story—subtly prepared for but still a surprise—leaves it ambiguous as to whether Graesler has really learned anything.

These stories, written over a span of seventeen years, rank among Schnitzler's best and most beloved. They show him to be a master of psychological modernism and of very different literary styles. From the down-to-earth colloquial style of "Lieutenant Gustl" to the flowing and lyrical style of "Casanova's Homecoming," each style expresses the personality, language, class, and culture of the memorable main character of the story. Schnitzler understands each one with the empathic grasp of a depth psychologist but nevertheless with a sharp and critical eye. Were all the men to some degree, even Lieutenant Gustl, seemingly so unlike him, self-representations? Like Casanova, Schnitzler had a reputation as a libertine; like Alfred, he suffered at times from an irresolvable ambivalence and guilt over an inability to choose between two women; like Graesler, he carried on relations with "sweet girls" of a lower class he perceived as loving and undemanding but who did not satisfy him; and like Gustl, he was oversensitive to imagined slights. His writing, he explained in a letter to a friend, was for him not only a means of expression and self-analysis but also a way of "sitting in judgment of himself."

MARGRET SCHAEFER

Berkeley, California
June 2006

Bachelors

The Murderer

A YOUNG MAN with a law degree, but not practicing his profession, lived by himself in comfortable circumstances after having lost both his parents. He was well liked and much in demand socially, but for more than a year now he had maintained a relationship with a girl from a lower social class who, like him, had no living relatives and so could afford to ignore the opinions of the world. Early in their relationship, Alfred had induced his beloved to give up her position as a secretary in a reputable Viennese department store, less out of kindness or passion than from a wish to enjoy his new happiness in as comfortable and undisturbed a manner as possible. And although for a long time he was happier in this relationship than he had ever been in earlier ones, surrounded as he was by her gratitude and love and able to enjoy their shared freedom in ease and comfort, he gradually began to feel that familiar restlessness which had always announced to him the inevitable end of an affair. This time, however, the end did not seem to be imminent, and uneasily he saw himself consigned to the fate of one of his old friends who had become entangled in a similar relationship some years ago, and was now a disgruntled family man forced to live a secluded and restricted life. And so many hours that should have given him the purest pleasure at the side of a graceful and gentle creature like Elise began instead to bring him boredom and anguish. True, he had the capacity and, he

3

liked to think, the consideration, not to give Elise any indication of these feelings, yet as a consequence he more and more frequently sought out the respectable bourgeois circles he had almost totally abandoned in the course of the past year. When the much-courted daughter of a wealthy factory owner approached him with obvious interest at a dance he chanced to attend, he suddenly saw the possibility of a relationship more appropriate to his station and his means. He began to experience what had begun as a lighthearted and casual adventure with Elise as a tiresome shackle that a young man with his assets should be able to cast off without qualms. But the smiling serenity with which she continued to receive him, her constant and devoted surrender in the now ever rarer hours of their intimacy, and the unsuspecting trust with which she released him from her arms into a world of which she had not the least inkling—all this not only forced the words of farewell he had resolved to say off his lips, but also filled him with an agonizing compassion whose barely perceptible outward expression could appear to a woman as guilelessly trusting as Elise only as a sign of a renewed and ever deeper love. As a result, Elise never believed herself more adored than at those moments when Alfred, after another meeting with Adele, returned to the quiet home consecrated solely to him and his faithless love, trembling with memories of sweet inviting glances, promising touches, and, eventually, the secret kisses of another woman. And so the next morning—and every morning thereafter—Alfred left Elise with a renewed pledge of eternal fidelity rather than with the words of farewell he had resolved to utter each time he came through the door.

And so the days passed with him carrying on both affairs simultaneously. Finally he faced only the decision as to which evening would be better for the now unavoidable confrontation with Elise: the day before or the day after his engagement to Adele. On the first of these evenings, with still another day left before the final deadline, Alfred arrived at his lover's door with the serene composure that the habit of his double life had by now made possible.

He found her propped up in a corner of the sofa, more pale than he had ever seen her. She didn't rise to greet him and offer her forehead and her lips for a welcoming kiss as she usually did, but merely acknowledged him with a tired and somewhat forced smile, so that Alfred suspected—with a feeling of relief—that the news of his coming engagement had, in the baffling manner of all rumors, reached her despite all his efforts to keep it secret. But in answer to his persistent questions he found only that from time to time Elise suffered from chest pains, a fact she had concealed from him because she had always recovered in a few minutes without assistance. This time, however, the aftereffects of an attack threatened to linger. Alfred, all too conscious of his guilty intentions, was so strongly moved by this revelation that he couldn't do enough to express his concern and offer proof of his kindness. And before the evening was over, without understanding exactly how it had happened, he and Elise had made plans for a trip together which they hoped would surely bring about a permanent cure of her condition.

Never did he love her as tenderly, and never was he so entranced by the thought of his own tenderness, as he was when he left her that night. On the ride home he seriously contemplated writing a farewell letter to Adele in which he would excuse his flight from their engagement and upcoming marriage as a duty imposed upon him by an instability in his nature that made him unsuited for lasting, tranquil happiness with anyone. The artful arrangement of what he would write pursued him into sleep; but by the time the morning light played over his bed through the openings in the blinds, he felt that the effort required was as foolish as it was superfluous. He was scarcely surprised that the image of his suffering lover of last night was now as insubstantial and distant as that of a woman left long ago, whereas the image of Adele stood before him wreathed in the perfume of infinite desire. Around noon he asked Adele's father for her hand, a petition which met with friendly consideration, though not with unconditional agreement. With good-humored ironic allusions to the suitor's youth and its many temptations, the father imposed the condition that Alfred should first go abroad for a year to test the strength and durability of his feelings for his daughter. To be sure of ruling out all possibility of self-deception, he even opposed the suggestion of an exchange of letters between the two of them. If Alfred then returned from his journey with the same intentions he had today, and if he found that Adele too retained the same feelings that she had today, he would not stand in the way of their immediate marriage. Alfred, who appeared to agree to these conditions only grudgingly, actually breathed an inner sigh of relief upon hearing them, seeing in them a desirable extension of the deadline for deciding his fate. After thinking it over for a few minutes, he declared himself ready to leave immediately, if only to hasten thereby the end of the imposed separation. At first Adele seemed to feel wounded by his unexpected and too eager acceptance of her father's conditions, but after a short consultation granted them by her father, Alfred induced his fiancée to admire his wisdom in matters of love and to release him into an uncertain future with vows of fidelity, even with tears in her eyes.

Alfred had scarcely reached the street outside when he began to consider the various opportunities he would have in the coming year to break off his relationship with Elise. But his tendency to settle the most difficult matters of his life in a passive fashion was so powerful that it not only overrode his vanity but also conjured up dark forebodings that his sensitive nature usually recoiled from. He thought it possible that Elise would grow cooler and gradually distance herself from him in the unaccustomed intimacy that travel made unavoidable. Even her heart condition might free him of her— of course, in a most unwelcome way. But soon he was able to ward off both this hope and this fear so completely that in the end he felt nothing but a childlike anticipation at the prospect of an exciting trip to far-off places in the company of a charming and doting creature. That evening, in the best of moods, he talked with his unsuspecting lover about the delightful prospects of the coming journey.

As spring was just beginning, Alfred and Elise first sought out the mild shores of Lake Geneva. Later in the season they moved up to cooler mountain heights, and later still they visited England to spend the late summer at a spa. In the fall they toured Dutch and German cities, then escaped the oncoming winter weather for the consolation and comfort of the southern sun. Until that time it wasn't just Elise, who had never gone beyond the outskirts of Vienna, who was gliding through this year of wonders on the arm of her beloved guide as though in a delicious dream, but Alfred as well. Although he remained aware that he was only postponing his future difficulties, he too had surrendered himself entirely to the delightful present, as though caught up by Elise's happiness. At the beginning of the trip he had taken care to avoid meeting anyone he knew and had stayed away from crowded promenades and grand hotel restaurants while with her; but toward the end of their journey he almost intentionally tempted fate and anticipated, almost with pleasure, a telegram from his bride-to-be accusing him of infidelity. Although he would then lose her whom he deeply desired, he would at the same time be rid of all the ambivalence, anxiety, and responsibility he now felt. But no telegram or any other news from home reached him, as Adele, contrary to Alfred's vain expectations, obeyed her father's injunction against writing, just as Alfred did.

Finally the hour arrived in which—at least for Alfred—the miraculous year came to an abrupt end. All at once it appeared to him completely devoid of magic—desolate, indeed more desolate than any other year of his life, a year in which time had simply stood still. It happened on a bright autumn day in the Botanical Gardens of Palermo when Elise, who had until then been alert, lively, and obviously blossoming, suddenly clutched at her chest, looked anxiously at her lover, and then immediately smiled again, as though she were conscious of a duty not to cause him any sort of inconvenience. But her expression, instead of moving him, filled him with a bitterness which of course he knew how to hide beneath a worried demeanor. He reprimanded her—without believing it himself—for having obviously concealed other such attacks from him; he claimed to be hurt that she evidently considered him heartless, and pleaded with her to come with him to find a doctor immediately. Yet he was secretly pleased when she rejected his suggestion because of her low opinion of the state of medicine in the country they were in. But when she suddenly, as though overcome with gratitude and love, brought his hand to her lips and kissed it in full view of the people passing by the park bench they were sitting on, he suddenly felt an intense wave of hatred flood him. Although first taken aback by this emotion, he soon managed to account for it by recalling the many hours of boredom and emptiness he was suddenly convinced had filled their trip. At the same time he experienced such a burning longing for Adele that, contrary to their strict agreement, he sent her a telegram that very evening begging her to send him a few words to Genoa, signing it "eternally yours."

A few days later he received her reply in Genoa. It said: "Yours for just as long." Keeping the crumpled-up paper—which despite its suspiciously lighthearted tone seemed to him to be the fulfillment of all his hopes—near his heart, he began the trip to Ceylon that was to be the final destination and the high point of their trip. Elise would have needed a more mistrustful nature to sense that it was merely the bold play of Alfred's imagination that now gave her more intense ecstasies of love than she had ever experienced before—to have guessed that it wasn't she who lay in his arms during the dark and silent nights on the ocean but the distant bride-to-be whom his intense longing had conjured up in living fullness.

Once they had at last reached the hot and glowing island, the dull monotony of this last of their destinations made Alfred realize that his overwrought imagination was beginning to fail him. He began to keep his distance from Elise and was deceitful enough to offer as the reason for his reserve a new and subtle sign of her heart condition that had occurred when she first stepped onto firm ground in Ceylon. She accepted this explanation, as she did everything he did, as a sign of his love, which had come to be the meaning and whole happiness of her life. And when she drove with him through rustling woods beneath the intense glow of an azure sky, securely snuggled against him, she had no idea that her companion wished only for the hour when he, alone and undisturbed by her presence, would have the opportunity to compose passionate words of love to a woman of whose existence Elise had no inkling nor would ever have. At such moments Alfred's longing for his far-off bride-to-be became so intense that he was able to forget the very features, even the voice, of the woman now at his side, the woman who belonged to him, the woman with whom he had traveled the world for almost an entire year. And when, on the night before their departure for home, he came out of his study to find Elise stretched out on the bed half-unconscious, he recognized with a small but almost sweet shiver of dread that what he thought was but a slight anxiety was in reality a never relinquished and dark glimmer of hope deep in his soul. Nevertheless, feeling genuine distress and concern, he didn't hesitate to send immediately for a doctor. The doctor, who came almost at once, gave the patient a shot of morphine for relief. To the alleged husband, who claimed for important reasons to be unable to postpone the suddenly inadvisable trip, he gave a note recommending the woman to the special care of the ship's doctor.

Almost at once, the fresh sea air seemed to have a beneficent effect on Elise. Her paleness vanished, her demeanor brightened, and her movements became freer than Alfred had ever seen. While earlier she had met even the most inoffensive friendly overtures with indifference, almost with hostility, now she opened up to the friendly conversation that accompanies life on board ship, and she accepted the respectful attentions of a few fellow travelers with satisfaction. In particular, a German baron who was seeking a cure for his chronic lung condition in the sea air spent as much time in Elise's company as he could without crossing the line into impropriety, and Alfred wanted to convince himself that Elise's encouraging behavior toward this most charming of her admirers was welcome evidence of her budding inclination toward him. But when Alfred once, with feigned anger, tried to upbraid Elise for her inordinately friendly behavior toward the baron, she explained to him with an embarrassed smile that all her accommodating behavior toward other men had no other purpose than to arouse his jealousy, and that she was indescribably happy that her little deception had succeeded so well. This time Alfred could no longer hide his impatience and his disappointment. He reacted to her confession, which she had thought would reassure and calm him, with unaccountably harsh words. She stood listening to him in dull incomprehension until she suddenly collapsed unconscious to the floor of the deck where they had been talking and had to be carried down to their cabin. The ship's doctor, who had been cautioned about her condition by the note from his colleague, did not feel it necessary to examine her more closely, and administered the same temporary relief that had worked before to calm her tormented heart. But he could not prevent subsequent attacks from happening for no apparent reason the next day and the day after that. Although the morphine never stopped working, the doctor could not disguise his fear that the illness was progressing and would have a bad end. He warned Alfred in appropriate but no uncertain terms that he should show his beautiful wife the utmost consideration.

Alfred, filled with sullen resentment against Elise, would have found it easy to obey the one admonition from the doctor that constituted a strict prohibition, if only Elise, consumed with longing, had not managed to draw him back to her again in a lonely hour late one night, as though it were a matter of mollifying him with tender affection. But when afterward she lay in his arms with half-closed eyes of ecstatic surrender, and he saw the bluish sheen of the waves outside the small cabin window beyond her moist forehead, he felt a smile creep to his lips from the deepest corner of his soul, a smile that he himself gradually recognized as one of scorn, indeed of triumph. But even when he, shuddering, slowly became conscious of his own dark hope, he told himself that the fulfillment of his wish would not only be his own salvation and the solution to all his worries, but that Elise herself, once she recognized the inevitability of her own death and were granted a choice in the matter, would wish nothing more than to die smothered by his kisses. And so when she, despite awareness of the danger she was in, seemed willing to offer herself to him more and more passionately and to risk expiring from and for love, he believed himself strong enough to accept her sacrifice. Enormous as it was, it would in the end be to the good of the lives of three people who were now so fatefully intertwined.

Thus night after night, as he observed the faint dimming of her eyes and the blissful expiration of her breath with simultaneous dread and anticipation, he began to feel all the more cheated when moments later her awakening glance gratefully sought his and the warm breath of her lips drank in his own with renewed passion. It seemed to him that his deadly deceit had only served to reinvigorate Elise with new and stronger life. She was now so certain of his love that whenever he left her to herself or with others for hours on end, so that he might climb to the highest deck of the ship to cool his feverish brow in the ocean wind, she trustingly stayed behind, and on his return answered his baffled, mad smile with eyes that lit up as though responding to a loving greeting.

In Naples, where the ship was scheduled to stop for a day before going directly on to Hamburg, Alfred hoped to find the letter that he had passionately begged Adele send to him while in Ceylon. The stormy weather provided him with a ready excuse for going on land without Elise in one of the rowboats readied for that purpose, in the company of other travelers. He drove to the post office, walked up to the counter, and gave his name, but retreated empty-handed. Even though he tried to calm himself with the idea that Adele's letter hadn't been sent in time or had gotten lost, the feeling of emptiness that overcame him at this disappointment made him realize that he could no longer contemplate a future without Adele. He had reached the end of his capacity for playacting, and his first thought was that immediately upon his return to the ship he would unsparingly tell Elise the truth. But he realized at once that he could not predict the consequence of such a confession. Not only might it strike Elise dead on the spot or drive her into madness or suicide, but the cause of some such event could scarcely be hidden and might compromise his relationship with Adele. Of course the same thing was to be feared if he saved his confession until the last possible moment, until the landing in Hamburg or even until their arrival in Vienna.

With such despairing thoughts—and at this point hardly even aware of their perfidy—Alfred walked up and down the seashore in the burning noontime sun. Suddenly he felt dizzy and nearly fainted. Suffused with anxiety, he sank down on a bench and remained there until the attack passed and the fog cleared from his eyes. Then he heaved a deep sigh of relief, as though he had just awakened; he knew immediately that in the incomprehensible moment when his senses had threatened to take leave of him, a terrible resolution that had long been growing deep inside him had clearly and pitilessly ripened. He now understood that he had to act in order to fulfill the ardent and dreadful wish he had all this time secretly nurtured. As though it were the culmination of long inner reflection, a complete and detailed plan of action arose fully formed from the depth of his being.

He rose and first went into the restaurant of a hotel, where he ate a hearty lunch with the best of appetite. Then he sought out three doctors, one by one, and presented himself to each of them as a very sick man tormented by unspeakable pain, one who was at the end of a supply of morphine to which he had been addicted for years. He took the prescriptions he was handed, filled them in several different pharmacies, and when he went back on board ship at sunset, he found himself in possession of a quantity of morphine that he knew was more than sufficient for his purpose. At dinner that evening, he related the story of an exploration of Pompeii that he had supposedly undertaken that day. In an overly enthusiastic tone, and with a sudden excessive delight in lying, as though he now wished to be truly satanic, he lingered for quite a while on a description of a quarter of an hour supposedly spent in the garden of Appius Claudius in front of a statue he had happened to read about accidentally in a guidebook, and which of course he had not seen at all. Elise sat at his side, with the baron across from her, and Alfred could not shake the impression that they were two ghosts staring at each other through empty eye sockets.

Later, as he had on so many other evenings, he strolled along the highest deck with Elise in the moonlight while the distant lights of the coast slowly faded. Since he felt himself momentarily weaken, he had to renew his resolve by imagining that it was Adele's arm that he held against his. The wave of passion that flooded him as he did so convinced him that the happiness that awaited him would not be too dearly bought even at the cost of the most terrible guilt. At the same time he felt something strangely like envy for the young creature at his side, who was fated to escape from the confusion of life and find release so soon, so unsuspectingly, and so painlessly.

When, back in the cabin, he took Elise into his arms for what would be the last time, it was with a nearly unbearable clarity of purpose and yet with desperate desire, all the while feeling himself to be the executioner of a fate not of his own making. He had only to reach out and overturn the glass that gleamed with a bluish cast on the bedside table for the drops of poison to seep harmlessly into the indifferent shipboard floor. But Alfred lay motionless and waited. He waited, his heart missing a beat, until finally he saw the familiar movement of Elise's hand as, with her eyes half shut, she reached for the glass one last time as she always did before falling asleep. With eyes wide open, motionless, he saw how she propped herself up, lifted the glass to her lips, and emptied its contents in one swallow. Then she lay back down with a soft sigh, resting her head on his chest, as she always did. Alfred felt a slow, dull hammering in his temples, and heard Elise's quiet breathing and the waves outside sighing against the bow of the ship as it floated on and time stood still.

Suddenly he felt a violent shudder pass through Elise's body. With both her hands she grasped his neck, and her fingers seemed to want to bore into his skin. Only then, with a sustained groan, did she open her eyes. Alfred freed himself from her embrace and jumped out of bed. He saw how she tried to get up, how she flailed her arms about in the empty air, cast a wild look about the cabin in the first light of dawn, then suddenly sank full length onto the bed and lay there completely motionless, breathing in short, shallow breaths. Alfred recognized immediately that she was fully unconscious and coolly asked himself how long she could continue in this state before the end set in. It occurred to him that right now she could perhaps still be revived, and with a dark awareness of tempting fate one last time, either to destroy the fruits of all his labor or to atone for it in one bold act of daring, he rushed to find the doctor. If the doctor recognized what had happened, he would lose the gamble, but if the doctor did not, he would pronounce himself free of all guilt and remorse forever.

When Alfred returned to the cabin with the doctor, Elise lay on the bed looking pale. Her eyes were half open and glassy, her fingers compulsively clutched the blanket, and drops of sweat glistened on her forehead and cheeks. The doctor bent down, put his ear to her chest, listened for a long time, nodded apprehensively, pushed her eyelids open, held his hand to her lips, listened again, shook his head, then turned to Alfred and informed him that Elise's death agony was over. With a genuinely mad look, Alfred beat his hands together over his head and sank down in front of the bed and remained there for a short time with his forehead pressed against Elise's knee. Then he turned and forlornly stared at the doctor, who offered him his hand with a sympathetic look. Alfred refused the doctor's hand. He shook his head and, with great inner clarity, whispered as though in tardy self-accusation, "If only we had followed your instructions." Then he sorrowfully hid his face in his hands. "I expected as much," he heard the doctor reprimand him mildly, as Alfred's eyes burned and glowed beneath his twitching eyelids in an overpowering sense of triumph.

The very next day, as shipboard protocol required, Elise's body was lowered into the sea, and Alfred felt himself surrounded by a general though silent and reserved sympathy for him, the widower. No one dared disturb him as he paced the upper deck for hours on end and gazed into the distance, which, unbeknownst to his shipboard companions, was for him suffused with the scent of blissful hopes. Only the baron sometimes joined him for a few moments in his wanderings, but he tactfully did not mention Alfred's bereavement. Alfred knew of course that it was only the baron's longing to feel himself in the circle of the beloved departed that moved the baron to accompany him. For Alfred, these moments were the only time he felt himself touched by the past in any way.

For he had otherwise succeeded in completely detaching himself from his deed and the meaning it might have for others. The image that stood before him as a living presence was that of the ardently desired and guiltily attained beloved. When he looked down into the water from the bow of the ship, he felt as though he saw her floating peacefully within sunken waves, which in the depth of their slumber were indifferent as to whether she had descended yesterday or a thousand years ago.

Only when he caught sight of the German coast did Alfred's heart beat faster. He planned to remain in Hamburg no longer than necessary to pick up the letter that surely awaited him there, then travel home on the next train. In his impatience, the long drawn-out process of disembarkation tormented him, and he breathed a deep sigh of relief, as though he had been rescued from some confinement, when his luggage was finally secured in the carriage and he was driving through the streets of the city on his way to the post office. It was a late spring afternoon with small, pink clouds. He gave the official his card, eagerly watched him go through letters, and had already readied his hand to reach for his when he received the reply that there was nothing for him—no letter, no card, no telegram. He put on a dubious smile and entreated the official to look again, in a tone so humble that he immediately felt ashamed. He attempted to make out the addresses on the letters by peering over the edges of the envelopes, and again and again imagined that he recognized his name in Adele's handwriting. Once or twice he even stretched his hand out hopefully, and each time he was forced to acknowledge that he had deceived himself. Finally the official put the packet of letters back into its cubicle, shook his head, and turned away. With exaggerated politeness Alfred took his leave and in the next moment found himself outside the door, half numb. The only thing clear to him now was that he could not possibly go on to Vienna without some news from Adele. For the moment he had to remain in Hamburg.

He drove to a hotel, took a room, and hastily wrote the following words on one of the message forms he found there: "No word from you. Incomprehensible. Stunned. Will be home the day after tomorrow. When can I see you. Answer immediately." He added his address and posted the telegram with a prepaid answer form. Coming into the hotel lobby, now already lit for evening, he felt two eyes resting on him. Sitting in an armchair with a serious expression on his face, a newspaper spread over his knees, was the baron from whom he had taken a hasty farewell on the boat. He nodded to Alfred without getting up. Alfred acted as if pleased by the unexpected meeting, even believed he really was, and told the baron of his intention to stay until the next day. Despite his pale cheeks and persistent cough, the baron maintained he felt fine, and later at dinner suggested that they go to a music hall together. Seeing Alfred's hesitation, he remarked, softly and with lowered eyes, that mourning had never yet awakened anyone from death. Alfred laughed, was immediately frightened by his laugh, believed that the baron had noticed his embarrassment, and realized that it would be best for him to accompany the baron. Shortly thereafter he sat with him in a private loge drinking champagne, watching through a cloud of smoke and haze as clowns and gymnasts practiced their art to the sounds of a shrill orchestra, and listening to half-naked women singing brazen songs. As though in the grip of a violent compulsion, he couldn't prevent himself from directing his taciturn companion's attention to the well-shaped legs and voluptuous breasts displayed on stage. He flirted with a flower girl, threw a yellow rose at the feet of a dancer who seductively shook her loose black hair at him, and burst out laughing when he saw the narrow lips of the baron twitch as though in bitterness and disgust. Later he felt as though hundreds of people were looking suspiciously at him from below, and that all the buzz and murmuring around him was meant for him alone. A cold shiver of fear ran down his back, but he calmed himself by remembering that he had downed a couple of glasses of champagne much too quickly. As he leaned over the balustrade, he noted with satisfaction that two heavily rouged women had engaged the baron in conversation. Breathing a sigh of relief as though he had been saved from some imminent danger, he stood up and nodded encouragingly at his companion as if wishing him success in his adventure, and soon he was walking back to his hotel alone in the cool night air down streets he had never seen before and would never see again, whistling snatches of a random melody and feeling as though he were in an unreal dream city.

When he awoke the next morning from a heavy, deep sleep, it took him a while to collect himself and realize that he was no longer on board ship, and that the white gleam over there was not Elise's morning robe but a curtain. With an enormous effort of will he suppressed the memory that threatened to surface, and rang for a servant. A telegram arrived with his breakfast. He let it sit on the tray while the waiter remained in the room, and felt as though this act of self-control deserved some kind of reward. Scarcely had the door closed again when he tore open the telegram with shaking fingers. At first the words swam before his eyes, but suddenly they stood there, gigantic and stiff: "Tomorrow at 11:00. Adele." He paced up and down the room, laughed through clenched teeth, and refused to let himself be put off by the cold, peremptory tone of Adele's reply. That was just her way. And even if everything at home were not quite what he expected, indeed, even if some uncomfortable revelations awaited him, what of it? He would still be standing face to face with her again, bathed in the light of her eyes and the sweetness of her breath, so that the monstrous deed had not been done in vain.

There was nothing to keep Alfred in the hotel, so he spent the short time before his train left walking about the city with his eyes wide open but seeing nothing. He left Hamburg for Vienna in the afternoon, staring hour after hour at the landscape flying past him out-side the window, suppressing with a well-practiced effort of will every thought, hope, and fear that threatened to rise up within him. When, in order not to attract the attention of his fellow passengers, he took up a book or a newspaper, instead of reading it he silently counted from one to a hundred, to five hundred, to a thousand. But as night fell, the yearning that consumed him broke through all his efforts to retain his self-control. He called himself mad to have mis-interpreted the absence of letters and the tone of Adele's last telegram, and could not fault her for anything except for obeying more zealously than he had the agreement her father had forced upon them. Even if she had in the meantime somehow found out that he had traveled with another woman, he felt that his love was strong enough to win her back again in the face of all the jealousy and bitterness she was likely to feel. So much did he succeed in mastering his waking dreams that in the long endless night of his journey he heard the melody of her voice, saw the outline of her form and features—even felt her kiss, more torrid and sweet than he had ever experienced it in reality.

Back home his apartment welcomed him with friendly com-fort. The carefully prepared breakfast placed before him tasted splendid, and for the first time in many days, it seemed to him, he was able to think with perfect calm of her who now slumbered in the silent ocean, delivered forever from all earthly misery. Some-times it seemed to him that the entire period between the landing in Naples and Elise's death was nothing but a fantasy born of his shat-tered nerves, and that what had happened was only—as the doctors had foreseen, even foretold—the natural outcome of the normal progression of her illness. Yes, the man who had craftily run from doctor to doctor and from pharmacy to pharmacy in that sun-baked foreign city, the man who had prepared the deadly poison with ghastly care, the man who just an hour before he poisoned her had lustily embraced the woman he planned to dispatch—that man seemed to him a completely different person from this man who now sat comfortably drinking tea between the walls of a familiar and ordinary bourgeois house. That man seemed to him much more powerful than he was, a man to whom he could look with shuddering admiration. Yet when he later caught sight of his own slim naked image in a mirror while climbing out of his bath, he suddenly became aware that it was indeed he and no one else who had done the incomprehensible deed. He saw his own eyes gleaming with a hard brilliance and felt himself now worthier than ever to clasp his waiting bride to his heart. With a smile of scornful superiority on his lips, he was more certain of her love than he had ever been before.

At the appointed hour on the following day he walked into the yellow room he had left a year ago almost to the very day, and a minute later Adele stood before him, as nonchalantly as if she had just said goodbye to him the previous evening. She gave him her hand and allowed him to give it a long kiss. What's preventing me from embracing her? he asked himself. He heard her talk in that husky voice he had heard just the night before in his dream, and realized he hadn't said a word yet but had only whispered her name as she walked up to him. She hoped he wasn't offended, she began, that she hadn't answered his beautiful letters, but there were things better said and done in person than in writing. Of course her silence should have alerted him to the possibility that many things had changed—the cool tone of her message had, she wanted to tell him right away, been quite deliberate. Because, about six months ago, she had become engaged to someone else. And she named someone Alfred knew. It was one of his many old friends about whom he had thought as little during the course of the past year as he had about anyone else he knew. He listened to Adele calmly, in a trance, staring at her smooth forehead and through it into the emptiness beyond, while in his ears there was a rushing like that of distant waves rolling across sunken worlds. Suddenly he saw a glimmer of fear in Adele's eyes and realized that he was deathly pale, looking at her with a terrifying gaze, and saying in a hard and toneless tone, "That can't be, Adele. You're mistaken. You can't do that."

The fact that he had finally spoken seemed to calm her. She smiled again in her direct manner and explained to him that it was not she who was mistaken, but he. For she could do whatever she wanted. She had not even been engaged to him; they had parted as free people, without any commitment to each other, she as well as he. And since she didn't love him anymore, but now loved someone else, that was the end of the matter. He had to understand and accept that; otherwise she would truly regret not following her father's advice to refuse to receive him this morning. And then she sat down across from Alfred, her slender hands crossed over her knees, her eyes bright and distant.

Alfred knew that he needed all his self-control not to do something foolish or dreadful. What exactly he wanted to do wasn't clear to him. Fall on her neck and choke her? Throw himself on the ground and moan like a child? But what good was it to think about what to do next? He had no choice, he was already defeated, and he had just enough presence of mind left to grasp Adele's hands when she wanted to leave and to implore her to stay: just a quarter of an hour! Hear him out! He could demand that much of her after all that had happened between them. He had a lot to tell her, much more than she could suspect, and she had to hear it. Because once she knew everything, she would also know that he belonged to her and she to him, him alone. She would know that she couldn't belong to anyone else, that he had won her through guilt and torment, that compared to his immense right to her, no one else had any—she would know that she was bound to him forever, just as he was to her. And on his knees before her, gripping her hands, his eyes locked into hers, he unrolled the contents of the entire past year before her eyes. He told her how he had loved another woman before he loved her and how he had traveled with her because she was ill and had no one on earth but him, how he had been consumed with the torment of endless longing for her, Adele, but how she, the other woman, had clung to him in her helplessness. And finally he told her how, at the end of his rope, out of love for *her, for her* whose hands he was now holding, out of a love stronger than anyone's on earth had ever been—how he had done away with the other woman, who would neither have wanted to live nor could have lived without him, had poisoned her with compassionate treachery, and how the poor creature was now sleeping underneath the waves of a distant sea—the sacrifice for a bliss that would be as peerless as the price of its achievement.

Adele had allowed her hands to remain in his and had not taken her eyes from his. She listened to what he said, but he couldn't tell whether she took it as a fairy tale about strange and alien beings or as a newspaper story about people who had nothing to do with her. Perhaps she didn't even believe what he said. In any case, whether it was the truth or a lie that came from his lips, it was clear that it made no difference to her. He felt more and more powerless. He saw all his words slide off her, empty and meaningless, and in the end, when he wanted to hear her say what he already knew, she only shook her head. He looked at her anxiously, knowing and yet not believing, with a demented question in his flickering eyes.

"No," she said with a frozen expression. "No. It's over."

And he knew that with this "No" everything was over. Adele's features remained completely motionless. They expressed not the slightest memory of former affection, not even horror—only a devastating indifference and boredom.

Alfred bowed his head, smiled emptily as though in agreement, stopped grasping at the hands that hung expressionless at her side, and turned around and left. The door behind him remained open, and he felt a cold breath of wind on his neck. As he went down the steps he knew there was nothing left for him to do but to end it all. He felt this to be so obviously true that he walked back to his house in the warm spring day in a leisurely and relaxed manner, as though headed to a much desired sleep after a night of dissipation.

But someone was waiting for him in his room. It was the baron. Without taking Alfred's proffered hand, he declared that he wished to talk with him only for a moment, and upon Alfred's curt but polite nod, he continued, "I find it necessary to tell you that I consider you a complete scoundrel." Right, thought Alfred. There was nothing to be said against this accusation. He answered calmly, "I'm at your disposal. Tomorrow morning, if that's satisfactory." The baron shook his head curtly: no. Now. He had prepared everything carefully, evidently while still on board ship—two young gentlemen from the German embassy were standing by, awaiting his further instructions, and he expected that Alfred, who after all was at home here, could easily arrange matters by evening. Alfred believed he could promise that. For a moment he was tempted to make a complete confession to the baron, but seeing the vast hatred that radiated from his cold face, he feared that his visitor already suspected the truth and might hand him over to the authorities. And so he chose to remain silent.

Alfred found his seconds without much trouble. One was Adele's fiancé, the other a young officer with whom he had once enjoyed many a lighthearted day. Before the sun set on the wooded banks of the Danube, a notorious spot for such engagements, he faced the baron. A calm which, after the turmoil of the past several days, he experienced as a profound joy enveloped him. When he saw the barrel of the pistol aimed at him and heard a distant voice count down three seconds, a sound that fell like three cold raindrops from the evening sky and echoed on the ground below, he thought about the unutterably beloved over whose decomposing body the rolling waves of the sea were flowing. And as he lay on the ground and something dark bent over him, embraced him, and would not let him go, he felt blessed that he, having atoned, was now dying for her, coming toward her, into that Nothing for which he had so long yearned.

Casanova's Homecoming

IN THE FIFTY-THIRD YEAR of his life, Casanova, now no longer
compelled to roam the world by the adventurousness of youth but by
the restlessness of approaching old age, began to feel such an intense
longing for his native city of Venice that he began to draw nearer and
nearer to it in ever tightening circles, like a bird gradually descending
from its airy heights in order to die. Again and again during the last
ten years of his exile he had petitioned the Grand Council for permission to return home. But while at first defiance and obstinacy, even a
grim pleasure in the task itself, had guided him in the crafting of his
sentences (a skill at which he was masterful), his words recently had
taken on an almost humble and pleading tone that clearly revealed a
painful longing and a genuine remorse. He felt all the more certain of
being granted his petition now that the sins of his earlier years were
by degrees slowly fading into oblivion. And of course it was not his
licentiousness, his quarrelsomeness, or his farcical swindles that had
most offended the Venetian town fathers but his freethinking. These
days it was the story of his amazing escape from the city's Lead
Chambers that was most often associated with his name. He had told
the story countless times and to great effect at the courts of princes,
in the mansions of aristocrats, at the dinner tables of the bourgeoisie,
and in houses of ill repute, and by now it overshadowed other malicious gossip about him. Just recently, in fact, he had again received

letters from influential men in Mantua, where he had been staying for the past two months, assuring the aging adventurer, whose inner as well as outer brilliance was gradually fading, that his fate would be decided in his favor very soon.

Since his financial resources had dwindled considerably, Casanova had decided to wait for his pardon in a modest but respectable inn where he had once stayed in happier years. There he wiled away his time—not counting a few earthly pleasures which he couldn't give up entirely—mostly in writing a polemic against the slanderous Voltaire, hoping that its publication would secure his position and his reputation with all right-thinking men in Venice.

One morning, as he walked outside the city walls trying to formulate a sentence that would annihilate the infidel Frenchman, he was overcome by a strange and almost physically painful agitation. The life of repetitive routine he had lead for the past three months—morning walks in the countryside outside the town walls, evenings spent in petty gambling with the so-called Baron Perotti and his pockmarked mistress, the attentions of his no longer young but still ardent innkeeper, even his study of Voltaire's works and the writing of his own audacious reply, which until then had seemed quite adequate—all seemed equally meaningless and repulsive to him here in the gentle, sweet air of this late summer morning. Muttering a curse without really knowing against whom or at what, he gripped the hilt of his sword and cast angry glances all round, as if invisible eyes were looking at him mockingly from the surrounding solitude. He did a sudden about-face and walked back toward the city, determined to prepare to leave town that very hour. For he was convinced he would feel better the minute he was closer to his beloved homeland, even if only by a few miles. He quickened his step to make sure of being back in time to secure a seat on the express mail coach that left for the east before sundown. He didn't have much else to do since he needn't pay a farewell visit to Baron Perotti, and half an hour was enough time in which to pack up his few meager belongings. He thought about his two rather threadbare garments, the shabbier of which he wore at the moment, and of his oft-mended, once-fine linen, which, along with a couple of boxes, a golden watch and chain, and a few books, were all that he now possessed. As he recalled earlier days when he had been an elegant gentleman well furnished with all sorts of necessary and unnecessary items as well as with a servant—who, to be sure, had usually been a scoundrel—and had driven through the countryside in a splendid coach, an impotent rage drove tears into his eyes.

Just then a young woman with a whip in her hand passed by in a little cart in which her drunken husband lay snoring between sacks of grain and various household odds and ends. At first she looked inquiringly and mockingly at Casanova, who walked in long strides beneath the bare chestnut trees lining the road and was approaching her with a contorted face, muttering inaudibly between clenched teeth. When he returned her look with a flash of anger, her eyes took on an expression of alarm, which, however, changed into one of amorous invitation as she passed and turned to look back at him. Casanova, who knew that fury and hatred gave the appearance of youth more readily than gentleness and amiability did, immediately recognized that he would only have to address the young wife suggestively to bring the cart to a halt and do whatever he pleased with her. But while the recognition of this fact improved his mood for an instant, it didn't seem worth the effort to lose even a moment on such a trivial adventure, and he let the peasant cart and its passengers continue to creak along unhampered down the dusty, hazy road.

The shade of the trees did little to alleviate the scorching heat of the rising sun, and Casanova was forced to slow his pace. The dust and dirt of the road covered him so thickly that the shabbiness of his garments and shoes was no longer visible. Judging by his dress and his bearing now, he could easily have been taken for a gentleman of rank who on a whim had decided to leave his stately coach at home and walk for once. He had almost reached the arched gateway near his inn when a heavy country carriage came lumbering toward him with a well-dressed and portly yet still relatively young man inside. The man's hands were clasped across his stomach, and, judging by his drooping eyelids, he seemed about to doze off when his glance happened to fall on Casanova. Suddenly he brightened with unexpected animation. His whole body seemed overcome with joyous excitement. He sprang to his feet too quickly, fell back into his seat, rose again, gave the driver a poke in the back to make him stop the carriage, and turned around in the still rolling vehicle to keep from losing sight of Casanova, all the time signaling with both hands and finally calling Casanova's name three times in a thin, high-pitched voice. Only when he heard the voice did Casanova recognize the man. He walked toward the carriage, then stopped, and, smiling, took the two hands that stretched out toward him, saying,

"Is it possible, Olivo—is it really you?"

"Yes, it's me, Signor Casanova—so you still recognize me?"

"And why wouldn't I? True, you've gained a little weight since I last saw you on your wedding day—but I suppose I've also changed a bit in the last fifteen years, if not in quite the same way."

"Why no!" exclaimed Olivo, "you've hardly changed at all, Signor Casanova! But it's been sixteen years—it was sixteen years only a few days ago! As you can imagine, we talked about you for quite a while on our wedding anniversary, Amalia and I . . ."

"Really," said Casanova warmly, "the two of you still remember me?"

Olivo's eyes brimmed with tears. He still held Casanova's hands and pressed them fondly, clearly moved. "We owe you so much, Signor Casanova! How could we ever forget our benefactor? And if we ever—."

"Let's not talk about that," interrupted Casanova. "How is Signora Amalia? And how is it possible that in the two months that I've been here in Mantua—I've been leading a rather retiring life, of course, but I still walk as much as I did before—how is it possible that I've never once run into either of you?"

"That's easy to explain, Signor Casanova! We haven't lived in town for a long time—I never really liked it, and neither did Amalia. Do me the honor, Signor Casanova, of coming into my carriage and riding home with me. In an hour we'll be at my house." When Casanova made a slight gesture of refusal, he added, "Please don't say no. Amalia will be so happy to see you again, and so proud to show you our three children. Yes, three, Signor Casanova. All girls. Thirteen, ten, and eight . . . so none of them is old enough—beg your pardon—to let her head be turned by Casanova."

Olivo laughed good-naturedly and was on the verge of simply pulling Casanova up into the carriage with him. But Casanova shook his head. For a moment he had been tempted to give in to his natural curiosity and take Olivo up on his offer, but now his impatience overcame him again with renewed force, and he assured Olivo that he was unfortunately obliged to leave Mantua on important business before nightfall. What business did he have in Olivo's house anyway? Sixteen years was a long time! Amalia would certainly not have grown any younger or more beautiful, and he could hardly expect the thirteen-year-old daughter to be interested in him at his age. The prospect of admiring Signor Olivo, who had once been a lean and eager student, in his new incarnation as a portly and ponderous country patriarch didn't tempt him enough to consider putting off a journey that would bring him ten or twenty miles closer to Venice. But Olivo didn't seem inclined to take no for an answer and insisted upon at least giving him a ride back to his inn, an offer that Casanova could not decently refuse. In a few minutes they arrived. The innkeeper, a well-endowed woman in her mid-thirties, greeted

Casanova at the entrance of the inn with an expression that could not but help make their amorous relationship obvious even to Olivo, whom she greeted as a familiar acquaintance. Olivo—as she promptly explained to Casanova—regularly supplied her with an excellent and well-priced wine that he grew on his estate. Olivo immediately complained to her that the Chevalier de Seingalt (since she had addressed Casanova by this name, Olivo did not hesitate to use the title as well) was so cruel as to reject the invitation of an old friend he hadn't seen in years with the ridiculous excuse that he must leave Mantua today and not a day later. The woman's startled look immediately informed Olivo that this was the first she had heard of Casanova's intention to leave, and Casanova was forced to explain that he had only pretended to have to leave immediately so as not to burden his friend's family with such a completely unexpected visit. Still, it was true that he was constrained, yes, obligated, to finish an important piece of writing in the next few days, and he knew of no better place to do so than at this excellent inn, in which he had a cool and quiet room.

At this Olivo declared that no greater honor could be granted his modest house than to have the Chevalier de Seingalt finish his work there. The rustic isolation of his estate could not but help such an undertaking. Also, there was no lack of scholarly tomes and reference books in the house, if Casanova needed them, because his niece, his stepbrother's daughter, a young but nevertheless highly erudite girl, had just arrived at their home with a trunk filled with books. If guests should drop by some evenings, the Signor Chevalier needn't disturb himself at all, unless a little pleasant conversation or a game of cards would be a welcome diversion after a day of labor. No sooner had Casanova heard about the young niece than he decided he had to have a look at the creature at close range, and finally, after a further show of reluctance, he gave in to Olivo's insistence, declaring, however, that he could on no account be away from Mantua for more than one or two days. He begged his dear innkeeper to promptly forward any letters that might come for him during his absence, as they might be of the utmost importance. After everything had been thus arranged to Olivo's great satisfaction, Casanova went to his room, prepared for the trip in a quarter of an hour, and returned to the dining room where he found Olivo having a lively business conversation with the innkeeper. Olivo rose, toasted her with a glass of wine and a significant wink, and promised that he would return the Chevalier to her safe and sound, if not tomorrow then the next day. But Casanova, suddenly distracted and eager to depart, took leave of the friendly innkeeper so coolly that as the carriage door slammed shut she whispered a parting word in his ear that was anything but an endearment.

While the two men drove along the dusty road beneath a blazing noonday sun, Olivo told Casanova the tediously detailed story of his life since he had last seen him: how he had bought a tiny piece of land near town soon after his marriage and had started a small vegetable stall; how he had gradually been able to add to his property and had begun more ambitious farming ventures; and how at length, thanks to his and his wife's industriousness and to God's grace, he had come so far as to buy the debt-ridden Count Marazzini's old and somewhat dilapidated palazzo and vineyard three years ago. Though not living in patrician splendor, he now lived comfortably with his wife and children on this estate. And in the last analysis he owed all this to the hundred and fifty gold pieces that Casonova had given his bride, or rather, her mother. But for this magical aid, his life would no doubt be the same today as it had been then: he would still be teaching reading and writing to ill-mannered brats. And probably he would have wound up an old bachelor and Amalia an old maid. . . .

Casanova let him ramble on but hardly listened. He recalled the adventure that had been only one of many he had carried on at the time. As it had seemed to him the most trivial of them, it had until now troubled his soul as little as his memory. He had been traveling from Rome to Turin or Paris—he couldn't remember which—when, during a brief stopover in Mantua, he had caught sight of Amalia one morning in a church. Her pretty but pale and somewhat tearstained face had attracted him, and he had gallantly addressed a friendly question to her. Trusting and well disposed toward him, as was everyone in those days, she had gladly poured out her heart to him. He found that she lived in meager circumstances and had fallen in love with a poor schoolteacher whose father, like her own mother, adamantly refused to consent to such an unpromising match. Casanova promptly declared himself ready to solve the problem. First he arranged to have himself introduced to Amalia's mother, and since she was a pretty young widow of thirty-six who could still lay claim to the attentions of men, he was soon on such intimate terms with her that he could persuade her to agree to anything he wished. Once her consent to the marriage had been won, Olivo's father, a merchant down on his luck, no longer refused his consent, especially since Casanova, introduced to him as a distant relative of the bride's mother, had generously offered to pay the wedding expenses and a part of the dowry. After that, of course, Amalia herself couldn't help demonstrating her gratitude to her noble benefactor, who seemed to her a messenger from another, higher world, in the way that her own heart as well as his wishes dictated. And when, the night before her wedding, she tore herself away from Casanova's embrace with glowing cheeks, nothing was farther from her mind than the idea that she might have wronged her bridegroom, who after all owed his good fortune entirely to the kindness and noble spirit of this marvelous stranger. Whether Olivo had ever found out about the length to which Amalia had gone out of gratitude to her benefactor; whether, if he had, he had taken her sacrifice as a matter of course and accepted it without retrospective jealousy; or whether he remained ignorant of it to this day—this was something that Casanova had never troubled himself about. Nor did he let it trouble him now.

It grew hotter and hotter. The carriage, with its poor springs and hard cushions, rumbled along and jolted its occupants painfully. Olivo's incessant, thin-voiced, good-natured chatter about the fertility of his land, the excellence of his wife's housekeeping, the wonderful qualities of his children, and the cordial and forthright relationships he had with both his peasant and his aristocratic neighbors, began to bore Casanova, and he asked himself irritably why on earth he had accepted an invitation that could bring him nothing but discomfort and ultimately probably disappointment. He longed for his cool hotel room in Mantua, where at this very hour he could be working undisturbed on his polemic against Voltaire. He had just decided to get out at the next inn they should happen to come across, hire any old carriage he could find, and return to his inn when Olivo let out a loud "Hullo!" He began to wave his hands in his characteristic way and, grabbing Casanova by the arm, pointed out a cart that had come to a stop next to theirs, as if by prearrangement. Three little girls jumped down, one after the other, so quickly that the narrow board that served them as a seat flew into the air and flipped over.

"My daughters," said Olivo, not without pride, turning to Casanova. And when Casanova began to rise from his seat, he continued, "Just stay where you are, my dear Chevalier. We'll be at my place in a quarter of an hour, and for that little while we can squeeze together in my carriage. Maria, Nanetta, Teresina—see, this is the Chevalier de Seingalt, an old friend of your father's. Come closer, kiss his hand. But for him you—"

He caught himself and whispered to Casanova, "I almost said something very stupid." Correcting himself out loud, he said, "But for him a lot of things would have been different."

The girls, black-haired and brown-eyed like Olivo, all, including Teresina, still very much children, looked at the stranger with direct,

somewhat peasantish curiosity. The youngest, Maria, was in all seriousness about to obey her father's command and kiss his hand. But
Casanova didn't allow it and instead took the face of each girl in his
hands and kissed it on both cheeks. Meanwhile Olivo exchanged a
few words with the young peasant who had brought the girls in the little cart, whereupon the fellow whipped up his horse and drove off toward Mantua.

Laughing and bickering good-humoredly, the girls sat down on
the backseat opposite Olivo and Casanova. They sat tightly
squeezed together, all talking at once, and since their father likewise
continued talking, Casanova at first had a hard time figuring out
what they were trying to say to each other. One name stood out: that
of a Lieutenant Lorenzi. According to Teresina, he had passed them
on horseback a short while ago, had promised to visit them this
evening, and had sent his respects to their father. The girls also reported that their mother had meant to come with them to meet their
father, but because it was so awfully hot, she had in the end decided
to stay home with Marcolina. As for Marcolina, she was still in bed
when they left home, and if they hadn't pelted her through her open
window with berries and hazelnuts from the garden, she would
probably still be asleep even now.

"That's not like Marcolina at all," Olivo said, turning to his
guest, "usually she's already sitting in the garden at six o'clock in
the morning if not earlier, studying until lunch. Of course we did
have visitors yesterday, and so we were up a little later than usual.
We had a little card game—not the kind of game the Chevalier is
used to, of course—we're simple people and we don't want to take
money away from each other. Since our good abbot usually partici-
pates, you can imagine that things don't get very sinful."

At the mention of the abbot, the girls laughed and began telling
one another God knows what, which made them laugh even more.
But Casanova merely nodded absentmindedly. In his imagination he

already saw Signorina Marcolina, whom he hadn't even met yet, lying in her white bed directly opposite her window, throwing off her bedclothes and revealing her half-naked body, and with drowsy hands warding off the hail of berries and hazelnuts flying in. Suddenly his senses were flooded by a rush of foolish passion. He was as certain that Marcolina was Lieutenant Lorenzi's lover as if he had seen them in the most intimate embrace, and he was as ready to hate the unknown Lorenzi as he was to desire the yet unseen Marcolina.

Through the shimmering haze of noon a square tower became visible looming above the greenish-grey foliage. The carriage turned off the main road into a side road. To the left, vineyards sloped gently uphill; to the right, the crests of ancient trees draped over the top of a garden wall. The carriage stopped at a gate whose weather-beaten wooden doors stood wide open. The passengers alighted, and at a signal from Olivo, the coachman drove on toward the stable. A broad avenue lined with chestnut trees led to the little castle, which at first glance looked somewhat bare, even neglected. The first thing that caught Casanova's eye was a broken window on the second story; and he couldn't help noticing that the battlements of the squat tower, which sat somewhat gracelessly on the building, were crumbling here and there. But the front door was finely carved, and as soon as he entered the entrance hall Casanova noted that the interior of the house was well maintained and in far better condition than might have been supposed from its exterior.

"Amalia," shouted Olivo, in a voice so loud it echoed from the vaulted ceiling. "Come down as fast as you can! I brought you a guest, Amalia—and what a guest!"

But Amalia had already appeared at the top of the stairs, though she was not yet visible to most of those who had just emerged from the bright sunlight into the dimly lit interior. Casanova, whose sharp eyes could still see well even in the dark, saw her before her husband did. He smiled and was aware that his smile made his face look younger. Amalia hadn't grown the least bit fat, as he had feared. She was still as slim and as youthful as ever. She recognized him instantly.

"What a surprise—how wonderful to see you!" she cried out without a trace of embarrassment, rushing headlong down the stairs and offering Casanova her cheek, whereupon he did not hesitate to hug her like a dear old friend.

"And I'm to believe, Amalia, that Maria, Nanetta, and Teresina are really your own flesh and blood? It would be possible, given the time that has passed, but—"

"And given everything else that happened," Olivo added, "you can take my word for it, Chevalier!"

"So it was your running into the Chevalier that made you so late, Olivo?" Amalia said, letting her eyes rest nostalgically on their guest.

"That's right, Amalia, but I hope there's something left to eat despite our late arrival?"

"Of course. We didn't sit down to eat all by ourselves, Marcolina and I, though we were very hungry."

"And would you mind being patient a little longer so that I can get some of the dirt of the road off my clothes and myself?" said Casanova.

"Of course; I'll show you to your room immediately," said Olivo. "I do hope you'll be happy there, almost as happy . . . ," he winked at him and added in a muted voice, "as in your room in Mantua, though there might be a thing or two missing here . . ."

He led Casanova up the stairs and into the gallery encircling the four sides of the entrance hall, where a narrow wooden staircase wound its way upward from one of the farthest corners. When he had reached the top, Olivo opened the door to the tower room, and, standing at the threshold, politely offered it to Casanova. A maid followed with his valise and went back down the stairs with Olivo, leaving Casanova alone in a simply furnished and relatively bare room which nonetheless contained every necessity. Its four tall, narrow bay windows offered expansive views in all directions of the sun-drenched plain with its green vineyards, brightly colored meadows, golden fields, white roads, light-colored houses, and dusky gardens. Casanova paid little attention to the view and got ready quickly, not so much out of hunger as out of a tormenting desire to see Marcolina face to face as soon as possible. He didn't even change his clothes as he wished to wait until evening to appear in greater splendor.

When he entered the wood-paneled dining room on the ground floor he saw seated at the amply laden table, next to his host and hostess and their three daughters, a graceful and petite young woman in a simple, flowing grey dress of a faintly shimmering fabric. She looked at him as frankly and as unself-consciously as if he were either a member of the household or a guest who had visited a hundred times before. That her eyes did not light up with that gleam which had so often greeted him in earlier days when he, unknown, had made his entrance in the captivating glow of his youth or in the dangerous beauty of his prime, was not a new experience for Casanova of late. Still, even now the mere mention of his name usually sufficed to elicit from women's lips an expression of belated admiration, or at least a slight twitch of regret at not having encountered him a few years earlier. Yet when Olivo introduced him to his niece as Signor Casanova, the Chevalier de Seingalt, she smiled no differently than she would have smiled at the mention of any utterly indifferent name devoid of any aura of adventure or mystery. Even when he took his seat next to her, kissed her hand, and slowed his eyes to shower her with gleams of delight and desire, her manner betrayed nothing of the demure satisfaction that might, after all, have seemed a fitting response to such a glowing tribute.

After a few polite pleasantries, Casanova gave his table partner to understand that he had been informed of her intellectual endeavors and asked her which field of knowledge she had chosen to study. Above all, she answered, she was interested in higher mathematics, to which she had been introduced by Professor Morgagni, the renowned teacher at the University of Bologna. Casanova expressed his amazement that a charming young lady should have an interest in such a difficult and at the same time so sober a subject, and received from Marcolina the reply that in her view higher mathematics was the most imaginative of all the sciences—indeed, the one most truly divine. But when Casanova asked for a more detailed explanation of what for him was a quite novel point of view, Marcolina modestly declined and commented that those present, especially her dear uncle, would much rather hear about the experiences of a widely traveled friend whom he hadn't seen in a long time than to listen to a philosophical discussion. Amalia wholeheartedly seconded this request, and Casanova, always happy to oblige in these matters, said nonchalantly that in the last few years he had been engaged mostly in secret diplomatic missions that had taken him to Madrid, Paris, London, Amsterdam, and St. Petersburg, to mention only the largest cities. He spoke of meetings and conversations, some serious and some amusing, with men and women of every station in life, and did not forget to mention the friendly reception he had received at the court of Catherine of Russia. He gave a very comical account of how Frederick the Great had almost made him a teacher at a cadet school for sons of Pommerian Junkers—a danger he had avoided by a timely escape. He told these and many other stories as though they had just recently happened, not, as was really the case, many years, even decades, earlier. To these tales he added a number of details of his own invention, scarcely even conscious of the lies he was telling, enjoying his own good humor as much as the rapt attention of his audience.

While he recounted these real and imaginary incidents, he almost felt he was still that glorious, bold, and radiant favorite of fortune, Casanova, who had traveled around the world with beautiful women, had been honored by the special favors of secular and spiritual princes, and had squandered, gambled, and given away thousands—and not the poor devil down on his luck who was supported by paltry remittances from former friends in England and Spain—amounts that sometimes failed to appear at all, so that he was forced to rely on the few miserable gold pieces he could win off Baron Perotti and his guests. He even forgot that right now his highest aim was to finish his once splendid existence in the city of his fathers, where he had been imprisoned and from which, after his escape, he had been banned—to return now as one of the least of its citizens, a mere scribbler, a beggar, a nothing.

Marcolina listened to him attentively like the rest, but with an expression appropriate to someone listening to moderately entertaining stories read from a book. That the man himself, the man who had experienced all this and much more, Casanova, lover of a thousand women, was sitting beside her did not register in her expression at all. Amalia's eyes, however, glistened with a different light. For her Casanova was still the same man he had once been. His voice was as seductive to her as it had been sixteen years ago, and he sensed that only a word from him, if that, would revive their old affair whenever he wanted. But what was Amalia to him now, when it was Marcolina he desired as he had never desired any other woman before? Beneath the faintly shimmering folds of the dress caressing her, he thought he could see her naked body; her budding breasts beckoned to him, and when she bent over to pick up a handkerchief that had fallen to the floor, Casanova's overheated imagination attributed such a suggestive meaning to her movement that he was near to swooning. It did not escape Marcolina that he inadvertently faltered for a moment in the middle of his story, nor that his gaze had begun to flicker strangely. And in her expression he read a sudden alienation and a protest, even a trace of disgust. He quickly regained his composure and was about to continue his story with renewed vigor when a portly clergyman, whom Olivo greeted as Abbot Rossie, entered, and Casanova immediately recognized him as the man he had met twenty-seven years earlier on a market boat going from Venice to Chioggia.

"You wore an eye patch," said Casanova, who seldom missed a chance to show off his excellent memory, "and a peasant woman with a yellow scarf recommended an ointment to you which a young pharmacist with a very hoarse voice happened to have with him on the boat."

The abbot nodded and smiled, flattered. Then, with a sly expression on his face, he walked right up to Casanova as though he had a secret to tell him. But instead he spoke out loud:

"And you, Signor Casanova, were there with a wedding party . . . I don't know whether as an ordinary guest or as best man, but in any case, the bride was looking at you with a much fonder look than she was looking at the groom. . . . A wind picked up, there was almost a storm, and you began to read an extremely racy poem."

"I'm sure the Chevalier did so only in order to calm the storm," said Marcolina. "I've never credited myself with magical powers," replied Casanova, "but I won't deny that after I began to read, no one worried about the storm anymore."

The three girls had surrounded the abbot. They had their reasons: from his enormous pockets he produced large quantities of delicious candies and popped them into the children's mouths with his pudgy fingers. Meanwhile Olivo was telling the abbot in great detail about how he had just found Casanova again. As though lost in reverie, Amalia kept her shining eyes riveted on her beloved guest's magnificent dark forehead. The children ran out into the garden, and Marcolina arose to watch them through the open window. The abbot brought greetings from the Marchese Celsi, who planned to visit his esteemed friend Olivo with his wife that evening, "his health permitting."

"Excellent," said Olivo. "Then we can have a little card game in honor of the Chevalier. I'm also expecting the Ricardi brothers, and Lorenzi is also coming—the girls ran into him today when he was out riding."

"Is he still here?" asked the abbot. "I heard a week ago that he was supposed to leave with his regiment."

Olivo laughed. "I suspect that the marchesa persuaded Lorenzi's colonel to give him an extension of his leave."

"I'm surprised that any officer from Mantua is being granted a leave right now," interjected Casanova. And he continued, fabricating: "Two friends of mine, one from Mantua, and the other from Cremona, left last night to march with their regiments toward Milan."

"Is there a war?" inquired Marcolina from the window. She had turned around; the features of her shaded face remained impossible to read, but there was a slight tremor in her voice that probably no one but Casanova noticed.

"Perhaps it won't come to anything," he said nonchalantly, "but since the Spaniards are acting belligerently, we have to be prepared."

"Does anyone know," asked Olivo with an air of importance, wrinkling his brow, "which side we'll be fighting with, the Spanish or the French?"

"I'm sure Lieutenant Lorenzi won't care either way," the abbot remarked, "as long as he finally has a chance to test his capacity for heroism."

"He's already done that," said Amalia, "He fought at Pavia three years ago."

Marcolina remained silent.

Casanova knew all he needed to know. He walked over to Marcolina and cast a searching glance over the garden. He saw nothing but a wild rolling meadow bordered by a row of stately, close-set trees within a surrounding wall, on which the girls were playing.

"What a magnificent estate," he said, turning to Olivo. "I'd be interested in seeing the rest of it."

"And I, Chevalier," replied Olivo, "would like nothing better than to take you through my vineyards and fields. Indeed, to tell the truth—just ask Amalia—in all the years since I bought this little place, I've wanted nothing more fervently than to welcome you as my guest on my own land and property. On at least ten occasions I was on the point of writing to invite you to come. But how could I trust that a message would reach you? If I happened to hear from someone somewhere that he had recently seen you in Lisbon, I could be sure that in the meantime you had gone to Warsaw or Vienna. But now that by some miracle I found you just as you were on the point of leaving Mantua, and succeeded in luring you out here—it wasn't easy, Amalia!—you are so miserly with your time that you—can you believe it, Signor Abbot, he won't grant us more than two days!"

"Perhaps the Chevalier will allow himself to be persuaded to stay longer," said the abbot, who was contentedly allowing a slice of peach to dissolve in his mouth. As he spoke, he cast a quick glance at Amalia in a way that led Casanova to infer that she had confided in the abbot more intimately than in her husband.

"I'm afraid I can't," said Casanova, formally, "—and I would be remiss if I kept this from friends who have shown such concern for my fate—but my fellow Venetians are on the verge of making somewhat belated but therefore all the more honorable amends for the injustice they did me years ago, and I cannot fail to heed their requests any longer without appearing ungrateful or even vindictive." With a wave of his hand, he dismissed the eager but respectful question that he saw forming on Olivo's lips, and hastened to add, "Well, Olivo, I'm ready. Show me your little kingdom."

"Wouldn't it be more advisable," Amalia interjected, "to wait until it's a little cooler? I'm sure that the Chevalier would prefer to rest for a while or to relax with a stroll in the shade." And her eyes sought Casanova's with a shy supplication, as though her fate would be decided a second time during such a walk in the garden.

No one objected to Amalia's suggestion, and everyone went outside. Marcolina ran across the sunlit meadow to join the children in their game of badminton. She was scarcely taller than the oldest of the three girls, and now, as her loosened hair flowed around her shoulders, she looked like a child herself. Olivo and the abbot seated themselves on a stone bench beneath the trees on the avenue near the house. Amalia continued to stroll at Casanova's side. When they were out of everyone's earshot, she began to speak to him in the same intimate tone of voice she had used with him long ago, as though she had talked to him just yesterday.

"So you're here again, Casanova! How I've longed for this day. I knew it would come one day."

"I'm here by pure chance," said Casanova dispassionately.

Amalia only smiled. "Call it whatever you like. You're here! In all these sixteen years I've dreamed of nothing but this day!"

"One has to assume," answered Casanova cooly, "that you've dreamed of a few other things in all this time—and not merely dreamed of them, either."

Amalia shook her head. "You know that's not so, Casanova. And you haven't forgotten me either, otherwise you wouldn't have accepted Olivo's invitation, seeing that you're in such a hurry to get to Venice!"

"What exactly are you implying, Amalia? That I came here to make a cuckold of your good, decent husband?"

"How can you say that, Casanova? If I were to be yours again, it would neither be a betrayal nor a sin!"

Casanova laughed out loud. "Not a sin? Why not a sin? Because I'm an old man?"

"You're not old. You'll never be old for me. It was in your arms that I felt ecstasy for the first time—and I'm certain that it's my fate to experience it for the last time with you as well!"

"The last time?" Casanova repeated scornfully, though he wasn't entirely unmoved. "My friend Olivo might have some objections to that!"

"Oh, that," answered Amalia, blushing, "that's duty—all right, maybe even a pleasure; but ecstasy it's not . . . and never has been."

They didn't walk all the way to the end of the avenue, as if avoiding the place in the meadow where Marcolina and the children were playing. As though by prior agreement, they retraced their steps in silence and soon were back at the house. One of the windows at the narrow end of the ground floor stood open. In the dim light at the far end of the room, Casanova saw a half-open drape, behind which the foot of a bed was visible. A pale, gauzy garment hung over a chair next to it.

"Marcolina's room?" asked Casanova.

Amalia nodded. And in a seemingly gay and unsuspecting tone, she asked Casanova, "Do you like her?"

"Yes, since she's beautiful."

"Beautiful and virtuous."

Casanova shrugged, as if indicating that he hadn't inquired about her scruples. Then he said, "If you were seeing me for the first time today, do you think you would you still be attracted to me, Amalia?"

"I don't think you look any different today than you did back then. I see you now—the way you were then, the way I've always seen you—the way I've seen you in my dreams."

"Just look at me, Amalia! These wrinkles on my forehead . . . the loose folds of my neck! And these deep furrows that run from my eyes to my temples! And here—look here in the corner of my mouth, I'm missing a tooth!—and he opened his mouth wide in a distorted grin. "And look at these hands too, Amalia! Just look at them! Fingers like claws . . . little yellow spots on the nails . . . and these veins here—blue and swollen—the hands of an old man, Amalia!"

She took his hands as he held them up to her and in the shade of the trees on the avenue kissed them reverently one after the other. "And tonight I'll kiss your lips," she said in a humble and tender manner that enraged him.

Not far from them, at the far end of the meadow, Marcolina lay in the grass, her hands behind her head, looking up into the sky as the children's shuttlecocks flew to and fro. Suddenly she reached up with one hand and seized a shuttlecock in midair. As she caught it and laughed with pleasure, the girls pounced on her. Her hair tossed wildly about as she tried unsuccessfully to defend herself.

Casanova trembled. "You'll kiss neither my lips nor my hands," he said to Amalia, "and you'll wait for me and dream about me in vain—unless I've possessed Marcolina first."

"What, are you mad, Casanova?" gasped Amalia in an injured voice.

"Then we have nothing to reproach each other with," said Casanova. "You're mad because you think you see the love of your youth in me, an old man, and I'm mad because I've taken it into my head that I must have Marcolina. But maybe we are both fated to retrieve our sanity. Marcolina shall restore me to youth—for you. So—plead my case with her, Amalia!"

"You're out of your mind, Casanova. It's impossible. She isn't interested in any man."

Casanova laughed out loud. "What about Lieutenant Lorenzi?"

"What about Lorenzi?"

"He's her lover. I'm sure of it."

"How wrong you are, Casanova. He asked for her hand, and she turned him down. And he's young—he's handsome—yes, I almost think more handsome than you ever were, Casanova!"

"He asked her to marry him?"

"Ask Olivo if you don't believe me."

"Well, it doesn't matter to me. What do I care if she's a virgin or a whore, a bride or a widow—I've got to have her. I must have her!"

"I can't give her to you, my friend." And he sensed from Amalia's tone of voice that she pitied him.

"Now you know what a despicable creature I've become, Amalia! Ten years ago, even five years ago, I would have needed neither help nor an advocate to plead my case, even if Marcolina had been the goddess of virtue herself! And here I'm trying to turn you into a go-between. If I were rich . . . yes, with ten thousand ducats I could. . . . But I don't have ten thousand ducats. I'm a beggar, Amalia."

"You wouldn't get Marcolina even for a hundred thousand! What does she care about money? She loves books, the sky, the meadows, the butterflies, playing games with children . . . and with her inheritance, though it's small, she has more than she needs."

"Oh, if only I were a prince!" Casanova cried—a bit theatrically as was his wont, especially when in the grip of a genuine passion. "If I had the power to throw men into prison, to have them executed. . . . But I'm nothing. A beggar—and a liar to boot. I've been begging the Venetians for a position, for a piece of bread, a place to call home! What's become of me? Don't I disgust you, Amalia?"

"I love you, Casanova!"

"Then get her for me, Amalia! I know you can do it. Tell her whatever you like. Tell her that I've threatened you. That you think I'm capable of setting your house on fire! Tell her I'm a madman, a dangerous madman who just escaped from the asylum, but that a virgin's embrace could cure me. Yes, tell her that."

"She doesn't believe in miracles."

"What? She doesn't believe in miracles? Then she doesn't believe in God, either. That's even better! I have influence with the archbishop of Milan! Tell her that! I can ruin her! I can ruin all of you. Yes, it's true, Amalia! What kinds of books does she read, anyway? Some of them must be on the Index. Let me have a look at them. I'll make a list. One word from me . . ."

"Quiet down, Casanova! Here she is. Don't give yourself away! Be careful how you look at her! Never, Casanova, never, I tell you, have I known anyone more chaste. If she had any idea of what I just heard, she would feel sullied, and you wouldn't see her for the rest of your visit. Talk to her. Go ahead, talk to her—you'll see. You'll beg me for forgiveness."

Marcolina approached with the girls, who ran past her into the house. But she paused in front of Casanova, as if out of courtesy to a houseguest, and Amalia deliberately withdrew. Casanova did indeed feel a breath of austerity and purity from those pale, half-parted lips, that smooth brow framed by her dark blonde hair, now carefully arranged again—a sensation he rarely felt with regard to a woman, and which he hadn't felt before in her presence either. And a feeling of reverence and surrender empty of desire flooded him. And with reserve, yes, even with the kind of deference one might use in addressing someone of higher rank, which couldn't help but flatter her, he asked whether she was planning to devote the evening hours to her studies. She replied that she wasn't in the habit of working regularly in the country but, as had just happened while she lay in the meadow looking at the sky, she couldn't prevent a certain mathematical problem that she happened to be working on from preoccupying her even during her free hours. But when Casanova, encouraged by her friendliness, asked her in a joking manner what sort of lofty and pressing problem it was, she answered somewhat scornfully that it had nothing to do with that famous Kabbala with which the Chevalier de Seingalt was said to have achieved great things, and that therefore he wouldn't know what to make of it.

It annoyed him that she spoke of the Kabbala with such unconcealed contempt, despite the fact that in his admittedly rare moments of inner reflection, even he was aware that the mystical number system called the Kabbala made no sense and had no legitimacy—that far from having any correspondence to natural reality, it was no more than an instrument whereby cheats and pranksters—roles of which he himself was master—could lead gullible fools by the nose. Nevertheless, against his own inner conviction, he now undertook to defend the Kabbala to Marcolina as a completely legitimate and valid science. He spoke of the divine nature of the number seven, to which, he claimed, there were many references in the Holy Scriptures; of the profound and prophetic meaning of numbers pyramids and of the new system of constructing them that he himself had invented; and of the frequent predictions he had made using his system. Had he not, a few years earlier, while in Amsterdam, persuaded the banker Hope, on the basis of just such a pyramid, to take over the insurance of a merchant ship believed to be lost, thereby earning him a profit of two hundred thousand gold guilders? He was so eloquent in defense of his preposterous theories that this time too, as often happened, he began to believe all the nonsense he was spouting. In the end, he went so far as to declare that the Kabbala was not merely a branch of mathematics but its metaphysical perfection.

At this point Marcolina, who had listened to him attentively and with apparent seriousness, looked at him with a half-pitying, half-mischievous expression and said, "My esteemed Signor Casanova" (she seemed to be purposely refusing to address him as "Chevalier"), "you seem to find it important to give me a prime example of your world-famous talent as an entertainer, for which I'm genuinely grateful. But of course you know as well as I do that the Kabbala not only has nothing to do with mathematics but is in fact a sin against its true essence. It bears no more relation to mathematics than the confused and deceitful prattle of the sophists does to the clear and lofty doctrines of Plato and Aristotle."

"Nevertheless," answered Casanova quickly, "you'll have to grant me, my beautiful and learned Marcolina, that even the sophists were far from being the despicable and foolish fellows one would assume they were from your all-too-harsh criticism. To take an example from the present—Monsieur Voltaire himself is an arch-sophist in his thinking and writing. And yet it wouldn't occur to anyone, not even to me, who must confess to being his resolute opponent—in fact, I won't deny that I'm now in the process of writing a polemic against him—to refuse his extraordinary talent the recognition it deserves. And let me hasten to add that I've not let myself be influenced by the extreme courtesy that Monsieur Voltaire had the kindness to show me on the occasion of my visit to Ferney ten years ago."

Marcolina smiled. "It is really very big of you, Chevalier, to have the largesse to judge the greatest mind of the century with such charity."

"A great mind—the greatest even, you say?" Casanova exclaimed. "To call him that seems to me to be inappropriate, if for no other reason than that with all his genius he is a godless man, yes, even an atheist. And an atheist can never be a great mind."

"As far as I'm concerned, Signor Chevalier, that isn't a contradiction at all. But first you'll have to prove that Voltaire is indeed an atheist."

Now Casanova was in his element. In the first chapter of his polemic he had collected a great number of passages from Voltaire's works, especially from the notorious *Pucelle*, which seemed to him particularly well suited for proving Voltaire's atheism. Thanks to his excellent memory, he was now able to cite them chapter and verse and to add his own counterarguments. But in Marcolina he had found an adversary hardly inferior to himself in knowledge and mental acumen. On top of that she was far superior to him in skill and clarity of expression, if not in eloquence. The passages that Casanova cited as evidence of Voltaire's spirit of mockery, skepticism, and atheism Marcolina adroitly and quick-wittedly reinterpreted as proofs of the Frenchman's scientific and literary genius as well as his indefatigable struggle for truth. Further, she boldly contended that doubt, mockery, and indeed even atheism itself, when associated with such a wealth of knowledge, such absolute honesty, and such great courage must be more pleasing to God than the humility of the pious, which was usually nothing more than an excuse for an inability to think logically, and often enough—there were plenty of examples—nothing but cowardice and hypocrisy.

Casanova listened to her with growing astonishment. Since he felt incapable of winning Marcolina over—all the less so as he realized how much a certain mood of his recent years, which he had grown accustomed to calling faith, threatened to disintegrate completely under her objections—he took refuge in trite generalities, arguing that views like those Marcolina had just expressed were a serious threat not only to the very foundation of the church but also to the state. From this he was able to make a clever transition into the field of politics, where, given his wide experience and knowledge of the world, he could be relatively sure of having an edge over Marcolina. But although she lacked Casanova's acquaintance with the notable figures in this realm and the details of court and state diplomacy, and therefore couldn't contradict him on individual particulars even when she was inclined to doubt the accuracy and reliability of his assertions, it was nevertheless clear to him from her remarks that she had little respect for either the princes of the earth or the institutions of the state. She seemed convinced that in things great and small, selfishness and lust for power not so much ruled the world as brought it into a state of hopeless confusion. Rarely had Casanova encountered such freedom and independence of thought in a woman, much less in a girl who was certainly not yet twenty. He remembered, not without a touch of melancholy, that in former, better days, his own mind had ventured along the same path that he now saw Marcolina take, and had done so with a self-conscious and rather self-satisfied sense of daring that he saw entirely lacking in Marcolina, who seemed completely unaware of the boldness of her thought. Utterly captivated by the uniqueness of her ways of thinking and expressing herself, he almost forgot that he was walking beside a young, beautiful, and most desirable creature, a forgetfulness that was all the more amazing as he was then all alone with her on the shady avenue, at a considerable distance from the house.

Suddenly, however, breaking off in the middle of a sentence she had just begun, Marcolina called out brightly, almost joyfully, "Here comes my uncle!"

And Casanova, as if to rectify a missed opportunity, whispered to her, "Too bad. I would love to go on talking to you like this for hours, Marcolina!" He was aware as he said these words that his eyes again lit up with lust, at which Marcolina, who despite her mocking attitude had adopted an almost intimate tone during their conversation, immediately renewed her reserve. Her expression again revealed the same wariness, indeed the same aversion, that had so deeply wounded Casanova earlier in the day.

Am I really so repulsive? he anxiously asked himself. No, he assured himself, answering his own question. That's not it. It's that Marcolina—isn't really a woman. She's a scholar, a philosopher, one of the wonders of the world, as far as I'm concerned—but not a woman. Yet he knew at the same time that he was merely trying to deceive, console, and save himself—and that all his attempts were in vain.

Olivo had reached them. "Well," he said to Marcolina, "didn't I do well to bring you someone with whom you could at last have as intelligent a conversation as you have with your teachers in Bologna?"

"Yes, Uncle—indeed, even among them," Marcolina answered, "there isn't one who would dare to challenge Voltaire to a duel!"

"Voltaire? The Chevalier has challenged him to a duel?" exclaimed Olivo, not understanding.

"Your witty niece, Olivo, is referring to the polemic that I've been working on recently. Something to while away idle hours. I used to have more sensible things to do."

Marcolina, paying no attention to this remark, said, "It's pleasantly cool for your walk now. Goodbye." She nodded curtly and hurried across the meadow back to the house.

Casanova suppressed an impulse to follow her with his eyes, and asked, "Is Signora Amalia coming with us?"

"No, Chevalier," said Olivo, "she has a number of things to attend to in the house—and this is the time of day she usually gives the girls their lessons."

"What an excellent wife and mother she is! You're a lucky fellow, Olivo."

"Yes, I tell myself the same thing every day," replied Olivo, his eyes growing moist.

They walked along the narrow side of the house. Marcolina's window was still open, and from somewhere deep within the dimly lit room the diaphanous bright gown shimmered. They followed the broad, chestnut-lined avenue until they came to the road, now completely in shade. They walked slowly up the slope along the garden wall; there, where the road made a sharp right turn, the vineyards began. Olivo led his guest between tall grape vines heavy with dark blue fruit and up to the summit of the hill, then contentedly gestured back toward his house, which lay quite deep below them. In the window of his room in the tower, Casanova thought he saw a female figure going to and fro.

The sun was near setting, but it was still rather hot. Beads of perspiration ran down Olivo's cheeks while Casanova's brow remained perfectly dry. Walking slowly on and going downhill now, they came to a lush meadow. Grapevines wreathed their way from one olive tree to the next, and tall golden sheaves of grain waved between the rows of trees.

"The sun's blessing," said Casanova appreciatively, "comes in a thousand different shapes."

Once again and with an even greater wealth of detail than before, Olivo told the story of how he had acquired this beautiful property piece by piece, and how a few good harvests and vintages had made him a well-to-do, in fact even a rich man. But Casanova was lost in his own thoughts and only now and then picked up a word of Olivo's in order to prove by some polite question or other that he was paying attention. Only when Olivo, chattering on about everything under the sun, began to talk of his family and finally of Marcolina did Casanova prick up his ears. But he didn't learn much more than he already knew. Marcolina had lost her mother early on, and her father, Olivo's stepbrother, had been a physician in Bologna. While still a child she had astonished everyone at her father's house with her precocious intelligence, and so by now everyone had had plenty of time to get used to her brilliance. Her father had died a few years ago, and she had lived ever since with the family of a distinguished professor at the University of Bologna, that same Morgagni whom Casanova had already heard about, who took it upon himself to turn his pupil into a great woman scholar. But she always spent the summer months at her uncle's. She had turned down any number of offers for her hand, among them one from a Bolognese merchant, one from a neighboring landowner, and one from Lieutenant Lorenzi. It appeared that she really was determined to devote her life entirely to the service of learning. As Olivo recounted this, Casanova felt his desire grow beyond all bounds, while the realization that it was as foolish as it was futile brought him to the edge of despair.

Just as they came from the meadow and the fields back onto the main road, they heard shouts coming toward them from a cloud of approaching dust. A carriage gradually materialized in which an elegantly dressed older man sat next to a somewhat younger, amply endowed, and heavily rouged woman.

"The marchese," Olivo whispered to his companion, "he's on his way to my house."

The carriage halted. "Good evening, my dear Olivo," the marchese called out, "Will you be so good as to introduce me to the Chevalier de Seingalt? For I have no doubt that I have the pleasure of seeing him standing here at this very moment."

Casanova bowed slightly. "I am he," he said.

"And I'm the Marchese Celsi—and this is the marchesa, my wife." The marchesa offered her fingertips to Casanova, who put them to his lips.

"Well, my good Olivo," said the marchese, whose thick red eyebrows, growing together over his piercing green eyes, did not lend a friendly aspect to his narrow and waxen-yellow face, "my good Olivo, we're all going the same way, namely to your house. And since it's less than a quarter of an hour from here, I'll get out and walk with you. You don't mind driving this little distance by yourself, do you?" he said, turning to the marchesa, who had in the meanwhile been examining Casanova with lascivious, searching eyes. Without waiting for his wife's answer, he nodded to the coachman, who immediately lashed the horses furiously, as though for some reason he had to get his mistress away as quickly as possible. In an instant, the carriage had vanished in a whirl of dust.

"It's already gotten around the whole neighborhood," said the marchese, who was a few inches taller than Casanova and unnaturally thin, "that the Chevalier de Seingalt has come to stay a few days with his friend Olivo. It must be glorious to bear such a famous name."

"You're very kind, Signor Marchese," replied Casanova. "It's true that I haven't yet given up hope of winning a name such as you describe, though at the moment I'm still far from it. A work I'm currently engaged in will bring me, I hope, a little closer to my goal."

"We can take a shortcut here," said Olivo, turning into a pathway that led directly to the wall of his garden.

"Work?" repeated the marchese in a doubting tone. "May one ask what kind of work you're referring to, Chevalier?"

"Since you ask, Signor Marchese, I feel compelled to ask what you meant when you referred to my fame," he said, looking arrogantly into the marchese's piercing eyes. He knew perfectly well that neither his romance *Icosameron* nor his three-volume *Refutation of Amelot's History of the Government of Venice* had brought him notable literary fame, but it was important to him to give the impression that he thought no other kind of fame worth striving for. He therefore deliberately pretended to misunderstand all of the marchese's subsequent remarks to the effect that by the name "Casanova" he meant a celebrated seducer of women, a gambler, a merchant, a political emissary, and all sorts of other things—everything but a writer, especially since he had never heard a word about either the refutation of Amelot or the *Icosameron*. Finally the marchese remarked with a certain polite embarrassment, "At any rate, there's only one Casanova."

"That too is an error, Signor Marchese," countered Casanova coldly. "I have brothers and sisters, and the name of one of my brothers, the painter Francesco Casanova, surely isn't unknown to a connoisseur like yourself."

It became apparent that the marchese had no claim to connoisseurship in this field either, so he turned the subject to acquaintances of his in Naples, Rome, Milan, and Mantua whom he thought Casanova might have met. In this connection he brought up the name of Baron Perotti, though in a rather contemptuous tone, and Casanova was forced to admit that he often did a little gambling in the baron's house. "Just for distraction," he added, "for half an hour's relaxation before going to bed. Otherwise I've pretty well given up that way of wasting time."

"I'd be sorry if that were true," said the marchese, "because I must admit, Signor Chevalier, that it's been a lifelong dream of mine to compete with you, not only at the gaming table but—in my youth—in other areas as well. Did you know, by the way, that—how long ago could it have been?—I once arrived in the Belgian resort of Spa on precisely the same day, indeed at the very hour, you had left? Our carriages passed each other. And I had the same bad luck in Regensburg. Would you believe that there I even stayed in the very room you had vacated just an hour earlier?"

"It's really unfortunate," said Casanova, flattered in spite of himself, "that some people's paths don't cross until too late in life."

"It's not too late yet!" exclaimed the marchese enthusiastically. "As far as certain other things are concerned, I'll gladly concede victory to you in advance, and it doesn't bother me much. But as for games of chance, my dear Chevalier, perhaps we're now at the age—"

Casanova interrupted him. "—At the age—you may be right about that. But unfortunately it's precisely in the field of gambling that I no longer have the pleasure of measuring myself against someone of your rank"—and he said this in the tone of a dethroned ruler—"because, despite my renown, my dear Signor Marchese, I'm now practically reduced to the condition of a beggar."

The marchese involuntarily lowered his eyes before Casanova's proud gaze, then shook his head incredulously, as though what he had just heard was an odd joke. But Olivo, who had followed the whole conversation with great interest, and had accompanied his marvelous friend's deft parries with approving nods, could hardly suppress a gesture of alarm. When they reached a narrow wooden door in the rear garden wall, as Olivo was turning the key in the creaking lock to let the marchese enter the garden before them, he grasped Casanova by the arm and whispered, "You must take back your last words, Chevalier, before you set foot in my house again. The money I've owed you for sixteen years is waiting for you. I just didn't dare to . . . Just ask Amalia . . . it's all counted out and ready, waiting for you. I was planning to hand it to you on your departure."

Casanova gently interrupted him. "You owe me nothing, Olivo. Those few paltry gold pieces were—as you know perfectly well—a wedding present that I, as a friend of Amalia's mother . . . But why even talk about it? What do I care about a few ducats?" Raising his voice so that the marchese, who had stopped a few steps ahead of them, would hear him, he added, "I stand at a turning point of my fortune."

Olivo exchanged glances with Casanova to make sure he approved, then said to the marchese, "You see, the Chevalier has been summoned back to Venice and will set out for home in a few days."

"To be more precise, " remarked Casanova as they approached the house, "they've been summoning me to return ever more urgently for quite a while now. But as far as I'm concerned, since the senators took their time to make up their minds, it's their turn to be patient now."

"You're certainly entitled to stand upon your dignity, Chevalier!" said the marchese.

As they left the avenue and crossed the meadow, now in full shade, they saw the rest of the company awaiting them near the house. Everyone rose and began walking toward them, the abbot leading the way between Marcolina and Amalia, followed by the marchesa alongside a tall, young, and beardless officer in a red uniform trimmed with silver lace and shiny riding boots. This could be none other than Lorenzi. The way he talked to the marchesa while scanning her white powdered shoulders as if they were merely samples of other attractions with which he was equally familiar, and even more so, the manner in which the marchesa smiled up at him with half-closed eyes, could leave even a novice no doubt as to the nature of their relationship nor their lack of concern in keeping it a secret. They didn't interrupt their quiet but animated conversation until they were face to face with those coming toward them.

Olivo introduced Casanova to Lorenzi. They appraised each other with curt, cold glances that offered assurances of mutual dislike; with fleeting forced smiles, both bowed without offering to shake hands, as this would have required each of them to take a step toward the other. Lorenzi was a handsome man with a narrow face and, considering his youth, strikingly sharp features. Lurking behind his eyes was something difficult to grasp, something indefinable that suggested caution to an experienced eye. For only a split second did Casanova wonder who it was that Lorenzi reminded him of. Then he realized that it was he himself as he had been thirty years ago who was standing before him. Can it be that I've been reincarnated in his form? he asked himself. But then I must have died. . . . And a shudder went through him: haven't I been dead for a long time? What's left of the Casanova who was once young, handsome, and happy?

Though she was standing right next to him, Amalia's voice broke into his musings as though from somewhere far away. She was asking how he had enjoyed his walk. Raising his voice loud enough for everyone to hear, he lavished the highest praise on the fertile, well-tended estate he had just wandered through with Olivo. Meanwhile, with the help of Olivo's two eldest daughters, the maid was laying the long table that had been set up on the lawn. The girls were bringing the necessary dishes, glasses, and other items from the house amidst a great deal of commotion and giggling. Gradually dusk began to fall, and a gentle cooling breeze swept through the garden. Marcolina rushed to the table to put the finishing touches on what the girls and the maid had begun. The others casually wandered about the garden and along the avenues. The marchesa was extremely polite to Casanova, and asked him to tell the famous story of his escape from the Lead Chambers of Venice, though she was aware—as she added with an ambiguous smile—that he had had much more dangerous adventures, which however he might be less inclined to recount. Casanova answered that although he had indeed experienced a variety of sometimes serious and sometimes amusing troubles, he had never really experienced the kind of life whose very essence was danger. For even though he had been a soldier for a few months during a time of unrest on the island of Corfu many years ago—really, was there any profession which fate had not conspired to thrust him into?!—he had never had the good fortune to be part of an actual campaign such as the one that Lieutenant Lorenzi was about to take part in—for which he almost envied him.

"Then you know more than I do, Signor Casanova," Lorenzi said in a bright and impudent tone, "indeed, more than my colonel does, as he just granted me an indefinite extension of my leave."

"Is that so!" exclaimed the marchese with uncontrolled fury, and added spitefully, "Just imagine, Lorenzi, we—or rather, my wife—have been counting so definitely on your leaving that she's invited one of our friends, Baldi the singer, to stay with us at our palazzo at the beginning of next week."

"That's fine," answered Lorenzi, unperturbed. "Baldi and I are the best of friends. We'll get along fine. Don't you think so?" he turned to the marchesa, his teeth flashing. "You'd better!" the marchesa said, laughing gaily.

As she spoke, she seated herself at the empty table. Olivo seated himself on one side of her and Lorenzi on the other. Amalia sat opposite them between the marchese and Casanova. Marcolina sat next to Casanova at one end of the long table, and Olivo sat next to the abbot at the other end. The evening meal, like dinner at midday, was simple but delicious. The two oldest girls, Teresina and Nanette, served the food and filled the guests' glasses with the excellent wine grown on Olivo's hillsides. The marchese and the abbot thanked the girls with playful and somewhat suggestive caresses that a stricter father than Olivo might have objected to. Amalia didn't seem to notice anything. She was pale and dejected looking, like a woman determined to be old because youth no longer holds any meaning for her.

Is that all that's left of my power? Casanova wondered bitterly, contemplating her profile. Maybe it's just the lighting that's making her look so gloomy, he thought, for only a single broad beam of light fell upon the guests from inside the house. Otherwise they had to be content with the glow of the setting sun. The crowns of the trees shut out the views with sharp black outlines, reminding Casanova of a mysterious garden where late one night many years ago he had waited for a lover.

"Murano," he whispered to himself, and trembled. Then he said aloud, "There's a garden on an island close to Venice, a convent garden, where I last set foot several decades ago—at night the scent there was just like the one here tonight."

"So you were a monk once too?" asked the marchesa jokingly.

"Almost," replied Casanova with a smile, and explained, truthfully enough, how as a boy of fifteen he had been given minor orders by the Patriarch of Venice but had decided soon afterward to set aside his cassock.

The abbot mentioned that there was nunnery nearby, and strongly urged Casanova to visit it if he had never seen it. Olivo heartily endorsed this recommendation, singing the praises of the somber but picturesque old building, the attractive setting, and the rich variety of the landscape along the way.

By the way, the abbot continued, the abbess there, Sister Seraphina—an extremely learned woman, a duchess by birth—had written him a letter (as the nuns in this particular convent were under a vow of perpetual silence) saying that she had heard of Marcolina's erudition and wished to meet her.

"I hope, Marcolina," said Lorenzi, addressing her directly for the first time, "that you won't let yourself be seduced into trying to emulate this noble abbess in other respects as well as in learning."

"Why should I?" rejoined Marcolina brightly. "Freedom can be maintained without taking vows—better, actually, since a vow is a form of coercion."

Casanova sat next to her. He didn't dare to touch her foot lightly with his, or to press his knee against hers. If he were forced to see that expression of horror and loathing in her eyes a third time, he would—he was certain of this—be driven to some act of folly. As the meal progressed and the number of emptied glasses grew, the conversation grew livelier, with everyone joining in. Once more Casanova heard Amalia's voice as though from afar, saying, "I've talked to Marcolina."

"You've talked—." A mad hope flared up in him.

"Calm yourself, Casanova. We didn't talk about you, only about her and her plans for the future. And I'm telling you one more time: she'll never belong to any man."

Olivo, who had put away a considerable quantity of wine, suddenly rose in his chair, glass in hand, and said a few clumsy words about the great honor that the visit of his esteemed friend, the Chevalier de Seingalt, had conferred on his humble home.

"But where is this Chevalier de Seingalt you're talking about, my dear Olivo?" asked Lorenzi in his clear, insolent voice.

Casanova's first impulse was to throw his full glass of wine into the impertinent fellow's face, but Amalia touched his arm lightly to restrain him and said, "Many people, Signor Chevalier, still know you only by your older and more famous name of Casanova."

"I didn't know," said Lorenzi with offensive earnestness, "that the King of France had conferred nobility on Signor Casanova."

"I was able to spare the king that effort," replied Casanova calmly, "and I hope that you, Lieutenant Lorenzi, will be content with the explanation to which the mayor of Nuremberg had no objection when I had the honor of explaining it to him in connection with an occasion with which I needn't bore the company." There was a moment of tense and silent anticipation. "The alphabet, as everyone will agree, is our common property. I picked out a few letters which I liked and made myself a nobleman without being under obligation to some prince or other who would hardly have been able to acknowledge my claims. So I'm Casanova, Chevalier de Seingalt. I'm sorry, Lieutenant Lorenzi, if the name does not meet with your approval."

"Seingalt—it's an excellent name," said the abbot, and repeated it several times, as though tasting it.

"And there's not a man in the world," exclaimed Olivo, "who has a better right to call himself Chevalier than my distinguished friend Casanova!"

"As for you, Lorenzi," added the marchese, "as soon as your fame has reached as far and wide as that of Signor Casanova, we'll call you Chevalier too, should you so desire."

Casanova, annoyed by the unwanted support from all sides, was just about to ask the others to refrain so that he could argue in his own defense, when out of the darkness of the garden two elderly, shabbily dressed gentlemen appeared at the table. Olivo greeted them with noisy effusions, delighted to defuse a dispute that was threatening to spoil the good mood of the evening. The newcomers were the brothers Ricardi, two bachelors who, as Casanova learned from Olivo, had once been well-off members of society but had experienced a run of bad luck in a series of investments and had finally withdrawn to their birthplace, the small neighboring village, where they rented a wretched little house. They were eccentric but harmless characters. Both Ricardis expressed their delight at renewing their acquaintance with the Chevalier, whom they had met in Paris years ago. Casanova couldn't recall meeting them. Maybe it was in Madrid?

"That's possible," said Casanova, but he knew he had never seen either of them before. Only the obviously younger one spoke; the older one, who looked as though he were at least ninety, accompanied his brother's words with incessant nodding and addled grins.

By now everyone had left the table. The girls had already disappeared. Lorenzi and the marchesa strolled across the meadow in the dusk, and Marcolina and Amalia were soon visible in the hall, evidently setting up for the evening's card game. What's the meaning of this? Casanova, now standing alone in the garden, wondered. Do they imagine me to be rich? Do they want to fleece me? All these preparations, including the marchese's ingratiating manner, the abbot's obsequiousness, and the appearance of the Ricardi brothers, seemed somehow suspicious to him. Wasn't it possible that Lorenzi was part of this intrigue? Or Marcolina? Or even Amalia? It occurred to him that the whole thing might be a trick his enemies were playing on him to make his return to Venice more difficult or even impossible at the last minute. But he quickly realized that the notion was absurd, if for no other reason than that he had no more enemies. He was nothing but an old fool down on his luck. Who would even care whether he returned to Venice or not? When he glanced through the open windows and now saw the men busily arranging themselves around the table on which cards and full wine glasses had been set, it became clear to him beyond any doubt that nothing more was in the offing than an ordinary innocent card game at which a new player would be welcome. Marcolina brushed against him as she walked by and wished him luck.

"Aren't you going to stay? Not even just to watch the game?"

"What point would there be in that? Good night, Chevalier de Seingalt—I'll see you tomorrow."

Voices from the interior called out into the garden. "Lorenzi"—"Signore Chevalier"—"We're waiting for you."

Casanova, standing dark in the shadow of the house, could see the marchesa trying to draw Lorenzi away from the open meadow and into the deeper shade of the trees. Once there, she pressed herself passionately against him, but Lorenzi tore himself roughly away from her and hurried toward the house. He met Casanova in the entry and with mock politeness gestured toward him to enter first. Casanova accepted the precedence without a thank-you.

The marchese was the first banker. Olivo, the brothers Ricardi, and the abbot bet such small amounts that the whole game seemed ludicrous to Casanova—even now, when his entire fortune consisted of no more than a couple of ducats. It seemed all the more ridiculous to him as the marchese raked in his winnings and paid out his losses in a grand manner, as though large amounts of money were involved. Suddenly Lorenzi, who hadn't taken part until now, threw down a ducat, won, let the doubled stake stand, won a second and a third time, and kept winning the continually doubled stakes with only occasional interruptions. The other men continued to bet petty coins just as they had before, and the Ricardis in particular grew highly indignant when the marchese seemed not to treat them with the same respect as he did Lieutenant Lorenzi. The two brothers played every hand together, and beads of perspiration rolled down the brow of the older one, who handled the cards, while the younger one, standing behind his brother, incessantly offered infallible advice. When his taciturn brother won, his eyes shone, but when his brother lost he looked despairingly up to heaven. The abbot, for the most part relatively indifferent, occasionally threw in a piece of proverbial wisdom—"Luck and women can't be coerced" or "The earth is round; heaven is vast"—and every now and then he cast a sly encouraging glance at Casanova and then at Amalia, who sat opposite him at her husband's side, as though it were important to him to get the two old lovers to pair off again.

But Casanova's only thought was that Marcolina was now slowly undressing herself in her room, and that, if her window were open, her white skin would be gleaming in the night. Seized by a desire so intense that his senses almost failed him, he was about to get up from his place next to the marchese and leave the room, when the marchese interpreted his movement as a decision to join the game and said, "At last—we were sure that you wouldn't want to remain a mere spectator, Chevalier." He dealt him a card, and Casanova staked all the money he had with him—nearly everything he had to his name—about ten ducats. He didn't count them but simply emptied his purse on the table, hoping to lose it all in one round. That would be a sign, a good omen—he didn't quite know what of, whether his speedy return to Venice or a look at the naked Marcolina—but before he had a chance to make up his mind, the marchese had already lost the hand to him. Like Lorenzi, Casanova then let the doubled amount stand, and luck stayed with him too, just as it had with the lieutenant.

By now the marchese no longer bothered to deal to the other players, and the taciturn Ricardi got up, offended, while his brother wrung his hands—and then the two of them withdrew to a corner of the room looking devastated. The abbot and Olivo accepted their fate more easily. The abbot ate sweets and repeated his little proverbs, and Olivo watched the course of the game excitedly. At length the marchese had lost five hundred ducats to Casanova and Lorenzi together.

The marchesa got up and winked at the lieutenant before she left the room with Amalia. She swayed her hips in a way that

Casanova found repulsive, and Amalia crept along beside her looking like a humble, aged woman. Now that the marchese had lost all his cash, Casanova became the banker and insisted, to the marchese's displeasure, that the others return to the game. The Ricardi brothers came back to the table in a flash, eager and greedy; the abbot shook his head—he had had enough; and Olivo joined merely because he didn't wish to be discourteous to his noble guest. Lorenzi's luck held, and when he had won four hundred ducats in all, he stood up and said, "Tomorrow I'll be happy to give everyone a chance for revenge. But now I'd like to ask your permission to ride home."

"Home!" exclaimed the marchese with a scornful laugh, having won back a few of his ducats. "That's a good way to put it! The lieutenant is staying at my house, you know," he said, turning to the others. "And my wife has already gone home. Have a good time, Lorenzi!"

"You know perfectly well," rejoined Lorenzi, without batting an eye, "that I'm riding straight to Mantua and not to your palazzo, where you were so kind as to put me up yesterday."

"You can ride to the devil for all I care!"

Lorenzi politely took his leave of the others and, to Casanova's amazement, left without offering a suitable retort to the marchese. Casanova returned to the game and won so often that the marchese was soon several hundred ducats in debt to him. What's the point of this? Casanova asked himself. But gradually the allure of the game seized him once more. I'm doing pretty well, he thought to himself. . . . I'll have a thousand soon . . . and that could turn into two thousand. The marchese will pay his debts. It wouldn't be bad to arrive in Venice with a small fortune in hand. But why Venice? Wealth means youth. Wealth is everything. Now I'll at least be able to buy her again. Who? There's only one woman I want . . . the one standing naked in the window—I know she is. . . . Maybe she's waiting for me to come after all. . . . She's standing in the window to drive me mad! And I'm here.

All the same, with an immobile face, he continued dealing the cards, not only to the marchese but also to Olivo and the Ricardi brothers, to whom, every so often, he slipped a gold piece they weren't entitled to. They made no objections. The noise of hooves resounded into the room from the darkness outside. Lorenzi, thought Casanova. . . . The noise reverberated from the rear garden wall, then gradually faded. But now Casanova's luck turned. The marchese bet higher and higher stakes, and by midnight Casanova found himself as poor as he had been before—in fact even poorer, since he had lost even the few gold pieces he had first ventured. Pushing the cards away with a smile, he arose and said, "Thank you, gentlemen."

Olivo stretched out both arms toward him, "My dear friend, do let's keep playing . . . you have a hundred and fifty ducats—have you forgotten? No, not only a hundred and fifty! All that I have—all that I am—everything, everything!" He was slurring his words now, as he hadn't stopped drinking the whole evening. Casanova refused his offer with an exaggerated courtly gesture. "Luck and women can't be coerced," he repeated with a bow toward the abbot, who nodded contentedly and clapped his hands. "Till tomorrow, then, my dear Chevalier," said the marchese. "The two of us will join forces to win the money back from the lieutenant."

The Ricardis, however, insisted that the game go on. The marchese, in an expansive mood, opened a bank for them. They bet the gold pieces that Casanova had allowed them to win. In a couple of minutes the marchese had won them too and firmly refused to go on playing with the Ricardis unless they could come up with cash. They wrung their hands. The older one began to cry like a child; the younger one kissed him on both cheeks to soothe him. The marchese asked if his carriage had returned, and the abbot said yes, he had heard it drive up half an hour ago. Thereupon the marchese offered the abbot and the Ricardi brothers a ride home, promising to drop them off at their respective houses—and they all left the house.

When they had gone, Olivo took Casanova's arm and assured him over and over again in a tearful voice that everything in this house belonged to him and was at his disposal. They walked past Marcolina's window. It was now not only shut but an iron grating had been closed over it, and a curtain drawn on the inside. There was a time, mused Casanova, when all such precautions would have been meaningless. They walked into the house. Olivo insisted on accompanying his guest up the creaking staircase and into the tower room, where he embraced him and said, "Tomorrow you'll get to see the nunnery. But sleep as long as you like; we won't leave too early, and anyhow we'll arrange everything to suit your convenience. Good night." He left, closing the door quietly behind him, but his footsteps on the stairs resounded throughout the house.

Casanova stood alone in his room, dimly lit by the light of two candles, and let his eyes roam from one to another of the four windows that faced in all directions. The view from each of them was almost identical, the landscape stretching out beneath him in a bluish haze. He saw broad plains with only slight elevations, except for an indistinct line of mountains to the north. A few isolated houses, farms, and some larger buildings could be seen here and there. From one of these, which Casanova assumed to be the marchese's palazzo, set on slightly higher ground, a light shone toward him. The room, which other than the freestanding wide bed contained nothing except a long table on which two candles were burning, a couple of chairs, and a commode with a gold-rimmed mirror, had been carefully arranged, and his valise had been unpacked. The shabby leather briefcase that held his manuscripts and that he kept locked had been placed on the table along with the few books he needed for the work he had brought along. Writing materials had also been provided. As he wasn't the least bit sleepy, he removed his manuscript from the briefcase and in the light of the candle read what he had most recently written. Since he had left off in the middle of a paragraph, it was easy for him to continue. He took up the quill and quickly wrote a few sentences, then stopped abruptly. What for? he asked himself, as if in a cruel flash of inner illumination. Even if I knew that what I'm writing now and what I'm going to write later would be glorious beyond all expectation—yes, even if I could really succeed in destroying Voltaire and in having my fame outshine his—would I not be ready to burn all these papers in an instant if by doing so I could but embrace Marcolina right now? Indeed, wouldn't I be prepared to swear never to set foot in Venice again for the same prize—even if they were to fetch me back in triumph?

Venice! . . . he repeated the word aloud, and it resounded in all its splendor—and in an instant it had regained all its old power over him. The city of his youth rose up before him suffused with all the magic of nostalgia, and his heart ached with a yearning more tormenting and more intense than any he remembered feeling. To renounce the idea of returning home seemed to him the most impossible sacrifice that fate could demand of him. How could he go on living in this poor and faded world without the hope, without the certainty, of seeing his beloved city again? After all the years and decades of wandering and adventure, after all the happiness and unhappiness he had experienced, after all the honor and all the shame, he must finally have a resting place, a true home. Could there be any other home for him but Venice? Or any other happiness than the consciousness of having a home again? It had been a long time since he had known happiness during his exile. He still had the power to grasp it but not the power to hold on to it. His power over others, over women as well as men, had vanished. Only in situations where he evoked memories were his words, his voice, his appearance still able to captivate; in the present, however, his power had fled. His time was past! And he admitted what he had been especially eager to conceal from himself: that even his literary accomplishments, including the polemic against Voltaire upon which he pinned all his hopes, would never achieve renown. It was too late for this too. If in his youth he had devoted time and patience to serious writing, he would have been—he was confident of this—a match for the best poets and philosophers, just as he would have risen to the greatest prominence as a financier or diplomat if he had had more perseverance and more forethought than he in fact possessed. But where had all his patience and his foresight gone, what had happened to all his plans for the future, whenever a new amorous adventure had beckoned?

Women—always women. Time and time again, he had cast everything aside for them—for aristocratic and for common women, for passionate and for frigid ones, for virgins and for whores. For one night in a new bed of love he had always been prepared to forfeit all the honors of this world and all the bliss of the next. But did he truly regret whatever he had forfeited in his life as a result of this perpetual seeking, this never—or always—finding, this earthly and divine flight from desire to pleasure, from pleasure to desire? No, he had no regrets. He had lived his life as no other man had—and wasn't he still living it today after his own fashion? Women were still everywhere on his path, even if they weren't quite as enamored of him as they once had been. Amalia? He could have her whenever he wanted, even right now, in her drunken husband's bed. And his innkeeper in Mantua—wasn't she head over heels in love with him and as devoured by tenderness and jealousy as if he were a handsome boy? And Perotti's pockmarked but well-built mistress—so intoxicated by the name Casanova that it sparkled for her with the lusts of a thousand nights—hadn't she implored him to grant her but one single night of love, and hadn't he spurned her like a man who could still choose whomever pleased him?

Of course there was Marcolina. Yes, women like Marcolina were now beyond his reach. Would she ever have been available to him? Yes, there were women of that sort. Perhaps he had met some of them in earlier years, but since there had always been other, more willing ones readily available, he had never so much as wasted a day sighing in vain. And since even Lorenzi had not succeeded in conquering her—as she had rejected the hand of this young man who was as handsome and as brazen as Casanova had been when young—perhaps Marcolina really was that wondrous being whose very existence on earth he had doubted until now: the truly virtuous woman.

At this point he let out a laugh so loud that it echoed around the room. "The bungler, the idiot!" he exclaimed aloud, as he often did when talking to himself. "He just didn't know how to take advantage of the situation. Or perhaps the marchesa is hanging on to him. Or maybe he just took up with her when he couldn't get Marcolina, the woman of real erudition, the"—And suddenly the idea struck him: tomorrow I'll read her my polemic against Voltaire! She's the only person who has the intelligence to understand it. I'll convince her. . . . She'll be full of admiration for me. Of course she will. . . . "Excellent, Signor Casanova! What a brilliant style you have, old fellow! By God . . . you've destroyed Voltaire . . . you brilliant sage!"

Like a beast in a cage, he paced back and forth, spitting out the words. He was seized by a terrible fury, against Marcolina, against Voltaire, against himself, against the whole world. It was all he could do to keep himself from bellowing at the top of his lungs. At length he threw himself down on his bed without undressing, and lay there with his eyes wide open, staring at the rafters on the ceiling where here and there silvery cobwebs gleamed in the candlelight. Then, as sometimes happened late at night after playing cards, images of cards raced through his mind one after the other until he finally fell into a brief and dreamless sleep. When he awoke, he listened to the mysterious silence around him. The eastern and southern windows of the tower were open, and the delicate, sweet aromas and vague noises that herald the approaching dawn wafted in from the garden and the fields. Casanova could no longer lie quiet; a powerful urge to move gripped him and drew him outdoors. Morning bird song called to him, and a cool breeze gently caressed his forehead. Casanova softly opened his door and moved cautiously down the stairs. With the skill acquired from long experience in such matters, he negotiated the creaky wooden staircase without a sound. From there he made his way down a stone staircase to the ground floor, then through the room where half-emptied glasses were still standing on the table, and out into the garden. Since it was impossible to walk silently on the gravel path, he stepped across it to the meadow, which now, in the early light of dawn, seemed to stretch into infinity. Then he crept into the avenue of trees that ran along the side of the house, to where he could see Marcolina's window. It was closed, barred, and curtained, just as he had seen it the night before.

Barely fifty feet from the house Casanova sat down on a stone bench. He heard a carriage drive by on the other side of the garden wall, and then everything grew quiet again. A fine grey haze hovered above the meadow, giving it the appearance of a transparent dark pond with a hazy edge. Once again Casanova recalled that long-ago night in the convent garden in Murano when he was young—or had it been some other night in some other garden? He couldn't remember exactly what night he was recalling—perhaps there had been a hundred such nights that his memory had fused into one, just as a hundred women he had loved sometimes merged into the image of one woman who loomed mysteriously in his mind. In the end, wasn't one night ultimately like any other night? And one woman like any other? Especially when it was past and gone? The phrase "past and gone" continued to hammer on his temples as though it were destined to become the heartbeat of his forlorn existence.

Suddenly it seemed to him that something rustled along the wall behind him. Or was it only an echo of something? Yes, it was a real sound, and it came from the house. Marcolina's window suddenly opened; the iron grating was pushed back and the curtain drawn to one side. A shadowy figure became visible against the dark interior. It was Marcolina herself, standing at the window in a white, high-buttoned nightgown, as though to drink in the pure morning air. Spellbound, Casanova hastily slipped behind the bench and peered over the treetops. He watched Marcolina as she looked vaguely into the dawn. Only after a few seconds did she appear to gather her drowsy attention into a focused gaze, which she slowly directed all around. Then she leaned out, as though she were looking for something in the gravel, and turned her head upward, her long hair falling, to gaze at a window on the upper story. She stood motionless for a while with her hands propped against both sides of the window frame, as though nailed to an invisible cross. Only then, as she was suddenly illuminated from within, could Casanova see her features clearly. A smile flitted around her lips, then instantly froze. Her arms fell to her sides, and her lips moved strangely, as though she were whispering a prayer. Once again her eyes slowly searched the garden, then she gave a quick nod, and someone who must have been crouching at her feet leapt over the windowsill into the garden—Lorenzi! He flew rather than walked across the gravel to the tree-lined avenue, crossing over it barely ten feet from Casanova, who held his breath as he lay beneath the bench. Lorenzi hurried along a narrow strip of grass near the wall to the other side of the meadow, where he disappeared from Casanova's view at the back of the garden. Casanova heard a door groan on its hinges—it had to be the one through which he, Olivo, and the marchese had returned to the garden yesterday—and then all was silent. Marcolina, who had stood motionless this entire time, drew a sigh of relief as soon as she was certain that Lorenzi was safely away, and closed the grating and the

window. The curtain fell back into its place as though of its own accord, and everything was as it had been before—except that now, as
though it had no more reason to delay, daylight dawned over house
and garden.

Casanova still lay under the bench with his hands stretched out
in front of him. After a while he crawled on all fours into the middle
of the tree-lined avenue to a spot where he couldn't be seen either
from Marcolina's window or from any other. Standing up with his
back aching, he stretched his body and limbs and finally felt restored
to his real self, as though he had been transformed from a beaten dog
back into a human being, albeit one who continues to feel the humiliation of the blows if not the bodily pain. Why, he asked himself,
didn't I go to the window while it was still open? Why didn't I leap
across the windowsill and into her room? Could she have resisted—
would she have dared to do so—the hypocrite, the liar, the slut? He
kept on swearing at her as though he had a right to, as though he had
been the lover to whom she had sworn fidelity and then betrayed. He
vowed to confront her face-to-face and to denounce her in the presence of Olivo, Amalia, the marchese, the abbot, the maid, and the
servants as nothing but a lustful little whore. As though rehearsing,
he recounted to himself everything he had seen in great detail and
took pleasure in inventing all kinds of other details that would degrade Marcolina all the more: he would say that she had stood naked
at her window and let herself be fondled indecently by her lover in
the morning breeze.

After he had vented his fury for the moment, he considered
whether he might not make some better use of his new knowledge.
Didn't he have her in his power now? Couldn't he now threaten her
into granting him the favor she'd been unwilling to grant him
freely? But this plan collapsed almost at once of its own accord, not
because Casanova recognized how contemptible it was but because
he was forced to admit even as he thought about it how utterly use-

less and pointless it was with someone like Marcolina. Why should his threats bother Marcolina, who didn't have to answer to anyone, and who was astute enough to drive him from her door as a slanderer and blackmailer if she wanted to? And even if for some reason she were willing to purchase the secret of her affair with Lorenzi from him with her body (though he knew, of course, that this was beyond the realm of possibility), wouldn't such a forced pleasure be a nameless torture for someone like him, who, when he made love, was a thousand times more concerned with giving pleasure than with receiving it, and so drive him to madness and despair? Suddenly he found himself standing at the door to the garden. It was locked. So Lorenzi had a master key to it! But who then—it suddenly occurred to him to ask—had he heard gallop off during the night after Lorenzi had excused himself from the card game? Obviously, a servant hired for the purpose. Casanova couldn't help smiling in approval. . . . They obviously deserved each other, Marcolina and Lorenzi, the philosopher and the officer. A glorious career lay ahead of them.

And who will be Marcolina's next lover? he asked himself. The professor in Bologna, in whose house she lived? Oh, what an idiot I am! That's already an old story! Who else? Olivo? The abbot? Well, why not? Or the young groom standing by the gate gawking when we drove up yesterday? Of course—it's all of them! I'm sure of it! But Lorenzi doesn't know. I have that advantage over him. Yet at the same time Casanova was convinced deep down that not only was Lorenzi her first lover, but that the night just past was the first one in which she had given herself to him. That didn't prevent him from continuing his spiteful, lewd fantasies while he circled the garden along the wall, however. At length he found himself back in front of the parlor door he had left open, and realized that for now there was nothing for him to do but sneak back into his tower room without being seen or heard. Cautiously he crept upstairs, and when he was back in his room he sank again into the chair in front of the table. The loose, unbound pages of his manuscript seemed to await his return. Involuntarily, his eyes fell on the half-finished sentence where he had left off: "Voltaire will be immortal, yes, but he will have paid for his immortality with his immortal soul—his wit has devoured his heart just as his doubt has devoured his soul, and so . . ." At that moment the red rays of the morning sun illuminated the room, falling on the page he held, setting it aglow. With a feeling of utter defeat, he let the page fall back onto the table.

Suddenly aware that his lips were dry, he poured himself a glass of water from the pitcher on the table. It was lukewarm and had a sickly sweet taste. Nauseated, he turned his head to one side and saw, staring back at him from the mirror on the wall above the dresser, a wan old face with disheveled hair hanging across its forehead. In a self-tormenting mood, he let the corners of his mouth droop even further, as though he were acting some cheap theatrical role. He mussed his hair to make it hang down even more sloppily, he stuck out his tongue at his own mirror image, croaked out a string of ridiculous invectives against himself, and finally, like a naughty child, blew the pages of his manuscript off the table. Then he began to abuse Marcolina again, and after he had heaped the most obscene insults on her, he hissed between his teeth: You think your happiness will last long? You'll get fat and wrinkled and old just like all young women—you'll become an old woman with flabby pendulous breasts and brittle grey hair, a toothless and stinking hag, and in the end you'll die! You could even die young! And then you'll decompose! Become a meal for worms! And to wreak his final revenge against her, he tried to imagine her dead. He saw her lying in an open casket, dressed in white, but he was unable to imagine her with any sign of decay. Instead the thought of her truly unearthly beauty worked him into a renewed frenzy. With his eyes closed, the coffin became her bridal bed and Marcolina lay there smiling with glowing eyes. As if to mock him, her slender pale hands tore the white garment she wore away from her tender breasts. But when he stretched his arms out toward her, yearning to throw himself on her, the vision dissolved into nothingness.

There was a knock at the door. Casanova started up as if from a heavy sleep to find Olivo standing before him. "What, you're at your desk already?" Composing himself instantly, Casanova answered, "I'm in the habit of devoting the early morning hours to my writing. How late is it?"

"It's eight o'clock," Olivo answered. "Breakfast is waiting for you in the garden. As soon as you wish, Chevalier, we can set out on the drive to the convent. But I see that the wind has scattered your papers." And he began to pick up the pages of manuscript from the floor. Casanova didn't interfere, as he had walked to the window and caught sight of the breakfast table that had been set up on the lawn in the shadow of the house. Sitting around it, all dressed in white, were Amalia, Marcolina, and the three little girls. They called a morning greeting to him. He had eyes only for Marcolina, who smiled up at him with bright eyes. She was holding a full plate of fresh, early-ripening grapes in her lap and popping one after the other into her mouth. All the contempt, all the anger, all the hatred in Casanova's heart melted away. All he knew was that he loved her. Intoxicated by the sight of her, he turned back to the room where Olivo was still kneeling on the floor gathering the scattered pages from beneath the table and chest. Casanova asked him not to bother any more but to leave him alone so that he could prepare for the outing.

"There's no hurry," said Olivo, brushing the dust from his breeches, "we'll easily be back in time for lunch. And in any case, the marchese asked if we could begin today's game early in the afternoon. Evidently he wants to get home before sunset.

"It doesn't matter to me what time you start the game," Casanova said, arranging the pages of his manuscript in the briefcase. "I won't be taking part in it in any case."

"Yes, you will," declared Olivo with an air of decision unusual for him. Placing a roll of gold pieces on the table, he continued, "Payment of what I owe you, Chevalier—belated, but it comes from a grateful heart." Casanova made a gesture of refusal. "You must accept it," Olivo insisted, "if you don't wish to insult me deeply. And besides, Amalia had a dream last night which will induce you—but she should describe it to you herself." And he left hastily.

Casanova counted the gold pieces; there were a hundred and fifty of them, exactly the sum he had given to the groom or the bride or her mother—he had forgotten who—fifteen years ago. The most sensible thing for me to do, he said to himself, would be for me to put the money in my pocket and take my leave, if possible without seeing Marcolina again. But when have I ever done the sensible thing? And what if I got a message from Venice in the meantime? . . . My excellent innkeeper promised to forward any mail for me immediately. . . .

Meanwhile the maid had brought up a large earthenware jug filled with cold water freshly drawn from the spring. Casanova washed himself carefully. Greatly refreshed, he dressed in the better and more formal of his two garments, the one he would have worn last night had he had time to change his clothes. But now he was delighted to appear before Marcolina more elegantly dressed, in a new version of himself, as it were, a better one than the previous day.

He made his entrance into the garden in a richly embroidered grey satin coat trimmed with wide Spanish silver lace, a yellow waistcoat, and cherry-red silk breeches. He carried himself with a noble though not too proud bearing and wore an affable though supercilious smile on his lips, his eyes shining as though with the fire of unextinguishable youth. To his disappointment, he found no one there but Olivo, who invited him to sit down at the table and share his modest breakfast. Casanova devoured milk, butter, eggs, and bread, followed by peaches and grapes which seemed to him better than any he had ever enjoyed. The three girls came running across the lawn, and Casanova kissed them all in turn, giving the thirteen-year-old the kind of caress she had accepted from the abbot the day before—but the gleam that began to sparkle in her eyes was, as Casanova quickly recognized, something more than that aroused by a harmless childish amusement. Olivo was delighted to see how well the Chevalier got along with his little girls. "Must you really leave us tomorrow? " he asked with shy affection.

"Tonight," said Casanova, but with a playful wink. "You know, my dear Olivo, how the senators in Venice—"

"They don't deserve you," Olivo interrupted him, animatedly. "Let them wait. Stay here with us until the day after tomorrow, no, better still, stay for a week."

Casanova shook his head slowly as he took little Teresina's hands and pretended to hold her prisoner between his knees. She gently pulled away from his grasp with a smile that had nothing childish in it as Amalia and Marcolina emerged from the house; Amalia wore a black shawl draped over a light-colored dress, and Marcolina wore a white shawl draped over hers. Olivo urged them both to join him in asking Casanova to stay. But when neither Amalia nor Marcolina said anything to second Olivo's invitation, Casanova replied, "No, it's impossible," in an exaggeratedly earnest and severe manner.

Walking along the chestnut-lined avenue toward the gate, Marcolina asked Casanova whether he had made any important progress on the essay that Olivo had found him working on early in the morning, as he had announced to everyone. Casanova was tempted to give her an ambiguous and sarcastic answer that would take her aback without giving him away, but he restrained his biting wit with the thought that anything done too hastily could harm his cause. And so he answered politely that he had only made a few revisions, impelled by the stimulating conversation he had had with her the day before. Everyone climbed into the shabby, lumbering, but otherwise comfortable carriage, with Casanova opposite Marcolina and Olivo opposite his wife. Unfortunately, the carriage was so roomy that despite the continual jostling and rattling, there was no chance for any accidental contact between the occupants.

Casanova asked Amalia to tell him her dream. She gave him a friendly, almost gracious smile; any trace of hurt feelings or anger had vanished from her features. Then she began, "I saw you, Casanova, drive by a white building in a magnificent carriage drawn by six dark horses. Or rather, I should say, the carriage had pulled up to the building and stopped before I knew who was in it—then you climbed down, dressed in a splendid, white, gold-embroidered coat of state, even more splendid than the one you are wearing today"—there was a friendly mockery in her voice—"and you were wearing—I'm sure of it—the same thin gold chain you're wearing right now and which I've seen you wear before!" (This chain, a gold watch, and a gold box embedded with semi-precious stones, which Casanova fingered as Amalia spoke, were the last trinkets of any value he still possessed.)

"An old man who looked like a beggar opened the carriage door—it was Lorenzi. But you, Casanova, you were young, very young, younger than you were back then." (She said "back then" quite nonchalantly, heedless that all her memories were coming back to her with a rustle of wings.) You bowed right and left, even though there wasn't a soul anywhere; then you entered through the door. It slammed shut behind you—I didn't know whether it was the storm or Lorenzi who had slammed it shut—so forcefully that the horses shied and raced off with the carriage. Then I heard shouting from nearby streets, as if people were trying to save themselves from being run over, but soon the carriage stopped. Yet you suddenly appeared at one of the windows in the house—I knew now that it was a casino—and bowed again in all directions, even though there was no one there. You turned to look over your shoulder, as though someone were standing behind you—but I knew no one was there either. All of a sudden I saw you at another window, on a higher floor, and the same thing happened again. You kept appearing successively on higher and higher floors—as though the building were growing toward infinity, and from every floor you bowed toward the street and talked to people standing behind you, though no one was really there at all. And all the while Lorenzi was running up the stairs behind you, flight after flight, without being able to catch up with you. He kept chasing you because you had forgotten to give him a tip. . . ."

"And?" asked Casanova, as Amalia stopped.

"A lot of other things happened, but I've forgotten them now," said Amalia.

Casanova was disappointed. Whether he was reporting a dream or a real incident, he would have tried to give the narrative an ending and a point. So now he said, a little dissatisfied, "How dreams turn everything around! Me a rich young man, and Lorenzi an old beggar!"

"As far as Lorenzi is concerned," said Olivo, "his wealth doesn't amount to much. His father is pretty well off, true, but the two of them don't get along very well." And without having to ask more questions, Casanova discovered that Olivo had met the lieutenant through the marchese, who had simply brought him along on a visit one day a few weeks ago. As to the nature of the relationship of the young officer to the marchesa—well, it wasn't necessary to spell it out to a man of the Chevalier's experience. And since the husband evidently had no objections, there was no reason for anyone else to be concerned about the situation either.

"I'm inclined to doubt whether the marchese is as unconcerned as you seem to think, Olivo," said Casanova. "Didn't you notice the mix of contempt and fury with which he treats the young man? I wouldn't bet on this situation ending well."

Even now Marcolina's expression and bearing remained impassive. She seemed not to take the least interest in all this talk about Lorenzi and appeared only to be quietly enjoying the view of the countryside. They were driving along a road that wound gently upward through a forest of olives and oak, and as they had now reached a place where the horses had to pull more and more slowly, Casanova got out to walk alongside the carriage. Marcolina talked about the lovely landscape around Bologna and about the evening walks she was used to taking with Professor Morgagni's daughter. She also mentioned that she was planning a trip to France next year in order to meet in person the famous mathematician Saugrenue at the University of Paris with whom she had been corresponding. "Perhaps I'll allow myself the pleasure," she said, smiling, "of stopping in Ferney to find out from Voltaire's own lips his reaction to the polemic of his most formidable opponent, the Chevalier de Seingalt." Casanova, who walked with his hand resting on the side rail of the carriage near Marcolina's arm, close enough to feel her puffy sleeve brushing against his fingers, answered cooly, "It matters less what Monsieur Voltaire thinks of my polemic than what posterity thinks, because only posterity will have the right to make a final judgment."

"Do you really believe," Marcolina inquired earnestly, "that in questions of this sort a final judgment is ever really possible?"

"I'm surprised that you should ask such a thing, Marcolina, since your philosophical—and if I may use the word here, your religious—views, though hardly indisputable as far as I'm concerned, seem to be absolutely grounded in your soul—assuming that you acknowledge the existence of such a thing." Marcolina, ignoring Casanova's barbs, calmly gazed up at the sky, spread out over the treetops in a deep dark blue, and answered, "Sometimes, especially on a day like this"—and to Casanova, knowing what he knew, her words conveyed the tremor of reverence from the depths of a newly awakened woman's heart—"I feel as though everything we call philosophy and religion is only a game of words, a noble one perhaps, but an even more pointless game than other kinds. We can never grasp infinity and eternity. Our path goes from life to death. What can we do but live in accordance with the law within each of our hearts—or else in rebellion against it? For rebellion and humility both come from God."

Olivo looked at his niece with shy admiration, then glanced anxiously at Casanova, who was searching for a reply that would make it clear to Marcolina that she both affirmed and denied God in the same breath, or that she had said that God and the devil were the same. But he realized that he had nothing but empty words to set against her feelings, and even these didn't come to him readily today. But his strangely contorted expression evidently aroused in Amalia the memory of the confused threats he had made yesterday, and she hastened to remark, "And yet Marcolina is truly devout, believe me, Chevalier." Marcolina smiled dreamily. "We're all devout in our own manner," Casanova said politely, looking straight ahead.

A sudden turn of the road and the convent was before them. The slender tops of cypresses towered over the high wall that encircled it. At the sound of the approaching carriage the gate swung open, and the gatekeeper, a man with a long white beard, greeted them reverently. They advanced to the main building through a set of arcades between whose columns an overgrown, dark-green garden was visible. A cool unfriendly breeze came toward them from the grey, unadorned, prisonlike walls of the convent. Olivo pulled the bell cord; a shrill ring immediately died away, and a heavily veiled nun silently opened the door and accompanied the guests into the bare and spacious reception room, which contained nothing but a few simple wooden chairs. At the back of the room was a heavy iron grating, behind which there was only a vague darkness. With a bitter heart, Casanova remembered the adventure that still seemed to him one of his most wonderful. It had begun in surroundings just like this: and the image of the two nuns at the convent in Murano, who had become close friends through their love for him and had together given him incomparable hours of pleasure, was resurrected from the depth of his soul. When Olivo began to whisper of the strict discipline imposed on the nuns here—once confirmed as novices, they were not allowed to show their faces unveiled before any man, and furthermore they were condemned to perpetual silence—he immediately suppressed the smile that flitted around his lips.

Suddenly the abbess was in their midst, as though she had materialized out of the darkness. She saluted her guests silently, and with an exceedingly gracious nod of her veiled head accepted Casanova's gratitude at being admitted to the convent along with the rest. But when Marcolina was about to kiss her hand, she folded the young woman in her arms. Inviting everyone to follow her with a wave of her hand, she led them through a small side room into a colonnade which encircled a quadrangular garden in full bloom. In contrast to the wildly overgrown outer garden, this one appeared to be tended with special care, and the many rich sun-drenched beds had a wonderful interplay of bright and pale colors. But intermingled with the heavy, almost intoxicating perfumes that streamed from the blossoming flowers was an unusual mysterious scent which evoked no responsive echo in Casanova's memory. Just as he was on the verge of mentioning it to Marcolina, he realized that the enigmatic, exciting fragrance that so aroused his senses was coming from her. She had draped the shawl she had worn over her shoulders across her arm, allowing the odor of her body to rise up from the nape of her loosened dress and mingle with those of a hundred thousand flowers. It was a scent kindred to them yet unique.

The abbess, still silent, led her visitors along a narrow path that wound back and forth between the flower beds like a delicate labyrinth. As she guided them, the joy she took in showing others the colorful splendor of her garden was evident in her light, quick step. As though determined to make them giddy, she moved faster and faster in front of them, like the leader of a lively folk dance.

But soon—Casanova felt as though he were waking from a confused dream—they were all back in the reception room. On the other side of the iron grating, dim figures hovered. It was impossible to say whether there were three or five or twenty veiled women wandering as aimlessly as startled ghosts behind the closely spaced thick bars. Only Casanova's acute night vision discerned human figures in the deep gloom. The abbess led her guests to the door, gave them a mute sign of dismissal, and then disappeared without a trace before they even had time to express their thanks. Just as they were about to leave the room, a woman's voice sounded from somewhere behind the grating—"Casanova!"—nothing but the name, but with a depth of feeling that Casanova could not remember ever having heard before. Was it a former lover who had just broken her holy vow of silence to breathe his name into the air for the last—or the first—time? Or was it someone he had never known? Did the voice tremble with the bliss of an unexpected reunion, the pain of an irretrievably lost love, or a lament that an ardent desire of long ago was fulfilled so late and so pointlessly? Casanova could not tell. He knew only that his name, so often tenderly whispered, passionately stammered, or joyfully shouted, had today for the first time penetrated his heart with the full resonance of love. Precisely for that reason he felt that any further inquiry would be both dishonorable and pointless—and he let the door close upon a secret he would never solve. Were it not for the timid and fleeting glances that the others exchanged with one another, indicating they had all heard the brief outcry, all might have thought it was a trick their ears had played on them. No one uttered a word as they walked to the gate through the covered arcades of the convent. Casanova followed behind with his head bent low, as though he had just come from a profoundly moving last farewell.

The gatekeeper awaited them outside and accepted their alms. The visitors climbed back into the carriage, which promptly started on the road home. Olivo looked embarrassed, Amalia distracted, and Marcolina completely unaffected. But the conversation she tried to strike up with Amalia about domestic matters seemed to Casanova all too forced. Olivo had to come to his wife's aid. But Casanova, who was extremely well versed in matters of the kitchen and the cellar, soon joined the conversation as he saw no reason to keep his knowledge and experience in these matters to himself rather than display them as further evidence of his many talents. Amalia now roused herself from her dreamy state and joined in. After the haunting adventure they had just shared, everyone, especially Casanova, took a certain comfort in such mundane matters. When the carriage reached Olivo's house and the smell of roasting meat and spices of all sorts greeted them invitingly, Casanova was in the midst of an appetizing description of a Polish meat pie, to which even Marcolina listened with a gracious domestic interest that Casanova found flattering.

In a strangely calm and almost gay mood, which surprised even him, he took his place at the table among the rest and courted Marcolina in the lighthearted, offhand manner appropriate for a distinguished old gentleman to adopt toward a well-bred young lady of good family. She accepted his attentions cheerfully and returned his pleasantries with perfect grace. It cost him as much effort to remember that this demure dinner companion was the same Marcolina from whose window he had seen a young officer emerge, obviously just moments after being in her embrace, as it did for him to believe that this delicate girl, who loved to roll around in the grass with other half-grown girls, was pursuing a learned correspondence with the famous Saugrenue in Paris. But at the same time he scolded himself for the ridiculous dullness of his imagination. Hadn't he realized on countless occasions that in the soul of every truly vital person not only contradictory but even apparently warring elements could coexist in perfect harmony? Take himself, for example—only a brief time ago he had been a deeply disturbed, even a desperate man, ready to do the most evil things. Wasn't he now gentle and kind, and in such a merry mood that he made Olivo's little daughters repeatedly split their sides with laughter? It was only his ravenous, almost animal-like appetite, which invariably overcame him at times of intense emotional agitation, that made him realize his emotional balance was by no means fully restored.

With the last course the maid brought in a letter for the Chevalier, just delivered by a messenger from Mantua. Olivo, who noticed that Casanova grew pale with excitement, ordered that the servant provide food and drink for the messenger, then turned to his guest with the words, "Don't mind us, Chevalier, go ahead and read your letter."

"With your permission," answered Casanova, and rose from the table with a slight bow, walked to the window, and opened the letter with well-feigned indifference. It was from Signor Bragadino, an old bachelor friend of his, now over eighty, who had been like a father to him in his youth. He had been a member of the Grand Council of Venice for ten years now, and appeared to be pleading Casanova's cause in Venice with more zeal than his other supporters. The letter, written in extremely delicate if somewhat shaky handwriting, read as follows:

My dear Casanova:
    I am delighted that I am finally in the agreeable position of sending you news which I trust will be substantially in accordance

with your wishes. The Grand Council, at its last meeting yesterday evening, not only declared itself ready to grant you permission to return to Venice but even expressed the hope that you expedite your return as quickly as possible, as it intends to take immediate advantage of the active gratitude you have pledged in so many letters.

Although you may not be aware of this, my dear Casanova (since we have been deprived of your presence for so long), the internal affairs of our beloved native city have recently taken a rather disturbing turn both politically and morally. Secret organizations opposed to our sovereign constitution and apparently even fomenting its violent overthrow have come into existence. As might be expected, the members of these organizations, which in harsher terms you might call conspiracies, are for the most part drawn from certain freethinking, irreligious, and in every sense lawless elements in the city. We are informed that the most shocking and downright treasonable conversations are occurring in public squares and coffee houses, to say nothing of what goes on in private. But in only the rarest of cases have we been able to catch the guilty parties in the act, or to secure definite evidence against them afterward. Confessions obtained by torture have proven so unreliable that a few members of our Grand Council have expressed the opinion that it would be better to refrain from such cruel and often counterproductive methods of investigation.

Of course there is no dearth of individuals willing to offer their services to the government for the good of the public order and the welfare of the state, but these are precisely the same people who, for the most part, are so well known to be staunch supporters of the existing regime that it is unlikely anyone would allow himself to be so carried away in their presence as to make a careless remark, let alone a treasonous speech.

In view of this, at last night's meeting one of the senators, whom I shall not name for the moment, expressed the view that a man who had the reputation of being without moral principles and a freethinker to boot—in short, a man like you, Casanova—would find a sympathetic welcome in the very circles which the government regards as suspect, and would, if he played his cards right, soon gain their confidence. Indeed, in my opinion, you would of necessity, as if by a law of nature, attract to you exactly those elements the Grand Council, in its indefatigable efforts on behalf of the public good, is most eager to render harmless and to punish as an example to others.

And so, my dear Casanova, we would take your service in this role not only as proof of your patriotic zeal but also as persuasive evidence of your complete repudiation of all those tendencies for which you had to atone by confinement in the Lead Chambers—a perhaps severe but not altogether unjust punishment, as you yourself grant today (if we can believe your epistolary assurances). If, in other words, you were prepared, immediately upon your return, to act in the manner suggested and to seek out those elements that I have sufficiently described above and insinuate yourself into their circles as someone who shares their views, and then to promptly furnish the Senate detailed and comprehensive reports of anything that struck you as suspicious or otherwise worthy of our attention, we would be disposed initially to offer you a monthly income of two hundred fifty lire, exclusive of extra remuneration in individual cases of special importance. Of course we would also cover any other expenses you might incur in the performance of your services (for example, the costs of treating this or that person to food and drink, small gifts for women, and so on) without hesitation or too close a scrutiny.

I do not in any way conceal from myself that you may have to overcome certain scruples before you can reach a decision to act in accordance with our wishes, but permit me as your old and sincere friend (who was himself young once) to remind you that it can never be regarded as dishonorable for a man to render his beloved fatherland a service necessary to ensure its secure existence, even if it were to be a service that casual and unpatriotic citizens might consider unworthy. Let me add, Casanova, that you are certainly a good enough judge of character to distinguish a mere thoughtless prattler from a real criminal, or a mocker from a true heretic, and it will be in your power to temper justice with mercy in appropriate cases, and to hand over to punishment only those who in your honest conviction deserve it. Above all, however, bear in mind that if you should reject the Grand Council's gracious proposal, the fulfillment of your most fervent wish—your return to your native city—is likely to be postponed for a long and I fear an indefinite period, and that I myself, if I may say so, an eighty-one-year-old man, would in all probability have to forgo the pleasure of ever seeing you again in my lifetime.

Since for understandable reasons your employment will be of a confidential rather than a public nature, I beg you to address your reply to me personally (I will take responsibility for communicating it to the Grand Council at the next meeting one week from today), and to do so as speedily as possible since, as I have already indicated, we are daily receiving applications from the most trustworthy persons voluntarily offering their services to the Grand Council out of love for their fatherland. Of course there is hardly one among them who can compare with you, my dear Casanova, in experience and intelligence. And if, in addition to all these reasons, you take my affection for you into account as well, I find it difficult to doubt that you will joyfully accept the call that has gone out to you from such a venerable and friendly a source as the Grand Council.

Until then, I remain, in undying friendship,

Your devoted Bragadino.

P.S. I will be happy, immediately upon receiving word of your decision, to issue you a remittance in the amount of two hundred lire via the Valori Bank in Mantua, for the defrayal of your travel expenses. The above.

Although Casanova had long finished reading the letter, he continued to hold it in front of him to conceal his deathly pallor and contorted features. The noise of the meal, the clattering of the plates, and the clinking of glasses continued as before, but conversation had entirely ceased. At length Amalia ventured to say timidly, "The food is getting cold, Chevalier. Won't you come and eat something?"

"No, thank you," said Casanova, revealing his face again, which, thanks to his extraordinary skill at disguising himself, he had been able to compose. "I've just received excellent news from Venice, and I must reply immediately. I hope you'll excuse me for leaving the table so abruptly."

"Suit yourself, Chevalier," said Olivo, "but don't forget that our game begins in an hour."

Casanova climbed up to his room and sank into a chair. His whole body broke out in a cold sweat, chills shook him, and he experienced such a feeling of nausea that he thought he would choke on the spot. For a time he was unable to think clearly, and it took all his energy to restrain himself—though he couldn't have said from what. After all, there was no one here in the house on whom he could vent his enormous rage, and he could still recognize the absurdity of the vague notion that Marcolina was somehow involved in the unspeakable humiliation he had just suffered. When he had succeeded in composing himself somewhat, his first thought was to take revenge on the scoundrels who assumed they could hire him as a police spy. He would sneak into Venice in some sort of disguise and stealthily do them all in—or at least the one who had come up with this miserable plan.

Could it have been Bragadino himself? Why not? He was an old man who had become so shameless that he dared write this letter to Casanova—so feebleminded that he thought that he, Casanova—Casanova! whom he had personally known!—would stoop to become a spy! Ah, clearly he didn't know Casanova anymore! No one knew him anymore, not in Venice nor anywhere else. But they would get to know him again! Granted, he was no longer young and handsome enough to seduce a virtuous girl—nor skillful and agile enough to escape from prison and perform acrobatics on rooftops. But he was still smarter than all the rest of them! Once back in Venice, he could do anything he pleased—it was just a question of getting there! Perhaps it wouldn't even be necessary to kill anyone; there were many other more clever and more devilish kinds of revenge than an ordinary murder. If, for example, he pretended to accept the Council's offer, it would be the easiest thing in the world to destroy the people he wanted to destroy instead of those the Great Council had in mind, those who doubtless were the finest Venetians of them all! What? Because they were the enemies of this vile government and were reputed to be heretics, they were to be put away in those very same Lead Chambers where he himself had languished twenty-five years ago—or perhaps even to die under the executioner's axe? He hated the government a hundred times more than they did, and with better reason! He had been a heretic all his life, and remained one today, with even more conviction than any of them! He had merely been playing out a twisted comedy and deluding himself in recent years—out of boredom and disgust. He believe in God? What kind of God was it who was gracious only to the young and left the old in the lurch? A God who, whenever he felt like it, transformed himself into the Devil and changed wealth into poverty, fortune into misfortune, pleasure into despair? You play games with us—and we're supposed to worship you? To doubt your existence is the only means we have—not to blaspheme you! Don't exist! Because if you do, I must curse you!

Clenching his fists and raising them heavenward, he sat up, and a detested name formed on his lips. Voltaire! Yes, now he was in the right mood to finish his polemic against the sage of Ferney. To finish it? No, to begin it! A new one! A different one—in which the ridiculous old codger would be shown up as he deserved to be . . . for his cowardice, his halfheartedness, his groveling. He an unbeliever? A man about whom it was lately said again and again that he was on the best of terms with priests and attended church and even went to confession on holy days? Voltaire a heretic? He was nothing but a windbag, a boastful coward—nothing else! But the terrible day of reckoning was at hand, a day after which there would be nothing left of the great philosopher but a clever little scribbler. How he puffed himself up, this good old Monsieur Voltaire. . . . "Ah, my dear Signor Casanova, I'm really quite upset with you. What do I care about the works of Merlin? You're to blame for my spending four hours over this nonsense."

"It's all a matter of taste, my esteemed Monsieur Voltaire! Merlin's works will still be read long after your *Pucelle* has been forgotten . . . and perhaps people will still value those sonnets of mine which you gave me back with such an insolent smile, without saying a word. But these are trifles. Let's not destroy a matter of such great importance because of our literary pride. What's at issue here is philosophy—and God! . . . We'll cross swords, Monsieur Voltaire! Just please do me the favor of not dying first!"

He was about to sit down and begin his work on the spot when it occurred to him that the messenger was waiting for his answer. He hastily composed a letter to that old fool Bragadino, a letter full of hypocritical humility and feigned delight: with joy and gratitude he accepted the mercy of the Grand Council and would expect the remittance by return mail so that he might have the privilege of prostrating himself at the feet of his benefactors, and above all at those of his honored old family friend Bragadino, as soon as possible.

As he was about to seal the letter, there was a soft knock on the door. Olivo's oldest daughter, the thirteen-year-old, entered to tell him that the whole company was assembled below and impatiently waiting for the Chevalier to join the game. There was a strange gleam in her eyes; her cheeks had turned rosy, and her lush blue black hair, as thick as a woman's, lay loose around her temples. Her little childlike mouth was half open. "Have you been drinking wine, Teresina?" asked Casanova, taking a long step toward her. "Yes, I have—how did you know?" She blushed more deeply and in embarrassment moistened her lower lip with her tongue. Casanova seized her by the shoulder and, breathing into her face, pulled her down and threw her on his bed. She looked at him with great helpless eyes from which the gleam had vanished. But when she opened her mouth as though to scream, Casanova's expression was so menacing that she was almost paralyzed with fear and let him do as he wished with her. Afterward he kissed her with tender ferocity and whispered, "Don't tell the abbot about this, Teresina, not even in confession. And when you have a lover later on, or a fiancé, or even a husband, he doesn't need to know about it either. In fact you should always lie, to everyone, to your father and mother and your sisters, too—that way you'll prosper in this world. Mark my words."

Teresina evidently took his blasphemies as a kind of blessing pronounced over her, for she seized his hand and kissed it with reverence, as she would a priest's. He laughed out loud. "Let's go," he said, "come with me, my little woman, we'll walk into the parlor arm in arm!" She acted coy at first but nevertheless smiled contentedly.

It was high time they left, as Olivo was just coming up the stairs frowning and looking flushed. Casanova inferred that the marchese or the abbot had aroused his suspicions by some coarse jibes about his daughter's prolonged absence. Olivo's expression brightened immediately when he saw Casanova standing in the doorway with his arm hooked into Teresina's, as if for sport. "I'm sorry to have kept you all waiting, my dear Olivo," said Casanova. "I had to finish writing my letter first." He held it up to Olivo as if displaying evidence.

"Take it," said Olivo to Teresina, smoothing her somewhat rumpled hair, "and give it to the messenger."

"And here are two gold pieces for the man," said Casanova. "Give them to him and tell him to hurry so that the letter will go to Venice with today's post—and have him tell the innkeeper there that I . . . will be back tonight."

"Tonight?" exclaimed Olivo. "Impossible!"

"Well, we'll see," said Casanova condescendingly. "And here, Teresina, here is a gold piece for you too." When Olivo objected, he added, "Put it in your money box, Teresina; the letter you have in your hands is worth a few thousand gold pieces." Teresina ran off, and Casanova nodded with delight. He had already possessed her mother and her grandmother, and now he particularly enjoyed paying the little girl for her favors under the very nose of her father.

When Casanova walked into the parlor with Olivo, the game was already under way. He acknowledged the group's effusive greetings with good-natured dignity and took his place opposite the marchese, who was banker at the moment. Through the open windows facing the garden, Casanova heard voices approaching outside: Marcolina and Amalia passed by, glanced into the room, and disappeared out of sight. While the marchese was dealing the cards, Lorenzi turned to Casanova with extravagant politeness and said, "My compliments, Chevalier. You were better informed than I was: our regiment is indeed under orders to march tomorrow afternoon."

The marchese looked surprised. "Why didn't you tell us before, Lorenzi?"

"I didn't think it was that important."

"Not to me, to be sure," said the marchese, "but to my wife. . . ! Don't you think?" He laughed in a repulsively hoarse way. "And actually, I have some interest in the matter as well. You won four hundred ducats from me yesterday, and now there may not be enough time for me to win them back."

"The lieutenant won money from us too," said the younger Ricardi. The elder, silent Ricardi turned around to look up over his shoulder at his brother, who stood behind him as he had yesterday.

"Luck and women . . . ," began the abbot. The marchese finished the sentence for him: "coerce them, if you can."

Lorenzi carelessly scattered his gold pieces on the table. "There they are. If you like, I'll stake everything on one card so you won't have to chase after your money for long."

Casanova suddenly became conscious of a certain sympathy for Lorenzi, though he was puzzled by it. But since he had considerable faith in his own powers of premonition, he was convinced the lieutenant would go down in the first round. But the marchese refused the high stakes, and Lorenzi did not insist on them, and so they resumed the game as they had before, with everyone betting only moderate amounts. After a quarter of an hour, however, the stakes began to grow, and soon Lorenzi had lost his four hundred ducats to the marchese. As for Casanova, luck didn't seem to bother about him one way or the other: he won, he lost, and he won again, in an almost ridiculously regular pattern.

Lorenzi breathed a sigh of relief when his last gold piece had made its way to the marchese, and rose from the table. "Thank you, gentlemen. This"—he hesitated for a moment—"will probably prove to be my last game in this hospitable house for a very long time. And now, my dear Signor Olivo, permit me to say goodbye to the ladies before I ride back into the city. I want to get there before sunset so I can prepare for tomorrow."

You shameless liar, thought Casanova. In the middle of the night you'll be back here—with Marcolina! Rage flared in him again.

"What?" exclaimed the marchese irritably. "It's still several hours till evening, and the game is supposed to be over already? If you like, Lorenzi, I'll have my coachman drive home and tell the marchesa that you'll be late."

"I'm planning to ride to Mantua," replied Lorenzi impatiently.

Ignoring this, the marchese went on, "There's still plenty of time. Put out some of your pieces of gold, even if it's but a single one." And he dealt him a card.

"I don't have a single gold piece left," said Lorenzi wearily.

"What!"

"Not one," repeated Lorenzi, as though disgusted by the whole topic.

"Never mind," exclaimed the marchese with a sudden and rather unpleasant pretense of amiability. "You can owe me ten ducats, and if necessary, more."

"All right, a ducat, then," said Lorenzi, and took up his cards. The marchese's hand won. Lorenzi kept on playing as though it were now a matter of course and soon owed the marchese a hundred ducats. Casanova took over the bank and had even better luck than the marchese. By now it had again turned into a game for three, and this time even the Ricardi brothers didn't protest. Along with Olivo and the abbot, they became admiring observers. Not one syllable was uttered. Only the cards spoke, and they spoke very clearly. By the luck of the game every last piece of cash went to Casanova. After an hour he had won two thousand ducats, ostensibly from Lorenzi, though they all came out of the marchese's pocket, leaving him without a penny. Casanova offered him whatever he wanted to keep on playing, but the marchese shook his head. "Thanks," he said, "but enough is enough. The game is over for me."

From the garden came the laughter and shouts of the girls. Casanova heard Teresina's voice above the rest, but he sat with his back to the window and didn't turn around. For Lorenzi's sake, he tried once more to persuade the marchese to resume the game, though he didn't know why. But the marchese refused with an even more decisive shake of his head. Lorenzi rose. "Permit me, Signor Marchese, to hand you the amount I owe you in person before noon tomorrow."

The marchese gave an abrupt laugh. "I'm curious to know how you're going to manage that, Lieutenant Lorenzi. There isn't a soul in Mantua or anywhere else who would lend you even ten ducats, much less two thousand, especially now that you're marching into battle and there is no guarantee you'll return."

"You'll have your money tomorrow morning at eight o'clock, Signor Marchese. I give you my word of honor."

"Your word of honor," said the marchese coldly, "isn't worth a single ducat to me, much less two thousand."

The others held their breath. But Lorenzi simply answered, apparently unmoved, "You'll give me satisfaction, Signor Marchese."

"With pleasure, Signor Lieutenant," answered the marchese, "as soon as you've paid your debt."

Olivo, profoundly disturbed, intervened, stammering a little, "I'll vouch for the sum, Signor Marchese. Unfortunately I don't have enough cash on hand to—but there is my house, my property"—and he made an awkward circular gesture.

"I won't accept your pledge," the marchese replied, "for your sake—you would lose your money." Casanova saw that all eyes were fastened on the gold that lay on the table in front of him. What if I were to vouch for Lorenzi? he thought. What if I paid for him? . . . The marchese couldn't refuse me. . . . Isn't it almost my duty? It's the marchese's gold, after all. But he said nothing. He sensed a vague scheme forming in his mind, a scheme that he needed time to develop.

"You'll have your money this evening, before nightfall," said Lorenzi. "I'll be in Mantua in an hour."

"Your horse might break its neck," answered the marchese, "and you too—in the end, on purpose."

"In any event," said the abbot angrily, "the lieutenant can't conjure up the money by magic." The two Ricardis began to laugh but quickly stopped.

"It's clear," Olivo said, turning to the marchese, "that first of all you have to let the lieutenant leave."

"Only if he gives me a deposit," exclaimed the marchese with flashing eyes, as if this new idea gave him some special pleasure.

"That's not a bad idea," said Casanova, a little distracted, as his scheme was ripening. Lorenzi pulled a ring from his finger and let it drop on the table.

The marchese took it. "This is good for a thousand."

"What about this one?" Lorenzi flung another ring in front of the marchese.

He nodded, saying, "Good for the same amount."

"Are you satisfied now, Signor Marchese?" asked Lorenzi, getting ready to leave.

"I'm satisfied," said the marchese, smirking, "all the more so as these rings are stolen." Lorenzi turned sharply, and clenched his fist above the table as though to bring it smashing down on the marchese. Olivo and the abbot seized his arm tightly.

"I know both these stones," said the marchese without moving from his seat, "even though they've been reset. Look, gentlemen, this emerald has a small flaw, otherwise it would be worth ten times as much. The ruby is flawless, but it's not very large. Both stones come from a piece of jewelry I once gave my wife. And since it's impossible to assume that the marchesa had them made into rings for Lieutenant Lorenzi, it's obvious that they've been stolen—that the whole piece has been stolen. Well, this is sufficient security for now, Signor Lieutenant, until later."

"Lorenzi!" cried Olivo. "We all give you our word that not a soul will ever know what has just happened here."

"And whatever Signor Lorenzi might have done," said Casanova, "you, Signor Marchese, are the greater scoundrel."

"I hope so," replied the marchese, "when one is as old as you and I, Signor Chevalier de Seingalt, one shouldn't allow one's self to be bested—at least in villainy—by anyone. Good evening, gentlemen."

He rose to his feet and left the room. No one responded to his farewell. For a short time the silence was so heavy that the laughter of the girls from the garden seemed unusually loud. Who could find something to say to Lorenzi that would reach his soul, standing as he was with his arm still raised above the table? Casanova, the only one who had remained seated, took an aesthetic pleasure in this nobly threatening gesture, now pointless but seemingly petrified, as if the young man had been turned into a statue. Finally Olivo turned to him with a soothing gesture, the Ricardis began to move toward him, and the abbot appeared to be formulating a speech. But suddenly a kind of tremor ran through Lorenzi's body, and, rejecting all attempts at intervention with a peremptory gesture, he nodded politely and left the room deliberately. Casanova, who in the meantime had wrapped the gold before him in a silk scarf, followed him at once. Without seeing the others' expressions, he sensed their conviction that he was now hurrying to do what they had expected him to do all along, namely, place his winnings at Lorenzi's disposal.

He overtook Lorenzi on the tree-lined avenue that led from the house to the gate, and said in a light tone, "May I have the pleasure of accompanying you on your walk, Lieutenant Lorenzi?"

Lorenzi, without looking at him, answered him in a haughty tone hardly appropriate to his situation, "As you please, Signor Chevalier, but I'm afraid you won't find me a very entertaining companion."

"Well, Lieutenant, you might find me all the more entertaining in return," said Casanova. "And if you have no objection, let's take the path through the vineyards, where we can talk undisturbed."

They turned off the road into the same narrow path along the garden wall that Casanova had walked the day before with Olivo.

"You're right in assuming," Casanova began, "that I'm inclined to offer you the money you owe the marchese. Not as a loan, because—you'll pardon me for saying so—I consider that an all too risky venture. But I could let you have it as—an all too meager compensation, to be sure—for a favor you may be able to do me."

"Go on," said Lorenzi coldly.

"Before I say more," replied Casanova in a similar tone, "I must state a condition you will have to agree to if this conversation is to continue."

"Name your condition."

"Give me your word of honor that you'll hear me out without interrupting me, even though what I have to say may arouse your displeasure or even your outrage and strike you as strange. After you've heard me out, it'll be entirely up to you, Lieutenant Lorenzi, to decide whether or not to accept my proposal. I'm entirely aware of its unusual nature. But I want you to answer it with a simple yes or no. And whatever you decide, yes or no—no one will ever find out what transpired here between two men of honor who are both also lost souls."

"I'm ready to listen to your proposal."

"You accept my condition?"

"I won't interrupt you."

"And you'll say nothing except yes or no?"

"Nothing except yes or no."

"Very well, then," said Casanova. And as they walked slowly up the hill between the rows of grapes in the sultry heat of the late afternoon, Casanova began: "Let's discuss this matter logically; that way we'll understand each other best. It's obvious that you have absolutely no chance of getting the money you owe the marchese by the prescribed deadline. There's also no doubt at all that he's made up his mind to destroy you if you don't pay him back. Since he knows more about you than he revealed today"—and here Casanova ventured further than he needed to, but he loved to spice up an otherwise pat little adventure by taking small risks—"the fact is that you're absolutely in the power of this old scoundrel, and your fate as an officer and man of honor is completely sealed. That's one side of the situation.

"On the other hand, as soon as you've paid your debt to him and have the rings back in hand—however they came into your possession—you're saved. For you to be saved means no less than that you'll have your entire future, which you have essentially foreclosed, back again—a future which, since you're young, handsome, and bold, will be filled with fame, fortune, and happiness. Such a prospect strikes me as magnificent enough—particularly when you consider that the only alternative is an inglorious, even a shameful, ruin—to sacrifice to it a moral prejudice that you've personally never even held.

"I know very well, Lorenzi," he added quickly, as though he expected to be contradicted and wished to forestall it, "that you in fact have no moral prejudices at all, any more than I do now or have ever had. What I'm going to ask of you is something I wouldn't have a moment's hesitation in agreeing to if I were in your position—just as I've never hesitated to act basely, or rather what fools like to call basely—if fate or even just a whim should happen to demand it. At the same time—like you, Lorenzi—I've always been ready to risk my life for less than nothing, and that makes us even. I'm ready to risk it now, in the event you don't like my proposal. We're cut from the same cloth, Lorenzi. We're brothers in spirit, and we may therefore expose our innermost souls to each other, proud and naked, without false shame. Here are my two thousand ducats. They are yours—if you can arrange for me to spend the night with Marcolina in your place. But let's not stop here, Lorenzi. Let's keep walking."

They walked through the fields, beneath the branches of low-hanging fruit trees where the grapevines, laden with berries, meandered. Casanova went on without pausing, "Don't answer me yet, Lorenzi—I haven't finished. My request would of course be not exactly monstrous but certainly hopeless and therefore pointless if it were your intention to make Marcolina your wife, or if Marcolina herself had hopes and desires along that line. But just as last night was your first night of love with her"—he uttered this assumption too as though he had absolute knowledge of its truth—"so tonight— insofar as it's humanly possible to know such a thing—is destined to be your last for a very long time, and most likely forever. I'm absolutely convinced that Marcolina herself, in order to save her lover from certain ruin, would be perfectly willing to grant this night to her lover's savior. Because, you see, she is a philosopher like we are, and therefore just as free of moral prejudice as we are. Nevertheless, even though I'm certain that she would pass this test, it isn't at all my intention to subject her to it. Because to make love to a submissive woman filled with inner resistance, especially in this case, wouldn't satisfy my desires. I want to enjoy a rapture so great that I would ultimately be willing to pay for it with my life—and such a rapture is possible only if I am not only a lover but also a beloved.

"Understand me here, Lorenzi. That's why Marcolina can't even suspect that it's me, not you, that she's clasping to her heavenly bosom. She must be absolutely convinced that it's you she's holding in her arms. To lay the groundwork for this deception is your task; to maintain it is mine. You won't have much difficulty persuading her that you must leave before dawn, and you won't have much trouble inventing a pretext for mute caresses this one time. To avert any danger of her discovering the truth later on, at a suitable moment I'll pretend to hear a suspicious noise outside the window and I'll take my cloak—or rather, your cloak, which of course you'll have to lend me for this purpose—and disappear through the window, never to return. Beforehand, of course, I'll have pretended to take my leave of the others. But halfway to Mantua, under the pretext that I've forgotten some important papers, I'll have the coachman turn around. I'll then enter the garden through the back door—you'll supply with me with the master key, Lorenzi—and creep to Marcolina's window, which will open at midnight. I'll have taken off my clothes, even my shoes and socks, in the carriage, and will wear only your cloak, so that when I suddenly take flight nothing will remain behind to betray either you or me. The cloak and the two thousand ducats will be at your disposal at five o'clock tomorrow morning at my inn in Mantua, so that you can throw the marchese's money at his feet even before the appointed hour. I pledge my solemn oath to do this. And now I'm finished."

Casanova stopped walking. The sun was near setting, and a gentle breeze rustled the tops of the golden shafts of grain. A red evening glow spread over the tower of Olivo's house. Lorenzi stopped too. Not a muscle stirred in his pale face as he gazed motionlessly into the distance over Casanova's shoulder. His arms hung limply at his side while Casanova—prepared for anything—gripped the hilt of his sword. Several seconds passed while Lorenzi remained rigid and silent; he seemed lost in quiet contemplation. But Casanova remained on guard, holding the scarf with the ducats in his left hand and the hilt of his sword in his right.

Casanova spoke again: "You've fulfilled my condition like a man of honor. I know it wasn't easy for you. Because even if we ourselves are free of moral prejudices, the world we live in is so poisoned by them that we can't wholly escape their influence. And just as you, Lorenzi, in the last several minutes were more than once on the verge of grabbing my throat, so I've been toying—I'll admit it—with the idea of just giving you the two thousand ducats as I would to any friend. For rarely, Lorenzi, have I been so strangely drawn to anyone as I was to you from the first moment we met. But if I'd yielded to this magnanimous impulse, I would have deeply regretted it a moment later—just as you, Lorenzi, in the second before you pulled the trigger to blow your brains out, would desperately regret having been such a fool as to throw away a thousand nights of love with countless new women for one single night after which no more nights—and no more days—could follow."

Still Lorenzi remained silent, and his silence persisted for minutes, until Casanova began to wonder how much longer his patience was to be tried. Just as he was on the point of turning away with a curt greeting, thus indicating that he understood Lorenzi to have rejected his proposal, Lorenzi, still silent, slowly reached into the pocket of his cloak and handed Casanova the key to the garden gate at the same instant that he, still on his guard, had taken a step back as if about to duck. Casanova's movement, which betrayed some fear, brought the merest flicker of a contemptuous smile to Lorenzi's lips. But Casanova was able to suppress his rising anger, knowing that its expression could destroy everything, and, taking the key with a nod, he merely remarked, "I assume I may consider this a yes. An hour from now—by then you'll have made arrangements with Marcolina—I'll await you in my room in the tower. There, in exchange for your cloak, I'll have the pleasure of giving you the two thousand gold pieces without further delay—first, as a sign of my trust in you, and second because I really don't know where I would keep the gold during the night."

They parted without further formalities. Lorenzi returned to the house the same way they had come, and Casanova took a route to the village. There, leaving a considerable deposit, he secured a carriage that would await him at ten o'clock that evening in front of Olivo's house to take him back to Mantua.

A short while later, after he had hidden his gold in a secure corner of his room in the tower, he went down into Olivo's garden, where he saw a sight that was by no means remarkable in itself but which in his present mood he found strangely touching. Olivo was sitting beside Amalia on a bench at the edge of the grass, his arm around her shoulders, while at their feet lay the three girls, tired out from the games of the afternoon. The youngest, Maria, had her head in her mother's lap and seemed to be asleep; Nanette lay stretched out on the grass at Amalia's feet, her arms behind her neck; and Teresina leaned against her father's knees while his fingers rested tenderly in her curls. As Casanova drew nearer, Teresina's eyes greeted him not with the look of lascivious collusion he had expected but with the open smile of childlike trust, as if what had happened between them a few hours earlier had been nothing but a harmless game. Olivo's face lit up in a friendly manner, and Amalia nodded a warm and grateful greeting. It was perfectly clear to Casanova that they received him as someone who had just performed a noble deed but who, out of a sense of tact, preferred that no mention be made of it.

"Are you really still determined to leave us tomorrow, my dear Chevalier?"

"Not tomorrow," answered Casanova, "but—as I said—this evening."

As he saw that Olivo was about to raise another objection, he said with a regretful shrug, "The letter I received today from Venice unfortunately leaves me no other choice. The entreaty addressed to me is in every way so honorable that any delay of my return would be a terrible, yes, an inexcusable discourtesy toward my noble benefactors." He begged to be allowed to withdraw into his room now so that he could prepare for his departure and thus be able to enjoy undisturbed the last hours of his stay within the circle of his kind friends.

Ignoring their protests, he returned to his room, where he first exchanged his splendid outfit for the simpler one that would have to do for the trip. He then packed his bag, all the while listening more and more anxiously for Lorenzi's footsteps with each passing minute. Even before the appointed time there was a sharp knock on the door, and Lorenzi entered in a voluminous dark blue riding cloak. Without a word, he lightly slipped the cloak from his shoulders so that it lay between the two men as a shapeless piece of cloth. Casanova removed his gold pieces from beneath one of the bolsters on the bed and spread them out on the table. He counted them carefully under Lorenzi's watchful eyes—which didn't take much time, as many of the gold pieces were worth more than one ducat—and gave Lorenzi the agreed upon amount after dividing the money into two different bags, a procedure that left a hundred ducats for himself. Lorenzi put the two bags of gold into his coat pockets and was about to leave without saying a word when Casanova said, "Wait, Lorenzi, it's possible that our paths in life will cross again sometime. If so, let it not be in anger. This was a business transaction like any other, and we're even now." He held his hand out to him. Lorenzi refused it and finally said his first words: "I don't remember that anything like this was included in our pact." Turning on his heels, he left.

So we're keeping strictly to the letter, my friend? thought Casanova. Then I can be sure I won't wind up duped in the end. Admittedly he hadn't seriously considered such a possibility. He knew from personal experience that men like Lorenzi had their own code of honor, a code whose laws couldn't be set down in neat paragraphs perhaps, but which left little doubt about its requirements in particular circumstances. He packed Lorenzi's cloak in the top of his bag

and closed it. He put the remaining gold pieces into his pockets, and
for one last time glanced around the room, which he was not likely
to see again. Then, hat and sword in hand and ready for departure,
he went down to the hall where he found Olivo, his wife, and his
children seated at a table already set for supper. At that instant, from
the direction of the garden, Marcolina also entered the room, which
Casanova interpreted as an auspicious sign. She greeted him with a
graceful nod. Supper was served. The conversation was slow and la-
bored at first, as though subdued by thoughts of Casanova's imminent departure. Amalia seemed conspicuously busy with her girls,
continually preoccupied with whether one or the other had received
too much or too little on her plate. Olivo began to talk irrelevantly
about a trifling lawsuit he had just won against his neighbor, and
about the upcoming business trip that would soon take him to Mantua and Cremona. Casanova expressed the hope that he would see
his friend in Venice before long. It was the one place where, curiously enough, Olivo had never been. Amalia had seen the marvelous
city in her childhood many years ago; she couldn't recall how she
had traveled there and remembered only an old man wearing a scarlet cloak who, after disembarking from a long, narrow boat, had
stumbled and fallen flat on his face.

"And you've never been to Venice either?" Casanova asked
Marcolina, who sat directly across from him, looking over his shoulder into the darkness of the garden. She shook her head but said
nothing. Casanova thought, If only I could show you the city where
I was young! Oh, if you had been young with me. . . . And another
thought, one more senseless than the last, crossed his mind: What if
I took you there with me now?

While all these unspoken thoughts ran through his mind, he
began to talk of the city of his youth with that ease he was able to
muster even in moments of extreme inner agitation. He spoke with
an artist's touch, as cooly as if he were trying to describe a painting.

But when he began to tell the story of his own life, his tone grew warmer, and he became a figure in the center of the painting, which only now came vividly alive. He spoke of his mother, the celebrated actress for whom her admirer, the great Goldoni, had written his splendid comedy *La Pupilla*; of his unhappy days in the boarding school of the skinflint Doctor Bozzi; of his childish love for the gardener's little daughter, who had later run off with a footman; of his first sermon as a young abbot, after which he had found in the sexton's collection basket not only the usual coins but also a number of love letters; of the mischievous pranks he had played with a few of his like-minded companions in the streets, taverns, dance halls, and casinos of Venice, sometimes masked and sometimes unmasked, while a violinist in the orchestra of the Theater San Samuele. He was able to tell of these high-spirited and sometimes alarming pranks without using a single offensive word—indeed, he spoke of them in a manner that transformed his tale into a kind of poetry, as though in consideration of the girls who, like the rest, including even Marcolina, hung on his every word. But gradually the hour grew late, and Amalia sent her daughters off to bed. Before they left, Casanova kissed each one with great tenderness, treating Teresina exactly as he did the two younger ones, and made them promise to visit him in Venice with their parents soon.

With the girls gone, he spoke with less restraint but continued to relate everything without suggestive innuendos and above all without vanity, so that his audience might have imagined they were listening to a soulful romantic rather than a dangerous seducer and wild adventurer. He told them of the mysterious woman who had traveled with him for weeks disguised as an officer and who one morning had suddenly disappeared; of the cobbler's daughter in Madrid, who in the intervals between their embraces had tried to turn him into a devout Catholic; of Lia, the beautiful Jewess of Turin, who bore herself on horseback better than any princess; of Manon

Balleti, charming and innocent, the only woman he had nearly married; of the terrible singer in Warsaw whom he had hissed on stage, after which he had had to fight a duel with her lover, General Branitzky, and flee the city; of Charpillon, the wicked woman who had made such a fool of him in London; of the storm-tossed midnight boat ride across the lagoons to the island of Murano to see the nun he adored, which had almost cost him his life; of Croce, the gambler, who, after losing his fortune at Spa, had bid him a tearful farewell on a country road and had set out toward St. Petersburg dressed just as he was—in silk stockings, an apple-green velvet jacket, and a walking cane. He told of actresses, singers, hat-makers, countesses, dancers, and chambermaids; of gamblers, officers, princes, ambassadors, financiers, musicians, and adventurers. So carried away was he by the rediscovered and revivified magic of his own past—so complete was the victory of his glorious though now irretrievable former life over the wretched shadows of his present existence—that he was on the point of telling the story of a pale and pretty girl who had confided her troubles in love to him in a twilit church in Mantua, completely forgetting that this girl, now sixteen years older, was the one who was sitting across the table from him as the wife of his friend Olivo, when the maid entered noisily and announced that his carriage awaited him at the gate.

Instantly, with his incomparable talent, sleeping or waking, for pulling himself together to meet any situation and do what was necessary, Casanova rose to make his farewells. Once more he warmly embraced Olivo, who was too moved to speak, and invited him to visit him in Venice with his wife and children. And when he approached Amalia to kiss her as well, she lightly fended him off and only gave him her hand, which he kissed respectfully. When finally he turned to Marcolina, she said, "You should write down everything you told us tonight—and a great deal more—Signor Chevalier, just as you did the story of your escape from the Lead Chambers."

"Do you really mean that, Marcolina?" he asked with the shyness of a young author.

She smiled in gentle mockery. "I suspect," she said, "that such a book might prove much more entertaining than your polemic against Voltaire."

That's probably true, he thought, but did not say so out loud. Perhaps I'll follow your advice someday. If so, you, Marcolina, will be the subject of the final chapter. This idea, and even more so, the thought that he would experience this final chapter that very night, made his eyes flash so strangely that Marcolina, who had given him her hand in farewell, withdrew it before he could press a kiss to it. Betraying neither disappointment nor anger, Casanova turned to go, and with one of those clear and simple gestures unique to him, he indicated to everyone that no one, not even Olivo, was to follow him.

With quick steps he hurried through the chestnut-lined avenue, handed a gold piece to the maid who had brought his luggage to the carriage, swung himself up, took his seat, and rode away.

The sky was overcast. In the village a few lamps still flickered from behind dirty windows, but once the carriage had left it behind, the only light that illuminated the night was the yellow glow of the lantern fastened to the shaft of the carriage. Casanova opened his bag, removed Lorenzi's cloak, flung it over himself, and under its cover cautiously undressed. He packed his clothing and his shoes and stockings in the bag and wrapped the cloak more tightly around himself. Then he called out to the coachman, "Hey, we have to go back!"

The coachman turned around, annoyed.

"I've forgotten my papers in the house. Do you understand? We have to go back."

And when the coachman, a surly, skinny, grey-beard, appeared to hesitate, Casanova added quickly, "Of course I'm not asking you to do this for nothing. Here you are!" And he pressed a gold piece into the man's hand.

The coachman nodded, muttered, gave his horse a superfluous lash of his whip, and turned the carriage around. As they drove through the village again, all the houses were now silent and dark. A little farther up the main road, the coachman made as if to turn into the narrower, gradually rising side road that led to Olivo's property.

"Halt!" cried Casanova. "We won't drive any closer, otherwise we'll wake everyone. Wait for me here. I'll be back soon. . . . If it should take a little longer, you'll get a ducat for every hour!"

The man seemed to understand what was afoot—Casanova noticed it by the way he nodded. He descended and hurried on, out of the coachman's sight and all the way past the locked gate and along the wall to the corner where the side road made a sharp right turn up the hill. He then took the path through the vineyards which, since he had walked it twice by daylight, he had no difficulty finding. Staying close to the wall, he followed the path around another turn halfway up the hill, then made his way across the soft grass of the meadow, concerned only about not missing the garden door in the dark of the overcast night. He felt his way along the smooth stone wall until his fingers touched rough wood, and soon he made out the outline of the narrow door. Quickly finding the lock, he inserted the key, opened the door, entered the garden, and closed the door behind him. On the other side of the meadow, the house seemed incredibly far off and the tower incredibly high. For a while he stood quietly and looked around. What for others would have been impenetrable darkness was to him no more than deep twilight. Since the gravel of the path hurt his bare feet, he walked across the meadow, which also had the advantage of muffling the sound of his footsteps. His tread was so light he felt as though he were soaring.

Did I feel any different, he asked himself, when I undertook similar adventures as a thirty-year-old? Don't I feel the same ardor of desire, and doesn't the same sap of youth course through my veins? Am I not still the same Casanova I was then? And since I am

Casanova, why should I be subject to the same wretched law that others are, the law of aging!

Growing steadily bolder, he asked himself: Why am I going to Marcolina in disguise? Even though he's thirty years older, isn't Casanova a better man than Lorenzi? And isn't she the very woman to understand this? Was it really necessary to commit this small act of dishonesty and to seduce someone else into committing a larger one? Wouldn't I have reached the same goal with a little more patience? Lorenzi will be gone tomorrow; I could have stayed on . . . five days . . . three—and she would have been mine, would knowingly have been mine. He stood close to the side of the house beneath Marcolina's window, still tightly closed, and his thoughts raced on: Is it too late now? . . . I could come back tomorrow or the next day . . . and begin the work of seduction—as an honorable man, so to speak. Tonight would be but a foretaste of future successes. Marcolina mustn't find out that I was here today—or find out only later, much later.

Marcolina's window was still tightly closed. There was no sign from within. It was probably a few minutes to midnight. Should he make his presence known in some way? Perhaps by lightly tapping on the window? No—since nothing of the sort had been prearranged, it might arouse Marcolina's suspicions. Better wait. It couldn't be much longer. The idea that she might recognize him instantly and see through the deception before it had succeeded crossed his mind, not for the first time, yet fleetingly, and merely as a remote possibility that was understandable and logical but not a serious concern. A rather ludicrous adventure of twenty years earlier crossed his mind. He had spent an exquisite night with an ugly old woman in Soluthurn believing that he possessed a beautiful young woman whom he adored—a woman who, to add insult to injury, sent him an insolent letter the next day in which she derided him for his mistake, which she had greatly desired and brought about with disgraceful cunning. He shuddered with disgust at the memory. It was the last thing he should have thought about just now, and he drove the repulsive image from his mind.

Well, wasn't it midnight yet? How long was he supposed to stand here pressed against the wall and shivering in the chill of night? Or perhaps he was waiting in vain? A dupe after all, despite everything? Two thousand ducats for nothing? Lorenzi behind the curtain with her—mocking him? He gripped the hilt of his sword, pressed against his naked body beneath the cloak—with a fellow like Lorenzi, one had better be prepared for unpleasant surprises. But then . . . at that instant he heard a soft creaking, and he knew that the grate on Marcolina's window was being drawn back. A moment later both wings of the window opened wide, though the curtain inside was still drawn. Casanova remained motionless a few seconds longer, until an unseen hand pulled the curtain to one side. Casanova took this as a sign to swing himself over the windowsill into the room and to close the window and the grate behind him. The gathered curtain had fallen across his shoulders, so that he had to crawl out from under it. He would have stood in absolute darkness if out of the depths of the room, as if awakened by his own glance, a faint shimmer had not shown him the way. Just three steps—and eager arms reached out toward him. He let his sword slip from his hands and his cloak from his shoulders, and he sank into bliss.

From Marcolina's sighs of rapture, the tears of bliss that he kissed from her cheeks, and the ever-renewed passion with which she received his caresses, he was soon convinced that she shared his ecstasy, which seemed to him to be of a higher, indeed, of a new and different kind than he had ever enjoyed before. Pleasure became reverence, and the most profound rapture became an intense consciousness. Here at last was what he had so often and so foolishly believed he had experienced before, and yet had never truly attained—fulfillment. Here, in Marcolina's arms. With this woman he could squander himself yet still feel inexhaustible. The moments of ultimate abandon and of new desire coalesced into a single moment of unimaginable spiritual ecstasy. Weren't life and death, time and eternity, all one on these lips? Was he not a god? Youth and Age merely a fable, invented by man? Home and exile, splendor and misery, fame and oblivion—insubstantial distinctions for the restless, the lonely, and the vain? And meaningless, if one were Casanova and had found Marcolina! As the minutes passed it seemed to him contemptible and ludicrous that he should abide by the timid resolution he had made earlier and flee from this miraculous night mute and unrecognized, like a thief. In the unwavering conviction that he was just as much the giver as the receiver of joy, he believed he was ready to risk disclosing his identity, though he was aware that he was playing for high stakes by doing so—stakes which, if he lost, he must be prepared to exchange for his life.

Pitch-darkness still surrounded him, and he could postpone his confession until the first light of dawn penetrated the heavy curtain, when Marcolina's reaction would determine his fate, his very life. Besides, wasn't this silent and blissful, sweetly oblivious union precisely what would bind Marcolina to him more and more inextricably, kiss by kiss? Hadn't the ineffable delights of this night transformed what had begun as deception into truth? Didn't she—this duped, beloved, matchless woman—already sense that it wasn't Lorenzi, a mere boy, an insignificant little creature, who was giving her this divine ecstasy, but a man—Casanova himself? He began to think it possible that he might be spared the desired and yet feared moment of revelation. He imagined that Marcolina, trembling, entranced, and transfigured, would whisper his name to him. And then—when she had forgiven him—no, had accepted his forgiveness—he would take her with him, immediately, this very hour. They would leave the house together in the grey morning, together climb into the carriage that waited at the curve of the road, and together drive away—and he would keep her forever. He would crown his life's work by having won her, the youngest, the most beautiful, the most gifted of women, through the overwhelming force of his inextinguishable personality. He would make her his own forever at an age when other men prepared themselves for a dismal old age. For she was his as no other woman before her had been. Now he was gliding down mysterious narrow canals, between palaces in whose shadow he was once more at home, under arched bridges over which blurry figures darted. Some of them waved to the couple from the balustrade and were gone before they could be recognized.

Now the gondola drew up to the marble staircase leading into the splendid mansion of Senator Bragadino, the only one festively lit. Masked guests were ascending and descending the stairs—some of them paused with inquisitive glances, but who could recognize Casanova and Marcolina behind their masks? He entered the hall with her. A high-stakes game was being played. All the senators, including Bragadino, were standing around the table in their crimson robes. When Casanova entered, they all whispered his name as though terror-stricken, for they had recognized him by his eyes flashing behind his mask. He did not sit down, nor did he take any cards, yet he joined in the game. He won. He won all the gold lying on the table, but it was not enough—the senators had to give him promissory notes. They lost their fortunes, their palaces, their crimson robes—they were beggars crawling around him in rags, kissing his hands. Nearby, in a scarlet ballroom, there was music and dancing. Casanova wanted to dance with Marcolina, but she had vanished. Once again the senators were sitting around the table in their crimson robes as before, but now Casanova knew that the hazards at stake were not those of a game of cards but the destinies of accused persons, criminals and innocents.

Where was Marcolina? Hadn't he been holding her wrist tightly the entire time? He ran down the staircase. The gondola was waiting. On, on, through the maze of canals. Of course the oarsman knew where Marcolina was, but why was he masked too? That wasn't the custom in Venice. Casanova wanted to take him to task, but he didn't dare. Is this how cowardly old men become? Onward, onward—what a gigantic city Venice had become in these past twenty-five years! At last the houses receded and the canal became broader—they were gliding between islands, and there stood the walls of the nunnery of Murano, to which Marcolina had fled. The gondola was gone—now he had to swim—how delightful! Meanwhile it was true that the children of Venice were playing with his gold pieces, but what did he care about the gold? . . . The water was now warm, now cool; it dripped from his clothing as he climbed up the wall.

Where is Marcolina? he asked loudly in the reception room, in ringing tones that only a prince would dare to use.

I'll summon her, said the duchess-abbess, and disappeared.

Casanova walked, flew, and flitted to and fro like a bat along the bars of the grating. If only I had known sooner that I could fly! I'll teach Marcolina too. Behind the bars female figures were floating. Nuns—yet they all wore secular clothing. He knew this, though he couldn't see them, and he knew who they were. It was Henrietta, the mysterious unknown woman, and Corticelli the dancer, and Cristina the bride, and the beautiful Dubois, and the accursed old woman from Solothurn, and Manon Balleti . . . and a hundred others—all except Marcolina!

You betrayed me, he shouted at the oarsman who waited for him in the gondola. He had never hated anyone on earth more than this oarsman, and he vowed to take an exquisite revenge on him. But wasn't it stupid of him to look for Marcolina in the Murano nunnery when she had gone to visit Voltaire? It was fortunate that he could fly, since he didn't have enough money left to pay for a carriage. He swam away, but the water wasn't as delightful as before—it grew colder and colder. He was adrift in the open sea, far from Murano, far from Venice—and there was no ship anywhere in sight. His heavy gold-embroidered garments dragged him down; he tried to strip them off, but it was impossible as he was holding in his hand the manuscript he had to give Monsieur Voltaire. Suddenly water filled his mouth and nose, and a fear of death seized him. He flailed about, there was a rattle in his throat; he screamed and with great difficulty opened his eyes.

A ray of morning light had broken through a narrow strip between the curtain and the window frame. Wrapped in a white nightgown which she held with both hands across her breast, Marcolina stood at the foot of the bed, contemplating Casanova with an expression of unutterable horror. Her look instantly awakened him completely. Instinctively he stretched out his arms to her in a gesture of appeal. In reply, Marcolina repulsed him with her left arm, clutching her nightgown to her breast even more convulsively with her right. Supporting himself with his hands on the mattress, Casanova raised himself halfway and stared at her. He was no more able to avert his eyes from her than she was able to avert hers from him. Rage and shame were in his; horror and shame in hers. And Casanova knew just what she saw, because he saw his image as if in an invisible mirror just as he had seen it yesterday in the mirror in his room in the tower: a yellowed, evil, deep-lined face with thin lips and piercing eyes— now looking three times worse than yesterday because of the excesses of the night, the anxious dream of early morning, and the shock of recognition upon awakening. The words he read in Marcolina's eyes were not "thief," "lecher," "villain"—these he would prefer a thousand times—but the one phrase that now crushed him more ignominiously than any term of abuse. For him it was the most terrible label of all, the one that passed a final judgment on him: old man!

If it had been within his power to destroy himself with a spell, at that moment he would have done it, simply to spare himself having to crawl out from beneath the blanket and display himself to Marcolina in all his nakedness. Such a picture had to be more loathsome to her than the sight of a disgusting animal. But Marcolina, as if gradually collecting herself, and clearly in order to allow him to do what he had to do as quickly as possible, turned her face to the wall. He seized the moment to leap from the bed, pick the cloak up from the floor, and wrap himself in it. He made sure he had his sword, and feeling that he had at least escaped the greatest disgrace of all, that of looking ridiculous, he began to wonder if he couldn't, through the skillful words usually at his command, put this whole wretched business into a different light, and to even somehow turn it to his advantage. From the nature of the circumstances, it was impossible for Marcolina to doubt that Lorenzi had sold her to Casanova—yet however profoundly she might hate Lorenzi at this moment, Casanova sensed that he, the cowardly thief, was a thousand times more hateful to her than Lorenzi. Perhaps there was some other way to achieve satisfaction. He could, for example, attempt to degrade Marcolina with mocking and lewd phrases full of innuendo. But this spiteful idea faded as the look on her face changed gradually from one of horror to one of infinite sadness, as if it wasn't only Marcolina's womanhood that had been desecrated, but as if during this night there had occurred a nameless and unforgivable violation of trust by cunning, of love by lust, of youth by age.

Beneath this gaze which, to his torment, momentarily reawakened everything that was still good in him, Casanova turned away. Without looking back at Marcolina, he went to the window, drew the curtain aside, opened the shutters and the grate, cast a glance around the garden still slumbering in the approaching dawn, and swung himself across the windowsill. Aware of the possibility that someone in the house might already be awake and see him from a window, he avoided the meadow and sought cover in the protective shade of the avenue. Passing through the garden door, he had barely shut it behind him when someone approached and barred his way—the gondolier. This was his first thought because he suddenly realized that the gondolier in his dream had been none other than Lorenzi. And there he stood. His silver-braided scarlet uniform glowed in the morning light. What a magnificent uniform, thought Casanova in his confused and weary brain—it looks quite new. And of course it's not paid for. . . . These mundane reflections brought him abruptly to his senses, and as soon as he was aware of the situation he felt glad. He assumed his proudest stance, gripped the handle of his sword more firmly, and said in a most cordial tone, "Don't you think, Signor Lieutenant Lorenzi, that it's a little late for this?"

"Not at all," answered Lorenzi—and at this moment he was more handsome than any man Casanova had ever seen—"since only one of us will leave this place alive."

"You're in too much of a hurry, Lorenzi," Casanova said in an almost tender tone. "Can't we postpone this at least until we get to Mantua? I would be honored to take you with me in my carriage. It's waiting at the turn of the road. There's something to be said for observing the formalities . . . especially in a case such as ours."

"We don't need any formalities. You, Casanova, or I—right now, at this very moment." He drew his sword.

Casanova shrugged. "As you wish, Lorenzi. But I must point out to you that I'd be forced to compete in a completely inappropriate costume." He threw open his cloak and stood there naked, holding his sword playfully in his hand. Hatred flashed in Lorenzi's eyes. "You won't be at any disadvantage with me," he said, and began to remove all his clothes with great speed. Casanova turned away and wrapped himself in his cloak once more, since despite the sun that broke gradually through the morning haze, it had become uncomfortably chilly. The few sparse trees at the top of the hill cast long shadows across the grass. For a moment Casanova wondered whether someone might come this way after all. But the path that ran along the wall to the rear garden door was probably used only by Olivo and the members of his household. It occurred to Casanova that these were perhaps the last minutes of his life; he was amazed at his own calm.

Monsieur Voltaire is lucky, he thought fleetingly, but in truth he was completely indifferent to Voltaire and wanted to recall lovelier images than that of the repulsive, birdlike face of the old writer. Incidentally, wasn't it strange that there were no birds singing in the crowns of the trees on the opposite side of the wall? The weather must be changing. But what did he care about the weather? He would rather think of Marcolina, of the ecstasies he had enjoyed in her arms, for which he would now pay dearly. Dearly? Cheap enough! A few years of old age—in misery and obscurity. . . . What was there left for him to do in the world? . . . Poison Signor Bragadino? Was that worth the effort? No, nothing was worth the effort. . . . How thin the trees were on top of the hill! He began to count them. Five . . . seven . . . ten. Don't I have something more important to do?

"I'm ready, Chevalier!"

Casanova turned around sharply. Lorenzi stood before him like a young god, magnificent in his nakedness. Everything base had been wiped from his face. He seemed equally ready to kill or to die. What if I were to throw away my sword? thought Casanova. What if I were to embrace him? He let his coat slip from his shoulders and now stood like Lorenzi, naked and slender.

In accordance with the rules of fencing, Lorenzi lowered his sword in salute. Casanova returned the salute. A moment later they crossed blades, and the morning light glinted like silver from sword to sword.

How long has it been, Casanova wondered, since I last crossed swords with an opponent like this? But he couldn't remember any of his serious duels, only the fencing practice he used to have with his valet Costa, that scoundrel who later absconded with a hundred and fifty thousand of his lire. All the same, thought Casanova, he was a fine fencer—and I haven't forgotten what I learned! His arm was sure, his hand was quick, and his vision was as sharp as ever. Youth and age are only fables, he thought. . . . Am I not a god? Are we not both gods? If anyone could see us now! There are women who would pay a high price for the privilege!

The blades bent, the points flashed, and at each touch of blade against blade the swords sang softly in the morning air. Was this really a fight? No, it was a fencing tournament. . . . Why this look of horror, Marcolina? Aren't we both worthy of your love? He's only a youngster, but I am Casanova! . . .

Lorenzi sank suddenly to the ground, thrust through the heart. The sword fell from his grip. He opened his eyes wide as if in utter astonishment. He lifted his head once more, his mouth twisting in pain, and then let it fall. His nostrils flared, and with a soft rattle in his throat, he died.

Casanova bent over him and knelt down beside him, saw a few drops of blood ooze from the wound, and moved his hand in front of Lorenzi's mouth—but there was no breath of life. A cold shudder ran through Casanova's limbs. He rose and put on the cloak. Then, returning to the body, he looked down at the fallen youth stretched out on the lawn in incomparable beauty. A soft rustling disturbed the silence; it was the morning breeze stirring the treetops on the other side of the garden wall.

What now? Casanova asked himself. Shall I call someone? Olivo? Amalia? Marcolina? What for? No one can bring him back to life!

He deliberated for a while with the cool composure always at his command in his most dangerous moments. It could be many hours before anyone found Lorenzi, possibly evening, perhaps even later. That will give me time, and that's the only important thing right now.

He still held his sword in his hand. Noticing Lorenzi's blood glistening on it, he wiped it on the grass. He thought of dressing the corpse, but that would cost him valuable and irrecoverable minutes. As though paying his last respects, he bent down once more and closed the dead man's eyes. "Lucky fellow," he murmured to himself, and dreamily kissed the murdered man on the forehead. Then he quickly rose and hurried along the wall, following it around the corner and downward toward the road. The carriage waited where he had left it, the coachman fast asleep on the box. Casanova was careful not to wake him. He climbed cautiously into the carriage, and only then called out, "Hey, let's go!" prodding him in the back. The coachman started, looked around, was astounded to find it already daylight, lashed the horses, and drove off. Casanova sat far back in the carriage, wrapped in the cloak that had once belonged to Lorenzi. Only a few children were to be seen in the streets of the village; evidently the men and the women were already at work in the fields. Once they had left the houses behind, Casanova breathed more easily. Opening his bag, he took out his clothes and began to dress himself beneath the cover of the cloak, not without concern that the coachman might turn around and notice his passenger's strange maneuverings. But nothing of the sort happened, and Casanova was able to finish dressing undisturbed, pack Lorenzi's cloak in his bag, and put on his own.

He glanced up at the sky and saw it had become overcast. He wasn't at all tired; on the contrary, his nerves were taut and he was overly alert. He considered his situation again from various angles and concluded that, though grave, it wasn't as dangerous as it might have seemed to anxious types. Of course he would be suspected of killing Lorenzi, but no one could doubt that it had been during an honorable duel—and besides, he had been confronted by Lorenzi and forced into this duel, and no one could consider him a criminal for having fought in self-defense. But why had he left Lorenzi lying in the grass like a dead dog? Well, no one could fault him for that, either: it had been his perfect right, almost his duty, to flee immediately. Lorenzi would have done the same.

But what if Venice turned him over to the authorities? As soon as he arrived, he would place himself under the protection of his patron Bragadino. Yet if he did so, wouldn't he be accusing himself of a deed that might otherwise never be discovered, or with which he might never be charged? What proof was there against him? Hadn't he been summoned to Venice? Who could say he went as a fugitive from justice? The coachman who had waited for him half the night? A few more pieces of gold would shut his mouth. Thus Casanova's thoughts ran in circles. Suddenly he thought he heard the pounding of horses' hooves behind him. So soon? was his first thought. He leaned his head out of the carriage window to look backward. The street was empty. They had driven past a farm, and it had been the echo of his own horses' hoofbeats. The discovery of this self-deception so quieted his apprehensions that he was convinced that all danger was over for good. The towers of Mantua loomed in front of him. . . . "Drive on, drive on," he said to himself, not wanting the coachman to hear his words. But the coachman, nearing his destination, now urged the horses on, and soon they were at the gate through which Casanova had left town with Olivo fewer than forty-eight hours earlier. He gave the coachman the name of the inn where he wanted him to stop, and after a few minutes the sign with the image of the golden lion appeared. When they stopped, Casanova leaped from the carriage.

His vivacious innkeeper was standing in the doorway, smiling broadly. She seemed in the mood to give Casanova the welcome of a sorely missed lover returning after an unwelcome absence. But Casanova glanced warily at the coachman, possibly a troublesome witness, and sent him off to eat and drink to his heart's content.

"A letter from Venice came for you yesterday evening, Chevalier," said the innkeeper.

"Another?" asked Casanova, mounting the stairs to his room.

The innkeeper followed him. A sealed letter lay on the table. Casanova opened it with great apprehension. A revocation of the Grand Council's offer? he wondered anxiously. But as he read, his face brightened. It was a few lines from Bragadino along with a draft for two hundred and fifty lire, so that Casanova wouldn't need to delay his trip for even one more day. Casanova turned to the innkeeper and with feigned irritation explained that he was unfortunately compelled to continue his journey instantly. Were he to delay, he ran the danger of losing the position that his friend Bragadino had procured for him in Venice—a position for which there were fully one hundred applicants. Noticing the storm clouds gathering in her face, he quickly added that he merely meant to secure his position and accept his mandate—that of secretary to the Grand Council of Venice. Then, once safely in office, he would immediately request a leave of absence to put his affairs in Mantua in order. They couldn't really deny him such a request. He would leave most of his few effects here at the inn, and then it would be entirely up to his dear, charming sweetheart to decide whether she would give up her business here and follow him to Venice as his wife. . . . She threw her arms around his neck and with moist eyes asked whether she couldn't at least bring a hearty breakfast to his room before his departure. He knew that she had in mind a farewell feast for which he felt not the least desire, but he agreed in order to be rid of her at long last.

As soon as she had gone downstairs, he took only the clothing and books he most urgently needed and packed them in his bag. Then he went down into the parlor where he found the coachman enjoying a generous meal, and asked him whether—for a sum double the usual price—he could leave immediately for the next postal station on the road to Venice with the same horses. The coachman agreed on the spot, and so for the moment Casanova was free of his greatest concern. Now the innkeeper, her face flushed with rage, entered to ask whether he had forgotten that his breakfast was waiting for him in his room. Casanova answered calmly that he had not forgotten it for a moment. At the same time he asked her, since he didn't have time himself, if she would be willing to go to the bank and get him the two hundred fifty lire against the draft he was about to give her. While she ran to get the money, Casanova returned to his room and with wolfish voracity began to devour the food that was set out for him. He didn't pause when she came back, but simply put the money she brought into his pocket. When he finished eating, he turned to the woman who, thinking her hour had finally come, had affectionately seated herself next to him and stretched her arms toward him in an unmistakable invitation. He embraced her fiercely, kissed her on both cheeks, clasped her to him, and just as she seemed ready to yield to him, exclaimed, "I must leave . . . goodbye!" He tore himself from her with such violence that she fell backward into the corner of the sofa. The expression on her face, a mixture of disappointment, rage, and impotence, was so irresistibly amusing to Casanova that, as he shut the door behind him, he couldn't help laughing out loud.

It couldn't have escaped the coachman that his passenger was in a hurry, but it was not his business to wonder about the reasons. He was sitting on the box ready to go when Casanova burst from the inn, and he whipped the horses furiously the moment his passenger was inside. He thought it best not to drive straight through the middle of town but skirted it to rejoin the main road on the other side. The sun was low in the sky, as it was still three hours before noon. It's likely they haven't even found Lorenzi's body yet, Casanova mused. He scarcely realized that he had killed Lorenzi himself. All he knew was that he was happy to be leaving Mantua farther and farther behind, and glad to have some rest for a while. . . . He fell into the deepest sleep he had ever experienced—one that, in a sense, lasted two whole days and nights. The short interruptions that were necessary for changing horses along the way, and those during which he sat in inns or walked up and down in front of post offices, exchanging casual bits of conversation with postmasters, innkeepers, customs guards, and other travelers, did not linger in his memory as individual events. Later the memory of these two days and nights merged with the dream he had had in Marcolina's bed. Even the duel between two naked men on a green meadow in early morning sunshine seemed somehow to belong to this dream, in which curiously enough he was sometimes not Casanova but Lorenzi—not the victor but the vanquished, not the fugitive but the fallen, the one whose pale youthful body the morning breeze caressed. Neither he nor Lorenzi were any more real than the senators in crimson cloaks who had crawled to him on their knees as beggars, nor any less real than the old man leaning over a railing of some bridge to whom he had tossed a few alms from the carriage. Had Casanova's power of reason not allowed him to distinguish between his real experiences and the ones he had dreamed, he could easily have convinced himself that he had fallen into a confused dream in Marcolina's arms from which he would not awaken until he caught sight of the Campanile of Venice.

It was on the third day of his trip that he again, from Mestre, saw the bell tower of Venice after more than twenty years of longing—a solitary grey stone mass looming out of the morning twilight as though from a great distance. Only a two-hour drive now separated him from the beloved city of his youth. He paid the coachman without knowing whether he was the fourth, fifth, or sixth one he had paid since leaving Mantua. Then, followed by a boy who carried his baggage, he hurried through the squalid streets to the harbor to catch the market boat that left for Venice at six in the morning just as it had twenty-five years ago. The boat seemed to have waited for him; he had barely seated himself on a narrow bench among petty traders, workmen, and women bringing their wares into town, when the boat began to move. The sky was overcast; a mist hung over the lagoons, and a smell of stagnant water, damp wood, fish, and fresh fruit was in the air. The Campanile loomed taller and taller; the outline of other towers emerged from the mist; church domes became visible. The beams of the morning sun danced on one roof, then another, and another. Individual houses became distinct and grew in height; boats large and small bobbed out of the mist, and greetings were exchanged from one to the other. The chatter around him grew louder. He bought grapes from a little girl and devoured them, spitting the blue skins overboard in the manner of his countrymen. He took up a conversation with someone who expressed his pleasure that the weather seemed to be finally clearing. What, it had been raining here for three days? He knew nothing about it, he had come from the south, from Naples and Rome. . . .

The boat had already entered the canals of the city's outskirts. Dirty houses stared at him with grimy windows that looked like vacant, hostile eyes. The boat stopped two or three times, and a few young men, one with a large portfolio under his arm, and some women with baskets got off. Now they were coming into more familiar territory. Wasn't that the church where Martina used to go to confession? And wasn't this the house where, in his own fashion, he had restored the pallid and deathly ill Agatha to rosy-cheeked health? And wasn't that house the one where he had beaten the good-for-nothing brother of the charming Silvia black and blue? And that small ochre house over there in that side canal, where a barefooted fat woman was standing on the steps as the water washed over them . . . Before he could remember what apparition from his distant past belonged there, the boat had entered the Grand Canal and was now slowly gliding down the broad waterway between the palaces that lined each side. Because of his dream, it seemed to Casanova that he had been down this route only yesterday. He disembarked at the Rialto, for he had decided that before visiting Signor Bragadino he would stow his baggage and secure a room in a small and modest hotel he recalled as being near there, though he couldn't remember its name. He found the building dilapidated, or at least more neglected than he had pictured it. A sulky waiter badly in need of a shave showed him to an uninviting room overlooking the blind wall of the house opposite. But Casanova didn't wish to lose any time, and as he had exhausted almost all his cash during the trip, he welcomed the cheap price of the room. He therefore decided to stay for the time being. He washed off the dust and dirt of his long trip and deliberated about changing into his finer suit, but in the end he decided to wear his more modest one, and then left the inn. It was only a hundred paces through a narrow little street and over a bridge to Bragadino's small and elegant palazzo. A young servant with a rather impudent expression took Casanova's name in a manner that implied he had never heard the famous name, but he came back from his master's rooms with a more civil demeanor and let the guest in. Bragadino was having breakfast at a table that had been moved near an open window. He started to get up, but Casanova wouldn't let him.

"My dear Casanova!" Bragadino exclaimed. "I'm so happy to see you again! Yes, who would have thought we'd ever see each other again?" And he held out both his hands. Casanova took them as though he were going to kiss them, but he didn't do so. He answered the warm greetings with words of passionate gratitude, in the somewhat grandiloquent manner he always adopted on occasions of this sort. Bragadino invited him to sit down and asked him whether he had had breakfast. When Casanova indicated that he hadn't, Bragadino rang for the servant and gave him the appropriate orders. As soon as the servant left the room, Bragadino said how gratified he was that Casanova had accepted the Grand Council's offer without reservation. He certainly wouldn't be sorry for deciding to devote his services to the fatherland. Casanova declared that he would consider himself fortunate merely to win the approval of the Grand

Council. And so he went on, keeping his thoughts to himself. Not that he felt any more hatred toward Bragadino now; rather he felt a little sorry for the ancient man who sat across from him with a thinning white beard and red-rimmed eyes, who had become a little simpleminded and whose cup trembled in his hands. When Casanova last saw him, Bragadino had probably been as old as Casanova was today, and he had already seemed ancient to him them.

The servant brought Casanova's breakfast. He needed little encouragement to indulge his appetite, since he had only had an occasional meager bite during his trip. Yes, he had traveled day and night from Mantua to get here—so eager was he to demonstrate his readiness to serve the Grand Council and to prove his eternal gratitude to his noble benefactors (he offered this by way of excusing the almost indecent gluttony with which he noisily slurped his steaming hot chocolate). Through the window, from the Grand and the smaller canals, the myriad sounds of Venetian life rose up, dominated by the monotone shouts of the gondoliers. From somewhere not far away, perhaps from the palazzo directly opposite—wasn't it Fogazzari's?— a beautiful, high soprano voice was practicing coloratura runs. The voice was obviously that of a very young woman, someone who hadn't even been born at the time of Casanova's escape from the Lead Chambers. He ate toast and butter, eggs, and sliced cold meats, continually excusing himself for his insatiable appetite while Bragadino looked on, pleased.

"I love it when young people have a good appetite!" he said. "And if I remember right, my dear Casanova, you've never failed in that regard!" He recalled a meal he had shared with Casanova in the early days of their acquaintance—or rather, a meal he had admiringly watched his young friend enjoy, just as he was doing today. He himself had been in no condition to eat then, as it was just after Casanova had thrown out the doctor who had almost sent poor Bragadino into an early grave with his incessant bloodletting. . . .

They went on talking about old times—yes, life in Venice had been better then.

"Not everywhere," said Casanova with a faint smile, alluding to the Lead Chambers. Bragadino waved away his remark with a dismissive gesture, as if to say this was not the hour to remember such petty unpleasantness. Besides, he, Bragadino, had tried everything possible to save Casanova from punishment, though unfortunately he hadn't succeeded. If only he had already been a member of the Council of Ten then!

Thus the conversation turned to political matters, and the old man, inflamed by his subject, seemed to regain much of the wit and liveliness of his younger years. Casanova learned many remarkable things about the intellectual movement that a segment of Venetian youth had recently become involved in, and about the dangerous intrigues that were beginning unmistakably to be revealed. Casanova was therefore well prepared when later in the evening that same day, which he had spent sequestered in his dismal room trying to calm his much disturbed soul by arranging and occasionally burning some of his papers, he made his way to the Café Quadri on St. Mark's Square, reputed to be the main gathering place of freethinkers and revolutionaries. There he was promptly recognized by an elderly musician, the former conductor of the orchestra of the San Samuele Theater where Casanova had played the violin more than thirty years earlier. Through him, in the most casual manner, he was introduced to a group of mostly young people whose names he remembered from the morning conversation with Bragadino as being especially suspect. But the name of Casanova did not appear to have the effect on them that he felt entitled to expect; indeed, most of them apparently knew nothing of Casanova other than that he had been imprisoned in the Lead Chambers a long time ago for one reason or another, perhaps even for no reason at all, and had escaped despite great dangers. The little book in which he had described his flight so vividly many years before wasn't completely unknown, true, but no one seemed to have read it with much attention.

It amused Casanova to think that it lay solely in his power to help each and every one of these young gentlemen gain firsthand knowledge of the living conditions in Venice's Lead Chambers and of the difficulties of escape. But far from giving any indication of such a malicious thought, he played the role of the charming and innocuous gentleman here as elsewhere, and soon he was entertaining the group in his inimitable fashion with stories of all sorts of lively adventures, describing them as experiences of his recent trip from Rome to Venice—stories that were true enough, but had in fact happened fifteen or twenty years ago. While his audience was still listening to him eagerly, someone came to announce the news that an officer from Mantua had been murdered near the country estate of a friend he had been visiting, and that thieves had stolen everything, including the shirt, off the victim's body. Since attacks and murders of this sort were common in those days, the story aroused no particular interest in this company, and Casanova resumed his narrative at the point where he had been interrupted—as though the Mantua affair concerned him as little as it did the rest of them. Suddenly freed from an uneasy feeling that he hadn't been quite willing to acknowledge, he was funnier and bolder than ever.

It was past midnight when, after a brief farewell to his new acquaintances, he left the café and walked alone across the broad, empty square. A sky empty of stars hung heavy with fog. With the sureness of a sleepwalker, without really becoming conscious that he was walking a route he hadn't traversed in a quarter of a century, he found his way through narrow streets between dark houses, and over narrow bridges under which dark canals flowed toward the eternal waters, back to his wretched inn, where the door was opened for him, sluggishly and inhospitably, only after repeated knocks. A few minutes later, overwhelmed by painful exhaustion, and tasting on his lips a bitterness that came from his innermost being, he threw himself half-undressed onto his uncomfortable bed in the hope of gaining his first sleep in the city to which he had so ardently desired to return after twenty-five years of exile—a sleep that would not come until the break of dawn when, heavy and dreamless, it finally took pity on the aging adventurer.

Lieutenant Gustl

HOW LONG is this thing going to last? Let me look at my watch . . .
it's probably not good manners at a serious concert like this, but
who's going to notice? If anyone does, he's not paying any more attention than I am, so I really don't need to be embarrassed. . . . It's
only a quarter to ten? . . . It feels like I've been at this concert for a
good three hours already. Well, I'm just not used to it. . . . What is this
piece anyway? I've got to look at the program. . . . Oh yes, that's
right: an oratorio! I thought it was a mass. Things like this really belong in church. Another good thing about church is that you can leave
whenever you want.—If only I at least had an aisle seat!—Ah well,
patience, patience! Even oratorios have to end some time! Maybe it's
really beautiful and I'm just not in the right mood. But how am I supposed to get in the mood? To think I came here to take my mind off
things. . . . I should have given the ticket to Benedek instead. He likes
this sort of thing. After all, he plays the violin himself. But then
Kopetzky would have been insulted. It was very good of him to give
me the ticket. He meant well. He's a good fellow, that Kopetzky!
He's the only one I can really trust. . . . His sister is singing in the
chorus. There are at least a hundred young women up there, all
dressed in black: how am I supposed to pick her out of the crowd?
It's because she's singing with them that Kopetzky got the ticket. . . .
Why didn't he come himself?—Actually, they're singing very well.

It's very inspiring—yes it is! Bravo! Bravo! . . . Yes, I'll clap too. The fellow next to me is clapping like a maniac. Does he really like it that much?—The girl over there in the box is very pretty. Is she looking at me or at the man with the blond beard over there? . . . Ah, a solo! Who's that? *Alto: Fräulein Walker, Soprano: Fräulein Michalek* . . . that's probably the soprano. . . . I haven't been to the opera for a very long time. I always enjoy going, even when it's boring. Actually, I could go the day after tomorrow, to *La Traviata*. Well, by the day after tomorrow I may already be dead! Oh, nonsense. I don't believe that myself! Just wait, you silk-stocking lawyer, I'll teach you to make remarks like that! I'll punch you in the nose next time. . . .

If I could only get a better look at that girl in the box! I'd like to borrow those opera glasses from the man next to me, but he'd probably eat me alive if I disturbed his reverie. . . . Wonder which section of the chorus Kopetzky's sister is in? Would I recognize her? I've seen her only two or three times. The last time was in the officers' mess. . . . Wonder if all those girls are respectable, all one hundred of them? Oh Lord! . . . "In collaboration with the Choral Society!" . . . Choral Society . . . funny! I always thought it had something to do with Viennese chorus girls. Well, actually, I always knew it was something else. . . . What beautiful memories! That time at the Green Door . . . what was her name again? And later she sent me a postcard from Belgrade . . . a beautiful city!—That Kopetzky is lucky. He's been sitting in a bar all this time, smoking his Virginia! . . .

Why does that fellow keep looking at me? I think he notices that I'm bored and don't belong here. . . . Hey, take my advice and don't look at me so impudently or I'll settle with you in the lobby afterward!—He's looking the other way already! . . . Funny, they get so intimidated when I glare at them. . . ! "You have the most beautiful eyes I've ever seen," Steffi said the other day. . . . Oh, Steffi, Steffi, Steffi!—It's really all Steffi's fault that I have to sit here listening to all this wailing.—Oh, this constant canceling of our meetings is really getting on my nerves! How wonderful this evening could have been. I'd really like to read Steffi's little note again. I've got it here, yes. But if I take it out of my pocket now, the fellow next to me will have my head! . . . Well, I know what's in it . . . she can't come because she has to go to dinner with "him." . . . That was amusing a week ago when she was with him at the Horticultural Society Café and Kopetzky and I were sitting across from her. She kept on flirting with me, giving me signals, the ones we had agreed on . . . and he didn't notice a thing—unbelievable! He must be a Jew. Of course, he's with a bank and he has a black mustache. . . . He's supposed to be a lieutenant in the reserves too! Well, in my regiment he'd never get that far! Funny they're still commissioning so many Jews—so what good is all this anti-Semitism anyhow? The other day at the club when that affair came up between the doctor and the Mannheimers . . . they say the Mannheimers are Jews, too—baptized ones, of course. . . . They don't look it, though—especially Mrs. Mannheimer . . . she's so blonde, has such a stunning figure. . . . It was pretty nice, that party. Great food, the best cigars. . . . Well, they've got money, after all!

Bravo! Bravo! It's got to be over soon now!—Yes, they're all getting up . . . it looks so grand—very impressive!—An organ too? . . . I love the organ. . . . Oh, I like that—very beautiful! It's really true, one should go to concerts more often. . . . I'll tell Kopetzky it was wonderful. . . . Will I see him at the café today?—Oh God, I don't feel like going there today at all. İ was so furious yesterday! Lost a hundred and sixty gulden in one sitting—damn it! And who won it all? Ballert, the one who doesn't need it. . . . It's all Ballert's fault that I had to come to this stupid concert. . . . Otherwise I could have played again today and maybe won something back. It's a good thing I gave my word of honor that I wouldn't touch another card for a month. . . . Mama will make a long face again when she gets my letter!—Well, let her go and see my uncle. He's loaded. A couple of hundred gulden mean nothing to him. If only I could get him to give me a regular allowance . . . but no, I've got to beg for every penny. It's always the same story: "last year the harvest was bad!" . . . Should I go down to visit him again this summer for two weeks? Actually, I'm always bored to death there. . . . If I could. . . . what's her name again? It's odd, I can't remember names at all! . . . Oh yes, Etelka! . . . She didn't understand a word of German, but that wasn't necessary . . . we didn't have to talk! . . . Yes, it would be quite good to have fourteen days of fresh country air and fourteen nights with Etelka or somebody else. . . . But I should spend a week with Papa and Mama again. . . . Mama looked awful last Christmas. . . . Well, by now she'll have gotten over the humiliation. . . . If I were her, I'd be glad that Papa has retired.—And Klara will get a husband yet. . . . Uncle will just have to donate some of his money. . . . Twenty-eight, that isn't so old. . . . I bet Steffi isn't any younger than that. . . . But it's amazing—*those* women stay young much longer. When one thinks about it: that Maretti recently in *Madame Sans-Gene*—she's thirty-seven if she's a day, and she looks . . . Well, I wouldn't have said no!—Too bad she didn't ask me . . .

It's getting hot in here! Still not finished? I'm looking forward to some fresh air! I'll take a little walk around the Ring. . . . I've got to get to bed early tonight so as to be fresh tomorrow afternoon! Funny how little I think about it; it doesn't bother me at all. The first time I did get a little upset. Not that I was afraid, but I was nervous the night before. . . . True, Lieutenant Bisanz was a tough opponent—and still, nothing happened to me! . . . That was a year and half ago already. How time flies! And if Bisanz didn't wound me, the lawyer certainly won't! Although sometimes it's precisely those amateurish fencers who're the most dangerous. Doschintzky told me that a fellow who'd never had a sword in his hand before came within a hair's breath of stabbing him to death. And Doschintzky is a fencing instructor with the militia now. Though he probably wasn't as good then as he is today. . . . The main thing is: keep cool. I'm not even mad at him any-more, and yet what an insult—unbelievable! If he hadn't been drink-ing champagne, he wouldn't have had the gall! . . . What an insult! He's obviously a socialist! They're all socialists, those loophole artists who pervert the law these days. What a mob . . . they'd abolish the whole army if they could! But they don't think about who'd help them if the Chinese were to invade. Idiots!—You've got to make an example of people like that. I was right. I'm glad I didn't let him get away with that comment. When I think about it, I get furious! But I behaved impeccably. Even the colonel said it was all absolutely cor-rect. The whole affair should stand me in good stead. I know a lot of people who would have let the fellow get away with it. Mueller, for sure—he would have tried to be "objective" or something like that. But being "objective" always makes one look stupid! "Herr Lieu-tenant!"—just the way he said "Herr Lieutenant" was offensive! "You'll have to grant me"—How did we get on the subject? Why did I let myself get involved in a conversation with a socialist? How did it all start, anyway? . . . As I recall, the brunette I took to the banquet was there . . . and then this fellow who paints hunting scenes—what's his name?—My God, he's the one to blame for the whole thing! He talked about our maneuvers, and then this lawyer joined us and said something I didn't like, something about us just playing at war or something like that—but I couldn't say anything just then. . . . Yes, and then the conversation turned to the cadet schools . . . yes, that was it. . . . And I told them about the patriotic rally . . . and then the lawyer said—not right away, but it grew out of my talk about the rally— "Herr Lieutenant, you'll surely grant me that not all of your comrades went into the military just to defend the fatherland." What gall! How does a fellow like that dare to say a thing like that to an officer's face! I wish I could remember exactly what I said in reply. . . .Yes, some-thing about people who stick their noses into things they don't under-stand. . . . Yes, right . . . then there was somebody who wanted to

smooth things over, an older man with a cold. . . . But I was too enraged! It was absolutely clear from the way he said it that the lawyer
meant me personally! All he had to add was that they kicked me out
of the *Gymnasium* and that was why they stuck me into cadet school.
. . . People like that just can't understand us military types, they're
just too stupid. . . . When I remember the first time I put on my
uniform—well, not everyone experiences a thrill like that. . . . Last
year, at the maneuvers—I would have given anything if it had been
for real . . . Mirovic told me he felt the same way. And then, when His
Highness rode up to inspect the troops, and the colonel addressed us
. . . you'd have to be a real louse if your heart didn't beat faster. . . .
And then along comes this pencil-pusher who never did anything in
his whole life except sit over a bunch of books, and allows himself to
make such an insolent remark! . . . Ah, just wait, my dear fellow—
unfit for battle, that's what I'll make you . . . yes, unfit for battle!

Well, what's going on? It's got to be over soon now . . . "Praise
the Lord, Ye, His Angels." . . . Yes, that's the final chorus. . . . Beautiful, there's no denying it, beautiful!—Oh no, I've completely forgotten the girl in the box, the one who started to flirt with me. Where is
she? . . . She must have left already. . . . That one over there is pretty
too . . . damn it, too bad I don't have a pair of opera glasses on me!
Brunnthaler is smart. He always keeps his with the cashier at the
café; you can't go wrong that way. . . . If only the young lady in front
of me would turn around just once! She sits there so demurely. The
woman next to her must be her mother.—Maybe I should think seriously about getting married. Willy wasn't any older than I am now
when he decided to take the plunge. There's something to be said in
always having a pretty little woman ready at hand at home. . . . Damn
it all that Steffi didn't have any time, today of all days! If only I knew
where she was, I could go and seat myself across from her again.
That'd be a good one! If he ever got wind of what's going on, he'd
palm her off on me and I'd have her hanging around my neck! . . .

When I think how much Fliess's affair with that Winterfeld woman is costing him! And all the time she's betraying him left and right. One day that's going to end with a big bang. . . . Bravo, bravo! Over, finally! . . . Oh, it feels good to get up and move again. . . . Well, not quite yet it seems! How much longer is it going to take him to put his opera glasses back in his case?

"Pardon me, pardon, may I get by?" . . .

What a mob! Better to let people through. . . . What an elegant woman . . . are those real diamonds? . . . This one is pretty. . . . the way she's looking at me! . . . Oh yes, my Fräulein, I'd be delighted! . . . Oh, her nose! . . . a Jewess. . . . There's another. . . . It's really amazing, half of them are Jews . . . one can't even enjoy an oratorio in peace these days. . . . So, here's the line. . . . Why is that idiot behind me pushing? I'll teach him a lesson. . . . Oh, an elderly man! . . . Who's that bowing to me over there? . . . Good evening, good evening! I've no idea who that was . . . the easiest thing would be to go to Leidinger's for supper . . . or should I go to the Horticultural Society Café? Maybe Steffi will be there. I wonder why she didn't write me where she was going with him? She probably didn't know herself. It's pretty awful, actually, such a dependent existence . . . poor thing! . . . Ah, there's the exit. . . . Well now, that's really a beauty! All alone? How she's smiling at me! That's an idea—I'll follow her! . . . So, now down these stairs. Oh, the major from the Ninety-fifth . . . he greeted me very politely. . . . So I wasn't the only officer here after all. . . . Where did that good-looking girl go? Ah, over there . . . she's standing by the staircase. . . . So, now to the check room . . . must make sure the little thing doesn't get away from me. . . . She's already got someone? What a miserable brat! Allows herself to be picked up by another man, and even so she's still smiling at me!—They're all worthless. . . . My God, what a crowd here at the checkroom! . . .

maybe I should wait a little bit longer. . . . There! Is that idiot going to take my number? . . .

"Here, number two hundred twenty four! It's hanging right there! What's the matter—are you blind? It's hanging right there! Well, thank God! . . . So, if you please!" . . .

That fatso is blocking off the whole wardrobe. . . .

"Please, let me by!" . . .

"Patience, patience!"

What did that fellow say?

"Have a little patience!"

I can't let that go . . . "Well, move over, already!"

"Come on, you'll get your coat!"

What did he say? Did he say that to me! That's going too far! I can't allow that! "Be quiet!"

"What did you say?"

Oh, what a tone of voice! That's the limit!

"Don't push!"

"You—shut up!" I shouldn't have said that; that was too rough. . . . Well, anyway, now it's done!

"What did you say?"

Now he's turning around. . . . Oh, I know him!—My God, that's the master baker who's always at the café. What's he doing here? He must have a daughter or some other relative at the Vocal Academy. . . . What's happening? What's he doing? It almost seems as if . . . yes, oh my God, he's grabbed the handle of my sword . . . is he crazy? . . . "You, sir!" . . .

"You, Lieutenant—you shut up!"

What did he say? My God, no one heard that, did they? No, he's talking very softly. . . . But why doesn't he let go of my sword? . . . Great God! . . . Now I have to get tough. . . . I can't get his hand off the handle . . . oh, not another scene now! . . . Isn't that the major standing behind me? . . . Does anyone notice that he's got the handle of my sword in his hand? Why, he's talking to me! What's he saying?

"Listen, Lieutenant, if you make the slightest fuss, I'll pull your sword out, break it, and send the pieces to the head of your regiment. Do you understand me, you stupid kid?"

What did he say? I must be dreaming! Is he really speaking to *me*? What should I say? . . . But the fellow is serious . . . he's really about to draw my sword out of the sheath. My God—he's actually doing it! . . . I can feel it, he's trying to pull it out! What's he saying? . . . For God's sake, not a big scene!—What's he saying now?

"But I don't want to ruin your career. . . . So, just behave yourself! Don't worry, nobody saw anything . . . everything's all right . . . And so that no one will think we've been fighting, I'm going to act very friendly to you!—I'm honored, Lieutenant, sir. It's been a real pleasure—I'm honored!"

My God, am I dreaming? . . . Did he really say that? . . . Where did he go? There he goes . . . I should pull my sword out and let him have it.—Heavens, I hope no one heard it. . . . No, he talked very softly, right into my ear. . . . Why don't I go over and split his skull open? . . . No, I can't do that, I can't do that . . . I should have done it right away. . . . Why didn't I do it right away? . . . I couldn't do it . . . he wouldn't let go of the handle, and he's ten times stronger than I am. . . . If I'd said another word, he really would have broken my sword. . . . I should be thankful he didn't talk any louder! If anyone had heard it, I'd have had to shoot myself on the spot. . . . Maybe it really was a dream . . . why is that man by the pillar over there looking at me like that?—Did he hear something after all? . . . I'll ask him. . . . Ask him? I must be crazy!—I wonder what I look like?—Does anybody notice anything?—I must be deathly pale.—Where is that s.o.b.? . . . I have to kill him! . . .

He's gone . . . the whole place is empty. . . . Where's my coat? . . . Why, I'm already wearing it . . . I didn't even notice. . . . Who helped

me on with it? . . . Ah, that one there. . . . I've got to tip him. . . . So!
. . . But what actually happened? Did it really happen? Did someone
really talk to me like that? Did someone really call me a "stupid kid"?
And I didn't cut him to pieces on the spot? . . . But I couldn't. . . . he
had a fist like iron. . . . I just stood there as though I were nailed to the
floor! . . . I must have lost my head, otherwise I would have used my
other hand to. . . . but then he'd have pulled my sword out and broken
it, and that would have been the end—that would have been the end of
everything! And afterward, as he walked away, it was too late . . . I
couldn't have run my sword through him from behind. . . .

What, I'm already on the street? How'd I get here?—It's nice
and cool here . . . ah, the breeze feels good. . . . Who's that over there?
Why are they looking at me? Maybe they heard something after all.
. . . No, no one could have heard a thing . . . I'm sure of it, I looked all
around right afterward! No one was paying any attention to me, no
one heard anything. . . . But he did say it, even if no one heard it. He
did say it! And I just stood there and took it, as if someone had hit me
over the head! . . . But I couldn't say anything, I couldn't do anything.
The only thing I could do was shut up, shut up . . . it's awful, I can't
stand it! I've got to kill him on the spot, wherever I happen to meet
him! . . . I can't believe someone said that to *me*! An idiot like that, an
s.o.b. like that—said that to me! And he knows me. . . . Oh my God,
he knows me, he knows who I am! . . . He can tell everyone what he
said to me! . . . No, no, he won't do that, otherwise he wouldn't have
talked so softly . . . he just wanted me to hear it. . . . But what's the
guarantee that he won't tell someone else today or tomorrow, that he
won't tell his wife, his daughter, his friends at the café?—Good God,
I'm going to be seeing him again tomorrow! When I get to the café tomorrow, he'll be sitting there as usual playing cards with Schlesinger
and the florist . . . No, no, that won't do, that won't do. . . . When I see
him, I'll cut him to pieces. . . . No, I can't do that . . . I should have
done it right then and there! . . . If only I could have! . . . I'll go to the

colonel and report the matter . . . yes, to the colonel. . . . The colonel is always very friendly—and I'll tell him: colonel, sir, I beg to report: he took hold of the handle of my sword; he wouldn't let go; it was exactly as though I were completely unarmed! . . . What would the colonel say?—What would he say?—There's only one answer: dishonorable discharge! . . .

Are those volunteer recruits over there? . . . How disgusting! At night they look like officers. . . . Oh, they're saluting!—If they knew—if they knew! . . . There's the Café Hochleitner. . . . Bet some of my fellow officers are in there; perhaps even someone I know. . . . What if I tell the whole story to the first fellow I run into, but as though it happened to somebody else? . . . I'm going completely crazy. . . . Why am I walking around here? What am I doing on this street?—Well, but where should I go? Wasn't I going to Leidinger's? Ha, ha, and sit down with a whole bunch of people? . . . I'm sure everyone would see what happened to me . . . yes, but I've got to do something . . . what am I going to do? . . . Nothing, nothing at all is going to happen—after all, no one heard a thing . . . no one knows a thing . . . at least at the moment. . . . What if I went to his house and begged him to swear not to tell anyone? . . . Ah, better to put a bullet through my head right away. . . . That'd be the best thing anyway! . . . the best thing? Why the best thing?—There's nothing else left for me to do . . . absolutely nothing . . . if I were to ask the colonel, or Kopetzky—or Blany—or Friedmaier—each of them would say, "You have no choice!" What if I were to talk it over with Kopetzky? . . . Yes, that would be the most sensible thing to do . . . if only because of tomorrow. . . . Yes, of course—because of tomorrow . . . around four in the afternoon in the cavalry barracks. . . . I'm supposed to fight a duel with the lawyer tomorrow at four in the afternoon . . . and now I can't even do it! I'm no longer qualified to fight a duel! . . . Nonsense! Nonsense! Not a soul knows, not a soul! There are plenty of people to whom much worse things have happened. . . . Look at all those stories about Deckener—when he and Rederow fought it out with pistols . . . in that case, the Court of Honor decided the duel could take place. . . . How would the Court of Honor decide with—would they consider me qualified to duel? . . .

"Stupid kid" . . . stupid kid . . . and I just stood there—! Good God, it doesn't matter if anybody else knows . . . I know, and that's the main thing! I feel I'm not the same person I was an hour ago—I know I'm not qualified to duel anymore, and that's why I've got to shoot myself. . . . Otherwise I'd never have a moment's peace again . . . I'd always be afraid that someone would find out about it somehow . . . and that someone would tell me to my face what happened today!—What a happy man I was an hour ago. . . . Kopetzy would have to give me that ticket . . . and Steffi, that bitch, would have to cancel our date—destiny hangs on things like that. . . . This afternoon everything was still fine and dandy, and now I'm a lost soul and have to shoot myself. . . . Why am I running like this? I'm not chasing anything. . . . What hour is the clock tower chiming? One, two, three, four, five, six, seven, eight, nine, ten, eleven . . . eleven, eleven. . . . I really should get something to eat! I've got to go somewhere anyway. . . . I could go to some little place where no one knows me—a man still has to eat, even if he shoots himself right afterward. . . . Ha, ha. Death is not child's play . . . who said that recently? . . . Oh, it doesn't matter. . . .

I wonder who'll be most upset? . . . Mama or Steffi? . . . Steffi . . . oh, God, Steffi . . . she can't show any emotion, or else "he" will show her the door. . . . Poor thing!—At my regiment—no one will have the least notion of why I did it . . . they'll all wrack their brains . . . why did Gustl commit suicide?—No one will guess that I had to shoot myself because of a miserable baker, an s.o.b. who just happened to have a stronger fist than me . . . it's just too, too stupid, too stupid for words!—And because of this, a fellow like me, a young, handsome fellow. . . . Well, afterward they'll all say: "He didn't have to kill himself over such a stupid little thing; what a shame!"—But if I were to ask any one of them now, they'd all give me the same answer. . . . And if I ask myself . . . damn it all . . . we're absolutely defenseless against civilians. . . . People think we're better off because we carry a sword . . . but if one of us ever makes use of it, they act as though we are born murderers. . . . No doubt it will be in the newspapers . . . "Young Officer Commits Suicide" . . . and how do they always put it? "Motive is shrouded in mystery." . . . Ha, ha! . . . "Mourners at his coffin are . . . " But of course it's true. . . . I always feel as though I'm telling myself a story . . . but it's true . . . I have to kill myself. There's nothing else I can do—I just can't risk that tomorrow morning Kopetzy and Blany will return my summons to the duel with the lawyer and tell me they can't be my seconds! . . . I'd be a bastard if I expected them to. . . . How could I be such an idiot as to stand there and let myself be called a stupid kid . . . by tomorrow everyone will know it . . . how could I think for even a second that a fellow like that baker wouldn't tell anyone . . . he'll tell everyone he meets. . . . His wife knows it already . . . tomorrow everyone in the café will know it . . . the waiters will know it . . . Schlesinger . . . and the cashier—even if he's decided not to tell anyone today, he'll tell everyone tomorrow. . . . And, anyway, even if he had a stroke tonight, *I'd* still know it. . . . I know it . . . and I'm not the sort of person who could go on wearing my uniform and sword when such a disgrace hangs over me! . . .

So, I've got to do it, that's all there is to it!—What difference does it make anyway?—Tomorrow afternoon the lawyer might run his sword through me anyway . . . it's happened before. . . . Bauer, that poor fellow, got a brain fever and was dead in three days . . . and Brenitsch fell off his horse and broke his neck. . . . No, when all is said and done, there's nothing else to do—not for me, not for me!— Yes, there are those who wouldn't take the whole thing so hard. . . .

God, what some people won't stoop to! . . . A butcher slapped Ringheimer in the face when he caught him with his wife, and Ringheimer had to resign his commission from the regiment, and now he's somewhere in the country and married. . . . I can't believe that there are women who would marry a man like that! . . . I swear I wouldn't shake hands with him if he came back to Vienna again. . . . So there you have it, Gustl, your life is over, all over, finished! Signed and sealed! . . . Now that I know, it's all quite simple. . . . So! I'm really quite calm. . . . Actually, I always knew if it really came to it, I'd be calm, completely calm . . . but that I'd have to kill myself because of such a . . . Maybe I didn't understand him correctly after all . . . maybe he actually said something quite different after all. . . . I was in a stupor because of all that singing and the heat . . . maybe I was temporarily out of my mind, and none of it's true? . . . not true, ha ha, not true! . . . I can still hear it . . . it's still ringing in my ears . . . and I can still feel in my fingers how I tried to get his hand off of the handle of my sword. . . . He's a brawny fellow, a real Atlas . . . though I'm not a weakling myself. . . . Franziski is the only man in the regiment stronger than me . . . .

Here's the Aspernbridge. . . . How much farther am I going to run?—If I keep on running like this, I'll be in Kragan by midnight. . . . Ha ha!!—My God, weren't we happy when we marched into Kragan last September! Only two more hours, and then Vienna. . . . I was dead tired when we arrived . . . I slept like a log the whole afternoon and by evening we were at Ronacher's . . . Kopetzky, Ladinser, and . . . who else was with us again?—Yes, right, the volunteer, the fellow who told all those Jewish stories on the march. . . . Sometimes they're nice fellows, those one-year volunteers . . . but they should only be substitutes—otherwise what sense does it make? All of us regulars have to work for many years while a fellow like that has to serve for only a year and gets the same status and reward as we do . . . it's an injustice!—But what do I care about all that now?—Why do I worry about stuff like that?—A common soldier on kitchen detail counts for more than me these days. . . . I'm not even of this world anymore. . . . It's all over with me. . . . Honor lost, all lost! . . . There's nothing left for me to do but load my revolver and . . . Gustl, Gustl, it seems to me you still don't really believe it, do you? Come to your senses. . . . There's nothing else you can do . . . no matter how much you wrack your brains, there's nothing else you can do! The only important thing now is to behave properly at the end, like an officer and a gentleman, so that the colonel will say: he was a fine fellow, we'll always honor his memory! . . . How many companies turn out for the funeral of a lieutenant? . . . I should really know that. . . . Ha ha! Even if the whole platoon or the entire garrison comes out and they fire off a twenty-gun salute, that still won't wake me up! . . . There's the café where I sat outdoors with Herr von Engel last summer, after the army steeplechase. . . . Funny, I haven't seen the man since then. . . . Why did he have a bandage over his left eye? I always wanted to ask him, but it wouldn't have been proper. . . .

There go two men from the artillery. . . . They probably think I'm following that woman into the carriage. . . . I've got to have a closer look at her . . . oh how horrible!—I'd like to know how someone like that can possibly make a living. . . . I'd rather . . . though in a pinch, the Devil will eat flies. . . . In Przemysl—afterward I was so horrified, I thought I'd never touch another female. . . . That was a ghastly time up there in Galicia . . . it was really a piece of luck that we came to Vienna. Bokorny is still stuck in Sambor and could be stuck there for another ten years, till he gets old and grey. . . . But if I'd stayed there myself, what happened today wouldn't have happened. . . . I'd rather get old and grey in Galicia than . . . than what? Than what?—What is it? What is it?—Am I crazy, that I keep on forgetting it?—Good God, I forget it every minute . . . whoever heard of anyone about to put a bullet through his head who keeps on thinking about all sorts of things that don't concern him anymore? My God, I feel as though I were drunk. Ha ha. What a high! A murderous high! A suicidal high!—Ha! I'm making jokes, that's good!—Yes, I'm in pretty good humor—I must have been born with it. . . . Really, if I were to tell anyone, he wouldn't believe me—I think if I had that revolver on me . . . I would pull the trigger right now—in a second it would be all over. . . . Not everyone has it so good—others have to suffer for months. . . . My poor cousin, she was sick for two years, couldn't move, had the most horrible pain. . . . How awful! . . . Isn't it better to do it oneself? You just have to be careful and aim well, so that an accident like what happened to the fellow who represented the cadets last year doesn't happen in the end . . . the poor devil, he didn't die, but he went blind. . . . Whatever happened to him? Where does he live?—Awful, to walk around like that—actually, he can't walk around, he has to be led—such a young fellow, he can't even be twenty today . . . he took better aim at his lover . . . she died immediately . . . unbelievable, the kind of things people shoot themselves for! How can anyone be jealous? . . . I've never felt anything of the sort my whole life. . . .

Hmm, Steffi's enjoying herself right now at the Horticultural Society Café, and then she'll go home with "him." . . . Not that I care, not at all! She has a nice arrangement—that little bathroom with the red lamp. When she entered in that green silk robe . . . I won't see that green robe ever again . . . nor Steffi either . . . and I won't ever go up that beautiful, broad staircase in the Gusshaustrasse again. . . . Fraulein Steffi will continue to amuse herself, as though nothing had happened . . . she won't even be able to tell anyone that her beloved Gustl killed himself. . . . But even so, she'll cry—oh yes, she'll cry. . . . Actually, a lot of people will cry. . . . Oh my God, Mama!—No, no, I absolutely can't allow myself to think about her. . . . Don't start thinking about home, Gustl, do you hear? . . . not even a little bit. . . .

Well, fancy that, I'm in the Prater Park already . . . in the middle
of the night. . . . This morning it would never have occurred to me
that I'd be walking in the Prater in the middle of the night. . . . Wonder what the night watchman over there is thinking? . . . Well, let's
just keep walking . . . it's quite beautiful . . . I don't feel like eating,
and I don't feel like going to the café either. The air is pleasant here,
and it's peaceful . . . very. . . . Well, soon it'll be very peaceful, as
peaceful as I could possibly want. . . . Ha ha!—But I'm altogether out
of breath . . . I must have been running like crazy . . . slow down,
slo-o-o-w down, Gustl, you won't miss anything, you don't have
anything to do—nothing, absolutely nothing!—What's this, am I
shivering?—It must be all the excitement . . . and then I haven't eaten
anything either. . . . What's that curious smell? . . . can anything be
blooming already? . . . What day is it today?—the fourth of April. . . .
It's been raining a lot in the last few days, yes . . . but the trees are
still almost bare . . . and how dark it is! Hah! It's enough to give you
the willies. . . . The only time in my life I was really scared was when
I was little, that time in the forest . . . but I wasn't that young, actually
. . . fourteen or fifteen. . . . How long ago was that?—Nine years?—
That's right.—I was a reserve at eighteen, a lieutenant at twenty . . .
and next year I'll be . . . what'll I be next year? What does that mean
anyway: next year? What does next week mean? What does the day
after tomorrow mean? . . . What's this? My teeth are chattering? Oh!
Well, let them chatter. . . . Lieutenant, you're all alone now, you don't
have to impress anyone . . . and it's bitter, it's bitter. . . .

I'll sit down on this bench here. . . . Ah!—Wonder how far I've
come? How dark it is! That place behind me there, that has to be the
second café . . . I was there once last summer, when our band was
giving a concert . . . with Kopetzky and Ruettner—and a few others.
. . . God, am I tired . . . I feel like I've been marching for ten hours.
. . . Well, it would be great, to sleep here. . . .—Hah! A homeless
lieutenant. . . . I really should go on home . . . though what would I

do at home? But then, what am I doing in the Prater?—Ah, what I'd really like is not to have to get up again—to fall asleep here and never wake up again . . . yes, that would be so easy!—But, Lieutenant, things aren't going to be that easy for you. . . . But how, and when?—I really should think the whole thing through properly . . . everything's got to be thoroughly considered. . . . That's how it is in life. . . . Well, now, let's consider. . . . Consider what?. . . . My God, how good the air feels here! . . . people should really go to the Prater more often at night. . . . Well, that should have occurred to me before; now it's all over—the Prater, the air, taking walks. . . . What's the matter with me?—Off with that cap; it feels as if it's pressing on my brain. . . . I can't even think straight. . . . Ah. . . . So!. . . . Now pull yourself together, Gustl . . . make your final arrangements! Tomorrow morning I'll end it all. . . . Tomorrow morning at seven . . . seven o'clock is a good time. Ha ha! . . . At eight, when training starts, everything will be over . . . but Kopetzky won't be able to teach, he'll be too shaken up . . . though maybe he won't know by then . . . it's possible no one will hear a thing. . . . They didn't find Max Lippay until the afternoon, and he had shot himself in the morning, and nobody had heard anything. . . . But what do I care whether Kopetzky will teach his classes or not?—Ha! So, seven o'clock it is!—Good . . . now, what else? . . . There's really nothing else to consider. I'll shoot myself in my room, and that'll be that! And on Monday, the body . . . I know one person who'll be happy about it: the lawyer . . . "Duel Cannot Take Place Due to Suicide of One of the Combatants." . . . Wonder what they'll say at the Mannheimers?—Well, he won't care very much. . . . But the wife, the pretty blonde . . . she didn't seem disinclined. . . . Yes, I think I would have had a chance with her if I'd only pulled myself together a little . . . yes, that would have been something altogether different than with that tart Steffi. . . . But the thing is, you can't be lazy with a woman like that . . . you have to court her, send flowers, talk seriously. . . . You can't just say, "Meet me tomorrow afternoon at the garrison!" . . . Yes, a respectable woman like that would have been really something. . . . The major's wife in Przemysl was hardly a respectable woman. . . . I could swear: Libitzky and Wermutek and that scruffy acting lieutenant—they all had her too. . . . But Frau Mannheimer . . . yes, that would have been quite different, that would have been classy company, it might almost have made a different man of me—it would have given me some polish—I would have been able to respect myself a little more.—But with me it's always those hussies . . . and I started so young too—I was still a boy that time when I had my first vacation back home with my parents in Graz. . . . Riedl was also there—it was a Bohemian woman . . . must have been twice my age—I didn't get home until early the next morning . . . what a look my father gave me. . . .

And Klara . . . I was really ashamed in front of her. . . . She was engaged then. . . . Why didn't anything come of that? Actually I didn't think much about it at the time. . . . Poor thing, she never had any luck—and now she's going to lose her only brother too. . . . Yes, you'll never see me again, Klara—it's all over! Well, little sister, I bet you didn't imagine you'd never set eyes on me again when you brought me to the station on New Year's Day!—And Mama. . . . Oh my God, Mama . . . no, I can't think of it. . . . When I think about it, I feel I might do something really contemptible. . . . Ah . . . what if I were to go home first . . . I could say I had a day's leave . . . and see Papa, Mama, and Klara once more before I make an end of everything. . . . Yes, I could catch the first train to Graz at seven and be there by one. . . . Hello, Mama. . . . Hi, Klara. . . . Well, how are you? . . . Well, this is a surprise! . . . But they might notice something . . . if no one else does . . . Klara will. . . . Klara's sure to. . . . Klara is so smart. . . . What a nice letter she wrote me recently, and I still owe her a reply—and the good advice she always gives me . . . such a kindhearted soul. . . . Wonder if everything would have turned out differently if I'd stayed home? I'd have studied economics, joined my uncle . . . they all wanted me to do that when I was a boy. . . . By this time I'd be married to some nice girl . . . maybe to Anna, who always liked me . . . and still does, I noticed the last time I was home, even though she already has a husband and two children. . . . I saw how she looked at me . . . and she still calls me "Gustl" like in the old days. . . . She'll get quite a shock when she finds out what sort of end I came to—but her husband will say: I saw it coming—what a scoundrel he was!—they'll all think it's because I was in debt . . . which isn't true at all, I've repaid everything . . . except the last hundred and sixty—and anyway, it will be there tomorrow. . . . I must arrange for Ballert to get those hundred and sixty gulden. . . . I'll have to write it down before I shoot myself. . . . It's terrible, terrible! . . .

What if I up and go away—to America, where no one knows me . . . in America no one will know what happened here this evening . . . no one will care. . . . In the papers recently there was a story about a Count Runge who had to leave because of some shady dealings, and now he has a hotel over there and doesn't give a damn about the whole business. . . . And in a few years I could come back . . . not to Vienna, of course . . . nor to Graz . . . but I could settle on the farm . . . and Mama and Papa and Klara would a thousand times rather have it that way, as long as I was alive. . . . And what do I care about all the rest? Who else really cares about me?—Except for Kopetzky, the rest of them could care less. . . . Kopetzky is the only one . . . and he had to be the one who gave me that ticket today . . . it's the ticket that's to blame for everything. . . . Without that ticket, I wouldn't have gone to the concert and none of this would have happened. . . . What did happen, actually? . . . I feel as though a hundred years have passed since then, yet actually it can't be more than a couple of hours. . . . Two hours ago someone called me a "stupid kid" and threatened to break my sword. . . . My God, I'm going to start screaming here in the middle of the night! Why did all this have to happen? Couldn't I have waited a little longer, till the checkroom was empty? Why did I have to say, "Shut up!" How did that slip out? I'm generally polite . . . even with my men I'm not usually so rude . . . but of course I was nervous—everything came at the same time . . . bad luck at cards, Steffi's eternal cancellations—and the duel tomorrow afternoon—and I haven't been getting enough sleep lately—and all that drudgery in the barracks—no one can stand that kind of pressure forever! Yes, I'd have gotten sick sooner or later— would have had to get a furlough . . . now it's no longer necessary— I'll get a long furlough now—a free one!—Ha ha!

How much longer am I going to keep on sitting here? It's got to be after midnight . . . didn't I hear the clock strike midnight earlier?— What's this . . . a carriage driving by? At this hour? Rubber tires—I can well imagine. . . . They're better off than me—maybe it's Ballert with Bertha. . . . Why should it be Ballert, of all people?—Oh well, just drive on!—That was a smart little rig His Highness had in Pzre-mysl . . . he always took it into town to see that Rosenberg woman. . . . Very sociable, His Highness—a true comrade, on familiar terms with everyone. . . . Those were good times . . . although . . . the place was pretty bleak and hot enough in the summer to kill you. . . . One single afternoon three people were hit by sunstroke . . . even the cor-poral in my platoon—what a helpful fellow. . . . In the afternoon we'd lie on our beds naked—and once Wiesner suddenly burst into my room; I must have been dreaming and stood up and drew my sword, which was lying next to me. . . . I must have been a sight. . . . Wiesner nearly died laughing—he's already a captain in the cavalry now. . . . Too bad I didn't go into the cavalry . . . but the old man wouldn't have it—would have been too expensive—and now it's all the same any-way. . . . Hmm, why?—Yes, I know, I know: I have to die, that's why nothing matters—I have to die. . . . So, how?—Look, Gustl, you came here to the Prater in the middle of the night where no one can bother you—so now you have time to think everything over calmly. . . . That's all nonsense about America and resigning your commission . . . you're much too stupid to take up something else—and if you lived to be a hundred and you recalled the time someone tried to break your sword and called you a "stupid kid" and you just stood there and couldn't do a thing—no, there's nothing more to figure out—what's happened has happened—and that business with Mama and Klara is all nonsense too—they'll get over it—people get over everything. . . .

How Mama wept and wailed when her brother died—and four weeks later she hardly thought about it any more. . . . She drove out to the cemetery . . . at first every week, then every month—and now she only goes on the anniversary of his death.—Tomorrow is the day of my death—April 5th.—Will they bring my body back to Graz? Ha ha! The worms in Graz will be delighted!—But that's no concern of mine . . . others can worry about that. . . . So what should I be concerned about? . . . Oh yes, the hundred and sixty guldens for Ballert—that's all—other than that, I have no arrangements to make.—Write letters? What for? To whom? . . . To say goodbye?—Well, damn it to hell, it's clear enough when somebody shoots himself!—People will soon notice that you've said goodbye all right! . . . If people only knew how little I cared about the whole thing, they wouldn't feel sorry for me . . . anyway, I'm no great loss. . . . And what did I get out of life anyway?—One thing I would have liked to do is fight in a war—but I'd have waited a long time for that. . . . I've experienced everything else. . . . Whether they're called Steffi or Kunigunde doesn't make any difference. . . . And I've heard all the best operettas—been to Lohengrin twelve times—and this evening I was even at an oratorio—and a baker called me a stupid kid.—Good God, that's enough already!—And I'm not even curious anymore. . . . So let's go home, slowly, very slowly . . . I'm really not in a hurry. Just a few more minutes rest here in the Prater, on a bench . . . homeless.—I'll never lie down in

a bed again—but I'll have plenty of time to sleep.—Ah, the air!—
I'll miss it. . . . "

Hey—what's going on.—Hey, Johann, bring me a fresh glass of water.
. . . What's happening? . . . Where . . . what, am I dreaming? . . . Oh my
head. . . . Oh for Christ's sake. . . . Damn . . . I can't get my eyes
open!—What, I'm fully dressed!—Where am I sitting?—Good God, I
must have fallen asleep! How could I possibly? It's already getting
light!—How long have I been sleeping—must look at my watch . . .
can't see a thing. . . . Where are my matches? . . . Damn, won't one
light? . . . Three o'clock . . . and I'm supposed to fight a duel—no, not
fight a duel—I'm supposed to shoot myself!—The duel isn't happening; I have to shoot myself because a baker called me a stupid kid. . . .
What, did that really happen?—My head feels so funny . . . my neck
feels like it's in a vise—I can't move—my right leg is asleep—Get up!
Up! . . . Ah, that's better!—It's getting lighter. . . . And the air . . . just
like it was that morning when I was on patrol and camped in the
woods. . . . That was a quite a different awakening—I had another day
before me then . . . I still can't quite believe it.
    Here's the street, grey, empty—I bet I'm the only person in the
Prater.—I was here once before at four in the morning, with
Pausinger—we were out riding—me on Captain Mirovic's horse and
Pausinger on his own nag—that was in May, last year—everything
was already in bloom—everything was green. Now everything is still
bare—but spring will soon be here—it'll be here in just a few days—
lilies of the valley, violets—too bad I won't be able to enjoy them any
more—any dirty Slav will able to enjoy them, but I have to die! It's
awful! They'll all sit around in the little outdoor café having supper, as
though nothing happened—just like we all sat around in the café the
evening of the day they buried Lippay. . . . And Lippay was so well
liked . . . in the regiment, they liked him better than they do me—so
why shouldn't they sit around in the café when I kick the bucket?—

It's really warm—much warmer than yesterday—and what a scent—
something must be in bloom already. . . . Will Steffi bring me flowers?—It won't even occur to her! She'll go out for a drive instead. . . .
Now if it were still Adele. . . . God, Adele! I don't think I've thought
about her for at least two years . . . what a scene she made when we
broke up . . . I've never seen a woman cry like that . . . actually, that
was the most beautiful thing that's ever happened to me. . . . She was
so modest, so undemanding—she really loved me, I swear she did.—
She was so different from Steffi. . . . Can't imagine why I gave her up
. . . what a jackass I was! I just got bored, I guess, that's all. . . . Going
out with the same girl every evening . . . then I got worried I might
never get away—what a nag.—Well, Gustl, you could have waited a
while—she was the only one who really loved you. . . . I wonder what
she's doing now? Well, what would she be doing?—By now she'll
have found someone else. . . . Yes, the arrangement with Steffi is more
convenient—when you only see someone now and then, someone
else has all the inconvenience and you get only the pleasant part. . . .
So I can't really expect her to come out to the cemetery. . . . Who'd go
there anyway, if he didn't have to!—Maybe Kopetzky, and that would
be it!—Oh, it's sad not to have anybody. . . .

But that's nonsense! I've got Papa and Mama and Klara . . . I'm
a son and a brother . . . but what else do we share? Yes, they love me,
but what do they really know about me?—That I'm in the military,
that I play cards, and that I run around with women . . . but anything
else?—That I'm sometimes disgusted with myself—that I never
wrote them—well, actually, I don't think I ever realized it myself.—
Ah, well, Gustl, why are you bringing all that up? Next thing you
know you'll start crying . . . disgusting! . . . March in step . . . this
way! Whether to a rendezvous or to duty or into battle . . . who said
that? . . . Ah yes, Major Lederer, in the canteen, when they were talking about Wingleder and how before his first duel he went pale—and
threw up. . . . Yes, whether going to a rendezvous or certain death, a

true officer doesn't reveal it either in his face or in his stride! So, Gustl—that's what Major Lederer said! Ha!

It's getting lighter and lighter . . . light enough to read. . . . What's that whistling? . . . Ah, over there is the North Train Station . . . there's the Tegetthoff Column . . . never saw it look so tall. . . . Over there the carriages are waiting. . . . But there's no one on the street except for the street cleaners . . . the last street cleaners I'll ever see . . . ha! Can't help laughing when I think about it . . . I don't understand why. . . . Does everyone do that once they know for sure? The station clock says half past three . . . the only question now is whether I shoot myself at seven railroad time or Vienna time? . . . Seven . . . well, why exactly seven? . . . As though it couldn't just as well be any other time. . . . I'm hungry—my God, I'm really hungry—no wonder . . . how long has it been since I ate anything? . . . Since—since yesterday evening at six, in the café . . . that's right! When Kopetzky gave me that ticket—a coffee with milk and rolls.—Wonder what the baker will say when he hears about it? . . . that damned s.o.b.—Ah, he'll know why—he'll catch on—then he'll understand what it means to be an officer!—A fellow like that can get into a fight right out in the open and nothing will happen, but if one of us gets insulted, even in private, he's as good as dead. . . . If only a fellow like that could stand up and fight a duel—but no, then he'd be more careful, he wouldn't risk anything like that. . . . And that s.o.b. will continue living, without a worry in the world, while I—I have to kick the bucket!—He's the one that's killing me! Yes, Gustl, mark my words, he's the one that's killing you! But he won't get away with it as easily as all that!—No, no, no! I'll write a letter to Kopetzky telling him everything, the whole story . . . or even better, I'll write to the colonel, I'll make a report to the regimental commander . . . an official report. . . . Just wait, you think something like that can remain a secret?—You're wrong there—written down it will be remembered forever, and then I'd like to see whether you'll dare show your face in the café again!—Ha!—"I'd like to see"—that's a good one!—There're a lot of things I'd like to see, only I won't be able to—it's all over!

Johann must be going into my room right about now; he'll notice that his lieutenant hasn't slept at home.—Well, he'll imagine all sorts of things, but that the lieutenant slept overnight in the Prater—God knows, he'll never imagine that! . . . Ah, there goes the Forty-fourth! They're marching out to the shooting range . . . let's let them pass . . . so, we'll stand right here. . . . Someone's opening a window up there—good-looking tart—well, at least I'd put on a little something if I were going to an open window. . . . Last Sunday was the last time. . . . That it would be Steffi, of all people, who would be the last one, I would never have dreamt. . . . Ah, God . . . that's the only real pleasure. . . . Well, in two hours or so the colonel will ride after them in his grand manner. . . . The top brass have an easy time of it—yes, yes, eyes right! Very good. If you only knew how little all this means to me! . . . Ah, that's not bad: it's Katzer . . . since when did he get transferred to the Forty-fourth?—Hello, hello! . . . What's he grimacing about? . . . Why is he pointing at his head? . . . My dear fellow, your skull is of very little interest to me. . . . Oh, I see! No, my dear fellow, you're wrong; I spent the night in the Prater . . . you'll read about it in the evening paper.—"Impossible!" he'll say, "I saw him only this morning in the Praterstrasse while we were on our way to the shooting range!"—Who'll get the command of my company?—wonder if they'll give it to Walterer?—Well, that'll be a good one—the fellow doesn't have any spunk, he should have become a cobbler. . . . What, the sun's coming up already?—It looks like it's going to be a beautiful day . . . a real spring day . . . damn it all!—this hack driver will still be alive at eight o'clock this morning, and I . . . come now, what's this? Hey, that would be funny—if I lost my nerve at the last minute because of a stupid hack driver. . . . What's going on, why is my heart suddenly pounding like that?—it can't be because of this. . . . No, oh no . . . it's because I haven't

eaten anything for so long. . . . Come now, Gustl, admit it to yourself—you're scared—scared because you've never done anything
like this before. . . . But that doesn't do you any good. Being scared
never helped anyone; everyone has to face up to it sooner or later,
and your turn happens to be sooner. . . . You were never worth much
anyway, so the least you can do is to behave decently until the end,
that much I demand of you!—Well, then, let's think things
through—I keep wanting to think things through . . . but really it's
all very simple: it's lying in the drawer of my nightstand, and it's
loaded too, so all I have to do is pull the trigger—that doesn't require any great skill!

The girl over there is already going to work in her shop . . .
poor girls! Adele was a shop girl too. A few times I went and picked
her up in the evening. When they work in a shop, they don't become
such tramps. . . . If Steffi belonged to me alone, I'd have her sell hats
or something like that. . . . Wonder how she'll hear about it?—in the
paper! . . . She'll be mad that I never wrote to her about it. . . . I think
I'm starting to lose my mind. . . . What do I care whether or not she
gets mad? . . . How long has our whole affair lasted anyway? . . .
Since January? . . . No, it must have been before Christmas . . . because I brought her back some candy from Graz, and she sent me a
little letter at New Year's . . . the letters I have at home—wonder if
there are any I should burn? . . . Hmm, the one from Fallsteiner—if
they found that letter . . . the fellow could get into trouble. . . . Why
should I worry about that?—Oh well, it's not that much trouble . . .
but I can't go tracking down the letter. . . . It's best to burn the whole
lot . . . who needs them anyway? It's all just a bunch of junk. . . . The
few books I've got I could leave to Blany.—*Through Night and Ice*
. . . too bad I can't finish it . . . haven't gotten around to reading
much lately. . . . What's that, an organ? . . . ah, from that church—
early mass—haven't been to one in a long time . . . the last time was
in February, when my whole platoon was ordered to attend. . . . But

that doesn't count—I was only keeping on eye on my men, to see whether they were reverent and behaved properly. . . . Should I go into that church? . . . maybe there's something to religion after all. . . . Well, today after lunch I'll know for sure. . . . Ah, "after lunch," that's a good one! . . . Well, all right, should I go in?—I think it would be a comfort to Mama if she knew I had! . . . Klara sets less store by it. . . . Well, let's go on in—it can't do any harm!

Organ playing—singing—hmm!—Wonder what it is?—I feel quite dizzy. . . . Oh God, oh God, oh God! I want someone I can talk to first!—What if I—went to confession? How his eyes would open wide—the priest—if I were to say at the end: my respects to you, Father; now I'm off to kill myself! . . . What I'd really like to do is lie down on the stone floor right here and bawl. . . . No, no, I can't do that! Though a good cry can really help sometimes . . . let's just sit down for a minute—but don't fall asleep again like in the Prater! . . . People who have a religion are better off. . . . Oh God, now even my hands are beginning to tremble! . . . If things continue this way, I'm going to get so disgusted with myself that in the end I'll have to kill myself out of pure shame!—That old woman over there—what's she praying for? . . . I could go over and say to her, "Ma'am, please include me in your prayers." . . . I never really learned how to pray properly. . . . Ha! It seems that dying makes you stupid!—Stand up! . . . What does that melody remind me of?—Good God! Last night!—Out, out of here, I can't stand it! . . . Shhh, don't make so much noise, don't let your sword clatter like that—don't disturb people at their prayers—

So! It's better outside after all. . . . Light . . . yes, it's getting later and later—if only it were over already!—I should have done it right away—in the Prater . . . one should never go out without a revolver. . . . If I'd had one yesterday. . . . Damn it all!—I could go into the café for breakfast . . . I'm so hungry. . . . Before, it always struck me as very odd that condemned people should have their breakfast in the morning and smoke their cigars before . . . Damn it all, I've never even smoked! Never had an urge to.—It's funny, but I really feel like going to my café. . . . Yes, it's open already, and none of our crowd will be there—and even if they are—it'll be seen as a sign of coolheadedness. "At six he was having breakfast at the café, and at seven he shot himself." . . . I feel altogether calm again . . . it's so pleasant to walk—and best of all, no one is forcing me. If I wanted to, I could still just chuck the whole thing. . . . America . . . what does that mean, "chuck the whole thing"? What does "chuck" mean? Maybe I have sunstroke! . . . Oh ho! Maybe I'm so calm because I still imagine I don't have to do it? . . . I do have to! I do have to! No—I want to!—Can you even imagine, Gustl, taking off your uniform and making a run for it? That damned s.o.b. would split his sides laughing—and even Kopetzky wouldn't shake hands with you anymore. . . . I think I'm turning red at the very thought of it.—That patrolman is saluting me. I've got to acknowledge him. . . . "Good morning!"—There, now I even said "good morning" to him, like an equal. A poor devil like him always appreciates that. . . . Well, no one has ever had much to complain of about me—off duty I've always been pleasant.—When we were on maneuvers, I gave my noncommissioned officers Britannica cigars—and one time during a drill, when I heard a man behind me muttering something about "this goddamned drudgery," I didn't report him—I just said, "You over there, watch out, one of these days someone else might hear that—and then you'd be in trouble!" . . .

The palace courtyard . . . who's on sentry duty today?—The Bosnians . . . they look smart.—The lieutenant colonel recently said that when we were down there in '78, no one would have believed that they would join us they way they did! . . . My God, I wish I could have taken part in something like that!—Now they're all getting up from the bench.—Good morning, good morning!—It's really disgusting that fellows like me miss all the action.—Would have been so much better to die with honor on the battlefield for the fatherland than like this. . . . Yes, counselor, you're getting off easy! . . . Wonder if someone else could take my place in the duel?—Great God, that's an idea—by heaven, that's what I'll do, I'll arrange for Kopetzky or Wymetal to fight the fellow in my place. . . . He shouldn't get away so easily!—Oh, well! Does it really matter what happens afterward? I'll never hear about it anyway!—The trees here are starting to bud. . . . I once picked up a girl here in the Volksgarten—she was wearing a red dress—lived in the Strozzigasse—later Rochlitz took her off my hands. . . . I think he's still with her, but he doesn't talk about it anymore . . . probably ashamed of it. . . . Steffi's probably still sleeping . . . she looks so sweet when she's asleep . . . as though butter wouldn't melt in her mouth!—Well, they all look like that when they're asleep!—I ought to write her a few lines . . . why not? Everybody does it, writes letters beforehand.—I should also write Klara that she should console Papa and Mama—the usual sentiments—and Kopetzky too. . . . Come to think of it, it seems to me it would be a lot easier if I had said goodbye to a few people. . . . And the report to the regimental command—and the hundred and sixty gulden for Ballert . . . still lots of things to do, in fact. . . . Well, no one's insisting I do it by seven . . . there's always enough time to be dead after eight! . . . Yes, and about death—as the saying goes—nothing's certain but . . .

The Ringstrasse here . . . I'll soon be at my café. . . . I think I'm actually looking forward to breakfast . . . unbelievable.—Yes, and after breakfast, I'll light myself a cigar, and then I'll go home and write. . . . First of all I'll write the report to the regimental command, then the letter to Klara—then to Kopetzky—then to Steffi. . . . What can I say to the little hussy . . . "My dear girl, you would never have thought." . . . Oh, what nonsense! . . . "My dear girl, how can I ever thank you" . . . "My dear girl, before I die, I don't want to miss the opportunity . . ." Oh well, letter writing was never my strong suit. . . . "My dear girl, a last farewell from your Gustl." . . . I'd like to see the look on her face! It's a good thing after all that I wasn't in love with her . . . it must be sad to really love someone and then . . . Come, Gustl, don't make a fuss, it's already sad enough. . . . After Steffi there would have been others, and finally someone who was worthwhile—a young girl from a good family, with a dowry—that would have been really nice. . . . I must write Klara in detail and explain to her why I couldn't have acted otherwise. . . . "You must forgive me, dear sister, and please, comfort our dear parents. I know I caused you a lot of worry and pain, but believe me, I've always loved all of you very much. I hope you'll be happy again, my dear Klara, and that you won't completely forget your unhappy brother." . . . Ah, better not write her at all! . . . It just makes me want to cry. . . . I can already feel my eyes beginning to tear when I think about it. . . . I'll only write to Kopetzky if I write at all—a comradely farewell, and I'll have him tell everyone else.—Is it six o'clock already?—Ah, no, half past, quarter to—what a charming little face! . . . It's that little scamp with the dark eyes I've seen so often in the Forianigasse!—Wonder what she would say?—But she doesn't even know who I am—she'll only wonder why she doesn't see me anymore. . . . The day before yesterday I made up my mind to talk to her the next time I saw her.—She flirted with me enough . . . how young she is . . . maybe in the end she's still a virgin!—Yes, Gustl! Don't put off until tomorrow what you can do today! . . . That fellow probably hasn't slept all night either.—Well, he'll just go home now and lie down—me too!—hah! Now it's getting serious, Gustl, yes it is! . . . Ah well, if there weren't that shiver of dread, there would be nothing to it—and on the whole, I have to say, I've behaved extremely well. . . . Ah, where to? Here's my café . . . they're still sweeping the place. . . . Well, let's go in . . .

Back there is the table where they always play tarok. . . . Strange, I find it hard to believe that the fellow who always sits there against the back of the wall could be the same fellow who

. . . There's not a soul here yet. . . . Where on earth is the waiter? . . . Hey! Here's one coming out of the kitchen . . . he's quickly slipping into his coat and tails . . . that's really not necessary for me! . . . Ah, but it is for him . . . he'll have to serve other people today too.

"At your service, Herr Lieutenant!"

"Good morning."

"So early this morning, Herr Lieutenant?"

"Ah, don't bother about my coat—I don't have much time. I might as well sit here with my coat on."

"And your order, Herr Lieutenant?"

"A coffee with milk."

"At once, Herr Lieutenant."

Ah, there are the newspapers . . . today's papers already? . . . Could there be anything in them? . . . What am I thinking of?—I do believe I wanted to check and see whether they mention that I've killed myself! Ha ha!—Why am I still standing? . . . Let's go sit near the window there. . . . He's already brought my coffee. . . . I'm going to draw the curtain; I don't like it when people look in. . . . Not that there's anyone walking by yet. . . . Ah, the coffee tastes good—not a bad idea, to have breakfast! . . . I feel like a new man—the whole trouble was that I didn't have any dinner last night. . . . Why is that fellow here again?—Ah, he's brought me the rolls. . . .

"Has the Herr Lieutenant already heard . . .?"

"Heard what?" Oh my God, does he know something about it already? . . . But nonsense, that's impossible!

"Herr Habetswallner . . ."

Who? That's the name of the baker . . . what's he going to say now? . . . Oh my God, he's been here already! Maybe in the end he was already here last night and told the whole story. . . . Why doesn't he go on? . . . He's still talking . . .

"—had a stroke last night, around midnight."

"What?" . . . I mustn't shout like that . . . no, I can't call attention to myself . . . but maybe I'm dreaming. . . . I have to ask him again. . . . "Who did you say had a stroke?" Splendid, splendid! I said that very nonchalantly! . . .

"The baker, Herr Lieutenant! . . . The Lieutenant must know him . . . you know, the fat one that played tarok next to the officers' table . . . with Herr Schlesinger and Herr Wasner the florist from across the street!"

I'm wide awake—all that checks out—but still I can't quite believe it—I have to ask him again . . . but very casually . . .

"He had a stroke, did he? . . . How did that happen? And how do you know about it?"

"But Herr Lieutenant, who should know it earlier than people like us—the rolls you're eating right now, sir, come from Herr Habetswallner's. The boy who delivers them at half past four every morning told us."

Oh my God, I can't betray myself. . . . I feel like shouting . . . like laughing . . . like giving Rudoph here a kiss. . . . But I have to ask him one more thing! . . . To have a stroke doesn't mean you're dead. I've got to ask whether he's dead . . . but very calmly, for why should the baker concern me?—I'll look at the paper while I ask the waiter . . . .

"Is he dead?"

"Why, of course, Herr Lieutenant. He died on the spot."

Oh how wonderful, how wonderful!—Maybe it's all because I went into the church . . .

"He'd been to the theater last night. He collapsed on the stairs—the house porter heard the noise . . . well, and then they carried him into the apartment, and by the time the doctor got there he was already dead."

"How sad. He was still in the prime of life"—I said that brilliantly—no one would suspect me of anything . . . and I really must restrain myself so that I don't start shouting or leap onto the billiard table. . . .

"Yes, Lieutenant, it's very sad; he was such a nice man. And he's been coming here for twenty years—he was a good friend of the proprietor's. And his poor wife . . ."

I don't think I've ever been as happy in my whole life! . . . He's dead—he's dead! No one knows a thing, and nothing's happened!— What incredible luck that I came to the café. . . . Otherwise I would have shot myself for nothing—it's like a stroke of fate. . . . Where is that Rudolf? Ah, he's talking to the janitor. . . . So, he's dead—he's dead—I still can't believe it! I'd like to go there and see for myself.— Maybe in the end he had a stroke out of anger, out of suppressed rage . . . ah, I don't care how it happened! It's all the same to me! The main thing is that he's dead, and I can go on living, and the world's all mine again! . . . Funny how I keep dunking the rolls that Herr von Ha- betswallner baked for me! Very tasty, Herr von Habetswallner! Splen- did!—So, now, I could really do with a cigar. . . .

"Rudolf! Hey, Rudolf! Don't spend all day with the janitor there!"

"I'm coming, Herr Lieutenant!"

"I'll have a Trabucco." . . . I'm so happy, so happy! . . . What shall I do now? . . . What shall I do? . . . I've got to do something, otherwise I'll have a stroke too, out of pure joy! . . . In a quarter of an hour I'll go over to the barracks and have Johann give me a cold rubdown. . . . There's weapons handling at 7:30, and drills at 9:30. . . . And I'll write Steffi and tell her she has to keep this evening free for me, no matter what! And this afternoon at four . . . just you wait, my dear fellow, just you wait! I'm in wonderful form . . . I'll make mincemeat of you!

Doctor Graesler

THE SHIP WAS READY for departure. Dr. Graesler, dressed somberly in an open grey overcoat and wearing a black armband, stood on the top deck facing the bareheaded hotel director, whose carefully parted brown hair barely stirred in the gentle coastal breeze.

"My dear doctor," the hotel director was saying to him in that condescending tone of his that Graesler found so irritating, "let me repeat that we're counting on having you with us again next year, in spite of the deeply distressing misfortune that befell you here." Dr. Graesler didn't answer. His eyes grew moist as he glanced shoreward toward the huge hotel with its white shutters, now tightly closed against the heat, gleaming in the sunshine. He let his gaze wander over the sleepy ochre houses and the parched gardens that crept toward the sparse ruins that crowned the hill in the heat of the noon sun.

"Our guests," the director continued, "some of whom will return next year, think highly of you, my dear doctor, and so we hope we can count on you to come back to the little villa"—he pointed to a bright, modest house near the hotel—"in spite of the painful memory it holds for you, all the more so since we unfortunately can't make number 43 available to you for the high season." And when Graesler shook his head mournfully, removed his stiff black hat, and smoothed his neatly combed, grey-blond hair, he persisted, "My dear doctor, time works wonders. And if you dread being alone in the little white house, there is a remedy for that. Why not bring a pretty little wife back from Germany with you?"

Graesler's only response was a faint raising of his eyebrows, but the director went on eagerly: "Oh, come on, they're a dime a dozen. A nice little blonde—of course it could just as well be a brunette—is probably the only thing you need to make your life perfect." Dr. Graesler raised his brows higher, as though his eyes were following retreating images of the past. "Well, think it over," said the manager affably. "One way or the other, single or married, you're welcome here. And on October 27 as we agreed, right? Unless you come then, you won't make it until November 10 because the steamer schedule, despite our best efforts, is still very inadequate. And since we open on November 1"—and now his voice grated like a drill sergeant's—"that wouldn't be good." He pumped the doctor's hand with a too eager handshake—a habit acquired in the United States—exchanged fleeting greetings with a passing ship's officer, and hurried down the stairs. A moment later he appeared on the gangway, where he gave a final nod to the doctor, who still stood gloomily at the balustrade of the top deck, hat in hand. A few minutes later the steamer pushed away from the land.

On the trip home, favored by beautiful weather, the director's parting words kept going through Dr. Graesler's mind. As he dozed in his comfortable deck chair on the promenade deck in the late afternoon, a plaid blanket over his knees, he sometimes had a dreamlike vision of a pretty, plump little woman in a white summer dress gliding through a house and garden. She had a red-cheeked doll's face that seemed familiar to him somehow—not from life but from some illustrated book or magazine. And this dream image had the mysterious power to exorcise the ghost of his dead sister, giving him the sense that she had departed from this world long ago and in a more natural manner than she actually had. Of course there were also hours, wakeful ones, heavy with memories, in which he experienced the terrible event again and again with intolerable vividness, as though it were happening in the present.

The disaster had occurred a week before. He had fallen asleep over his medical journal in the garden after lunch, as he often did. When he awoke, he deduced from the palm tree's long shadow, which had spread from beneath his feet to the other side of the gravel path, that he must have slept for at least two hours. This put him in a bad mood, as he was tempted to see it as a sign of diminishing vigor at forty-eight. He rose, thrust the journal under his arm, and, longing for the refreshing spring breezes of Germany, walked slowly toward the small house he shared with his sister, who was a few years older than he. He saw her standing at one of the windows, which struck him as strange, as usually during the hottest hours of the day all the shutters were closed tight. And when he came nearer he noticed that she wasn't smiling at him as he had thought she was from afar, but kept her back turned to him and was absolutely still. With a certain uneasiness that he didn't understand himself, he rushed into the house. Hastening toward his sister, who seemed to lean motionless against the window, he saw with horror that her head hung forward, that her eyes were wide open, and that there was a cord around her neck that had been fastened to the top of the window frame. He shouted Friederike's name but at the same time reached for his pocketknife and cut through the cord, causing her lifeless form to sink heavily into his arms. He shouted for the maid, who rushed in from the kitchen with no idea of what had transpired, and with her help carried his sister to the sofa. He immediately began all the efforts to revive her that he knew from his profession, while the maid rushed to get the hotel director. But by the time he arrived, Dr. Graesler, realizing that all his efforts were useless, had already sunk to his knees beside his sister's lifeless body, exhausted and stunned.

At first, he had racked his brains trying to find an explanation for her suicide, but in vain. That this dignified, aging spinster with whom he had lightly chatted at lunch about their approaching departure from the island should suddenly have gone mad seemed improbable to him. It was more likely that Friederike had been troubled with suicidal thoughts for a long time, perhaps even for years, and had for some reason chosen this undisturbed afternoon to carry out a plan that had developed gradually. It had occurred to him from time to time that her calm, quiet manner might conceal a gentle melancholy, but he had usually been too preoccupied by the demands of his work to worry much about it. Only now, upon reflection, did he gradually realize that he had rarely seen her truly happy since childhood.

He knew little about her early years, as he had been a shipboard doctor for many years and so was almost continually away from home. Fifteen years ago, shortly after he had left the service of the Lloyd Line, and their parents had died in quick succession, she had left their small-town family home to keep house for him wherever he happened to be. By then she was well into her thirties, though she had preserved such a youthful and graceful figure and such mysterious, dark, and sparkling eyes that she had no lack of admirers. Emil sometimes had good reason to fear she might be taken away from him by a late marriage to one of them. But with the passage of years even the last of her chances had vanished, and she had seemed to accept her lot without complaint. Now, though, her brother thought he remembered numerous reproachful glances, as though she held him partly responsible for her lack of happiness. Perhaps a consciousness that she had missed her life had grown all the keener the less she expressed her feelings, until at last she had preferred a quick end to the nagging pain of that realization. Of course by doing so she had put her unsuspecting brother in the position of having to worry about domestic details which he had heretofore been spared by her care, and at a time of life when it is difficult to acquire new habits. And so toward the end of his trip, despite all of his mourning, a comforting feeling of estrangement from the deceased, who had left him so totally unprepared for the future and so completely alone in the world without as much as a goodbye, crept into his heart.

2

After a brief stop in Berlin, where he reminded a number of consulting medical professors that he was available for the new spa season, Dr. Graesler returned to the health resort nestled within wooded hills where he had practiced professionally for the past six summers. He was warmly welcomed by his landlady, the elderly widow of a businessman, and was delighted with the modest wild flowers with which she had decorated the house for his arrival. With some uneasiness he walked into the small room his sister had occupied the previous year, but found himself not as deeply saddened as he had feared. As a matter of fact, life was quite tolerable from the very beginning of his stay. The sky was uniformly limpid and clear, and the air had the gentle warmth of spring. Sometimes, for example, when he breakfasted on his little balcony and the blue flowered pot from which he now poured his own coffee glistened in the morning sun, he even had a feeling of comfortable contentment that he had not experienced in his sister's company for several years. He took his other meals in the well-appointed dining room of the town's main restaurant with some of the town's leading citizens, old acquaintances with whom conversation was easy and sometimes even entertaining. His practice was promising from the start, and there were no cases so grave as to tax his sense of professional competence.

Thus the early weeks of summer passed without incident, until one July evening, after a full and busy day, a messenger who dashed away as fast as he had come summoned Dr. Graesler to the forest ranger's lodge, a good hour's drive from town. The doctor was not pleased—he was not as a rule eager to take on local residents as patients, as their care gave him neither fame nor financial reward. Still, as he drove up the valley along the pleasant country road bordered first by attractive country villas, then by golden fields of grain lying in the cool shade of hills, and finally by a forest of tall beech trees, he began to feel such a sense of well-being that when he caught sight of the ranger's appealing lodge, a place he recognized from walks he had taken in earlier years, he almost regretted that the drive had ended so soon. He asked the carriage driver to stop at the side of the road and walked up to the house by way of a narrow walkway bordered by sapling pines. The house had a friendly air; while the setting sun gleamed on the red roof, it greeted him with twinkling windows and a huge pair of antlers over the front door. A young woman whose face seemed familiar to him came down the wooden steps of a wide side porch that was remarkably spacious in proportion to the house. She shook hands with him and explained that her mother had had an attack of acute indigestion.

"She's been sleeping peacefully for an hour," she continued. "The fever must have gone down. At four o'clock this afternoon her temperature was still a little over one hundred. And as she's been feeling ill since yesterday evening, I permitted myself to send for you, Herr Doctor. I hope it's nothing serious." And she looked at him pleadingly, as though the gravity of the case depended entirely on his judgment.

He met her gaze with appropriate concern. Then, of course, he recognized her. He had seen her several times in town but had assumed she was one of the summer visitors.

"Well, if your mother is sleeping peacefully now," he said, "it probably isn't serious. If you can give me some more details, Fräulein, perhaps we won't have to wake her needlessly."

She invited him out to the porch and offered him a chair while she remained standing in the doorway to the house. In a frank and direct manner she described the course of her mother's illness. From her report, he was sure it was nothing more than passing indigestion. Still, he had to ask several medical questions and was surprised by the straightforward and frank manner with which she described and elaborated on natural bodily processes. He was unaccustomed to hearing young women talk with such candor, and while listening to her he fleetingly asked himself whether she would have been as candid had he been younger. He guessed her to be not less than twenty-five, though it might be that her large tranquil eyes gave him the impression that she was older than she was. She wore her blonde braids pinned high on her head with a plain silver comb. Her clothing was simple and provincial, but her white belt was fastened with an intricately gilded clasp. What struck the doctor most of all, even as somehow suspect, were her elegant, high-heeled doeskin shoes, which exactly matched the light brown color of her stockings.

She was still giving him her report and Dr. Graesler was still sizing her up when a call of "Sabine!" came from inside the house. The doctor rose and the young woman ushered him through a large dining room where it was already growing dark, and then into another, lighter room where the patient, wearing a white cap and dressing gown, sat up in one of two beds. She looked at the new arrival with surprised but otherwise alert and cheerful eyes.

"Dr. Graesler," Sabine introduced him, then quickly walked to the head of the bed, where she tenderly touched her mother's forehead.

The woman, who looked well nourished, friendly, and not at all elderly, shook her head disapprovingly. "I'm pleased to meet you, Herr Doctor," she said, "but why, dear—"

"It does seem that my visit here is superfluous," the doctor remarked as he took the patient's outstretched hand and felt her pulse, "all the more so since your daughter"—he smiled faintly—"appears to possess an amazing amount of medical knowledge. But now that I'm here . . ."

With a shrug of her shoulders, the woman submitted to her fate, and Graesler undertook a closer examination that Sabine watched calmly and attentively. Afterward Dr. Graesler reassured both patient and daughter. But difficulties arose when he attempted to put the patient on a restricted diet for a few days. She protested vigorously, insisting that she had cured former attacks of this sort, which she characterized as nervous in nature, with a meal of pork with sauerkraut and a certain kind of bratwurst, which, alas, was not to be found in this part of the world. True, she had let Sabine keep her from having a hearty meal at lunch, and that was probably the cause of her fever. At first the doctor thought she was joking, but in the course of the conversation he realized that the mother, in complete contrast to her daughter, had a view of medical science that was not merely uninformed but completely unorthodox. She ridiculed the virtues of the healing waters of the health resort, and even claimed that the water bottled for export was merely ordinary well water to which salt, pepper, and probably other more dubious seasonings had been added. Dr. Graesler, who felt obliged to defend the reputations of the particular spas where he practiced and also partly responsible for their successes and failures, could not completely suppress a sense of offended pride. Yet he refrained from flatly contradicting the patient and contented himself with an exchange of understanding smiles with the daughter, which he felt supported his own view in a dignified way.

When he was ready to leave and outside again with Sabine, he once more emphasized that her mother's illness was completely benign. Sabine agreed with him; yet, she added, some conditions that were benign in younger people merited closer attention in older ones. That was why she had felt obliged to send for a doctor, especially as her father was away.

"Your father is away on a tour of inspection?" Dr. Graesler inquired.

"What do you mean by that, Herr Doctor?"

"On a tour of inspection through the district?"

Sabine smiled. "My father isn't actually a forest ranger, and this house hasn't been a ranger's lodge for a long time. It's still called that because until six or seven years ago the ranger for the prince's estate did in fact live here. So just as everyone still calls this house the ranger's lodge, so everyone in town calls my father "the ranger" even though he was never anything of the sort in his entire life.

"Are you the only child?" Dr. Graesler asked as Sabine accompanied him back to the road along the narrow path between the pines as if it were a matter of course.

"No," she answered. "I have a brother. He's much younger than I am, only fifteen. Naturally, when he's home on vacation, he spends all his time in the woods. Sometimes he even sleeps outdoors." And when the doctor shook his head disapprovingly, she added, "Oh, it's nothing to worry about. I used to sleep out there myself now and then. Not very often, of course."

"Only near the house, I take it?" the doctor asked, a little anxiously. "And," he added hesitatingly—"when you were little, I suppose?"

"Oh no, I was already seventeen when we moved here. We hadn't lived in this part of the country before, but only in the city . . . in various cities."

They had now reached the road, and the coachman was ready to depart. Respecting her reserve, the doctor decided not to ask any more questions. But as Sabine shook his hand, he felt the need to continue talking.

"If I'm not mistaken, haven't we seen each other several times in town?"

"Of course we have, Herr Doctor. I've known you by sight for quite a while. Of course, sometimes I don't come into town for weeks. Last year, as a matter of fact, I exchanged a few words with your sister, at Schmidt's. She's come back with you again, I suppose?"

The doctor looked down. By chance his gaze fell on her shoes, but he averted his eyes and looked beyond her. "My sister didn't come back with me," he said. "She died three months ago, in Lanzarote." He felt a pang in his heart, but saying the name of the distant island somehow consoled him.

Sabine's only reply was, "Oh." They stood in silence for a while, until Dr. Graesler forced a smile and offered Sabine his hand.

"Good night, Herr Doctor," she said gravely.

"Good night, Fräulein," he answered, and swung himself up into the carriage. Sabine stood until the carriage began to move, then turned to go. Dr. Graesler followed her with his eyes—with a slightly bowed head and without looking back, she walked toward to the house along the path between the pines, now lit by a ray of light from the house. At a turn in the road her image disappeared from sight. The doctor leaned back and looked up at the sky, where a few scattered stars glimmered in the twilight. He thought of former times, of younger and happier days when he had had the love of many a pretty young woman. He thought of the engineer's widow from Rio de Janeiro, who left the steamer on which he worked as a physician in Lisbon, ostensibly to buy something in town—and never returned, even though she had a ticket to Hamburg. He could still see her in her black dress waving affectionately to him from the carriage that took her from the harbor to the city just before she vanished forever. He remembered the lawyer's daughter from Nancy, to whom he had become engaged at St. Blasien, the first spa at which he had practiced. She had suddenly returned to France with her parents because of an important lawsuit, and he had never heard from her again. Next he remembered Lizzie, from his student days in Berlin. She had shot herself, partly on his account; he remembered when she had reluctantly shown him the blackened spot beneath her left breast, and how, far from being touched, he had felt only annoyance and boredom. And then there was the charming, domestic Henriette, whose small apartment in the upper story of a house overlooking the Alster he had visited for many years whenever he returned to Hamburg from one of his long sea voyages, finding her always as cheerful and as open and willing as when he had left her—though he never found out, nor really cared, how she spent her time in his absence. Many other things also passed through his mind, less agreeable ones, and some so disreputable that he couldn't understand how he had let himself go in for them. As a whole, however, his feeling was one of regret that his youth had passed and with it the right to expect more from life.

As the carriage rolled on between the fields, the hills loomed taller and darker, and twinkling lights shone from the little villas. On a balcony he saw a man and a woman embracing more intimately than they would have in the light of day. From a porch where a small company sat at supper came the sound of loud conversation and laughter. Dr. Graesler began to feel hungry and looked forward to his supper at the Silver Lion. He told the driver to hurry.

Once at the table where his acquaintances were already seated, he drank one more glass of wine than he usually did, because he knew from previous experience that when he felt a little uneasy, as he did tonight, the wine made life seem sweeter and more carefree. He had originally planned to talk about his visit to the ranger's house, but for a reason that wasn't clear to him, he refrained. And the extra glass of wine didn't have its customary effect. Dr. Graesler rose from the table feeling even more melancholy than he had when sat down, and went home with a slight headache.

3

The next few days Dr. Graesler walked the town's main street more than usual in the vague hope of meeting Sabine again. Once, when his waiting room happened to be empty during office hours, he hurried down the stairs on a hunch and took a quick, though futile, walk to the spa's pump room and back. That same evening at his supper table he casually mentioned that he had recently been called to the ranger's lodge, and then listened eagerly and a little pugnaciously for the disparaging words, warranted or not, that men are apt to say about women when they are by themselves and in a jovial mood. But there was so little response to his news that he concluded that the Schleheim family was of no interest to them. There was merely a casual mention that the so-called ranger had relatives in Berlin, and that the daughter, who obviously was not regarded as a particular beauty, spent the winter months with them from time to time.

A few days later, late in the afternoon, Dr. Graesler decided to go for a walk that would take him gradually into the vicinity of the ranger's lodge. From the road he saw the lodge standing impassively in the shadow of the woods, and on the porch he noticed the figure of a man whose features he was unable to discern. Pausing for a minute, he felt the urge to walk up to the house and present himself as though he happened to find himself there by accident and wanted to inquire about Frau Schleheim's health. But he realized immediately that such an action was incompatible with his professional dignity and might create a false impression. When he returned from his walk more tired and disgruntled than he would have thought possible from such a trivial disappointment, and didn't see Sabine in town over the next few days either, he began to hope, in the interest of his own equanimity, that she had gone away for a time or even for good.

One morning, while he breakfasted on his sunny balcony, though with far less enthusiasm than he had the first few days after his return, he was notified that a young man wished to see him. Almost immediately a strapping young man in a bicycling suit appeared. He resembled Sabine so much in both appearance and bearing that the doctor couldn't help greeting him like an acquaintance.

"The younger Herr Schleheim?" he asked in a tone more of conviction than of inquiry.

"Yes, that's me," the young man answered.

"I recognized you immediately because of your resemblance to—your mother. Won't you sit down? I'm still at breakfast, as you see. What's the matter? Is your mother sick again?" He felt as though he were talking to Sabine.

The younger Schleheim remained standing, his cap politely in hand. "Mother is doing fine, thank you. Ever since you had that heart-to-heart talk with her, she's been more careful about what she eats."

The doctor smiled. It was clear to him that Sabine, in order to give greater authority to her own warnings, had ascribed them to him. Suddenly it occurred to him that this time it might be Sabine herself who was ill, and he recognized by the unexpected quickening of his pulse that her health mattered to him. But before he had a chance to ask, the boy said, "It's father this time."

Dr. Graesler drew a sigh of relief. "What's the matter with him? Nothing serious, I hope."

"That's what we'd like to know, Herr Doctor. He's changed so much lately. Perhaps it's not exactly an illness. He's fifty-two years old, after all."

The doctor involuntarily wrinkled his brow. In a chilly tone, he asked, "Well, what's giving you cause for worry?"

"Father has been having attacks of dizziness lately, Herr Doctor. Then yesterday, when he tried to get up from his chair, he almost fell and rescued himself only with difficulty by holding on to the edge of the table. And we've noticed for a long time that his hands tremble when he lifts up his glass to drink."

"Hmm." The doctor looked up from his cup. "I gather your father lifts up a glass pretty often, and that there isn't always just water in it—?"

The young man looked at the floor. "Sabine thinks that does have something to do with it. Also, he smokes all day long."

"Well, my dear young man, age may not have much to do with his problem. So your father wants me to visit him?" he added politely.

"Unfortunately, it's not that simple, Herr Doctor. We don't want father to know that you're coming on his account, as he won't hear of consulting a doctor. Sabine wondered whether the whole thing couldn't be arranged so that it seems as if you met him by chance."

"By chance?"

"For example, if you were to walk past the lodge as you did the other afternoon, Sabine could call you over from the porch and invite you to stop by. Then, after you came in—well, we'd have to improvise from there."

The doctor felt his face flush. Stirring his empty cup, he said, "I don't often get the chance to take a walk. But the other day, yes, I did happen to pass by the lodge." He recovered his self-possession and looked up. To his relief, he saw the young man's gaze resting on him quite guilelessly. He continued in his most professional tone, "Well, if there's no other way, I'll follow your suggestion—of course, we won't get very far with a conversation on the porch. I can't really say anything without doing a thorough examination."

"Of course, Herr Doctor, we know that. We hope that father will eventually come to consult you of his own accord. But if you could only get to know him first! You have such wide experience,

Herr Doctor! Perhaps you could manage to come over one of these days after your office hours? Of course, the sooner the better— today, if possible!"

Today—Graesler repeated to himself—I could see her again today! How wonderful! But he said nothing, consulted his appointment book, shook his head, and pretended to ponder insuperable difficulties. Suddenly he took a pencil and with an air of resolution crossed out an imaginary entry and on the next page wrote the first word that occurred to him, "Sabine." In a cool but cordial tone, he said decisively, "Very well, let's say today between five thirty and six. Is that good for you?"

"Oh, Herr Doctor . . ."

Graesler rose, protested the boy's expressions of gratitude, sent his regards to his mother and sister, and shook his hand. After leaving the balcony and going into his office, he watched from his window as the young Schleheim came out of the entryway with his bicycle, settled his cap firmly, and disappeared around the corner. If I were ten years younger, thought the doctor, I would imagine that this was all a pretext of Sabine's to see me again. And he sighed softly.

Not long after five o'clock, wearing a light grey suit on which his state of mourning was indicated by a black armband around his left arm, he left the house. He planned to have the carriage stop near the lodge, and then walk the rest of the way. But he had traveled only a little beyond the villa district when, to his pleasant surprise, he saw Sabine and her brother walking toward him on the narrow path that ran alongside the road. He jumped out of the carriage, which was proceeding up the hill ploddingly, and shook hands first with Sabine and then with the boy.

"We're so very sorry," began Sabine, with some agitation. "We simply couldn't get father to stay home, and he's not likely to be back until late this evening. Please accept my apologies and don't hold it against us." The doctor tried to look annoyed but failed, and said lightly, "Don't worry about it." He looked at his watch and wrinkled his brow, as though trying to decide what to do instead, but then he looked up and had to smile. Sabine and her brother stood on the side of the road looking like two schoolchildren expecting a scolding. Sabine wore a white dress and carried a broad-brimmed straw hat that hung by a yellow ribbon from her left arm. She looked much younger than she had the first time he had seen her.

"It's such a hot afternoon," the doctor said, almost reproachfully, "and you walked so far to meet me. That really wasn't necessary."

"Herr Doctor," said Sabine, a little embarrassed, "to avoid any misunderstanding, I must above all emphasize that we'll of course regard this unsuccessful call, like the other one, as a professional visit. . . ."

The doctor interrupted her hastily. "Please, Fraulein. The fact is that even if your scheme had worked today, I wouldn't have regarded it as a professional visit anyway. For the time being I beg you to consider me simply as a fellow conspirator."

"If you want to take it that way, Herr Doctor," answered Sabine, "you'll make it impossible for me—"

Dr. Graesler broke in again: "I had intended to go driving in the country today anyway. Perhaps you'll permit me to have the pleasure of putting my carriage at your disposal? Or if you'll allow me to accompany you, perhaps I can use the opportunity to see how your mother is." He felt himself to be quite a man of the world, and made a fleeting resolution to practice at a larger resort next year, though in fact he had never succeeded in such places.

"Mother is doing very well," said Sabine. "But if you really don't have any other plans this evening, Herr Doctor, what if"—and she turned to her brother—"we showed him our forest, Karl?"

"Your forest?"

"That's what we call it," said Karl. "It really is ours. None of the clients of the spa come out this far. Parts of it are just like a primeval forest."

"Well, I should certainly have a look, then," said the doctor. "I'll be delighted to take you up on it."

Dr. Graesler directed the carriage to park in the vicinity of the lodge, then followed the brother and sister down a trail so narrow they had to walk single file. They passed first through fields of wheat as high as a man's head, then across meadows, and from there into a dense forest.

The doctor remarked that although he had come to the area every summer for six years, he still didn't really know it. But that had been his fate—as a physician with the Lloyd Line, all he had ever seen was the coast, or at most the port towns and their immediate surroundings. His profession had almost always prevented him from exploring the surrounding countryside in greater depth. Karl's eager questions about the distant lands he had seen and the many sea voyages he had taken put him in the role of world traveler, enabling him to speak with an animation and a gaiety not usually at his command.

When they came to a clearing that afforded an appealing view of the town, where the glass ceiling of the resort's pump room now glittered in the rays of the setting sun, they decided to rest for a while. Karl flung himself full length on the grass, and Sabine sat down on the trunk of a fallen tree. But Dr. Graesler, who didn't wish to soil his suit, remained standing and continued to speak of his trips. His voice, usually somewhat hoarse despite his frequent attempts to clear his throat, seemed even to him to have acquired a new and unaccustomed clarity and softness, and he found himself listened to with an interest and sympathy he had not enjoyed for a long time. Finally he offered to accompany the brother and sister back home, so that their father, if he had returned by now, would readily believe that they had had a chance encounter. This would provide a simple way of striking up an acquaintance with him.

Sabine nodded curtly in a way characteristic of her, assenting more decisively than she could have with words. On the ever-broadening trail that led gently downhill toward the house, it was now Karl who led the conversation, spinning plans of travel and exploration whose boyish adventurousness had been obviously influenced by books he had recently read. Sooner than the doctor expected, they reached the garden fence where they saw the back of the white house with its six narrow, uniform windows gleaming faintly between tall pines. On the grass between the house and the fence stood a long roughhewn table with chairs and a bench.

Since Karl had run ahead to assess the situation, the doctor and Sabine were left alone beneath the pine trees for a while. They looked at each other, and the doctor smiled a little shyly. When Sabine's expression remained serious, he glanced slowly around, remarked, "How peaceful it is here," then cleared his throat.

Karl appeared at an open window and beckoned energetically. The doctor assumed a mien of professional seriousness and accompanied Sabine through the garden to the porch, where they found the ranger and his wife listening to their son's account of the afternoon's meeting. Graesler, still misled by the designation "ranger," had expected to see a bearded, stout man wearing a hunting jacket and holding a pipe in his mouth. He was much surprised to find a slender, clean-shaven man with black, carefully parted hair only just beginning to turn grey, greeting him with a friendly but somewhat theatrical formality. Dr. Graesler began the conversation by praising the beautiful forest, with whose glory Karl and Sabine had just now acquainted him. And during the course of a conversation that followed about how slowly the town was developing as a health resort despite its appealing surroundings, Dr. Graesler measured the master of the house with a professional eye. But he couldn't detect anything of note beyond a certain restlessness of gaze and a frequent scornful twitching at the corners of his mouth. Dr. Graesler was preparing to leave when Sabine announced supper, but the ranger, with exaggerated cordiality, wouldn't permit it. And so the doctor soon sat with the family at the table lit by a green-shaded lamp hanging from the wooden ceiling. He mentioned the coming Saturday afternoon tea at the Kursal and, turning to Sabine, asked her whether she ever took part in such affairs.

"Not in the last few years," replied Sabine. "I used to when I was younger"—And in reply to Graesler's smile of protest she added hastily—and, it seemed to him, significantly—"I'm already twenty-seven."

The father made a sarcastic remark about the small-town life of the health resort, and began to talk with great animation about the magic and bustle of great cities. From certain of his remarks it became clear that he had once been an opera singer and had given up this profession only recently. He spoke of various artists with whom he had worked, of patrons who had thought highly of him, and finally of the doctors to whose bad treatments he attributed the premature loss of his baritone voice. As he did so, he downed one glass of wine after another, until suddenly he seemed completely exhausted and looked like an old, worn-out man.

The doctor realized it was time to go. Sabine and Karl accompanied him to his carriage and asked anxiously what he thought of their father. Dr. Graesler said that if he were to venture an opinion tonight, he would say that there was nothing seriously wrong with him. But he expressed the hope of observing him more closely, or even better, of giving him a proper examination, without which, as a conscientious physician, he couldn't make a definite diagnosis.

"Don't you think," Karl said as he turned to his sister, "that it's been a long time since father was as talkative as he was tonight?"

"Yes, that's true," Sabine agreed, turning to Dr. Graesler with a grateful look. "He liked you right away—that was obvious."

The doctor modestly waved aside the compliment, and at their request he promised to come again in a few days. He got into the carriage while the two stood at the side of the road, watching as it drew away. The doctor drove home beneath a cool, starry sky. Sabine's trust filled him with satisfaction, all the more so since he had reason to believe that it wasn't inspired solely by his medical skill. He knew that in the last few years he had grown tired of his work and more indifferent toward his patients—often enough he lacked true human sympathy for them. Today, however, he felt once again the loftiness of his calling—a calling he had chosen with enthusiasm in the far-off days of his youth, but of which lately he had not always proved himself worthy.

4

The next day, when Doctor Graesler opened the door to his waiting room, he was surprised to see Herr Schleheim seated among his patients. Since he had been the first to arrive, he followed the doctor into his office straightaway. The former singer's first request was that his family never know of his visit. After Graesler agreed to this, Herr Schleheim did not hesitate to speak freely about his complaints and to submit to a complete examination. Dr. Graesler discovered no serious bodily illness, but it was obvious that Schleheim suffered from a deep emotional disturbance. Graesler felt this wasn't surprising in someone who had been forced to give up a brilliant career in his prime and could not find sufficient compensation either from his family or from his own inner emotional resources. But the opportunity to express himself frankly and openly obviously did Schleheim good, so he was delighted when the doctor genially suggested that rather than seeing him as a patient, he would much prefer to drop in at the lodge and chat with him as a friend whenever he happened to be strolling in the neighborhood.

When Dr. Graesler availed himself of this arrangement on the following Sunday morning, he found Herr Schleheim all alone in the house. Schleheim hastened to explain that he had thought it better to tell the family about his consultation with the doctor after all, and about the positive outcome of his physical exam, if only to rid himself of the worried looks and the tedious talk about his health with which they had nearly driven him mad. Dr. Graesler agreed that the young people's concern might have been a little exaggerated, but he praised their solicitude. Schleheim readily agreed and added that he had nothing to complain about as far as they were concerned—except that they were such honest and kind people. "That's why," he added, "neither of them will get much out of life. They probably won't even really get to know it." And his eyes shone with the pale memory of long past and perhaps disreputable adventures.

They had only just seated themselves on the bench in front of the house when the remaining members of the Schleheim family arrived, all dressed in their Sunday best and looking all the more *petit bourgeois* because of it. Sabine, apparently aware of this, hastened to remove her beribboned hat with a sigh of relief and then smoothed her hair.

The doctor was invited to stay for lunch. The conversation at table remained strictly superficial, and when the possible retirement of the director of one of the sanatoriums near town was mentioned, Sabine's mother casually asked Graesler if he was interested in the position, as it might give him the opportunity to systematically enforce his infamous hunger cure. Graesler smiled and remarked that he never aspired to a position of that sort. "I'm not willing to give up my personal freedom," he said. "Though I've practiced in this town for six years in a row and will probably continue to do so in the coming years, the responsibilities of a director would destroy my pleasure not only in this town but even in my work."

Through a barely perceptible nod, Sabine seemed to express her sympathy for this point of view. Otherwise she seemed well informed about the affairs of the sanatorium, and declared that the place could be much more profitable than it had been under the current director, who had grown old and neglectful. She also said that she thought every doctor would prefer to practice at a sanatorium because only in such a place was a really lasting relationship between doctor and patient possible, and therefore, the opportunity to use treatments that were really effective because they had been studied and controlled.

"Well, you have a good point there," Dr. Graesler said with the kind of reserve he considered appropriate for an expert speaking to lay persons. Sabine did not miss the tone. Blushing slightly, she quickly added, "Well, you know I worked as a nurse for a while in Berlin."

"Really!" exclaimed the doctor, temporarily at a loss as to how to respond to this revelation. He fell back on platitudes, "A beautiful, a noble calling! But what a serious and difficult one! I can well understand how your home in these beautiful woods drew you back."

Sabine said nothing, and the rest, too, remained silent. Dr. Graesler, however, suspected that he had approached the place where the key to the modest riddle of Sabine's life lay hidden.

After dinner Karl, as though it were his God-given right, insisted on a game of dominoes in the garden. He challenged the doctor to play, and soon, while the mother dozed over her needlework in a comfortable chair beneath the pines, the game was in full swing. Dr. Graesler remembered certain oppressive Sunday afternoons with his melancholy sister, and felt as though he had miraculously escaped a gloomy phase of his life. And when Sabine, noticing his distraction, reminded him through a smiling glance or a light touch on the arm that it was his turn to play, he felt her little intimacies to be a faint promise.

The dominoes were cleared away and a flowered tablecloth spread over the table once again. And since a carriage could not be obtained today, Dr. Graesler had to walk home and so had time only for a quick cup of coffee before it grew too late in the evening to visit those of his patients who couldn't do without him even on a Sunday. The memory of Sabine's smile and the gentle pressure of her hand cheered him so that he would not have complained had the road home been even hotter and grimier.

Nevertheless he thought it better to let some time pass before he visited the lodge again. It was easier for him to wait than he thought it would be — his profession had begun to interest him again. He not only kept up the clinical records of his patients with more care, but he also began to study medical books and journals in order to fill in the gaps in his theoretical knowledge that had formed over the years. And even though he was aware that his doing so was due to Sabine's influence, he resisted entertaining serious hopes of winning the young woman. Whenever he dreamed of wooing and winning Sabine and pictured life with her at his side, the disagreeable figure of the hotel director in Lanzarote would appear to him unbidden, and he would see the impertinent smile with which the director would receive the aging doctor and his young wife at the entrance to the hotel. This image appeared persistently, as if Lanzarote were the only place Graesler could practice his profession in the winter, as if the director were the only person in the world who could threaten his newly married life.

One morning at the end of the week, Graesler ran into Sabine shopping in town. She asked why he hadn't come for such a long time. "So few people come to visit us," she said, "and even fewer can carry on a decent conversation. Next time you must tell us more about yourself and your adventures. We'd love to hear more about all the things you've done." A look of quiet yearning lit up her eyes.

"If you think that life in the world out there is so interesting, Fräulein Sabine, why do you shut yourself away here in the peace and quiet of the country?"

"It may not be forever," she answered simply. "And anyway, I've already had a chance to experience a different kind of life. I can't think of anything better than what I have right now." And the yearning in her eyes dimmed.

5

Graesler did not undertake his next visit to the lodge unprepared. He searched his memory for incidents worth recounting and at first was a little dismayed that a life so outwardly eventful seemed on closer examination to be so devoid of actual content. Still, there were a few incidents that might be considered actual adventures: once on a distant South Sea island he had been present when natives attacked and killed one of the ship's mates; a pair of lovers had committed suicide on the high seas; a cyclone had hit his ship in the Indian Ocean; he had once landed at a Japanese port that had been destroyed by an earthquake only the day before; and he had once spent the night in an opium den, though the end of this story would have to be edited a bit for family consumption. And all this could be made more exciting in the telling. In addition to these stories, he could recount his vivid memories of a number of patients at various health resorts—various swindlers and eccentrics, and even a Russian grand duke who was murdered after having a presentiment of it the summer before.

As a result, when on one pleasantly warm summer evening at the Schleheims, he began to tell a story in response to a casual question from Karl as he leaned idly on the balustrade of the porch, he noticed that many of his forgotten memories grew brighter and more vivid as he talked, and that much that he had long forgotten welled up again from the depths of his soul. He was further surprised to discover a talent he didn't know he possessed: he found himself able to invent freely whenever his memory threatened to fail him. But he didn't take himself to task too harshly for this because it gave him a plea-sure he had not enjoyed for a very long time: that of being the center of attention in a sympathetic circle as he brought into the dreamlike peace of the forest lodge the seductive echo of a life that had mostly faded even for him.

On a later occasion, while Sabine and her mother received visitors in the garden—a rare occurrence—he sat alone on the porch with the old singer. Schleheim was talking more energetically about his former life at municipal theaters and the opera houses of minor courts than ever before—his tone implied a rich and proud life, a life he regretted losing. After the premature loss of his voice, his well-to-do father-in-law, a wine merchant from the Rhineland, had offered him a chance to go into business with him. But he had decided instead to retreat into nature and solitude so that he would not be constantly reminded of his loss, as he would be in a city. There was less in such an environment to hinder his enjoyment of what was left him: the pleasures of domesticity—he did not say this without irony—and the admirable qualities of his children, which once again he seemed almost to deplore.

"If only Sabine," he remarked gloomily, "had inherited my temperament as well as my talent, what a future she could have!" And he told Graesler that when Sabine was in Berlin, where she had stayed with relatives of his wife—very bourgeois sort of people— she had studied voice and dramatic art but had given them up because of her distaste for the loose morals of her fellow students.

"Fräulein Sabine," Graesler remarked—nodding in assent— "has a truly pure soul."

"Yes, she does! But what good is that, my dear doctor, compared to the immense prize of knowing life in all its heights and its depths! Isn't that better than keeping one's soul pure?" He looked into the distance and continued in an irritated tone, "So one day she overturned all her—or rather all my—plans for art and fame and—conscious of the marked contrast, I'm sure—enrolled instead in nurse's training, for which she suddenly believed she had a vocation."

The doctor shook his head. "But it seems that this profession didn't completely satisfy her either. If I understood her correctly the other day, didn't she give it up after a few years?"

"Thereby hangs a tale," Schleheim answered. "When she was a nurse she met a young doctor, to whom she became engaged. A very promising young doctor, it was said, with the most excellent prospects. I myself never had the chance to meet him. . . ." He finished rapidly and softly, since Karl had just then walked in on them. "Unfortunately, the young man died."

"Died," Graesler repeated to himself, but without any real sympathy.

Karl announced that coffee was being served beneath the pines. The men went into the garden, and the doctor was introduced to the other visitors, a widow and her two daughters, both a little younger than Sabine. Dr. Graesler and the ladies knew each other by sight, and a lively and spontaneous conversation soon unfolded over coffee and cake. The two young women claimed that every afternoon at a quarter to three, a time when they were usually busy sewing, they saw the doctor leave his usual restaurant from their window. They insisted they saw him take his pocket watch out every day, hold it to his ear, shake his head, and hurry back to his house. What was so important at home every day? asked the younger girl with twinkling eyes. Office hours? What a joke! Everyone knew that real patients never came to this so-called health resort. The interesting young man who was always being wheeled to the tavern in his wheelchair was really an actor from Berlin, hired by the resort management to play the invalid every summer season in return for room and board. And the elegant lady with the seventeen hats was not an American or even an

Australian, as the visitor list claimed, but as European as the rest of them. That was why yesterday evening, as she sat on a bench in the Kurgarten with the officer in civilian clothes who had come to visit her from Eisenach, she spoke with an unmistakable Viennese accent. Graesler made no attempt to vouch for the authenticity of the American lady, who was another doctor's patient, but he could vouch for the French couple who had traveled everywhere and thought this the most beautiful spot in the world. At this point the older sister began earnestly to praise the beauty of the woods and the hills surrounding the town as well as its friendly atmosphere, which was at its best, she believed, when all the visitors had left.

"You should really spend a winter here sometime, Doctor," said Frau Schleheim in agreement, turning to the doctor, "then you'd see how charming it can be here." Dr. Graesler didn't answer, but everyone saw mirrored in his eyes the distant places they had never seen and probably never would.

Later, when everyone prepared for an afternoon walk, the master of the house declared that he preferred to stay at home to continue reading a book on the history of the French Revolution, a period in which he had a special interest. At first the little group walked closely together, but later, as if by design, Graesler was given a chance to go ahead with Sabine. He felt surer today in her company than he had before—more secure, superior, and intimate. It seemed possible to him that Sabine had been closer than her father and her mother suspected to the young doctor who had been her bridegroom and who had then died. In that case he could think of her as a young widow, which would help somewhat in bridging the difference in their ages.

The pleasant day ended with a supper to the sound of the resort orchestra on the large terrace outside the Kurhaus. Herr Schleheim joined them, dressed so elegantly, almost foppishly, that the doctor could not picture him as just having emerged from the horrors of the French Revolution. Sabine's friends admired his appearance teasingly but genuinely while Sabine, if the doctor interpreted her expression correctly, did not find her father's attire wholly to her taste. Aside from that, everyone was in the best of spirits, and the younger of the two girls did not miss the opportunity to make sly comments about the other guests. She promptly espied the lady with the seventeen hats, who sat at an adjoining table in the company of three younger men and one older one, bobbing her head to and fro to the rhythm of a Viennese waltz in a manner that was anything but Australian.

When Dr. Graesler felt a foot fleetingly touch his, he was almost shocked. Sabine? No, it couldn't be. And he wouldn't have wished for it either. It had to be the mischievous little miss sitting opposite him and wearing a particularly innocent expression on her face. Since the gentle contact stopped immediately, it could of course have been accidental. It was as characteristic of Dr. Graesler that he was inclined to accept this interpretation as it was that he would gain so little satisfaction from it. An excessive modesty, yes, even a certain self-depreciation had always been his worst fault; otherwise he probably wouldn't be practicing here in this ridiculous little resort town but would be a distinguished physician at a grand spa like Wiesbaden or Ems. Even though Sabine looked at him with frank friendliness from time to time, and once even smilingly raised her glass to him, he grew more and more melancholy with every drop. His drooping mood seemed gradually to infect the whole company. The two older women became noticeably tired, the younger girls' conversation stopped, and even the singer, looking gloomily around, silently lit up a big cigar. By the time the company finally broke up, Graesler felt that never in his whole life had he been so lonely.

6

Karl's school vacation was over, and Frau Schleheim took him back to Berlin, from where she returned after a few days with an upset stomach, as expected. Dr. Graesler, now called upon in his professional capacity again, came to the lodge every evening and continued to do so even after Frau Schleheim had fully recovered. It often happened that he spent hours alone talking with Sabine, sometimes in the house or outdoors. Her parents, attributing a welcomed understanding to them, were happy to stay out of the way. Graesler told Sabine about his youth, about his native city with its many towers and its ancient wall, and about the house where he had lived with his parents. It was an old-fashioned kind of place whose rooms were always ready and waiting to welcome him—and until recently, his sister too—for a short spring or fall visit. And when Sabine listened to him sympathetically, he couldn't help but picture how delightful it would be to take her home with him, and how surprised his old friend Boehlinger, a lawyer—the only person who still formed a connection between him and his hometown—would be when he saw her.

As fall arrived early and with special force that year, most of the spa's clients fled before the season's end and, except for those he spent at the lodge, Graesler found his hours leaden and empty. He was so alarmed at the prospect of resuming his lonely, meaningless, and hopeless life of wandering that he sometimes felt quite determined to make a formal proposal to Sabine. But instead of asking her directly, for which he couldn't find the courage, he made inquiries—as though leaving it to fate to decide—about whether Dr. Frank's sanatorium, which Sabine had mentioned again, was really for sale and what the terms were. Finally, when he wasn't able to find out anything definite, he went directly to Dr. Frank, whom he knew personally. He found a grumpy old man in a dirty-yellow linen suit, looking more like an eccentric farmer than a doctor, sitting on a white bench in front of the sanatorium and smoking a pipe. Graesler asked him point-blank whether there was any truth to the rumors that he wanted to sell the place. It turned out that Dr. Frank had merely dropped hints of his intentions here and there and was also awaiting a nod from fate. In any case, he would like nothing better than to sell his place soon, as he wanted to spend the few years still left to him as far away from invalids, both real and imaginary, as possible, and recover from the hundreds of thousands of lies he had been forced to tell in the course of his professional career. "You can take it over," he said, "you're still young"—an assertion that Dr. Graesler countered with a melancholy gesture of dissent.

He took a look at the building but to his regret found it even more run-down and dilapidated than he had feared. The few patients whom he met in the garden, the hallways, and the inhalation therapy rooms seemed neither satisfied nor hopeful, and they greeted their doctor with a mistrust verging on hostility. But when he stood on the little balcony of the director's private house and looked out across the garden and over the inviting valley beyond it toward the gently rising hills, he was suddenly seized by such an intense yearning for Sabine that for the first time he realized with utter certainty that he loved her. He wished for nothing more than to stand on this very spot with his arms around her and to plan with her, his wife and companion, to renew and beautify the whole property. He needed all his self-control to feign indecisiveness and to depart without coming to an agreement with Dr. Frank, who in any case seemed completely indifferent.

At the lodge that evening he thought it best to say nothing about his visit to the sanatorium, but the very next day he took his friend Adelmann, an architect and one of his daily companions at the Silver Lion, to the sanatorium for an expert opinion. It turned out that the needed repairs would be less extensive and less costly than Dr. Graesler had feared. Indeed, the architect said he could make the institution as good as new by the first of May of the following year. In the presence of Dr. Frank, Graesler continued to act as if undecided, and left with the architect, who once they were alone strongly urged him to proceed with this advantageous purchase.

That same evening, as warm as if it were summer again, Graesler sat with Sabine and her parents outside on the porch and began as if in passing to talk about his conversation with Dr. Frank. He portrayed it as a chance conversation, saying he had happened to be walking in front of the institution with the architect just as Dr. Frank came through the gate. Herr Schleheim also thought the terms of the sale most advantageous and urged Dr. Graesler to forgo practicing in the south this winter and give this important matter his immediate attention. But Dr. Graesler wouldn't hear of it. He couldn't give up his contract with Lanzarote on the spur of the moment, and he was sure that if he left the matter in the hands of a competent man like Adelmann, he could leave without worry. At this Sabine, in her simple and direct fashion, offered to supervise the work during his absence and to give him regular reports about its progress. Soon after this her parents, as if by previous arrangement, disappeared into the house, and Sabine and Graesler strolled as usual up and down the tree-lined walkway that led from the house to the road. She had so many suggestions about the remodeling of the building that it seemed she had already thought a great deal about it. Most important, she argued, was the hiring of a lady—a genuine lady, she added—as chief administrator, because it was from the lack of social cachet that the institution had chiefly suffered in recent years. Graesler felt with a pounding heart that these words were the cue for his declaring himself, and he was on the verge of doing so when Sabine, as though to prevent him, hurriedly added: "An advertisement in the paper is the best way for you to do that. If I were you, I wouldn't even hesitate to travel some distance to get the appropriate person for such an important post. You've got plenty of time to do this at the moment. Most of your patients are already gone, aren't they? . . . When exactly are you thinking of leaving?"

"In four or five days. First, of course, I must go home—to my hometown, I mean. My sister didn't leave a will, and I need, my old friend Boehlinger wrote me, to settle a few things. But before I leave I want to take another close look at the sanatorium. Of course I can't make a final decision without discussing the matter with Boehlinger first." He went on guardedly and awkwardly for a while, all the time profoundly dissatisfied with himself, as he was well aware that the situation demanded clarity and resolution. As Sabine was persistently silent, he considered it best to plead a professional engagement and take his leave. He held her hand for a few moments, then suddenly raised it to his lips and pressed a fervent kiss to it. Sabine did not object, and when he looked at her afterward she looked happier and more cheerful than before. But he couldn't say anything else just then. He let go of her hand, climbed into the carriage, wrapped a blanket around his knees, and drove off. When he turned to look back, he saw Sabine standing motionless in the pale light. But it seemed to him that she was gazing somewhere else, into the night, the void—not in the direction in which he was driving and gradually disappearing from her view.

7

Without really looking forward to it and almost as a matter of duty, early the next morning Dr. Graesler set out in a grey drizzle to inspect the sanatorium for the third time. On this occasion he had to content himself with being taken around by a very young medical assistant, a doctor whose strained politeness was probably meant not so much for the old director as for the presumed new one. He seized every opportunity to indicate his familiarity with the most up-to-date therapeutic methods, voicing his regret that so far there had been no opportunities to use them. Today the entire building seemed to Dr. Graesler even more run-down and the garden more neglected than it had been before. And so when he finally sat down across from Dr. Frank in his bare office, where he found him eating breakfast among a litter of bills and other papers, he told him that a final decision had to await his return from his hometown, around three weeks from now. Dr. Frank received this statement with his usual indifference and remarked only that of course he too would not feel obligated in any way. Graesler did not object, and when he was back on the street and walking toward town beneath his open umbrella, he felt a sense of renewed freedom. His umbrella dripped with heavy rain, and the hills were shrouded in thick fog. It had become so cold that his fingers began to freeze, and he had to put on his gloves while holding his umbrella—not the easiest thing to do. He shook his head disapprovingly. Would he ever get used to spending the late fall and winter in this so-called temperate zone, now that he had grown used to a southern climate? He almost wished he could tell Sabine that very evening that the sanatorium had been snapped up from under his very nose by a more decisive buyer—whom he really didn't envy!

Upon his return to his flat he found a letter addressed to him in Sabine's handwriting. His heart suddenly skipped a beat. What could she have to write to him about? There was only one possibility—she was asking him to stop coming. That hand kiss yesterday—he knew right away—had spoiled everything. It was not the sort of thing he could carry off well. He must have looked the perfect fool. Suddenly he found that the envelope was open—Graesler hardly knew how—and he read:

Dear friend!

I trust I can call you that. I know you're coming again tomorrow evening, but I wanted you to have this letter first. For, unless I write to you, it may be that you'll leave the same way that you've left these many days and evenings, and will finally leave for your trip without having said anything, and in the end you'll persuade yourself that you've acted wisely and correctly. So there is nothing left but for me to speak—or rather, since I can't bring myself to do that, to write you what is in my heart. Well then, dear Dr. Graesler, my dear friend Dr. Graesler, I'm writing this down, and you'll read what I've written and perhaps be a little pleased and not consider it too unfeminine—and I feel I can write this—it would not be unwelcome to me, not at all, if you were to ask me to be your wife. There you have it. Yes, I'd like very much to be your wife. For I feel a deeper and warmer friendship for you than I've ever felt for anyone else. No, it isn't love. Not yet. But it's something akin to love and something that may very well grow into love one day. Whenever you talked about leaving in the last few days, I felt an odd tug in my heart. And when you kissed my hand this evening, it was very beautiful. But when you left and drove away into the darkness, I suddenly felt as though it were all over, and was truly afraid that you would never come again. Of course, that mood has passed. Those were only night thoughts, so to speak. I know you're coming again, tomorrow evening. And I also know that you like me as much as I like you. One doesn't have to say that kind of thing in words. But sometimes I feel that you suffer from a certain lack of self-confidence. Isn't that true? I've thought about why you might be that way, and I think it comes from the fact that you've never stayed long enough anywhere to put down roots, and have never in your whole life taken the time to wait for someone to develop a deep tie to you. Yes, I think that may be it.

But perhaps there's another reason for your hesitation. It's a little hard for me to write this to you, but since I've started, I'm not going to stop halfway now. As you know, I was once engaged. It was four years ago now. He was a doctor, like you. My father probably mentioned him to you. I loved him deeply, and it was a terrible blow to me to lose him. He was so young. Only twenty-eight. At the time I thought everything was over for me, as people tend to think at such times. But in the interest of truth, I must confess to you that he wasn't my first love. Before him I had a passion

for a singer. That was at a time when my father, with the best intentions, was trying to force me into a way of life for which I was
not naturally suited. It was the most passionate experience I ever
had in my life—though I can't exactly call it an "experience." It
wasn't an "experience," only a feeling. The whole thing ended
rather stupidly. The man fancied he was dealing with the sort of
creature he was accustomed to in his own circle, he behaved ac-
cordingly, and that was the end of it. But the strange thing is that I
still think about this man much more often than I think about my
fiancé, who was so dear to me. We were engaged for six months.
Which brings me to something I find a little hard to say. Do you
know what I think, dear Dr. Graesler? That you suspect something
that isn't true, and that's why you hesitate. Of course on the one
hand it's proof of your fondness for me. But it's also—please forgive me for saying it—a little pedantry and vanity on your part. Of
course I realize that this kind of vanity and pedantry is common
among men. But I want to tell you that you don't need to worry
about that at all. Do I have to spell it out even more clearly? Well,
my dear friend, I mean that I have no confessions to make regarding my past. When I stop to think about it, my relationship with
my fiancé was rather strange. I don't think that in six months he
kissed me more than ten times.

It's amazing what you can write to a good friend in the middle of the night, especially when you know you don't have to send
it in the end. But there would be no point in my writing this letter
if I didn't write down frankly whatever came into my head. Despite what I just told you, my fiancé was very dear to me. Perhaps
it was because he was so serious, so melancholy. He was one of
those doctors—there aren't many of them—who suffer all the misery they witness. So life was terribly difficult for him. Where
would he have found the courage to be happy? Well, I thought I
would be able to teach him how to be happy in time. I believed I
could. But fate decreed otherwise. I'll show you a picture of him

sometime. Naturally I've saved it. I don't have a picture of the other man, the singer, anymore. I had one that he didn't give to me—I had bought it in a poster shop before I even met him.

But how I do go on! It's already past midnight. And here I am still sitting at my desk writing, and I don't feel like stopping. By the way, I hear my father pacing up and down below. He's been having restless nights again. We haven't concerned ourselves very much with him recently—you and I, I mean. I want to change that. Oh, and that reminds me of something else that has just occurred to me. Please take it in the spirit in which it is meant. About the sanatorium—my father says that in case you can't at the moment put your hands on the necessary cash, he'll be happy to help you out. In fact, I think he'd like to have a financial stake in the business. And while we're on the subject of the sanatorium, and if you understand what I'm driving at in this letter (and I think I've made it fairly clear!), you can save yourself the trouble of placing ads and traveling to interview people, because I can confidently recommend myself as manager of the institution.

Wouldn't it be wonderful, my dear Dr. Graesler, if we could work together in this institution as comrades—I almost said colleagues? I must confess that I've been interested in the sanatorium for a long time. Longer than its future director! Its location and its grounds are really wonderful. It's such a pity that Dr. Frank has neglected it like this. Another mistake is that for some time now he's been taking on all sorts of patients who don't belong there. I think the place should once more be reserved exclusively for nervous disorders—excluding serious mental illnesses, of course.

But I'm straying too far now. There's plenty of time to discuss all this—at least until tomorrow, even if we shouldn't come to an understanding about the rest. And in any case you could use some of your travel time to spread the word about the sanatorium in Berlin and other big cities. I still know some professors in Berlin from my time there as a nurse, and perhaps they'll remember me.

Oh, I can see you smiling at this. Never mind. I know this is not an ordinary letter. Not at all. Malicious people might say something about a woman throwing herself at a man. But you aren't such a malicious person, and you'll take the letter in the spirit in which it was written. I'm very fond of you, my friend—perhaps not romantically like in novels, but still I mean it from the bottom of my heart! Partly too, I feel bad that you're roaming about the world so all alone. I might not be writing this letter if your sister were still alive. She was a good woman, I know that. And perhaps I'm also fond of you because I admire you as a doctor. Yes, I really do. Some people might find your professional manner a little cold. But that's just your façade, I think. Deep down, I know you're really sympathetic and kind. The essential thing is that you inspire confidence, as you did in my mother and my father—and that, after all, is how it all began, my dear Dr. Graesler.

When you come tomorrow—I don't want to make it hard for you—just smile or kiss my hand again the way you did tonight, and I'll know. But if all this is just my imagination, please tell me frankly. You needn't worry about it. I'll give you my hand in friendship and will cherish the memory of the beautiful hours we had together this summer. I'm not immodest enough to think I have to become a Frau Doctor or a Frau Director—that kind of thing really isn't very important to me. And please understand— even if you marry someone else and bring another woman back with you next year, some beautiful stranger from Lanzarote, an American or an Australian (but a genuine one!)—my offer to supervise the remodeling of the sanatorium stands if you take it over. Because these are two fundamentally different things which do not depend on each other.

Well, now it's really time for me to stop. I'm quite curious to know whether I'll send you this letter tomorrow morning. What do you think? Well, goodbye. Auf Wiedersehen!

Best regards—and whatever happens, I remain
Your friend
Sabine.

Dr. Graesler sat contemplating the letter for a long time. He read it a second and a third time, and was still uncertain as to whether its contents made him happy or sad. This much was clear: Sabine was willing to become his wife. She was, in fact, as she had herself written, almost throwing herself at him. At the same time she admitted that what she felt for him was not love. Indeed, she regarded him with an all too discerning, one might say even critical, eye. She had correctly pointed out that he was a vain, cold, and indecisive pedant—all qualities that he didn't deny having but which Fräulein Sabine would scarcely have noticed and certainly wouldn't have pointed out had he been ten to fifteen years younger. And he asked himself: since she had not failed to notice his faults from a distance, and didn't hesitate to mention them in her letter, what would happen later when the intimacy of daily life inevitably revealed his many other faults? He would have to be continually on his guard in order to maintain his integrity. To find it necessary to constantly watch himself, to act a part, so to speak—which would be far from easy at his age—would be almost as difficult as transforming a morose, finicky, comfortably set-in-his-ways old bachelor into a charming and gallant young husband. It would succeed at the beginning, of course. She was certainly sympathetic toward him, even, one might say, full of maternal tenderness. But how long would that last? No longer than it would take for another romantic singer or melancholic doctor or some other seductive male to show up and win her favors, all the more easily once marriage had made her riper and more experienced.

The wall clock struck half past one, long past the usual lunch hour. Conscious of his obsession with time, he hurried to the inn. At his table he found the architect and one of the city councilmen sitting in their usual corner over coffee and cigarettes. The councilman nodded toward him portentously and greeted him with the words, "Well, I hear we can congratulate you."

"What for?" said Dr. Graesler, startled.

"You've bought Dr. Frank's sanatorium."

Relieved, Graesler said, "Bought it? Not at all. Not yet, anyway—it depends on a lot of things that aren't settled yet. The place is in a terrible state, after all. It practically needs to be rebuilt from the ground up. And our friend here"—he studied the menu and pointed fleetingly at the architect—"keeps raising the estimate. . . ."

The architect protested vehemently that he really didn't want to profit from the project; and as far as the repairs to the place were concerned, they were easy to make. If the contract were drawn up at once, the place would be as good as new by the middle of May at the latest.

Dr. Graesler shrugged and was quick to remind the architect that only yesterday he had indicated the first of May as the completion date. Anyway, everyone knew what happens with renovations of this kind—the construction time and the costs were always more than estimated—and he didn't quite feel up to such a project at his stage of life. Also, the owner was asking a ridiculous price for it.

"And who knows," he added—jokingly of course—"how do I know that you, my dear Adelmann, aren't in cahoots with him?" The architect's temper flared at this suggestion. The councilman tried to smooth things over, and Dr. Graesler tried to apologize, but the genial atmosphere had been ruined and could not be repaired; the two men—the architect and the councilman—soon left the doctor sitting alone and feeling dissatisfied with himself. He didn't touch his last course and rushed home, where a patient who was about to depart for the winter and in need of his final instructions awaited him. The doctor prescribed the winter regimen impatiently, accepted his fee with a bad conscience, and felt a dull resentment not only against himself but also against Sabine, who had not failed to point out his indifference toward his patients in her letter. He went out onto his balcony, relit his cold cigar, and looked down into the miserable little garden, where despite the gloomy weather his landlady was as usual sitting on a white bench with her knitting and her sewing basket at her side. As recently as three or four years ago this rather elderly lady had had unmistakable designs on him—or so said Friederike, who always believed her brother to be surrounded by eager old maids and widows ready to pounce on him. God knows that was an exaggeration. But he was born to be a bachelor—all his life he had been an eccentric, an egotist, and a prig. Sabine knew this, as was all too obvious from her letter, and yet for various reasons, the least of which was love, she claimed to be throwing herself at him. Had she really thrown herself into his arms, the matter would be very different. In truth, the letter rustling in his pocket was hardly a love letter at all.

The carriage that took him to the lodge every evening was announced. Dr. Graesler's heart beat faster. He couldn't conceal from himself that there was only one thing for him to do now—to rush to Sabine, gratefully grasp the loving hands she so warmly and unreservedly held out to him, and ask the lovely creature to marry him— even if his happiness would last only a few years or even months. But instead of rushing headlong down the stairs, he remained rooted to the spot where he stood. He felt the need to clarify something in his mind once and for all but couldn't quite figure out what it was. Suddenly it occurred to him: he had to read Sabine's letter one more time. He removed it from his breast pocket and went into his consulting room where her words could sink in once again without distraction. And he read. He read slowly, with anxious attention—and felt his heart grow cold. Everything warm and heartfelt in the letter now seemed cool to him, even mocking, and when he came to the passage where Sabine pointed out his reserve, his vanity, and his pedantry, it seemed to him that she intentionally repeated what she had unjustly accused him of in her letter. How could she call him a pedant and a prig, he who had been ready to forgive her gladly if she were guilty of a misstep? So far from perceiving this, she attributed his holding back to just this. So little did she know him! Yes, that was it. She didn't understand him. And with this realization a new light suddenly illuminated the riddle of his existence. It was now clear to him that no one had ever really understood him. No one, neither man nor woman. Not his parents, not his sister, nor his colleagues, nor his patients. His reserve was taken for lack of feeling, his sense of order for priggishness, his seriousness for pedantry. That was why he, a man with neither dash nor sparkle, was destined to lifelong solitude. And because he was that sort of man and on top of that so many years older than Sabine, he neither could nor ought to accept the happiness she offered him—or believed she could bring him—a happiness that probably would never be real. He hastily snatched up a piece of stationery and began to write:

"My dear Fräulein Sabine! Your letter moved me deeply. How can I thank you, I, a lonely old man."

Oh, what nonsense, he thought, tore up the letter, and began anew:

My dear Sabine!

I've received your letter, your beautiful, lovely letter. It has moved me deeply. How can I thank you? You're offering me the possibility of a happiness I had hardly dared to dream of, and that is why, let me just say it plainly, that is why I don't dare accept it—at least not right away. Give me a few days to think it over, to contemplate my happiness, and, my dear Sabine, ask yourself again whether you are really and truly prepared to entrust your lovely youth to me, a much older man.

Perhaps it's a good thing that I must return to my hometown for a few days, as you know. I now intend to go a few days sooner, tomorrow morning instead of Thursday. We won't see one another for about two weeks, and that will give both of us time enough to think things through and come to a clear decision. Unfortunately, dear Sabine, I can't express myself as beautifully as you do. If you could only see into my heart. But I know you won't misunderstand me. I think it's better if I don't come to the lodge today. I'd rather take my temporary leave of you with this letter. At the same time I beg you for permission to write to you, and beg you to write to me. My address at home is Am Burggraben 17. As you know, I intend to confer with my old friend Boehlinger, a lawyer, about the sanatorium. So for the present I won't take your father up on his kind offer. Do convey my sincerest thanks to him. Besides, it's probably a good idea to get an outside architect's advice on the project, though of course this is not intended as a criticism of the one here. But all this can be considered when the time comes. For now, my dear Sabine, goodbye. Give my regards to your parents. Please tell them an urgent telegram from my lawyer has called me away a few days earlier. In two weeks then. When I return I hope to find everything the same as it is now as I depart. With what impatience I will await your answer! Now I must close. I thank you. I kiss your dear hands. Goodbye! Till we meet again!

Your friend,
Dr. Graesler.

He folded the letter. Several times while writing he had felt tears in his eyes from vague emotions for himself and for Sabine. But now that he had reached a temporary decision, his eyes were dry and he was perfectly composed as he sealed the letter and handed it to the coachman to deliver to the lodge. From his office window he watched the carriage leave. And just as he was about to call the coachman back, the words died on his lips, and the carriage was soon out of sight.

Then he began to prepare for his imminent journey. There was so little time and so much to do that at first he thought of nothing else. But later, when it occurred to him that by now his letter would be in Sabine's hands, he quite literally felt a pang in his heart. Would she send an answer right away? What if she simply got into the carriage and came to fetch him, the indecisive bridegroom? Then she could truly say that she was throwing herself at him! But her love wasn't strong enough to withstand such a test. And she didn't come. Not even a letter. And much later, at dusk, he saw the carriage drive by with another fare. Graesler slept very restlessly that night, and the next morning, chilled to the bone and in a dour mood, he rode to the station while the rain rattled sharply against the hood of the open carriage.

8

An agreeable surprise awaited Dr. Graesler upon his return to his hometown. Even though he had announced his arrival only at the last minute, he found his rooms not only in good order but much more comfortably furnished than during his last visit. He remembered now that Friederike had been here alone for a few days last fall and had purchased various household items and furniture. She had also arranged for competent workmen to undertake renovations which she had supervised throughout the winter months through a correspondence with Boehlinger. As Graesler walked through the apartment a second time and finally entered the room that opened into the courtyard and had belonged to his sister, he sighed softly — in deference to the caretaker, a printer's wife, who accompanied him through the house, but also in sincere mourning for the dear departed, who would never see the familiar room and its attractive new furnishings and lighting.

While unpacking, Dr. Graesler walked aimlessly around his rooms: he occasionally picked up this or that book from the library, only to put it back unread; he looked down into the narrow, nearly deserted street, where the streetlamp was mirrored in the wet pavement; he sat in the old desk chair he had inherited from his father and read the newspaper. All the while he realized with wistful surprise that he felt as distant from Sabine as if they were not only separated by many miles, but as if the letter in which she had offered him her hand—and which had driven him away—had arrived not yesterday but many weeks ago. When he took it out, it seemed to exhale a harsh and disquieting scent. Anxious about having to read it again, he locked it away in a drawer.

The next morning he asked himself what he might do with himself that day and on the days following. He had long ago become a stranger in his hometown. Most of his friends had passed away, and his ties to the few who remained had gradually weakened, though his sister, whenever she had happened to be here, had usually called upon a few elderly people who had belonged to their parents' circle. As a matter of fact, Graesler really had no business here at home other than to talk with Boehlinger, a task that was not in the least urgent.

Upon leaving his apartment, he first took a walk through town, as he always did when returning home after being away a long time. Usually such a walk gave him soothing feelings of nostalgia, but today, beneath the leaden grey sky, he felt nothing of the sort. With no feeling of any kind he walked past the old house from whose tall and narrow tower window his childhood sweetheart had once greeted him with secret nods and smiles as he had gone back and forth to his *Gymnasium*. He was indifferent to the murmur of the fountain in the autumnal park which had been developed on the old town moat. And when, as he came out of the courtyard of the famous old town hall, he caught sight of the ancient, dilapidated little house in the hidden little street around the corner, and behind whose windows with their typical red curtains he had had his first pitiful sexual adventure followed by weeks of terror, he felt as though there was nothing left of his entire boyhood but a few torn and dust-covered fragments of experience.

The first person he spoke to was the white-bearded tobacconist in the store where he bought his cigars. When the man effusively expressed his sympathy regarding his sister, Graesler hardly knew what to say, and left the shop in dread of meeting other acquaintances and having to listen to the same meaningless phrases. But the next person he met didn't recognize him, and when he encountered a third, who looked as if he meant to stop and talk, Graesler passed him by with a barely civil greeting.

After lunch, which he took in a familiar old inn, which unfortunately had been extravagantly redecorated, he went to see Boehlinger, who had been informed of his arrival in town. Boehlinger greeted him in a calm, friendly manner, and after a few words of condolence asked for the details of Friederike's death. Lowering his eyes and speaking softly, Dr. Graesler told his old friend the sad story. When he looked up again, he was surprised to find sitting across from him a stocky, elderly man looking wan and worn—a man whose beardless face was preserved in his memory as youthful and vigorous. Boehlinger was at first profoundly saddened. He remained silent for a long time, then finally shrugged his shoulders and turned to his desk, as if to demonstrate that even after such a terrible event there was nothing for the living to do but set themselves resolutely to the tasks of the day. Then he opened a drawer and removed Friederike's will and other important documents and proceeded to discuss the details of her estate. As the lawyer made clear at the end of his explanation, the deceased had left behind considerably more funds than Graesler had expected, and as he was her sole heir, he was now in a position to live modestly but comfortably on the interest from the estate without having to practice medicine. But the very disclosure of this possibility made Graesler realize that he wasn't yet ready for retirement, that in fact he had been born with a vigorous drive for activity.

Making this emphatically clear, he told his old friend about the sanatorium and about how he had entered into serious negotiations for its purchase just before leaving the resort town. The lawyer listened attentively, asked him to clarify many details, and seemed at first to approve of the doctor's plans. But in the end he hesitated to advise his friend to go ahead with them. The undertaking, he pointed out, would require, apart from the necessary medical expertise which of course Dr. Graesler possessed to an eminent degree, also certain administrative and business skills which Dr. Graesler had not yet had the opportunity to practice. The doctor, who had to admit that Boehlinger's reservations were justified, now wondered if this were not the right time to speak of Fräulein Schleheim, who would be more than capable of managing the business aspects of the project. But he felt that the old bachelor sitting opposite him was the last person who would understand so strange an affair of the heart. Graesler knew all too well that Boehlinger never missed a chance to speak slightingly, even cynically, about women, and Graesler could not have tolerated calmly a flippant remark about Sabine.

Boehlinger had not made a secret of the experience that had made him so contemptuous of women. One year at the town's annual masked ball, where respectable citizens rubbed shoulders not only with theater people but with persons of even more dubious moral standing, Boehlinger had quite casually won the supreme favors of a lady who no one in their wildest dreams thought capable of such wanton conduct. The woman, who had not dropped her mask even in the ecstasy of passion, believed that her identity then and ever after had remained a secret. But by a strange coincidence, Boehlinger had discovered the identity of his lover that night. And because he had told Graesler about his adventure but had consistently refused to divulge the woman's name, there wasn't a female creature in town, girl or woman, whom Graesler did not at one time or another suspect of being the one—and the more spotless the lady's reputation, the more he suspected her.

This adventure was responsible for Boehlinger's determination never to enter into an intimate relationship, let alone a marriage, with any of the women in town. And so he, a highly esteemed lawyer in a town that greatly prized respectability and morality, was forced to gather experience by short and mysterious trips out of town—experiences that would naturally only confirm his bitter attitude toward the fair sex. It would have been unwise therefore to draw Sabine's name into the conversation, doubly so since he had for the time being spurned the pure sweet creature who had thrown herself into his arms, and thus perhaps lost her forever. Graesler therefore said little more about his plans for the future and evaded the matter by explaining that he wished to wait for further reports from the architect. Finally he invited his boyhood friend, albeit less warmly than he had meant to, to call on him at his house on Burggraben as soon as he could, which caused him to remember that he owed him thanks for his supervision of the wallpapering of the house. Boehlinger modestly declined his thanks but said he looked forward to seeing the place again, which was filled with memories of days long ago for him too. They shook hands and looked into each other's eyes. Those of the lawyer moistened, but even so Graesler did not experience the pleasant nostalgia he had vainly expected throughout the day and which might have redeemed this unpleasant hour.

A minute later he was standing in the street with a feeling of agonizing inner emptiness. The sky had cleared, and it had become warmer. Dr. Graesler walked along the main street, stopping to look at a few shop windows and feeling mildly pleased that even his hometown was finally showing the influence of modern taste. Fi-

nally he went into a haberdashery to buy a hat and a few other trifles. This time, instead of the kind he usually picked, he chose a soft
hat with a broad brim. A glance in the mirror assured him that it was
more becoming to him than the stiff hats he usually wore, and when
back on the street, he was certain that women and girls gave him
friendlier glances. As dusk began to fall, it suddenly occurred to him
that a letter from Sabine might have arrived, and he hurried home to
find a number of letters, mostly forwarded to him from the resort—
but nothing from Sabine. Disappointed at first, he realized that he
had expected the improbable, indeed the impossible, and he left the
house again to resume his aimless walking. Later, on a whim, he decided to board a horse tram that had stopped right next to him, and
to ride a short distance. He stood on the rear platform of the car and
remembered, with a touch of nostalgia, that where there were now
suburban houses, there had been open fields and farmland in the
days of his boyhood. Most of the passengers gradually disembarked,
and it struck him then that no conductor had asked him for fare.
Looking around, he encountered two eyes that met his with friendly
mockery. They belonged to a young, rather pale girl who, dressed
simply but charmingly in a light dress, had probably been standing
next to him on the platform the whole time. "You're wondering why
no conductor has come around," she said, tossing her head back and
looking cheerfully up at Graesler as she held the brim of her black
straw hat.

"That's true," he said, a little stiffly.

"There is no conductor," the young girl explained. "But up
ahead, there, near the driver, is a box where you're supposed to drop
your ten-cent coin."

"Thank you," said the doctor, and made his way to the front and
did as he was told. He returned to the platform and said, "Thank you
very much, Fräulein; that's really a very practical arrangement—
especially for crooks."

"Crooks wouldn't have a chance. We're all honest people around here."

"I'm sure you are. But what would the other passengers have taken me for?"

"For a stranger, which is what you are, isn't it?" She looked at him inquisitively.

"Well, you could call me that," he answered. He looked up, then turned to her again. "What kind of stranger do you take me for?"

"Of course now I can tell that you're a German, perhaps even from near here. But at first I thought you were from afar, from Spain or from Portugal."

"Portugal?" he repeated and involuntarily touched his hat. "No, I'm not a Portuguese. But I've been there," he added casually.

"I thought so. You've traveled a lot?"

"A bit," answered Graesler, and his eyes lit up with the memory of foreign lands and seas. He noticed with satisfaction that the young girl's expression now held a certain admiration and curiosity. Then, quite unexpectedly, she said, "I've got to get off here. I hope you have a pleasant stay in our town."

"Thank you, Fräulein," Graesler said, and tipped his hat. The young girl disembarked and now nodded at him from the street with greater familiarity than would be expected after such a short acquaintance. Following a bold impulse, Graesler also jumped off the tram, which had just started to move, and went up to her. She had stopped in surprise. "Since you were good enough to wish me a pleasant stay just now, Fräulein," he said, "and since our acquaintance has begun so promisingly, perhaps . . ."

"Promisingly?" the girl interrupted him. "What do you mean?"

That sounded like a genuine rebuff, and so Graesler continued in a more modest tone: "I mean—Fräulein, your conversation is so charming, it would really be a pity—"

She shrugged lightly. "I'm almost home, and I'm expected for dinner."

"Just a quarter of an hour?"

"I really can't do it. Good evening." She turned to go.

"Please, not yet," Dr. Graesler exclaimed anxiously. "We don't want to end our acquaintance so abruptly."

The girl stopped and smiled. She turned back toward him and looked at him from beneath the brim of her black straw hat.

"Of course not," she said. "If I should see you anywhere, I would recognize you at once—you're the man—from Portugal."

"But what if I begged you, Fräulein, to give me the pleasure of talking with you for an hour?"

"An hour? You must have a lot of time on your hands."

"As much as you would like, Fräulein."

"Unfortunately, the same isn't true of me."

"It isn't always true of me, either."

"But you're on vacation now?"

"In a way, yes. You see, I'm a doctor. Allow me to introduce myself. Dr. Emil Graesler—born here and now back home again," he added hastily, as if acknowledging some guilt.

The young girl smiled. "You're from here?" she said. "My, how you disguise yourself! A person had better be careful with you!" She looked up at him and shook her head.

"But when can I see you again?" Graesler asked, this time more urgently.

She thought for a moment, and then said, "If it really wouldn't bore you too much, you can walk me home again tomorrow evening."

"Delighted, delighted. And where may I meet you?"

"The best thing would be for you to stroll up and down the street across from the store where I work, Kleimann's glove shop, Wilhelmstrasse 24. We close at seven. Then, if you like, you can ride home with me on the tram again." She smiled.

"Is that really all the time you can give me?"

"What can I do? I have to be home at eight o'clock."

"You live with your parents, Fräulein?"

She glanced up at him again. "Well, I suppose I must tell you who I am. My name is Katharina Rebner, and my father is a post office employee. And there, you see, there in the third story where you see an open window, is where we live—my father, my mother, and I. I have a sister who's married, and she's coming to see us tonight as she always does on Thursdays. And that's why I have to go right home."

"Today—but surely not every day?" Dr. Graesler put in quickly.

"What do you mean, Herr Doctor?"

"You don't spend all your evenings at home, do you? Surely you have friends you visit . . . or you go to the theater?"

"People like me don't often get to places like that." Suddenly she nodded in a friendly way to a man who walked on the other side of the street. He was dressed simply, in the manner of a skilled workman. He was no longer young and carried a package. He acknowledged her greeting curtly, evidently without noticing Graesler.

"That's my brother-in-law. That means my sister is already home. So now I really must go."

"I hope my having come so near your house with you won't make trouble for you?"

"Trouble? Happily, I'm of age, and at home they know who they're dealing with. Well, goodbye then, Herr Doctor."

"Till tomorrow!"

"Yes."

Dr. Graesler repeated, "Seven o'clock in the Wilhelmstrasse."

She remained standing and seemed to contemplate something. Suddenly she looked up at him and said hastily, "Seven o'clock, yes. But"—she hesitated—"you did mention the theater—and you won't be angry with me if—"

"Why should I be angry with you?"

"I mean, since you mentioned it before—if you were to bring tickets for the theater with you, that would be very nice. I haven't been in such a long time!"

"I'll be only too glad to! It would make me very happy to do that small favor for you."

"But please don't get expensive seats, the sort you're probably used to. I wouldn't like that."

"Don't worry about it, Fräulein—Fräulein Katharina."

"You're sure you're not angry with me, Herr Doctor?"

"But—Fräulein Katharina, angry—?"

"Well, goodbye then, Herr Doctor," and she gave him her hand. "Now I really must hurry. Tomorrow I don't have to be home so early." She turned around so quickly that he couldn't make out her expression when she said this, but there was a hint of promise in her voice.

As soon as Dr. Graesler was back home, Sabine's image returned to him with powerful longing. He had an irresistible impulse to write to her, if only a few lines. So he wrote her that he had arrived safely, had found his house in perfect order, had had a long but inconclusive talk with his old friend Boehlinger, and that tomorrow, in order to make good use of his time, he would visit the hospital where an old student friend from his student days now headed a ward, as he had probably mentioned. He signed these hasty lines "In heartfelt friendship, Emil." Once more he hurried outside to take the letter to the train station personally so that it would go out with the evening post.

9

The next morning, just as he had told Sabine he would, Dr. Graesler went to the hospital. He was cordially welcomed by the chief physician, and he then asked permission to accompany members of the staff on the day's rounds. He followed the doctors with an interest that gratified him. He asked for fuller information about the courses and treatments of the more notable cases, and he didn't hesitate to add a dissenting opinion at times, always with the self-deprecating preamble, "Insofar as it's possible for us health resort doctors to keep in touch with the advances of scientific medicine . . ." At lunch he joined a few assistant physicians at a modest restaurant across the street from the hospital, and he so enjoyed talking to his young colleagues that he decided to come back often. On the way home he bought the theater tickets. At home he leafed through medical books and journals, more and more distractedly as the hours passed, partly in expectation of a letter from Sabine, partly in vague imaginings of how the coming evening would go. To prepare for all eventualities, he decided to have a cold supper and a couple of bottles of wine at the ready—this didn't commit him to anything, after all. He made the necessary purchases, arranged for their delivery, and at a couple of minutes before seven he paced up and down the Wilhemstrasse. This time he did not wear yesterday's romantic hat but rather—in order to be less conspicuous and also, he imagined, to test the genuineness of Katharina's feeling—his usual stiff black hat.

He was looking at a window display when he heard Katharina's voice behind him: "Good evening, Herr Doctor." He turned around, shook her hand, and was delighted to see her so well-dressed and attractive that anyone would take her for a well-brought-up, middleclass girl—which, as the daughter of a civil servant, in fact she was, Graesler hastened to remind himself.

"What do you suppose my brother-in-law took you for yesterday?" she began promptly.

"I have no idea . . . for a Portuguese too?"

"No, not that. He thought you were a chorus conductor. He said you looked exactly like a conductor he once knew."

"Well, did you tell him I was something better—or something worse?

"I told him what you really are. Yes, I did. Was that all right?"

"I have no reason to make a secret of my profession. Did you also tell your family that you were going to the theater with me tonight?"

"That's none of their business. And, besides, no one asked me. Anyway, I could go there alone if I wanted to—don't you think?"

"Of course. But I like it better this way."

She looked up at him, putting her hand to the brim of her hat as was her custom. "It's no fun alone. The theater is only really fun when you're with someone. Someone has to sit next to you who laughs when you laugh, someone you can look at and—"

"And what? Go on."

"And whose arm you can squeeze when it's especially delightful."

"I hope it's particularly delightful tonight—I'm at your disposal in any case."

She laughed lightly and quickened her pace, as if worried she would miss the beginning.

"We're early," said Dr. Graesler, when they had reached the theater. "It won't start for another fifteen minutes."

She didn't listen. With her eyes sparkling she led the way to the first tier, hardly noticed when he helped her off with her jacket, and only when they were seated in the third row did she look at him gratefully.

Dr. Graesler glanced about the moderately full auditorium for a sight of anyone he knew. Here and there he saw a face he recognized, but no one was likely to recognize him in the dim light of the auditorium.

The curtain rose. The play was a vulgar modern farce. Katharina enjoyed it immensely and often laughed out loud, but without turning to Graesler. In the first intermission he bought her a box of bonbons, which she accepted with a grateful smile. During the second act she nodded at him from time to time when she found something particularly funny. Dr. Graesler was a little distracted and not paying close attention to the play when he suddenly felt a pair of opera glasses leveled at him from one of the boxes. He recognized Boehlinger and greeted him without embarrassment, completely ignoring his old friend's smiling and knowing look of inquiry. During the last intermission, as he strolled with Katharina through the lobby, he suddenly took her arm, which she allowed without protest, and gave her his opinion of the acting in a soft and insistent way, as if sharing a delicious secret with his charming companion. He was a little disappointed not to see Boehlinger. The bell for the last act rang, and when Graesler was again sitting next to Katharina, he moved so close to her that their arms touched. And because she didn't draw away, he felt that a more and more intimate relationship was gradually being established between them. Afterward, at the check room, he ventured a fleeting touch of her hair and cheeks as he helped her into her coat.

Standing outside in front of the theater, she looked up at him from under her hat and said, in a tone that wasn't very serious, "Well, I've got to be getting home now."

"But first," he skillfully interposed, "you'll do me the honor of taking a little supper with me, won't you Fräulein Katharina?"

She looked at him dubiously for an instant, then gave a quick, earnest nod of assent, as if understanding more than he had actually said. And like lovers whose footsteps are hastened by passion, they hurried arm in arm though the dark streets toward his home.

When they arrived at his apartment and he turned on the light in his study, Katharina glanced around and looked at the pictures and the books with curiosity.

"Do you like my place?" he asked.

She nodded.

"It's a very old house, isn't it?"

"Three hundred years, at least."

"But everything looks so new!"

He was happy to show her the other rooms. She liked the furniture and the way it was arranged, but when they went into his sister's room, she looked at him with suspicion.

"Don't tell me you're married after all," she said, "and your wife is merely away?"

He smiled, then passed his hand over his forehead and explained to her in a muffled voice that this newly redecorated room had been intended for his sister, who had died just a few months ago in a southern country. Katharina looked at him searchingly. Then she moved closer to him, took his hand and stroked it caressingly, making him feel wonderful. He turned off the light and they went into the dining room. Only now was she prevailed upon to remove her hat and her jacket. But after that she was quickly at home. When he began to set the table, she wouldn't allow it, insisting that it was her task. At her playful demand, he seated himself in a chair at the other end of the room and observed with some emotion the wifely way in which she prepared for the evening meal and moved about his kitchen and dining room as if she had kept house there for a long time. Finally they both seated themselves at the table. She served, he poured the wine, and they ate and drank. She talked with delight about the evening and was amazed to hear that Graesler rarely went to the theater, which was for her the height of human pleasure. He explained to her that the conditions of his occupation gave him few opportunities for such amusements, as he changed his residence every six months and had in fact just returned from practicing at a small German spa. And he would soon travel across the sea to a distant island where there was no winter, where tall palm trees grew, and where people drove in quaint little carriages through a yellow land beneath a burning sun.

Katharina asked him whether there were a lot of snakes there.

"One can protect oneself against them," he said.

"And when do you have to go back there?"

"Soon. Would you like to come along?" he asked in jest, but in the mood induced by the consumption of several glasses of wine in quick succession, he felt there was a hint of seriousness in it.

Without looking at him, she answered him calmly, "Why not?"

He moved closer to her and put his arm gently around her shoulder. She pushed it away, which did not displease him. He rose, determined from then on to treat Katharina like a lady, and politely asked her permission to light a cigar. As he smoked, he walked back and forth across the room and spoke seriously and impressively of the strange course of a man's days, not one of which could be predicted. He told her about all the places in the north and the south to which his work had led him, and hinted at the places where it might take him still. Once in a while he stopped next to Katharina, who was eating dates and nuts, and gently put his hand on her brown hair. She listened to him with interest, occasionally interrupting him with eager questions. At times her eyes lit up with a peculiar mocking expression that made Graesler talk even more eagerly and knowingly. When the clock on the wall struck midnight, Katharina arose as though it were an irrevocable signal to leave. Graesler pretended to be upset, though at heart he felt a certain relief. Before Katharina left, she cleared the table, returned the chairs to their proper place, and tidied the room. At the door, she suddenly raised herself up on tiptoe and offered him her lips.

"That's because you've been so well behaved," she said, and again there was that peculiar mocking gleam in her eyes. They went down the stairs by the light of a flickering candle that Graesler carried. At the corner there was a carriage for hire. Graesler got in with Katharina; she leaned against him, and he put his arm around her. In this manner they rode silently through the deserted streets, until, when they were near Katharina's house, Graesler impetuously pulled the young girl toward him and covered her with passionate kisses.

"When will I see you again?" he asked as the carriage came to a stop a little distance from Katharina's door.

She promised to come again the next evening. She disembarked, asked him not to accompany her to the door, then disappeared into the shadow of the houses.

The next morning Dr. Graesler did not feel the least desire to visit the hospital. But later, as he walked in the park in the cool, clear, autumn sunshine at an hour when everyone else was at work, he felt a pang of conscience, as though he had to answer not only to himself but also to someone else. That someone, he knew, was Sabine. The idea of Dr. Frank's sanatorium suddenly overtook him. He began to think about all kinds of possible renovations, considered the installation of new spa rooms, and drafted proposals in far more convincing language than had ever before been at his command. He vowed to return to the resort and settle the matter the instant he heard from Sabine. If she didn't answer his last letter, everything would be over, at least between Sabine and him. As for the sanatorium, there was no reason, actually, to make its purchase dependent on her behavior. In fact, it wouldn't be a bad idea—on the contrary, it would be a devilishly good idea—to move into the beautifully renovated place with a new Frau Director, if possible one who didn't regard him as an egotistical, pedantic bore. If it should please him to choose Fräulein Katharina as his companion, then, certainly, no one could say he was a pedant or a prig!

He sat down on a bench. Children ran past him. A mellow autumnal sun shone through the russet foliage. From a distant factory, a whistle signaled the noon hour. This evening, he thought. Is my youth returning? Is there still time for such an adventure? Shouldn't I be on my guard? Should I go away? Right now—take the next boat to Lanzarote? Or—back to Sabine? To the creature with the pure soul? Hmm! Who knows how her life would have turned out if the right man had come along at the right moment—not a shameless tenor or a hangdog doctor. . . . He got up and went to have lunch in the town's most elegant restaurant, where he wouldn't be bothered by the young doctors' shoptalk as he had been yesterday. Everything else could be decided later.

10

That afternoon he had just seated himself at his desk and opened his anatomical encyclopedia when there was a knock on the door; the printer's wife, the woman who kept house for him, entered. With profuse apologies, she asked if the Herr Doctor couldn't perhaps do her the favor of giving her a few pieces of clothing from his poor deceased sister's wardrobe. Graesler frowned. This woman, he said to himself, would never have had the cheek to make such a shameless request if I hadn't had a female visitor in my house last night! He answered evasively that he intended to give all such things to deserving charities in his sister's memory, and that in any case he didn't have time at the moment to look into the matter and therefore couldn't promise anything. It turned out that the woman had brought the key to the attic just in case, and she handed it to the doctor with an officious smile, thanking him before she left as effusively as if her request had already been granted. Since Graesler now had the key in his hand and was secretly pleased to find a way to pass the time, he decided into go up to the attic. He had not been there since childhood. He went up the wooden staircase, opened the door, and walked into a narrow room which was so dimly lit by the slanted window in the roof that he only gradually oriented himself. Forgotten and useless odds and ends stood in the dark corners, but the middle of the room was filled with boxes and trunks. The first one he opened appeared to hold nothing but old curtains and linens, and Graesler, who had no intention of unpacking and arranging things, let its lid fall shut. The long coffinlike box that he now opened seemed to promise more interesting things. Graesler saw all sorts of papers, from legal documents to old letters, and large and small packages tied with string. On one of the smaller packages he read: "From father's estate." Dr. Graesler hadn't realized that his sister had so carefully preserved this sort of thing. He took up a second package, this one sealed three times, on which was written in large letters, "To be burned unread." Dr. Graesler shook his head sadly. My dear Friederike, he vowed, your wish shall be fulfilled at the first opportunity. He replaced the package, which probably contained diaries and innocent love letters from her girlhood, and opened a third trunk. It was filled with all types of fabric—scarves, shawls, ribbons, and yellowed lace. He picked up a few pieces and let them run through his hands; he thought he recognized some of them as his mother's or even his grandmother's. His sister had worn a few of them, especially in her younger days, and he remembered that she had recently worn the beautiful Indian shawl with the green embroidered foliage and flowers, the gift of a wealthy patient. The shawl, as well as a number of other things, was quite unsuitable for the printer's wife or for a charity—but it was just the right thing for a pretty young woman who was cheering up a lonely old bachelor and sweetening the few hours he had at home. He closed the trunk with particular care, hung the shawl over his arm, smoothed it out, and with a lighthearted smile carried it down from the attic, which was now gradually sinking into darkness.

He didn't have to wait long before Katharina arrived. She was a little early, having come directly from the shop without freshening up, as she remarked apologetically and merrily. Dr. Graesler was glad she was here; he kissed her hand, and with a humorous, exaggerated bow, presented her with the shawl, which lay on the table ready for her.

"What on earth is that?" she asked with an air of surprise.

"Something to make you look beautiful," he answered, "though you don't exactly need it."

"You shouldn't have," she exclaimed, lifting up the shawl and letting it slide through her fingers. She put it around her shoulders, studied herself in the mirror with delight, and finally turned to Graesler, looked up at him, took his head in her hands, and drew his lips to hers.

"A thousand thanks," she said.

"That's not enough for me."

"A million, then."

He nodded.

"Thank you," she said, and gave him her lips to kiss. He took her in his arms and told her that he had picked out the beautiful shawl from among the things in the attic this afternoon, and that he was sure there were many others in the boxes and trunks up there that would be just as becoming to her as this. She shook her head, as though she would never again accept such a costly gift. He asked her how she had enjoyed last night, and whether she had had to work hard in the store today, and after she had told him everything he wanted to know, he gave her a report of his day as if she were a dear old friend. He told her that he had played hooky from the hospital and had instead lounged about in the park, remembering his far-off childhood when he had played within the old overgrown walls. Then he told her other stories about his past, especially—half by chance and half by design—about his adventures when he was a doctor aboard ship. When Katharina interrupted him with eager childlike questions about the appearance, dress, and customs of strange people in distant lands, about coral reefs and storms at sea, he felt as though he had to translate the things he had just told to good effect in a better circle into a language suitable for a more naive but therefore more appreciative audience. And he unconsciously adopted the tone and manner of a fa-

vorite uncle who seeks to delight and stir children with tales of remarkable adventures told in the dark.

Katharina, who sat next to him on the sofa with her hands in
his, had just gotten up to prepare supper when the doorbell rang.
Graesler started. What could it be? His thoughts raced. A telegram?
From the ranger's lodge? Sabine? Was her father ill? Or her mother?
Or did it have something to do with the sanatorium? An urgent inquiry from the owner? Was someone else interested in buying it? Or
could it be Sabine herself? What on earth would he do if it were her?
Well, she wouldn't take him to be an old prude anymore. But young
women with pure souls don't ring at bachelor's doors so late in the
evening. The bell rang again, shriller than the first time. He saw
Katharina's eyes on him, questioning but unperturbed. All too unperturbed, it suddenly seemed to him. It could have something to do
with her. Her father? Her brother-in-law—the alleged brother-in-
law? A scam? A blackmail attempt? Ah! It served him right. How
could he have let himself in for such an affair! An old fool, that's
what he was. But they wouldn't succeed. He wouldn't let himself be
intimidated. He had faced plenty of dangers and overcome them.
Damn it all, a bullet had just missed him on that South Sea island. A
handsome young, blond naval officer had fallen down dead next to
him. "Don't you want to see who it is?" asked Katharina, and
seemed surprised at his strange expression.

"Of course," he said.

"Who can it be, this late?" he heard her ask—the hypocrite—
when he was already at the living room door. He closed it behind
him and looked through the peephole of the front door into the hallway. A woman he didn't recognize stood there bareheaded, with a
candle in her hand.

"Who is it?" he asked.

"Excuse me, is the doctor at home? Please, I'm Frau Sommer's
maid."

"I don't know any Frau Sommer."

"She's the one on the first floor. Her little girl is very ill. Could I speak to the doctor?"

Graesler drew a breath of relief. He remembered that a widow by the name of Sommer lived here in the building with her little seven-year-old daughter. She must be the attractive woman in mourning whom he had met on the staircase only yesterday—he had turned to look at her almost without thinking.

"I'm Dr. Graesler. What is it?"

"If you'd be so good as to look at her, the little girl is very hot and keeps on crying."

"I don't practice here in town. I'm only here on a visit. I'd rather you asked another doctor."

"It's not easy to get someone so late at night."

"It isn't so late."

A gleam of light from an open door suddenly fell on the lower landing.

"Anna," someone whispered.

"That's Frau Sommer," said the servant quickly.

She rushed to the railing.

"Madam?"

"What's taking you so long? Isn't the doctor at home?"

Graesler also walked over to the railing and looked down. The woman at the bottom of the staircase, her face indistinct in the half light, raised her hands to him as if to a savior.

"Praise God! You'll come, Herr Doctor, you'll come right away, won't you? My little girl . . . I don't know what's the matter with her."

"I'll—I'll come, of course. Just a moment, please. I must bring my thermometer with me. Just a minute, madam—"

"Thank you," came the whisper, as Dr. Graesler closed the door behind him. He went quickly into the room where Katharina waited for him expectantly; she leaned against the table looking at him. He felt a profound tenderness toward her, all the more so because of his despicable earlier suspicions. She seemed so touching, almost angelic. He walked up to her and stroked her hair.

"Bad luck," he said. "They're asking me to come to see a sick child here in the building, and I can't possibly refuse. There seems to be nothing left but to put you in a cab."

She took his hand, which still rested on her hair.

"You're sending me away?"

"Not willingly, believe me. Or—would you really be patient enough to wait for me?"

She stroked his hand.

"If it doesn't take all night."

"I'll be as quick as I can. You're very, very sweet."

He kissed her on the forehead and hastened into his office to retrieve his doctor's bag, which was always at hand; then he encouraged Katharina to enjoy her supper and turned back to look at her from the doorway. She gave him a friendly nod, and he hurried down the stairs, cheered by the happy expectation of a loving reception from a sweet young thing when he returned from a somber professional visit.

Dr. Graesler found Frau Sommer at the bedside of her little girl, who tossed feverishly as he entered. After a few preliminary questions, he conducted a thorough examination, then informed the mother that a rash could soon break out. The mother was in despair. She had lost another child three years ago, and only six months ago her husband had died suddenly while abroad on a business trip; indeed she hadn't even seen his grave. What would become of her if she were robbed of the one thing she had left? Dr. Graesler explained that at the moment there was no reason for alarm. It could be a simple case of sore throat, but even if it were something more serious, such a well-nourished and strong-looking child would have enough resistance to overcome it. He gave her other reassurances as well, and was pleased to see that his reasonable words had their desired effect. He prescribed what was necessary, and the servant was sent to a nearby pharmacy. In the meantime, Graesler remained at the patient's bedside, feeling the child's pulse minute by minute and often putting his hand on the child's hot, dry forehead, where it sometimes met with the hand of the worried mother. After a lengthy silence, she began to ask anxious questions again, and he took her hands paternally and spoke to her kindly—thinking that Sabine would be pleased with him. At the same time he noticed in the muted light of the green-shaded ceiling lamp that the young widow's housedress revealed a graceful figure. When the maid returned, he rose and repeated what he had already explained—that unfortunately he could not continue to take care of the child as he was leaving town in a few days. The mother begged him to attend to the child at least until he left town. She had had bad experiences with the local doctors, whereas he had immediately inspired her confidence. If anyone could save her child, she felt, it was he. And so he promised to come again tomorrow morning, and, after he had watched quietly at the little girl's bedside for a few moments longer and she had begun to breathe more easily, he shook the mother's hand warmly and left, followed by her grateful, fervent glances.

As quickly as he could, he rushed up to the second floor, unlocked his door, and entered the dining room. He found it empty. So she didn't have much patience after all. It was only to be expected. And just as well, perhaps, as the child downstairs was probably developing an infectious disease. That had probably occurred to her as well. Of course, Sabine wouldn't have fled in such an event. In any case, Katharina evidently had taken the time to enjoy the supper! He contemplated the table with the remains of the meal on it, and his lips twitched contemptuously. It wouldn't be a bad idea, he told himself, if he were to go back downstairs and keep the pretty widow company. He felt that, even now, at the bedside of her feverish child, he could do anything he wanted with her, and the depravity of such a notion gave him a pleasant thrill. "But I won't go downstairs," he said to himself, "I am and always will be a prude—for which Sabine would probably forgive me in this case."

The door to his office was open. He stepped in and turned on the light. Of course, Katharina wasn't there either. But switching the light off, he noticed a gleam of light coming from beneath his bedroom door. A faint hope stirred within him. He hesitated; whatever might happen, it did him good to bask in the warmth of such an expectation for a moment. Now he heard a rustling sound in the room. He opened the door and there was Katharina, sitting on his bed, looking up at him from a big volume that she was holding both hands.

"You're not angry with me?" she said simply. Her brown, softly curling hair fell loosely over her pale shoulders. How beautiful she was! Graesler stood motionless in the doorway. He smiled, for the book on the bedspread was his anatomical encyclopedia.

"What's that you picked out?" he asked, approaching her bashfully.

"It was lying on your desk. Should I not have taken it? Sorry! But I would probably have fallen asleep if I hadn't taken it, and I'm so hard to wake up." Her eyes smiled, not mockingly this time but with an air of surrender. Graesler sat down on the bed next to her, drew her to him, and kissed her on the neck. The heavy book shut with a snap.

11

The next morning, while Dr. Graesler visited his little patient, whose illness now clearly revealed itself as scarlet fever, Katharina disappeared from his apartment. But she appeared again early in the evening and, to Graesler's great surprise, she carried a suitcase. She had mentioned the night before that she was entitled to three weeks' vacation every year, and hadn't yet used it this summer as if in premonition that she should save it for now. Upon hearing this in the intoxication of their first embraces, he had invited her on a little honeymoon trip. But now, when she arrived fully prepared for a trip and greeted him cheerfully with the words, "Here I am. If you like, we can go straight to the station," something in him revolted against the offhand way in which she was claiming a piece of his life, and he was happy to plead that his professional responsibility for the little girl would keep him in town for the next few days. Katharina wasn't particularly perturbed by this and immediately chatted on about other things. She showed him her pretty new yellow shoes and told him all about the head of her firm, who had just returned from Paris and London with new merchandise. As she talked, she went about the room straightening up a few books here and there and tidying up his desk while Graesler, standing at the window, watched her silently, moved somehow. As his glance fell on her little suitcase, which stood on the floor looking melancholy and ashamed, a measure of pity came over him at the thought that the good creature would soon have to take it away again. At first he avoided saying anything about it, but later, as he sat in his desk chair and she sat on his lap like a child with her arms around his neck, he said,

"Does it have to be an out-of-town trip? Why not just spend your vacation here at home with me?"

"Well, that wouldn't be possible, would it?" she answered weakly.

"Why not? Isn't it lovely here?" He pointed through the window to the distant hills on the horizon, and added jokingly, "I'll make sure you're satisfied with your room and board." And with sudden decisiveness he stood up, offered Katharina his arm, and led her into his sister's room. He switched on the hanging lamp, so that a soft reddish glow suffused the room, and with a sweeping gesture he offered her everything that she could see as if it were a gift for her. Katharina was struck dumb, and finally shook her head earnestly.

"Wouldn't you like it?" Graesler asked tenderly.

"But it's impossible," she answered in a hushed voice.

"Why? It's quite possible." And as though her only objection was a superstitious one, he explained, "Everything here is brand new, even the wallpaper—it didn't look half as nice before." And with hesitation he added, "Perhaps everything was meant to happen this way."

"Don't say that," she said, as though frightened. Then she looked around the room and her face brightened as she stroked the flowered chintz of the armchair that stood near the bed. Her eyes fell on the light muslin curtains that had been pulled back around the dressing table to reveal a pretty toilet set and a number of cut-glass bottles. As she stood there absorbed in what she saw, Graesler hurried out of the room and returned a few seconds later with her little suitcase. She turned to him, gave a little start, then smiled half incredulously. He nodded to her; she shook her head, and then, as if finally persuaded, she held out her arms to him. Touched, he put down the little suitcase and clasped her proudly to his breast.

A wonderful interlude followed, the equal of any Graesler had enjoyed in his youth, if not better. Like a happy pair of newlyweds, they spent most of the day within their own four walls, assiduously waited upon by the printer's wife. She accepted the situation— which was, after all, quite unusual for the town—with equanimity as Dr. Graesler had in the meantime gratified her immodest wish for a number of items from his sister's wardrobe. In the evenings the couple walked arm in arm, tenderly pressed against one another, through the quieter streets of the town, and once, early on a sunny

afternoon, they drove into the country in an open carriage, quite unconcerned by the possibility of encountering one of Katharina's relatives who thought the girl was staying at a friend's house in the
country. One day, while they were still at table, Boehlinger called on
them. Dr. Graesler, who had worried about admitting him, was afterward all the more pleased he had received him, as the lawyer treated
his charming companion most politely, addressing her as "madam."
After quickly taking care of the business matter that had brought
him there, Boehlinger upon leaving lightly kissed Katharina's hand
with the cool grace of a man of the world. After this incident
Graesler was filled with a heightened tenderness for Katharina, who
had played the part of lady of the house to perfection.

12

Dr. Graesler visited his little patient every morning, after which he
took a thirty-minute walk to minimize the risk of infecting Katharina. The illness, which had begun so alarmingly, took a surprisingly
easy course. After the anxiety of the first few days, Frau Sommer
proved to be a sociable, cheerful, and talkative person who, whether
by chance or design, was not too careful about whether the robe in
which she received her daughter's physician every morning was as
carefully closed across the bosom as strict respectability would dic-
tate. She never neglected to inquire after Graesler's "little friend," as
she liked to call Katharina. And she asked whether he intended to
take his sweetheart with him to Africa—this being the place she had
fixed upon as Graesler's winter destination—or whether he already
had a beautiful woman there, perhaps even a black one, who awaited
him with longing. Once she even insisted on giving him a cone of
chocolate cookies as a gift for Katharina, which he however refused
for fear of infection. Katharina, on the other hand, made derisive remarks about the young widow, which despite the fact that they were

motivated in part by jealousy, didn't seem entirely off the mark to Graesler. It appeared that during her husband's lifetime Frau Sommer's reputation had not been wholly above suspicion. He had been a traveling salesman, seldom at home with his wife. And as she had brought the little girl into her marriage, it was not certain if he was the girl's father. Katharina found all this out from the printer's wife. She talked with her more often and more intimately in the late afternoon hours when Dr. Graesler was not at home than he found suitable.

He once tried to make his beloved aware of the inappropriate nature of this intimacy, but since Katharina seemed scarcely to understand his misgivings, he didn't bring the matter up again—he didn't wish to darken their few remaining days of happiness with domestic discord. In any case, he was determined to regard this experience merely as a lovely adventure that would have no future consequences. Whenever she asked with modest curiosity and seeming indifference about his winter plans and about the climate and social life of the island of Lanzarote, he answered as briefly as possible and turned the conversation to another topic in an attempt to avoid raising hopes he had no intention of fulfilling. In his unwavering desire to enjoy these brief weeks without any clouds, he asked her little about her past. Content to live in the present, he was delighted not only with the happiness he enjoyed but even more so with the happiness he gave.

Nevertheless, as the days and nights progressed, a longing for Sabine began to stir powerfully within him, especially in the early morning hours when Katharina still slept at his side. He thought about how much happier he would be, how much more worthy his life would be if, instead of this pretty little shopgirl—who had certainly had two or three lovers in addition to the bookkeeper to whom she had been engaged, who lied to her parents and gossiped with the housekeeper—if instead of this insignificant creature, whose charm and kindness he didn't deny, it were the blonde head of that wonderful creature that lay on the pillow beside him—the one who with a pure soul had offered to be his life's companion, and whom he had spurned out of a completely unjustified lack of self-confidence. He was certain she had taken his timid and foolish letter as a definitive rejection. And in fact, that's what he had intended. But couldn't he make amends for what he had done in awkwardness and haste? Or was it possible the feelings that Sabine had expressed toward him in such a considerate manner were now completely extinguished and could not be rekindled? Hadn't he set a time limit for consideration of the matter—and wasn't she now, by not writing to him, merely complying with his request? Wasn't her silence in fact the very mark of what was noble and true in her? And if, at the end of the time limit he himself had set, he went to her and laid his final, well-considered, and therefore much more valuable consent at her feet— would he really find her a different person from the one he had left? In the peace and quiet of the lodge no other suitor was likely to have approached her, and in any case her pure heart would not have been disturbed either by a foolish but well-meant letter, nor by the sudden onset of a new passion. These anxious thoughts were nothing but the last flickers of his lonely and timid personality, to which self-confidence and trust had been miraculously restored by a wonderful stroke of fate. More and more it seemed to him that Katharina's true mission was to lead him back to Sabine, in whose love the entire meaning of his existence lay. And the more trustingly and unconditionally Katharina offered him her sunny young heart, the more impatiently and hopefully he yearned for Sabine.

As October drew to an end, external circumstances also demanded a decision. Dr. Graesler thought it advantageous to advise the owner of the sanatorium that he would call on him in a few days and settle the affair. Since no answer came, he sent a telegram asking whether he could count on meeting Dr. Frank on such and such a day.

When even this telegram did not elicit a reply, he was annoyed, but not alarmed, as he remembered what an irritable and impolite curmudgeon the old man was. As for writing to Sabine and announcing his arrival, he felt incapable of doing so after what had happened—he would simply go to her, stand before her, take both her hands in his, and read his redemptive answer in her clear eyes.

13

The date on which Katharina's vacation ended and she had to leave Graesler's house and return to her parents had naturally been fixed at the outset. But as if by mutual agreement, neither of them said a word about the ever more imminent day. And Katharina betrayed so little awareness of the coming separation that Graesler began to worry whether this clingy creature, who one evening had turned up uninvited with her little suitcase, was contemplating spending the rest of her life with him as his companion. As a result, he began to hatch a plan to flee the house and the town one morning as she slept. Inconspicuously, he began to make preparations for his departure. In addition to the Indian shawl and a few modest trinkets, he had given his beloved a number of items of his sister's, saving the more valuable jewelry for Sabine. But on a rainy afternoon two days before his intended departure, while Katharina rested in the room he had given her, as she often did at this time of day, something impelled Graesler to go back up to the attic for a final memento for her, one that would not only salve his conscience but might even comfort her a little after his disappearance. As he rummaged around in the attic, opening one trunk after another, turning over and examining various silks, linens, picture albums, veils, handkerchiefs, ribbons, and laces, he accidentally came across the package of letters that Friederike had directed be burned unread. For the first time, as though he suspected he wouldn't return to this room for a long time, if ever, he felt a tinge of curiosity. He laid the package aside, telling himself that he would put it in a safe place and leave it to a later heir to open without scruples for the wishes of an unknown and long dead person. Afterward, he took a few pretty little things for Katharina, among them a fine amber necklace and a piece of gold oriental embroidery—which, like so many other things, he had never seen Friederike wear—and brought them down along with the heavy package of letters. He put everything on his desk before going into Katharina's room.

When he entered the room, he saw her sitting in the armchair, completely wrapped in the reddish-brown Chinese dressing gown with richly worked gold dragons that he had recently given her. She had fallen asleep over a volume of an illustrated novel, her favorite literature. Touched at the sight, Graesler avoided waking her, returned to his study, and seated himself at his desk. Half lost in thought, he fiddled with the loose threads of yarn that encircled the package of letters until the seals cracked and broke. He shrugged his shoulders. Why not? he said to himself. She is dead, and I don't believe in personal immortality. And even if, against my expectations, there is one, Friederike's soul on high won't take it amiss. There aren't likely to be any dreadful secrets in the letters anyway.

He had soon unwrapped the cover and found a great many letters inside, carefully stacked and separated from one another by sheets of white paper. It was soon evident that they had been carefully arranged. The first one Graesler took up was more than thirty years old and written by a young man named Robert, who evidently had the right to address Friederike in very intimate terms. The content made it clear that this Robert had been a family friend, yet for the life of him Graesler couldn't figure out who he had been. There were about a dozen letters from him: love letters, but really quite innocent ones, and of no great interest to Graesler. The next batch dated from the period when Graesler was sailing around the world as a ship's physician and coming home only briefly every two years.

Now the letters were in various handwritings, and at first Graesler couldn't understand what all these passionate assurances, vows of fidelity, allusions to happy hours, outbursts of jealousy, warnings, vague threats, and fierce vituperations meant, and even less what this furious business could possibly have to do with his sister. He was on the point of deciding that these letters were addressed to someone else, perhaps to one of Friederike's friends who had entrusted them to her for safekeeping, when he suddenly recognized a familiar handwriting. From that and other indications he soon recognized that there was no doubt that all these letters were from Boehlinger.

Soon the interwoven threads of this strange narrative began to unravel, and it became clear to Graesler that more than twenty years ago, when she was already a fairly mature woman, his sister had been secretly engaged to Boehlinger, and that Boehlinger, on account of a previous love affair of Frederike's, had continually postponed the wedding. As a result, Friederike, whether out of impatience, caprice, or revenge, had betrayed him. She had in the end sought a reconciliation with him, but Boehlinger had responded only with outbursts of scorn and contempt. The tone of his last letters was so immoderate, so abusive, that Graesler couldn't understand how a tolerable relationship, in the end even a sort of friendship, had developed between the two.

As his feeling while reading was one of suspense rather than amazement, it was with heightened curiosity that he examined the remaining letters to find out what other secrets they might reveal about Friederike. There were not many letters left, but as these were now written in many different hands, Graesler inferred that after this point Friederike had saved only samples of her correspondence and not the whole of it. A few letters were comprised of nothing but ciphers and numbers, evidently symbols of a secret understanding. After a gap of a few years there followed letters from the period when Friederike had lived with him. There were even letters in French and English, and two in what he took to be a Slavic language, which Graesler was unaware his sister knew. Some of the letters were from suitors, others expressed gratitude. Some were cautious and respectful, others unambiguously passionate. Here and there he saw the vague shadow of one or another of his patients, whom he, an unwitting panderer, had introduced to Friederike. But the last letter, burning with passion, chaotic, and death-haunted, left no doubt that its author was the nineteen-year-old consumptive boy in the final stages of disease whom Graesler had sent home to Germany to die. He asked himself whether his apparently quiet and respectable sister, now revealed as an experienced, passionate woman, had not contributed to the poor boy's all too early demise. For a moment his image of his dead sister was marred by a combination of brotherly disappointment—that she had considered him unworthy of her confidence, and, like Sabine, had obviously thought him a prig—and his anger that to others he must have been as ridiculous as a deceived husband. But in the end, all of this was outweighed by a feeling of satisfaction that Friederike had not wasted her life, that he could feel free of any responsibility for her death, and that she had taken her life because it no longer offered her the pleasures she had once enjoyed in abundance.

And when he examined the letters once more, picking one up here and there and reading a few lines at random, it dawned on him that not everything he had just learned was as new to him as it seemed at first glance. He had witnessed many of the incidents himself without realizing their full significance, or feeling himself entitled to interfere with the freedom of a woman over the age of thirty—for example, the little affair between Friederike and a French captain many years ago at Lake Geneva that one of the letters alluded to. As for Friederike and Boehlinger, of course, it hadn't escaped him that a strong affection existed between the two of them as far back as the distant days of their childhood, though circumstances had prevented him from knowing about their later intimacy. And so it was quite possible that the strange looks that Friederike had sometimes given him in the last few years had not been, as he had then feared, accusations and reproaches but rather pleas for forgiveness for concealing all her feelings and experiences from him and living with him as a complete stranger. Yet he too had told her only of the most harmless of his feelings and life experiences, and had concealed from her everything that would have appeared just as questionable if written about in letters "to be burnt unread." Consequently he felt he had no right to bear her a grudge for the same reserve that he himself had been so careful to observe.

Suddenly Katharina stood behind him and put her hands over his eyes.

"You?" he asked as if waking up.

"I've already been here twice," she said, "but you were so absorbed in what you were doing I didn't want to disturb you." He looked at his watch. It was eight thirty. He had been absorbed in the story of his sister's life for four hours.

"I was just reading some of my poor sister's old letters," he said, pulling Katharina into his lap. "She was a strange woman."

For an instant he thought of telling Katharina something of the story in the letters, but he realized immediately that he would wrong his sister's memory to tell her story to a creature who not only didn't have the wherewithal to understand it but who might even think there were similarities between Friederike and her. So he pushed the letters aside with a gesture that relegated them to the past, and in the tone of a man emerging from dark dreams into a bright present, he asked Katharina what she had been doing with herself. She reported she had read more of her serialized novel, had once again carefully polished the silver and the glass bottles on the dressing table, and had altered some of the buttons on the Chinese robe. She also admitted that for half an hour she had gossiped on the stair landing with the printer's wife, defending her as a good and competent woman even though the straitlaced Herr Doctor didn't like her. Of course Graesler was displeased that Katharina enjoyed gossiping with a person of such low station, and that she had stood on the landing in her dressing gown. But he told himself it wouldn't be very long now; in a few days he would be far away in a worthier, purer environment. He would never see Katharina again, and his future visits to his hometown would be very brief, since from now on the sanatorium would, he hoped, demand his year-round presence and attention. While he was thinking all this, he held Katharina on his lap and mechanically stroked her face and her neck. But suddenly he noticed that she was looking at him attentively and sadly.

"What's the matter?" he asked.

She only shook her head and tried to smile. He was touched and surprised to see tears in her eyes.

"You're crying," he said softly, feeling surer of Sabine at this moment than he ever had done.

"Nonsense," answered Katharina, and jumped up. She put on a cheerful face, opened the door to the dining room, and pointed at the table ready for supper. "Will the Herr Doctor permit me to remain in my robe?"

This reminded him that he had again brought her something from the attic. He found the amber necklace slipped in among the letters on his desk, and clasped it around her neck.

"Yet another present?" she asked.

"Yes, but that's the last," he said, immediately regretting the remark, which sounded more serious than he had intended. He wanted to make amends. "I mean . . ."

But she raised her hand, as if telling him not to speak. They sat down to supper. Suddenly, after a few bites, she asked, "Will you think about me sometimes when you're in the South?"

It was the first time she had alluded to the coming separation, and Graesler was a little dismayed. She noticed, because she quickly added,

"Just say yes or no."

"Yes," he said, with a forced smile.

She nodded as though perfectly satisfied, filled their glasses with wine, and went on chatting in her usual gay and naive manner as though there were no parting in sight—or as if it didn't much matter whether they parted or not. Later on, she wrapped the Chinese robe tightly around her body, then let it fall and flow freely over her limbs as she twirled and danced around the room, holding the robe with the gold-embroidered dragons in one hand and a glass of wine in the other, laughing brightly with brimming eyes. Finally, Graesler took her in his arms and carried her into Friederike's dimly lit room. There he embraced her with an ardor in whose secret depth he felt the dull rancor toward her who had left him behind—his sister, the liar—flicker and die away.

14

The next morning, while Katharina was still asleep, Graesler rose from her side in order to visit his little patient one last time. She was doing splendidly but was not yet allowed out of bed. To prevent the news of his imminent departure from reaching Katharina by way of the printer's wife, he assured the patient's friendly mother that he expected to be in town for another week. Frau Sommer smiled, saying,

"I can quite understand that saying goodbye to your little friend will be hard for you! What a charming creature! How wonderful she looks in that Chinese robe you gave her!" The doctor frowned and busied himself with little Fanny, who was combing her doll's blonde hair with childlike earnestness. A few days before he had begun to tell the child about some wild animals that had traveled with him on a ship from Australia to Europe on their way to a circus. And ever since the little girl had refused to let him go until he had told her the whole tale again with complete descriptions of the lions, the tigers, the panthers, and the leopards, whom he had sometimes watched as they were being fed on the lower decks. But today he kept it brief as he still had a number of things to do before his departure the next morning. To the little girl's disappointment, he suddenly stood up, but was held up at the door by Frau Sommers's questions regarding the treatment of the child, questions he had already answered a hundred times. His impatience wasn't lost on her, but she tried to delay his departure by standing close to him, almost touching him, as she always did, and looked up at him with grateful, tender eyes. At last he succeeded in getting away and hurried down the stairs to the street. He had told Katharina only that he had a lot of things to do in town, and that he had to visit the hospital again—just enough to ensure that she wouldn't become impatient and he could prepare for his trip. He went to the hospital, took his leave of the senior physician, bought a few things in town, arranged for his luggage to be forwarded, and finally called on Boehlinger, with whom he had to settle some business matters. The lawyer seemed scarcely to notice his restlessness, and along with a few pieces of good advice offered him his best wishes for the success of the negotiations for the sanatorium. Boehlinger avoided, deliberately it seemed, any more intimate allusions, and it was not until Graesler was already outside on the stairs that it occurred to him that he had just spoken with one of his sister's lovers. But he was anxious to get home for the final lunch with Katharina. He wanted to spend his last few hours with her undisturbed, careful not give her any sign of his intentions, and then tomorrow morning, while she still slept, he planned to take a silent leave of her by means of a letter in which he would also include a small gift of money.

When he entered the dining room he found only one place setting. The printer's wife appeared and reported with malicious delight that she herself had laid the table at the behest of the young lady, who begged to be excused. Graesler's expression frightened her so much that she quickly left the room. He hurried into his study, where he found a sealed letter from Katharina. He opened it and read,

My dear, my dearest Doctor! It was so lovely with you. I'll think of you a lot. But I know you're going away tomorrow, and I'd better not disturb you today. I hope all will go well with you. If you come again next year—but you'll have forgotten me long before then. I do hope you'll have a pleasant ocean voyage. And many, many thanks for everything.

Your loyal Katharina.

Graesler was as touched by her clumsy childish handwriting as by the warmth of her words. "What a dear, sweet thing," he said to himself. But he wouldn't let himself weaken. He returned to the dining room, had his meal brought in, and busied himself between courses by writing in his engagement book so that he wouldn't have to talk to the printer's wife, whom he dismissed immediately after the meal.

Then he wandered from one room to the next. Everything was in perfect order. Everything that belonged to Katharina had been removed, and no trace of her was left except a subtle scent, especially in the room that had been hers for the last three weeks. Otherwise, though everything was as it had been, the whole apartment now seemed intolerably empty and cold to him. He suddenly felt so lonely that he wondered if he shouldn't throw all his other hopes and possibilities to the wind and just fetch Katharina back from her parents' house. But he immediately saw the imprudence, yes, the foolishness of such an impulse, whose satisfaction would imperil his entire future and forever destroy a happiness which was now so near. And all of a sudden the image of Sabine lit up his soul with marvelous brilliance. It occurred to him suddenly that there was nothing now to keep him from leaving this very evening, and that he could see Sabine as early as tomorrow morning. But he abandoned this thought—he didn't want to appear in front of his beloved exhausted and unkempt after what might be a sleepless night. He decided to use the extra time at his disposal to prepare the ground for a favorable reception by writing a letter announcing his visit. But when he sat down at his desk and took up his pen, he found himself unable to formulate a single sentence that expressed or even approximated his feelings. So he contented himself with a few but significant words, as if dashed off in the heat of passion:

"I am coming to you tomorrow evening. I hope for a kind reception. Longingly, E.G."

Then he wrote a telegram to Dr. Frank saying he would be there early the next morning and hoped to have a message about whether construction could begin on November 15. He personally dispatched both the letter and the telegram, returned home, cleared away some things, put others in order, and then packed his bag, into which he put a small cameo with the head of a goddess set in gold. During the night he woke up a half-dozen times from nightmares in which it seemed to him that everything was lost—Sabine and Katharina, the sanatorium, his property, his youth, the warm sun of the South, and the ivory cameo—if he overslept in the morning and missed the train.

15

It was a warm and sunny afternoon in late autumn when Dr. Graesler arrived back at the health resort. In front of the railroad station there were at least half a dozen carriages from various hotels waiting for new arrivals. The coachmen called out the names of their hotels, but without conviction, as few tourists came so late in the season. Dr. Graesler drove to his house and directed the coachman to wait. He asked for his mail. He was annoyed that there was no reply from Dr. Frank, and bitterly disappointed that there was no word from Sabine. He asked his obliging housekeeper about news of the city and its surrounding suburbs without learning anything of importance, not even, as he had feared, about events at the ranger's house. It was already nightfall when he drove up the valley beneath a starless sky along the familiar road that ran between now deserted villas and gloomy hills to the lodge. Suddenly he knew with pitiless clarity something that until that very moment he had foolishly tried to conceal from himself: that he was about to make a desperate and probably hopeless attempt to regain the favor of that splendid being he had lost, half from rashness, half from cowardice.

While he uselessly searched his mind for irrefutable words of justification and irresistible words of love, the carriage stopped abruptly—or so it seemed to Dr. Graesler—in the middle of the road. Suddenly, as though the lights in the house had just been turned on, a ruddy gleam fell across the path to the street. He disembarked, and slowly, in order to calm the violent beating of his heart, he walked up to the entrance. His ring was promptly answered. At the same time the door of the living room opened and Frau Schleheim came out while Sabine, looking up from her book, remained calmly seated at the table.

"How good of you," said the mother, extending her hand to him cordially, "to take pity on us two poor forsaken women."

"I took the liberty of writing Fräulein Sabine that I was coming."

"Welcome back," said Sabine, who by now had also gotten up, and she gave him her hand in a friendly manner. He tried to read her gaze, which met his directly, too directly. He inquired after the master of the house.

"He's traveling," answered Frau Schleheim.

"And may one ask where he is?" asked Graesler, as he seated himself at Sabine's invitation. Frau Schleheim shrugged.

"We don't know. This happens from time to time. But he'll be back in a week or two. We're used to it," she concluded with a meaningful look at her daughter.

"Are you planning to stay for a while, Herr Doctor?" asked Sabine.

He looked at her, but her look did not answer his. "It all depends," he said, "probably not very long—just until I have settled my affairs."

Sabine nodded as if absentmindedly.

The maid came in to set the table. "You'll stay with us for supper?" asked the mother.

He hesitated. Again his glance questioned Sabine.

"Of course the Herr Doctor will eat with us. We counted on his staying," she said.

Graesler felt: it's not loving kindness she's showing me—pity, perhaps. And he nodded his head in mute consent.

They were all silent now, and since the silence was especially painful to Graesler, he began to speak rapidly. "First of all I must look up Dr. Frank. Would you believe, ladies, that he didn't even answer my last letters? But I still hope that we'll come to an agreement."

"Too late," interjected Sabine cooly, and Graesler quickly realized that she referred not only to the lost business opportunity. "Dr. Frank decided to keep the place himself. He's already been busy renovating. Your friend Herr Adelman is in charge of the work."

"He's not my friend," said Graesler, "otherwise he would certainly have let me know." And he shook his head heavily and slowly, as if in his architect he had suffered a bitter disappointment.

"Under these circumstances," remarked Sabine politely, "I suppose you'll go south again?"

"Of course," answered Graesler hastily. "To good old Lanzarote. The climate here! Who knows whether I'd still be up to a European winter?"

It occurred to him that, given the poor steamer connections to and from the island, he would not be able to get there before mid-November, and that he might find his position already filled, as he had neither written that he was coming nor that he was resigning. Well, fortunately he no longer depended upon working there. If he liked, he could take a vacation for six months or even more, and if he were economical he could give up his practice altogether. But the thought of that alarmed him. He was not capable of living without a profession. He had to work, heal people, lead the life of an honorable, active man. And in the end perhaps he was destined to lead that life with this splendid and noble woman at his side. Perhaps she merely wanted to punish him a little for his hesitation and was testing him.

And so he explained that he had not yet made any definite arrangements, that he was still waiting for a letter from Lanzarote accepting the new, more advantageous terms he had proposed to the administration. If these were refused, he would spend the coming winter studying at various German universities. Oh, and he had not been idle in his hometown, either. Not only had he visited the hospital often but he had even engaged in private practice, though just by accident, to be sure. It involved a child, a dear little girl of seven, the daughter of a widow who lived in his apartment building. He couldn't refuse. It was quite a serious case . . . scarlet fever. But now the child was out of danger. Otherwise he couldn't have left.

As he talked he tried to recall Frau Sommer's image but instead kept seeing the woman with the doll's face from an illustrated magazine, the one that had filled his dreams during his long voyage home from Lanzarote. Evidently there was some resemblance—yes, of course, hadn't it struck him immediately? Sabine seemed to listen to his reports with a growing interest but, he feared—because of his uneasy conscience—with little credence. Abruptly, apropos of nothing, she began to speak of her two friends, whom Graesler must remember. The younger one had become engaged to a late summer visitor from Berlin. They were all going to Berlin for the wedding, and, the mother remarked, they planned to take the opportunity to immerse themselves in city life again as they had not been able to for a very long time.

Once again, and more urgently, almost imploringly, Graesler's eyes met Sabine's: How are things between us? But her eyes remained impenetrable, and even though during the course of the evening she became friendlier, yes, softer even, he felt that he had as good as lost her. But his pride rebelled against accepting the silent dismissal she seemed to intend for him, and he was determined to ask her for a private meeting before he left. When he rose and with forced gaiety alluded to the possibility of a Christmas meeting in Berlin, Sabine also stood, and it was apparent that she intended to accompany him outdoors, as usual. And so they walked side by side beneath the pines and toward the road where the carriage waited, just as they had in happier days. But they walked in silence.

All of a sudden, almost involuntarily, Graesler stopped and asked, "Are you angry with me, Sabine?"

"Angry?" she answered tonelessly. "Why should I be angry?"

"My letter—I know—my miserable letter!"

In the dark he saw only that she winced and gestured dismissively, so he hastened to explain, floundering more and more hopelessly with every word. She had misunderstood his letter, completely misunderstood it. It was his conscientiousness, his sense of duty that had made him write the letter. Oh, if only he had followed his heart, his passion! For he had loved her, adored her, from the very first moment that he saw her beside her mother's sickbed. But he hadn't had the courage to believe in his own luck. After such a joyless, lonely, restless life as his! He had not dared to hope, not dared to dream. An old man like him! Almost an old man. Of course he knew that it wasn't the number of years that made for age. He had learned to see that in the endless weeks of their separation. . . . But her letter, her wonderful, heavenly letter, oh, he hadn't been worthy of it. . . .

His words poured out confused and tangled, and he knew he wasn't finding, couldn't find, the right ones because the way between his lips and her heart was blocked. And as he finally, hopelessly, ended with a stifled cry, "Forgive me, Sabine, please forgive me!" he heard her say as though from a great distance.

"I don't have anything to forgive you for. But it would have been better if you hadn't spoken. I had hoped you wouldn't. Otherwise I would have asked you not to come."

Her voice sounded so hard that Graesler suddenly felt fresh hope. Wasn't it wounded love that made her so unforgiving? Wounded love—but love nevertheless? Love that she still felt, but was ashamed of? And so he resumed with fresh courage:

"Sabine—I won't ask you anything but this—let me come again next spring and ask you once more."

She interrupted him. "It's rather cold here. Goodbye, Dr. Graesler." And despite the darkness, he thought he saw a mocking smile on her face as she added, "I continue to wish you all the best."

"Sabine!"

He took her hand and tried to hold her back. She withdrew it gently. "Have a good trip," she said, and her voice resounded once more with the lovingkindness that was now lost to him forever. She turned away, and without quickening her pace she walked resolutely and irrevocably back into the house and disappeared through the doorway.

Graesler stood stock still for a little while, then hurried to the carriage, climbed in, wrapped himself in a coat and blanket, and rode homeward through the night. Defiance awoke in his heart. Very well then, he said to himself, if that's what you want, you are driving me into another woman's arms. You'll have your way. More than that, I'll rub your nose in it. . . . Before I go south, I'll bring her here for a few days. I'll drive past the lodge with her. You'll have to see her! You'll have to meet her! You'll have to talk to her! Allow me to present my bride to you, Fräulein Sabine! Not as pure a soul as you, Fräulein, but not as cold, either! Not as proud, but kind. Not as chaste, but sweet! Her name is Katharina—Katharina . . .

He spoke the name out loud. And the farther the carriage drove from the lodge, the more fervent his longing for Katharina became, and soon it changed into the wonderful, secure joy that he would soon—tomorrow, tomorrow evening—hold her in his arms again. How astonished she would be to find him waiting for her at seven o'clock in the evening in the Wilhelmstrasse! He wanted it to be a surprise. And a still greater one awaited her! Because he was not an old pedant. He had only one wish, to be happy, and he would take his happiness where it was offered him so warmly, so unconditionally, and in such a womanly way. . . . Katharina . . . How good it was that he had seen Sabine again. Only now did he know for sure that Katharina was the right woman for him—she and no other.

16

The next evening, only an hour after his arrival, he waited on the street corner from which he could not fail to see Katharina leaving the glove shop. Two other salesgirls emerged from the store entrance one after the other, the shutters were lowered, the stock boy left, the outside light was turned off—but there was no sign of Katharina. Strange. Very strange. Her vacation was over, wasn't it? So what could be keeping her from work? A sudden jealousy flared up in him. No doubt—she was with someone else. Probably with an old flame for whom she again had time now that the old doctor from Portugal with the Indian shawls and the amber necklaces had gone. Maybe it was someone completely new. Why not? That kind of thing can happen very quickly with people like us, don't you agree, Katharina? Where are you? Probably in the theater! Isn't that how it starts? The first evening, theater and supper together, the second evening — everything else! She's probably done that a number of times. But that the story should begin again the very next day, that really is too much! That miserable creature, for whose sake he had lost someone like Sabine! Gone off with the shawls and the hats and the robe and the jewelry, and in the end even making fun of the old fool from Portugal with some young fellow. . . . His thoughts raced on in this vein, and with deliberate self-torture he dismissed the possibility of more innocent reasons for Sabine's nonappearance. What to do now? The most sensible thing to do would be to go home and just forget about it, but he didn't have that much self-control.

He decided to walk in the direction of the district where she lived and to position himself near her house to wait for her. He would soon find out who it was she had taken up with — unless of course she had already installed herself in her new lover's apartment. . . . But that wasn't likely. She wouldn't so soon find another fool who would take such a creature, such a cunning, gossiping, uneducated, lying little vixen, into his house. His contempt for her knew no bounds, and he gave himself up to this feeling with a certain voluptuous satisfaction. Do you find that priggish, my Fräulein? His thoughts suddenly turned to the distant Sabine, against whom he now also felt a powerful resentment. Well, I can't help it. No one can get out of his own skin, be it man or woman. One woman is born to be a whore, the other to be an old maid, and a third, despite the best of upbringings in a good middle-class German family, leads the life of a coquette, hoodwinks her parents and her brother, and kills herself when she can't find any more willing lovers. As for me, God made me a pedant and a prude. But by God, it isn't the worst thing in the world to be a prude! If one doesn't play the prude toward certain women, they make a fool of you. The fact is, I'm not enough of a prude, for if a certain Fräulein had put off her tryst and had come out of her shop at seven o'clock as she should have, I would have taken her with me to Lanzarote as Frau Doctor. You would have enjoyed that, Herr Hotel Director! But that won't happen. Thank God I'm going back there as alone as when I left, if I go at all, which I haven't yet decided. In any case, I won't get there by October 27, as you ordered, even if I could! I'll go to Berlin first, then perhaps to Paris, and really enjoy myself like I've never enjoyed myself before. And he imagined himself in places of ill repute with half-naked women who danced wild dances. He planned monstrous orgies as a kind of demonic revenge on the wretched sex that had treated him so maliciously and so faithlessly—revenge on Katharina, on Sabine, and on Friederike!

Meanwhile he had unwittingly arrived at Katharina's apartment building. An unpleasant wind had arisen and swept the dust through the mean little street. Here and there windows were hastily being closed. Graesler looked at his watch. It was still a good while till eight. How many hours stood before him? How would he pass the time? It could be ten, eleven, or twelve o'clock, even tomorrow morning before the Fräulein came home.

The thought of tramping up and down the street for hours in the wind and rain—the first drops had already begun to fall—for an uncertain end was highly disagreeable. And now he began to heed a faint inner voice that had been trying to be heard for some time: what if in the end Katharina were already at home? Perhaps she had left the shop earlier—though that was unlikely on the first day after her vacation. Or perhaps her vacation wasn't over yet, and she was spending her last free day with her family. He didn't quite believe this either, but these conjectures relieved his mind, all the more so since it would be easy enough to ascertain the truth. All he had to do was to walk up three flights and ask at Herr Rebner's door whether his daughter, Fräulein Rebner, was at home. That wouldn't be too unseemly. A family in which the daughter returned from the country with twice as much luggage as she had left with wouldn't be all that particular. And if she were not at home, he could find out what pretext she had used for spending the evening out. If she were at home, well, all the better—everything would be all right, he would have her again and could make all the necessary arrangements for tomorrow and the next day and the days after that. If she were home, everything that had been running through his head was nonsense. He would owe her a mute apology for what he had attributed to her while in the wretched mood for which someone else was far more to blame than she. So it was in the best of moods that he stood before the door of her flat.

He rang. A small elderly woman in a housedress covered by an apron opened the door and looked at him in surprise.

"Excuse me," said Graesler, "is this Herr Rebner's place?"

"To be sure. I'm his wife."

"Of course. Yes. I'd like to—I wonder if I could perhaps have a word with Fräulein Katharina. For I had the pleasure—"

"Ah," Frau Rebner interrupted him, obviously pleased, "You must be the Herr Doctor whom Katharina met while she was staying at Ludmilla's in the country—the one who gave her the lovely shawl?"

"Yes, I am. My name is Dr. Graesler."

"Of course—Dr. Graesler—she told us about you . . . yes. I'll find out if she can see you. She's in bed. She came back yesterday and must have caught a cold."

Graesler was appalled.

"In bed? Since when?"

"She hasn't been up all day. She probably has a little fever too."

"Have you called a doctor, Frau Rebner?"

"Oh, no. She ate a hearty breakfast. She'll be all right soon."

"Perhaps you'll allow me, since I happen to be here—I think Fräulein Katharina wouldn't object to having me take a look at her."

"Well, fine, since you're a doctor—it might be a good thing to do."

And she led him through a large unlit room into a smaller one where Katharina lay in bed. There was a candle on the nightstand which flickered over the white, wet cloth that lay folded over Katharina's forehead. Her eyes were completely hidden.

"Katharina," exclaimed Graesler. With apparent effort, she moved the cloth from her eyes, which were expressionless and dull.

"Good evening," she said with a weak smile, but seemed barely conscious.

"Katharina!" He hastily pulled down the covers and slipped her nightgown away from her shoulders. He saw a dark red rash. Her fever was very high, and her prostration extreme. Graesler did not need to undertake a more thorough examination to recognize that Katharina's illness was scarlet fever. Holding one of her hands in his, he felt deeply distressed and guilty, and he sank down on the chair next to her bed.

At that moment her father arrived home and was hardly through the door when he exclaimed, "Why, what's all this fuss about? You've actually called a doctor—"

His wife went up to him. "Not so loud," she said, "her head hurts. It's the doctor she met at Ludmilla's."

"Oh," said the father, coming closer. "I'm pleased to make your acquaintance. Here I send my daughter to the country for a holiday at great expense, and now she comes home sick. Well, I suppose it's nothing much, is it, Herr Doctor? She probably sat outdoors too late in the evening at this time of year. Didn't you, Katharina?"

Katharina didn't answer and drew the cloth back over her eyes. Dr. Graesler turned to the father. He was a rather short, stocky man with dull eyes, almost bald, and with a grey mustache turned up at the corners. "It's not a cold," said Graesler. "It's scarlet fever."

"But Herr Doctor, that's impossible. That's a children's disease. Her sister had it when she was five. She would have caught it then if she were going to get it."

The father's overly loud words appeared to clear Katharina's mind, and she said, "The Herr Doctor must know better than you, father. He'll make me well again, won't he?"

"Yes, Katharina, I will, I will," said Graesler, loving her more at this moment than he had ever loved any human being in his life. Later, as he gave his instructions, Katharina's sister appeared with her husband, who first greeted the doctor with a wink but who soon disappeared with his wife into the adjoining room when he realized the gravity of the situation. Graesler quietly explained to the parents that he would stay the night, as the first night was of critical importance in cases of this sort. If he watched her all night he might be able to avert the dangers whose first signs would escape untrained eyes.

"Well, Katharina," said the father, stepping toward her bed again, "aren't you the lucky one. Not many people have a doctor like that. But Herr Doctor," he said, drawing Graesler toward the door, "I had better tell you right away, we're not wealthy people. Even if she stayed in the country, it was only as a guest of Ludmilla's, as you must have noticed. We merely had to pay her ticket there and back."

His wife told him to stop talking and sent him off to the living room, realizing that it was time to leave Katharina alone with her doctor.

Graesler bent over the sick girl, stroked her cheeks and her hair, kissed her on the forehead, assured her that she would be well again in a few days, and that she must come back to him. He would never let her out of his sight again and would take her with him wherever fate took him. He had been drawn back to her by a tremendous force, and she was his child, his beloved, and his wife. He loved her, loved her as no one had ever been loved before. But even as she smiled content-edly, he realized that his words no longer penetrated her conscious-ness and that the things going on around her were to her no more than dim and fleeting shadows. He realized that days were beginning in which every hour would be filled with awful dread for a beloved who was now the prey of an invisible enemy. He resolved to arm himself for a desperate struggle which he already knew was useless.

17

For three days and three nights Graesler sat at Katharina's bedside almost without interruption. She never fully regained consciousness, and her feverish soul left her on a gloomy November evening. Two days later, during which Graesler was completely occupied with the arrangement of all the dreary matters attendant upon a death, she was buried. Graesler walked behind her coffin without saying any-thing that wasn't absolutely necessary to her relatives, who despite their shared sorrow had remained completely distant from him. He stood rigidly by the grave as the coffin was lowered into it and then, without even saying goodbye, he left the cemetery and drove back to his apartment. He lay on the sofa in his study until evening, plunged into a dreamless, heavy sleep. It was dark when he awoke. He felt so alone, more alone than he had ever felt before, more alone even than after the death of his parents or his sister. Suddenly his life had lost all meaning. He went outside into the street without knowing what to do with himself, without knowing where he should go. He hated everyone, hated the city, hated the world, and hated his profession, which in the end had done nothing but destroy the one creature who had been destined to bring happiness to his declining years. What was there left for him on earth? His only consolation, his only success in life, was that he was in a position to abandon his profession and never again exchange a word with another human being.

The streets were damp, and frost covered the grass of the city park where he happened to find himself. He looked up. Shredded clouds were racing across the sky. He felt exhausted, tired not only of his aimless wandering but also of his own company, which he suddenly found unbearable. Going home and spending another hopeless and lonely night in the place where he had been happy with Katharina seemed completely impossible. He couldn't bear the thought of going over and over his fate with the same inadequate and threadbare words without getting some human response, some sympathy and consolation from someone. He realized that if he did not find someone with whom he could share his anguish this very hour he would begin to sob and scream and curse God right here in the open. His old friend Boehlinger was really the only one who would do, and so he set out for Boehlinger's house. He feared that he wouldn't find him at home, but for once fortune was on his side, and he found the attorney seated at his file-covered desk wearing a Turkish dressing gown, veiled in tobacco smoke.

"You're here again already?" Boehlinger said, receiving him. "What's the matter? It's rather late!" He glanced at the wall clock. It was ten o'clock.

"Excuse me," said Graesler hoarsely. "I hope I'm not disturbing you."

"But of course not! Won't you sit down? Have a cigar?"

"Thanks," said Graesler, "but I can't smoke right now. I haven't even had dinner."

Boehlinger looked at him with a wrinkled brow. "So," he said, "it appears that something important has happened. Did something happen with the sanatorium?"

"Nothing happened with the sanatorium."

"Ah, so that fell through? But that isn't what has hit you so hard, is it? Tell me! You wouldn't have come as late as this without a good reason—of course I'm delighted to see you anytime—but go on, tell me what this is about. Or should I guess? Woman trouble?" He smiled. "Infidelity?"

Graesler made a dismissive gesture. "She's dead," he said harshly, and suddenly stood up and paced up and down in the room.

"Oh," said Boehlinger. And he fell silent. When Graesler passed near him again, Boehlinger seized his hand and pressed it several times. But Graesler sank into a chair with his head in his hands and sobbed bitterly, sobbed as he had not sobbed since childhood. Boehlinger waited patiently and smoked his cigar. Now and then he glanced at a document on his desk and made a note or two in the margin. After a while, when Graesler seemed a bit calmer, he asked gently, "How did it happen? She was so young."

Graesler looked up. He twisted his mouth into a contemptuous smile. "She certainly didn't die of old age! Scarlet fever. And it was my fault. My fault!"

"Your fault? Did you bring it home from the hospital?"

Graesler shook his head, leapt up, and paced up and down the room again, lifting his arms up in despair. He took a deep breath. Boehlinger leaned back in his chair, and observed him. "How about telling me the whole thing? Perhaps it would make you feel a little better."

And Dr. Graesler began to tell the story of the last few months, awkwardly at first, but then more and more fluently. Sometimes walking up and down, sometimes standing in a corner, at a window, or leaning against the desk, he talked not only of Katharina but also of Sabine, of his hopes and his fears, of his renewed youth and his dreams here at home and at the resort—and how it had all come to naught in the end. Sometimes he had the feeling that both Katharina *and* Sabine were dead and that it was he who had killed them. Occasionally Boehlinger interjected a curious or sympathetic question. And when his friend's story became clear to him, he turned to him with the question, "Did you really come back with the intention of marrying her?"

"Absolutely. Yes. Do you think her past should have prevented me?"

"By no means. It's women with a future who are generally not preferable." And he stared into space.

"You may be right," said Graesler, and, looking straight at him, he added, "Which reminds me, there was something else I wanted to tell you—" He broke off.

His tone took Boehlinger aback. "What do you mean?"

"I read your letters to Friederike, yours—and those of others."

"Oh?" said Boehlinger, unperturbed, but with a wry smile. "That was long ago, my friend."

"Yes, it was long ago," repeated Graesler. And feeling the need to express his opinion of the affair briefly and once and for all, he added, "Of course, reading the letters made it clear to me why you didn't marry her after all."

At first Boehlinger looked at him uncomprehendingly. Then, with the corners of his mouth twitching, he said, "Oh, you think it was because—because she—deceived me? That's how the phrase runs. Good lord, what a fuss one makes about things like that when one is young. In reality she only deceived herself and I—I deceived myself! Yes, especially the latter. Well, now it's too late, isn't it?" And both remained silent for a while.

"It was long ago," said Graesler once more, as if from a deep sleep. An intense exhaustion had overwhelmed him, and his eyelids fell shut. He started when Boehlinger took him by the hand and warmly urged him to stay the night, which was already far gone. He even offered him his own bed. But Graesler chose to lie down fully dressed on the sofa in the smoke-filled room, and fell instantly into a deep sleep. Boehlinger spread a blanket over him, opened both windows to air out the room, arranged the files on his desk, closed the windows again, and left his sleeping friend alone in the room.

When Graesler awoke he found Boehlinger standing over him with a benevolent smile. "Good morning," he said kindly—like a doctor to a sick child who has just awakened from a healing sleep, thought Graesler. A cool autumn sun shone into the room. Graesler felt he must have slept a very long time, and asked what time it was just as the noon bells began to chime. He rose and reached for his friend's hand. "Thanks for your hospitality. It's time for me to go home now."

"I'll go with you," said Boehlinger. "It's Sunday, and I don't have to go to the office. But first you'll have breakfast. And there's also a bath waiting for you."

Graesler gratefully accepted. After the bath, which refreshed him considerably, he went into the dining room, where breakfast awaited him. Boehlinger sat beside him and served, and in an obvious attempt to distract his friend from his melancholy thoughts, he chatted away, relating all sorts of trivial political and local news. What do I care about the world, thought Graesler, or about this town, or other people? Yes, if Sabine could be restored to life—I mean Katharina! he corrected himself immediately—Sabine is still alive . . . so to speak. He smiled without quite knowing why.

The two friends left the house. The streets were alive with people strolling in their Sunday best, and Boehlinger exchanged greetings with many of them. They walked past the glove shop in the Wilhelmstrasse. Graesler regarded the closed shutters with hostility and horror. Finally they arrived at Graesler's building. "If you have no objection, I'll accompany you upstairs," said Boehlinger. At that moment a pretty plump woman in widow's clothes whose severity was moderated by the appealing and lighthearted tilt of her hat, came through the door. She was holding a little girl's hand, and her eyes lit up in surprise when she saw the doctor. "Look who's coming!" she exclaimed delightedly to her daughter. But Graesler's eyes widened in horror when he recognized Frau Sommer, and he gave the child a darting but completely uncontrolled look of hatred. Without the slightest greeting he walked by mother and child and entered the building. But Boehlinger noticed that the woman, who still held her daughter's hand, remained standing at the door, looking at his friend in astonishment, almost in despair. With a disapproving shake of his head he followed Graesler up the stairs, determined to ask for an explanation. But even before the door to his flat had closed behind him, Graesler burst out, "That was the child! That was the mother and the child. It was that child's fault! Katharina had to die, and I cured that child!"

"You can't talk of fault here," said Boehlinger. "As awful as the situation is, it's not the little girl's fault — and still less the mother's. Your behavior just now must have been totally incomprehensible to her."

"Of course she doesn't know what's happened," said Graesler.

"You looked at her as though she were a ghost. And the way you looked at the little girl—! You should have seen the mother's face. She was frightened to death."

"I'm sorry about that. But she'll get over it. I'll explain when I get the chance."

"You should certainly do that," Boehlinger said, and in a rather inappropriately cheerful tone he added, "all the more so as she's a very pretty and appetizing little woman." Graesler wrinkled his brow and gestured dismissively. Then he begged Boehlinger to excuse him: he wanted a few moments to go through his mail, which he had neglected since his return. He couldn't suppress a faint hope that Sabine might have written to him, calling him back, though he realized the utter ridiculousness of such a thought. There was not a single line from her nor anything else of the slightest importance.

Afterward he went with Boehlinger to a local restaurant and in the dim light of a warm and cozy nook and over a bottle of good

Rhine wine, his friend advised him not to give himself up to useless sorrow but to resume his work as soon as possible. Graesler promised to notify Lanzarote this very day of his arrival at the end of the month. He was confident he would be welcome. Later, over coffee and cigarettes, they talked of Friederike. While Boehlinger listened with half-closed eyes, slowly blowing rings of smoke into the air before him, her brother spoke of her with emotion, praising her thoughtfulness and loyalty. He even intimated that when she redecorated and refurnished her rooms, she had not been thinking of herself, but rather, in a spirit of presentiment and generous self-sacrifice, of another woman who might become her brother's helpmeet and beloved. Boehlinger merely nodded; every now and then he gave his old friend, who had never been so loquacious, a look of astonishment not unmixed with pity. Finally his attention wandered and he seemed a trifle impatient. He stood up suddenly and took his leave in a rush, with the excuse that he had an engagement that evening.

Graesler walked home alone. Restless, he paced up and down in his room and felt his grief gradually turn to boredom. He sat down at his desk and wrote the hotel management in Lanzarote that though he would arrive a little later this year, he was sure it would not cause the management much inconvenience since few visitors arrived at the island before the middle or end of November. When he completed the letter he was finished with his day's work. He took his hat and walking stick, left his flat again, and when he passed Frau Sommer's door in the hallway, hesitated a moment but then rang the bell. She opened the door herself and received him far more cordially than he had a right to expect, even with an exclamation of delight. He had come, he promptly said, to apologize for his strange behavior this morning. Perhaps Frau Sommer had already heard of the tragedy that had befallen him and so would be ready to forgive him. But she knew nothing, nothing at all, and she invited him into the living room. There he told her that his dear little friend, the one she had seen standing on the staircase in the Chinese robe with the gold-embroidered dragon only a few weeks ago, had died after a short illness. Only after Frau Sommer asked sympathetically did he add that the young girl had been carried off by scarlet fever. There were many cases of scarlet fever in town, yes, one could almost speak of an epidemic. He added that a connection between the illness of his girlfriend and that of little Fanny was all the more uncertain as Fanny's illness had been so mild that he now doubted the accuracy of his diagnosis. And he took the little girl, who had just run in, between his knees. He stroked her hair and kissed her on the forehead. Than he cried quietly to himself, and when he looked up again, he saw tears in the young widow's eyes.

The next day he visited Katharina's grave, where there were still a few modest wreaths with ribbons. Frau Sommer and the little girl accompanied him, and while Graesler stood in silence with a bowed head and Frau Sommer looked at the inscriptions on the ribbons of the wreaths, the little girl folded her hands in a silent prayer. On the way home they stopped for a while at a café, and Fanny came home with a large cone of bonbons.

Henceforth Frau Sommer looked after the bereaved bachelor with unobtrusive kindness; he spent many hours, in fact every evening, in her flat and brought the little girl, of whom he grew more and more fond, all sorts of toys, including wild animals made of wood and papier-mâché. Fanny insisted that he tell her tales about them as if they were real but enchanted beasts. And every day in word and deed Frau Sommer showed her growing gratitude for all the affection the doctor lavished upon her fatherless child.

Less than a month had elapsed since Katharina's death when Dr. Emil Graesler arrived on the island of Lanzarote accompanied by Frau Sommer, now Frau Graesler, and little Fanny. The director was standing on the gangway, bareheaded as usual, his plastered brown hair barely stirring despite the coastal breeze. "Welcome,

Doctor!" he shouted, greeting the arrivals in that American accent that had so irked Graesler the year before. "Welcome! You've made us wait a little, but we're all the more pleased to have you back. The villa is of course ready for you, and I hope that Frau Graesler will also like it here with us." He kissed her hand and patted the little girl's cheek.

The air was drenched in sunshine, as if on a summer day. They all walked up toward the white hotel gleaming in the sun. The manager and the young wife led the way in lively conversation, followed by Dr. Graesler and little Fanny, who was wearing a wrinkled white linen dress and a white silk ribbon in her black hair. Graesler held her small soft hand in his own and said to her, "Do you see the little white house with all the open windows? That's where you're going to live. Just below it—of course you can't see it right now—there's a garden with wonderful strange trees such as you've never seen before . . . and you're going to play beneath them, and when it's snowing and people are freezing elsewhere, the sun will be shining here just like it is today." He went on talking to her in this manner, continuing to hold her small hand in his, its gentle pressure bringing him more happiness than any other touch he had ever known. The little girl, looking up at him eagerly, listened to his every word.

Meanwhile the Herr Director continued his conversation with the young wife. "The season has opened auspiciously," he remarked. "You husband will have plenty to do. For on the fourth of next month we are expecting his Highness the Duke of Sigmaringen with his wife, children, and entourage. . . . We have a blessed spot of earth here. A perfect little paradise. And as the writer Ruedenau-Hanson, a regular guest here in our island for the last twelve years, remarked . . ."

And the wind that always blows across the shore, even on the calmest days, blew away his next words and the next and many more like them.